YUMA PRISON CRASHOUT

YUMA PRISON CRASHOUT

A HANK FALLON WESTERN

WILLIAM W. JOHNSTONE

and J. A. Johnstone

PINNACLE BOOKS
Kensington Publishing Corp.
www.kensingtonbooks.com

PINNACLE BOOKS are published by

Kensington Publishing Corp.
119 West 40th Street
New York, NY 10018

PUBLISHER'S NOTE
Following the death of William W. Johnstone, the Johnstone family is
working with a carefully selected writer to organize and complete
Mr. Johnstone's outlines and many unfinished manuscripts to create addi-
tional novels in all of his series like The Last Gunfighter, Mountain Man,
and Eagles, among others. This novel was inspired by Mr. Johnstone's
superb storytelling.

All Kensington titles, imprints, and distributed lines are available at special
quantity discounts for bulk purchases for sales promotions, premiums,
fund-raising, educational, or institutional use. Special book excerpts or
customized printings can also be created to fit specific needs. For details,
write or phone the office of the Kensington sales manager: Kensington
Publishing Corp., 119 West 40th Street, New York, NY 10018, attn: Sales
Department; phone 1-800-221-2647.

PINNACLE BOOKS, the Pinnacle logo, and the WWJ steer head logo are
Reg. U.S. Pat. & TM Off.

ISBN-13: 978-0-7860-4490-0
ISBN-10: 0-7860-4490-X

First printing: August 2018

10 9 8 7 6 5 4 3 2

Printed in the United States of America

Electronic edition:

ISBN-13: 978-0-7860-4210-4 (e-book)
ISBN-10: 0-7860-4210-9 (e-book)

CHAPTER ONE

For about ten seconds, perhaps as many as fifteen, Harry Fallon considered letting the inmates have at the fat weasel. After all this time, Fallon wondered if he would have enjoyed watching those butchers rip apart Captain Clyde Daggett. Maybe even those rioting prisoners would let Fallon join them. Because when the sweating, flushed captain of the guards ran up to him, Fallon could feel the lashes that Daggett had laid on his bare back, and the knots on Fallon's head seemed to throb again from the leather-wrapped stick Captain Daggett carried when making his rounds. The brute often used that club to remind the convicts at the Illinois State Penitentiary—better known as Joliet, the city where it had been built back in 1858—that he, all five-foot-five and two hundred pounds of him, was boss in the washhouse, the cell blocks, the yard, the chapel, the cemetery, the work details, and here in the prison laundry.

"Hide me, Fallon!" Daggett cried.

Fallon watched the tears rolling down the fat man's cheeks, mingling with the beads of sweat that quickly broke into rivers that flooded down the crevasses in the guard's face.

"For God's sake, Fallon, hide me!"

That was asking a lot. Outside, Fallon heard the screams, the ringing of the bells, the reports of shotgun blasts, and the incessant *rat-tat-tat* from the Gatling guns on the north and west walls. Outside, men were being butchered, and Fallon didn't know who was doing the killing. Most likely the guards. When Fallon heard about the planned eruption of violence—nothing remained a secret among the hardened inmates at Joliet—he even briefly considered joining the boys. But the boys wouldn't trust him, Fallon knew, and he understood something else.

Those prisoners who dared to revolt, to make a desperate but doomed attempt at freedom, would not stand a chance. They would be cut down, slaughtered. Likely, the inmates knew that too. They just didn't give a damn anymore.

"Fallon!" the fat figure begged.

Reason returned to Fallon's mind. Reason and humanity, which he thought he had lost after ten years in this inhumane place.

"In here," Fallon heard himself saying—words that should have surprised him, but nothing shocked him anymore. Fallon nodded at the cart of laundry in front of him.

Daggett blanched. "Are you crazy?" he said.

"Then to hell with you!" Fallon barked. Why was he even helping the brute? By hiding Daggett, Fallon would be putting his own life in jeopardy. Outside, the Gatling gun silenced. A roar came from several prisoners, like a Rebel yell from charging Confederate soldiers during the late War of the Rebellion.

The bark of the Gatling gun resumed, and the victorious yells turned into the shrieks of bullet-riddled, dying men.

Footsteps sounded outside, and just before the door smashed open, Captain Daggett dived into the cart, pushing it against Fallon's body. The inmate, in his tenth year of a fifteen-year sentence, stopped it with his body. He had always been lithe but strong and sturdy. Ten years in Joliet had hardened his muscles even more. Quickly, he tossed several black-and-white-striped shirts and pairs of relatively clean pants over the pathetic, fat pig. The guard had dropped his grip on the billy club, and Fallon picked that up and deftly slipped it inside the waistband of his own coarse prisoner's pants near the small of his back. He pulled his striped shirt up and let it fall, covering the weapon.

Almost immediately, six men barged into the laundry. The last one slammed the door.

"Where's Daggett?" the first man roared.

Fallon recognized him immediately. Joe Martin, six-foot-two, sentenced to thirty years for myriad charges, maybe another fifteen to go before he could be released. He was shirtless, bleeding from both nostrils, missing his right ear and two fingers on his left hand. The ear had been severed in a fight with Hume something-another—Fallon couldn't remember the man's last name—that brawl had happened before Fallon arrived at the Illinois pen. The way Fallon had most often been told the story went something like this: a few days after the fight, Hume somehow got a makeshift knife stuck between his ribs, and Martin had gotten ten more years added to his original sentence. The fingers Martin had chopped off himself, scuttlebutt had it, to get out of a work detail. The busted nose was the only recent injury, and Fallon could imagine what had become of the guard who had landed that punch.

"Where is he?" Martin demanded.

Fallon nodded at the door that led to the yard.

"C'mon!" Martin shouted, and moved toward the heavy door that led to the exercise yard. Fallon watched the horde run, and he tried to stop from sweating, even though the laundry became a furnace this time of year and no one would notice sweat. Hell, by this point, everyone in Joliet— guards, the warden, and the prisoners—were drenched with sweat. So, most likely, were the people on the other side of the prison's stone walls.

The newcomers to the laundry wore desperation on their faces. No pistols, no firearms, that Fallon could see— and if these men had managed to get a shotgun or a re- volver, they would not be hiding those at this point in their futile game. Two held sticks like the one Fallon had pro- cured. The others had the makeshift knives, forged in the factory, smuggled in through the prison walls, carved out of wood or stolen from the kitchen, or paid with bribes to trusties and corrupt prison guards. Fallon even had a handmade knife sheathed in his left brogan. He doubted if any prisoner in Joliet did not have a knife or something similar.

In a place like this, if you weren't armed—or if the in- mates didn't think you carried a weapon—your life wasn't worth spit.

"Wait, Joe!"

Fallon frowned at the grinning man, the prisoner bring- ing up the rear of Martin's gang.

Baldheaded, rail-thin, pale, pockmarked Dan Watrous, better known among prisoners, guards, the warden, and even the chaplain as the Deacon. An Old Testament, fire- and-brimstone preacher awaiting a date with a hangman in roughly three weeks.

Martin stopped, angrily spun around, and cursed the Deacon, who never took his eyes off Fallon.

"It's Fallon," the Deacon said.

"So what? I want Daggett!"

"Fallon's a lawdog. Remember?"

"Yeah, I've heard that bandied about. But he ain't never turned a key on me, Deacon," Martin said. "And never turned ag'in me in the years he's been here."

"Till now," the Deacon said.

The Gatling gun fell silent again, but not the shotguns and not the screams. But that was outside, or in the main cell block. Those places Fallon had no control over, and he felt his control in the laundry slipping from his grasp.

The Deacon smiled, spread his arms, and said in a mocking voice, "We are in the Garden of Gethsemane, Deputy Marshal Hank Fallon. And we have come for you."

Fallon heard the muffled gasp of Daggett beneath the laundry. No one else appeared to have caught it, and Fallon said, "You want to avenge your brother, Watrous, come ahead."

Blood turned the pale man's face a beet red. "Don't you mention Jimmy to me, lawdog."

Of all the prisoners in Joliet to try to escape through the laundry room, to go chasing after the cowardly brute Daggett, the Deacon had to be one of them. Fallon had never met Dan Watrous until the baldheaded killer came to Joliet, to be housed briefly, for no more than six months, before he was to be returned to Effingham, Illinois, to hang for rape and murder. The Deacon had never set foot in Judge Isaac Parker's courtroom in Fort Smith, Arkansas, thirteen years earlier, to testify to the character of his brother, Jimmy Watrous, or even offer an alibi, or beg Judge Parker for mercy. Parker, on the other hand, was not a man known to be prone to show mercy to a man charged with running poisonous whiskey in the Creek Nation and for killing a deputy United States marshal while resisting arrest. Fallon, however, had not killed Jimmy Watrous. He had merely put a .44-40-caliber Winchester bullet in the kid's thigh, testified the truth, the whole truth, and nothing but the truth as a witness to the murder of federal deputy J. T. Oakes, and Fallon had identified the young Watrous as the killer. Judge Parker had sentenced him. The hangman had pulled the lever on the gallows.

"You got a personal feud with Fallon, that's your business," Martin told the Deacon. "All I want is Daggett, and to get out of this hellhole."

"Then you best hurry," Fallon said. The gunfire outside now echoed with whistles in addition to the screams, curses, and bells. All intensified. "Your window's closing."

"C'mon!"

The Deacon started his sermon, that he would wash his hands after he turned Fallon over to the people, the people being Joe Martin and the other convicts, but no one listened to him. No one but Harry Fallon.

Martin resumed his hurried march toward the door. Fallon never took his eyes off the Deacon. Feeling the sweat darkening the back and the armpits of his shirt, Fallon also felt something that steadied his nerves and almost reassured him that he might live through the next few minutes: the billy club pressing against his buttocks and backbone.

Two of the men—the redheaded Irishman who had burned down a saloon in Chicago, and the old man who had ridden with the Reno brothers back when he was a fool green kid—slowed, keeping their eyes on Fallon. The Deacon touched the edge of the laundry cart, and he even looked down at the freshly laundered clothes. Fallon almost held his breath, but somehow kept his cool, and trained his cold brown eyes on the men as they passed.

Once he had reached the door, Joe Martin placed his hand on the handle. Two others, the one-eyed Italian from Springfield and the burly brute who had derailed a Burlington Route express in Adams County a year ago, waited by the door, listening to the violence outside.

They hesitated, uncertain.

Planning a riot, a slaughter, and with luck a prison break was one thing. Living through it was altogether something else.

The old man spit on the clothes and moved as fast as his brittle bones could take him. The redhead stopped abruptly, grinned like the simpleton he was, and reached for the shirt the Reno gang member had just spit on.

"Hey, Joe!" the kid yelled. "You want a clean shirt?"

Fallon's one chance was that the coward underneath the laundry would keep his wits.

In his gut, he knew that would not happen.

The shriek beneath the clothes startled the redhead. He dropped the shirt, stepped back as if the cart held slithering serpents ready to strike. Fallon began stepping back, as well, away from the inmates. All this while Captain Daggett tried to climb out from the laundry, turning over the cart onto the hard, stone floor.

"What the . . . ?" Martin stepped away from the door.

"God help me! God help me! God help me!" Daggett tried to scramble to his feet, but his brogans slipped on the pants of men he had abused, and down he went.

"It's Daggett!" the old man who had ridden with the Reno brothers shouted, and brought up his blade.

There was no time for Fallon to think. Thinking left men dead. Besides, Fallon's silence had just betrayed Joe

Martin, and Joe Martin showed about as much mercy as Judge Parker.

Fallon's left hand jerked up his shirt from the back. His right gripped the handle of the club, and he stepped forward, bringing the leather-wrapped stick around, slamming it across the Deacon's jaw. The man's face contorted, and blood and teeth splattered the overturned cart as down he went.

From the corner of his eye, Fallon spotted the petrified captain of guards crawling over laundry, trying to find his footing. Fallon let the momentum of his swing carry him around. Then he brought the stick up and down, smashing the Irishman's wrist. Bones snapped. The kid screamed. The metal and wood knife dropped onto the side of the cart.

The Reno lifer rushed toward him, started his thrust of his pike toward Fallon's ribs. But Fallon proved to be too fast. Where he found that speed, he could not fathom, but men could summon up anything when they had no other choice. The club swung, caught the old-timer in his throat, smashing the larynx and sending the man against the tubs of dirty water. Water sloshed over the edges. The lifer stood there, clutching his throat, sucking for air that would not come. He was dead before he toppled onto Captain Daggett.

"You—" An angry scream replaced Joe Martin's voice. He and the burly man turned away from the door and rushed toward the mangled and dead inmates, terrified guard, and Harry Fallon.

Only the one-eyed Italian kept his wits. This wasn't his fight. One way or the other, he just wanted to get out of Joliet, and, serving a life sentence, this was his only chance. He jerked open the door and disappeared outside, leaving the door open.

The Gatling spoke its ugly sound. Fallon figured the Italian died quickly, but died trying to escape this repugnant place, and not to kill just to kill before you died.

Fallon shifted the nightstick to his left hand. His right grabbed the knife the Irishman had dropped onto the overturned cart. He raised it, meaning to gut the burly man, who was running ahead of Joe Martin. Instead, the Irish punk came up. The redhead was full of surprises. He drew a butcher knife from his boot, and, gripping the knife with his good hand, lunged toward Fallon.

CHAPTER TWO

Fallon reversed course. He ducked underneath the redhead's swing. With his right hand, Fallon slashed with the blade. It was luck, nothing but pure luck, but Fallon took it. The blade somehow caught the Irishman across his throat, and the redheaded punk spun around, falling to his knees, slipping in the lake of blood that came from his gushing jugular. Almost at the same time, Fallon brought the stick up with his left hand. The heavy club caught the charging brute between his legs. The big man's blade came down, slicing into Fallon's back, but the ugly cur had lost his grip on the blade and now he staggered to his right—right into Joe Martin's path.

The leader of the riot crashed into the burly man, caromed into the dying, throat-cut Irishman, and slipped on the blood himself.

By then, the Deacon had come up, his face masked in agony, blood spilling from his busted jaw. Fallon swung the stick and caught the other side of the killer's face. Down again went the Deacon who was bound for the gallows.

Bullets began peppering the wall behind the open door,

splintering the shelves of soap and sponges, and the wall, followed by the sound of ricochets zinging into stacks of clean clothes and piles of dirty laundry.

Martin and the brute were recovering. Captain Daggett had managed to get at least to his knees. Keeping his make-shift knife and stick, Fallon moved.

"Get going, Daggett!"

Fallon kicked the guard's buttocks. The fat jackass went down, but this time came up quickly. Daggett glanced behind him. Fallon pointed toward the rear of the building.

"That way."

"But . . . the . . . door . . ." He stared with hope at the open door, the one the Italian had run out of to be cut down by one of Joliet's two Gatlings.

"Your pals are shooting without looking," Fallon snapped. "You want to die, go ahead."

The man saw the murderous inmates stirring behind Fallon. He turned.

"Storeroom!" Fallon shouted.

Terrified, Daggett ran for his life.

Harry Fallon followed right behind him.

Once he reached the door, Daggett jerked the handle. The door did not budge.

"It's . . . locked!" Daggett wailed. He whirled around, desperate. If any color remained in his terrified face, it vanished.

Without looking, Fallon pounded the door with the club.

"Open up!" he screamed. "Quickly! Open the damned door!" He whacked the door harder.

"What?" Daggett sniffed, not comprehending.

"You're not the first guard to run here," Fallon said. He slammed the stick against the door again. Then he swore at the futility.

And now those cowardly guards refused to open the

door, to risk dying themselves to save Harry Fallon and Captain Daggett. Well, Fallon couldn't blame them for that. Given the same circumstances, he might have done the same thing. No, he would never have done that. Even ten years in the Illinois State Penitentiary hadn't stolen everything from his soul.

"Oh my God!" Daggett dropped to his knees, clasped his hands. "Don't kill me, Joe. Please, please, God have mercy, don't murder me . . . don't . . . kill me . . . like . . ."

Fallon turned around, knife in one hand, baton in the other.

"Like a dog?" Joe Martin laughed. "*Like a dog*. Ain't that what you always said to me, you miserable swine? Ain't that what you said to every man you ever abused."

The Deacon mumbled something no one could understand, spitting out more blood and bits of teeth and tongue.

"No, you'll die, Cap'n. But first this Judas will die . . . like the dirty, lying lawdog he once was, before he became a dog like me and all them others."

The Deacon seemed to try to smile, but his busted jaws and mangled mouth refused to cooperate.

The brute brought his knife up quickly, slashed. Daggett screamed, wet his britches, stumbled back against the door to the storeroom, and fell onto the floor. He covered his head with his arms. He shivered.

Fallon leaped back, feeling the knife's blade rip into his coarse shirt. The nightstick whooshed across the air, and the big man sucked in his gut as he ducked back himself. Fallon took in a deep breath, faked a lunge with the knife, stepped back, and almost tripped over Daggett's quivering body.

Now, Fallon heard nothing except his own ragged breaths and the pounding of his heart against his ribs. The gunfire and terrifying noise outside of the laundry had not ceased. Fallon just couldn't hear that reckoning anymore. What happened outside was of little matter to Fallon. The only thing that mattered was right here, right now, between Fallon, Martin, and the big convict.

Fallon slashed out with nightstick and knife, watching the men dodge, and then he made a dash away from the storeroom, and the cowering Daggett, toward the tubs of water and the dead man whose throat Fallon had crushed. The killers, ignoring Daggett—as Fallon had hoped, though not that hard—came after him. Fallon stopped, went around one of the tubs, and watched the two men charging. He dropped both knife and stick at his feet, grabbed the edge of the table on which the tub sat, and somehow managed to overturn table and tub. Water splashed onto the floor, and both Martin and the big man slipped on the soapy foam.

Down they went. Fallon reached down, picking up his two weapons, and moved to his left. The burly man recovered first, and he still held his knife. Fallon took a chance, shifted his grip on his own blade, and let the weapon sail. It caught the man in his chest, but the blade was too small to make a fatal wound. In fact, the big man did not even seem to notice the knife stuck just beneath his rib cage.

He started to stand, but slipped again on the suds and wetness. Cursing as he fell, he landed hard on his chest. He grunted, pushed himself up, and then dropped into the suds. The big man did not move, but Fallon noticed the water beneath the convict turning red. Redder. Redder. Fallon understood what had happened.

When the big man fell in the soapy water, he landed hard, and the force pushed that little knife deeper into his chest, puncturing his heart, perhaps, or his lung, or something. Enough to kill the murdering rogue.

That left only Joe Martin to deal with. Unless, it struck

Fallon, others who had joined the riot remained alive and were heading for the laundry at this very moment. Fallon didn't give that another thought. If it happened, it happened. Right now, the only person Fallon needed to worry about was Joe Martin.

Joe Martin, soaking wet, was on his feet. He held a knife and a studded stick, and he stepped up to the man lying facedown in the bloody water. He glanced at the dead man, spit into the water, and waded through the wet mess.

"I'm going to kill you, lawdog," Martin said.

The blade shot out. Fallon parried it with his billy club. He let Martin take the offensive, and he backed away, between the buckets and bins, the carts used to haul laundry here and there. Stick against stick, knife slashing this way and the other. Like two fencers in one of those swashbuckling adventure novels set in old France or among pirates in the Caribbean. Fallon had hoped that Martin would give up on this folly, that he might remember that his only chance now was to somehow get out of Joliet, that even if he killed Fallon and Daggett, he would soon be dead himself, gunned down by the guards already angered by the callous murder of many of their own.

Martin's blade slashed deep into Fallon's left arm, maybe halfway between elbow and shoulder. Blood stained his tattered, wet sleeve, dribbled over his fingertips. The knife he held became more difficult to grip.

He had circled back toward the storeroom, where Daggett had gathered himself and huddled against the thick door, still locked, gripping his knees with his hands, trying to pull himself into some invisible ball.

The studded stick swung toward Fallon, who ducked, felt it tear a few strands of hair from his head, and slam against the door. Daggett shrieked. Fallon brought the blade up, but Martin dropped his own blade and grabbed a tight hold on Fallon's wrist. The killer's fingers squeezed like a mechanical vise. The studded stick came back toward Fallon's head, but then both men were tripping over the quivering form of Captain Daggett.

They landed hard on the floor, Martin on top of Fallon, but Fallon rolled away from Daggett and the storeroom, taking Martin with him. Fallon stopped, came up, and brought a knee toward the convict's groin. Martin blocked it with his studded stick. The convict swung up his fist, but Fallon ducked beneath it and brought the nightstick down on Martin's throat.

Martin died with his larynx crushed, too, and died with hate-filled eyes staring into Fallon's cold brown ones.

Realizing that it was over—for now—Fallon dropped back. He was on his knees, straddling the dead man, and now every muscle in his body screamed in agony. The pains in his various wounds multiplied. He could hear again, the *rat-tat-tat* of the Gatling gun, the shouts, the whistles, and all of the inhumanity. Mostly, he could see Joe Martin and the others that Hank Fallon had killed. And he could hear the sniffles of the brutal captain.

Shouts came from everywhere, and Fallon slowly understood that it was all over. The riot had ended. Ended badly for many prisoners, and who knew how many guards. Yet Fallon was alive. So was Daggett.

"Fallon," Daggett gasped.

Fallon did not, could not, answer.

"Fallon. You saved my life . . ." The man was slowly regaining his grip on reason.

"Fallon. Listen. I'll do anything you want, anything. I'll do whatever I can to see you get . . . I don't know . . . parole, pardon, maybe to a better prison, a reduced sentence. I'll do anything. Anything. Just don't . . . for God's sake . . . please . . . man . . . don't let anybody know that I showed yeller. Don't tell them I was a coward. Promise me."

Repulsion. Gall. Hatred. Remorse. Exhaustion. Sick. Miserable. Self-loathing. Disgust. Fallon felt all of those. Then, because he had spent ten years in this hellhole, living in a cell infested by rats, he felt the way most men here felt.

He felt nothing. Not one damned thing. Nothing at all.

CHAPTER THREE

"Drop the damned gun, you son of a bitch!"

Slowly, Fallon turned toward the open door. He stared down the barrel of the shotgun at one of the guards, the new, pockmarked youngster who had started his job just two weeks back, held in shaking arms. The kid's uniform was soaked. Fallon didn't know if it came from an enormous amount of sweat, or if the warden had called in that pumping engine from the firehouse down the street to turn the hose on the inmates. He knew one thing. He didn't have a gun. Didn't even hold the club or a makeshift knife anymore. So he just stared at the kid, as three other guards rushed in.

"No!" Captain Daggett rose quickly. "Hold your fire, men. It's all right. We're safe. The inmates here are dead."

Daggett grabbed the stick Fallon had used to kill Joe Martin and banged it on the door to the storeroom. "It's all right. We're in control. You can open the door and come out now, you damned yellow-backed cowards."

A bitter, mirthless laugh escaped Fallon's lips. He shook his head. He had to give Captain Daggett credit for one thing. The man recovered quickly, and he thought amazingly fast for a man who had barely escaped a brutal death, who had been paralyzed by fear just moments ago.

The door to the storeroom did not open. Fallon wondered if the men inside could hear.

Cautiously, the new guards, led by the potbellied man named Goodman, moved around the wreckage of the laundry. The boy holding the shotgun lowered the weapon and brought up the rear. Their whispers reached Fallon's ears as the men saw the dead prisoners, but the men did not seem shocked. Probably, after all that had happened outside, nothing would surprise these men ever again.

"Captain," Goodman said. "Did you . . . kill . . . all of these . . . ?"

Another guard finished the sentence. "Yourself?"

"Yes," Captain Daggett said, but stiffened at the lie. His eyes flashed toward Fallon, and the fear returned, but only briefly. He made a quick correction, but not a complete one.

"No. No. Not all. Fallon here. He helped. He killed this one . . . and that one . . . and helped me with Joe Martin."

"Why'd you do a thing like that, bucko?" Goodman asked. His breath stank of breakfast and vomit.

"Fallon was once a deputy United States marshal," Daggett explained quickly, fearing Fallon might answer Goodman's question with the truth. Fallon had no intention of answering.

Goodman rolled his eyes. "Like old habits are hard to break. Something like that, Fallon? Or did you . . . ?"

"Goodman," Daggett said hoarsely. He found a clean prisoner's shirt and wiped his face, then dropped the striped cloth onto the soapy and bloody floor. "Lay off Fallon. I mean it. If not for Fallon, I'd be dead."

At least, Fallon thought, that much was true.

"What the hell are we supposed to do?" said another one of the guards.

"Get Fallon back to his cell."

"His cell? Those bastards set that whole block on fire." Fallon didn't know who said that. He was too busy staring at Captain Daggett.

"Then get him to another cell. Any cell." Daggett turned. The door to the storeroom was finally opening. "Or better yet, we can leave Fallon here. For now. Till the warden figures out . . ."

"The warden's dead," the youngster said.

"No, he ain't," Goodman corrected. "That was the deputy warden Klaus. Got shot off the west wall."

"I thought . . ."

So it would go. Rumors. Lies. The men whose lives Fallon had saved stepped out of the storeroom, uncertain, faces drained of color, eyes rimmed red from tears and pressure and fear.

"In here, Fallon." Captain Daggett held open the door. "In here. Just for a while. Till we can figure out what Warden Cain wants. All right?" The captain of the guards was asking Harry Fallon for permission.

Fallon didn't answer. He returned to the form of a prisoner, not a federal lawman. He lowered his eyes, stared at the floor. You did not look a guard in his eyes—not if you knew what was good for you. Fallon walked through the opening and stood between the shelves, barrels, and kegs the guards had used to barricade themselves in, to prevent the door from being opened.

"Fallon," the captain of the guards whispered. "Remember what I said. I won't forget you. I promise you."

As Fallon sat on one of the overturned barrels, the door closed, sending Fallon back into a world of midnight. They'd leave a guard outside. Maybe two. And Fallon knew that, most likely, other inmates would soon join him. Those who had lived through the nightmare.

Two days later, eight armed guards escorted Fallon and five others out of their new cells. They looked down as they walked to the exercise yard. Fallon and the old trusty named Langendorf stopped by the pine box, which they lifted—Langendorf gasped in pain at the weight—and carried the box through the front gates.

They loaded the coffin in a buckboard, and then came back through the gate to find another coffin. The other four prisoners also worked in pairs.

Twelve coffins. It had seemed a lot worse. Twelve prisoners dead. Hell, Fallon had killed most of those himself. But sixteen more were in the prison hospital, and two others had been transported to nearby Chicago, where they could get better care. The assistant warden and three other guards were also dead, but they would not be buried in the prison cemetery. Some of these men would lie in this flowerless, not hallowed, ground only briefly, till relatives or loved ones came to dig up the body and take the poor soul, no longer suffering, to rest among his own.

Once the coffins had been loaded, the guards escorted the men on wagons to the graveyard. There, Fallon took a shovel. He wondered if this was Captain Daggett's payment. Letting him bury the men he had killed.

"How come they let us out?"

The boy with the pickax, the starry-eyed kid from Springfield, Honest Abe Lincoln's home, looked around.

Fallon didn't answer; he just let the shovel dig up earth.

"I mean . . . why's the graveyard beyond the walls?"

"You're in Joliet for the length of your sentence," Fallon answered. "Ten years. Fifteen. Or life."

The kid stared. Fallon looked at him.

"The prison has you for life," Fallon said. "But not after you're dead."

The boy turned around, but Langendorf and Fallon both barked out a short rebuke.

Turning back, the kid asked, "What?"

"Don't look," Fallon said.

"At what?"

"The outside," Langendorf told him. Meaning, Fallon knew, what the outside of Joliet looked like. What the free world looked like.

"But . . ."

Fallon said, "Our guards will think you're uppity, getting some notions. Maybe will want to try to escape. You don't want that. Don't look. Just dig."

The kid asked no more questions.

"Enjoy it though," the trusty Langendorf said, and laughed his laugh of a man dying from consumption. "You're breathing free air." He drew in as much breath as his mangled lungs could hold, coughed, cursed, and tried to laugh it off.

But Fallon knew how much it meant to men like Langendorf. The chance to get beyond Joliet's walls. To breathe free air. Fallon stopped to adjust his work gloves and drew in deeply. The old, dying lunger was right. The air was different. It felt better. It felt fresher. Free.

He dug.

Langendorf and the boy left Joliet two days later. They would spend some time in the Joliet jail till the burned wreckage of the cell block had been rebuilt. A few of the more hardened prisoners were escorted to Chicago, to be housed in the damp, tough jail there. Fallon found himself left behind, put in another wing in another cell. The cell was meant for two prisoners. It housed five more, not including Fallon. Six men. Straw for beds. One slop bucket.

"Scuttlebutt has it that you saved Daggett's life."

Fallon leaned in his corner of the cell, the one that didn't have the disgusting slop bucket that hadn't been emptied in two days. Fallon's legs were pulled up. His back pressed against the wall. It wasn't comfortable, but at least he didn't have to fight for straw for a bed. He could sleep in this sitting position. And no one would be able to stick a knife in his back.

The cell was dark. Lights out had been sounded four hours earlier, as though there had even been light here. You didn't get a candle. Inmates with candles had a tendency to set cells afire. When the sun went down, you slept. Or you remained awake to stay alive.

"I heard the same thing."

He knew the voice. Diego Valdez, who had spent twenty years in prison and would never get out of Joliet alive.

"I hear you cut out Joe Martin's heart and ate it raw."

"Joe Martin had no heart."

Valdez laughed. "Maybe so, but he was a friend of mine."

"No, he wasn't. That's why you're still alive. If you liked Martin, you would have been with him. Then I would have killed you too. And I would have cut out your heart and eaten it raw. If I could have found the puny damned thing."

Valdez laughed again. "Well, maybe I will cut out your heart, lawdog."

"If you can find it."

Someone cursed both Valdez and Fallon from near the slop bucket, told them to shut up, that he wanted to sleep. Another man cursed the inmate sleeping next to him for kicking him in his sleep. Fallon tried to make himself more comfortable, at the same time attempting to make himself a smaller target for a rock or knife thrown in his direction.

"Sleep well, *gringo*," Valdez said.

"*Gracias*," said Fallon, and he knew he was safe. At least from Diego Valdez. Of the twelve hundred or thirteen hundred prisoners still in Joliet, Diego Valdez would be the happiest to have Joe Martin now outside the prison walls, lying beneath the sod in the cemetery. The death of Joe Martin made Diego Valdez king of the yard, or at least the leader of the Mexicans, Italians, and Spaniards in prison. The Irish had their own leader. So did the Germans. The Northern whites had a couple of leaders, and the few Southern whites had their own version of General Nathan Bedford Forrest.

Fallon did not sleep though. The man by the slop bucket would be the reason Fallon kept awake, not Diego Valdez. Fallon had arrested that man, much younger then, for running liquor in the Indian Territory. His name, Fallon remembered, was Joey Kurth. That had gotten him a year or two, courtesy of Judge Parker, but Joey Kurth had not reformed. He had been arrested again, for running whiskey and resisting a federal officer, and was in Joliet for five more years. He had not forgotten Fallon.

Fallon sighed. The Lord works in mysterious ways. That's what the parson had said the Sunday before the riot. Fallon didn't know what the Good Lord had planned for Harry "Hank" Fallon, but the ways were mysterious. He tried to figure out how the hell he came to be in the corner of a darkened cell he shared with five cutthroats.

CHAPTER FOUR

Fifteen, twenty years ago, no one would have been surprised to hear that Harry Fallon was in prison. His mother always warned him, "The devil's got his hand on you, boy—both hands, looks like—and he's a-gonna lead you to ruin. Which is his purpose." His pa never said much of anything, but when neighbors or the preacher mentioned Harry's wild streak, Pa would say, "Jail, prison, been knowed to turn a body around."

"So has a hangman," Fallon overheard that hard-shell sky pilot reply one time.

Hell, Fallon figured it too. And once he left home at fifteen, he had spent a few nights in jails. Mostly for disorderly conduct, public drunkenness, or disturbing the peace. He was quite good at disturbing the peace. Then, down around Gonzales, Texas, he hired on with Old Bill Porter, who was herding twenty-two hundred head of longhorn cattle to Newton, Kansas. Fallon rode drag, ate about his weight and the weight of all the horses in his string in dust. Once the crew got paid off in Newton, the boys decided to cut loose.

They must have done a right fine job of it, because Fallon

woke up the next morning lying on the floor of the cell in his own vomit and with a knot on his head the size of a goose egg. Fallon couldn't remember a thing after having a whiskey, and the trail crew's *segundo*, Josh Ryker, suggesting that the streetlamps sure made inviting targets for their .45s.

Thirty days and fifty dollars later, he and Ryker rode back to Texas. They rode the grub line that fall and winter, gambled some in Fort Worth, tried hunting buffalo up around Fort Griffin, and rounded up cattle down along the Frio River in the spring. A few months later, they drove another herd to Kansas, this one to Wichita.

Another jail. Another headache. Another fine and sentence from a frowning judge, only this time he had to muck stalls and empty spittoons in the mornings and replace streetlamps in the afternoon, before returning to the damp, hard, hot, stinking cell at night.

Once out, he joined another buffalo-hunting outfit and wound up at a place in the Texas Panhandle called Adobe Walls. The Comanche, Kiowa, and other Plains Indians just about set his sun that time—along with all the other hunters at the Walls, but Fallon learned something about himself during that hard fight.

"You shoot steady, boy," a mustachioed gunner named Bat Masterson told him. "With that Sharps Big Fifty and that .45 Colt. Who taught you?"

"Nobody taught me a thing," Fallon said.

"Hank's just a natural," Billy Dixon said as he reloaded his Sharps. "Just like me and you, Bat."

Almost getting his hair lifted by Indians, and not cottoning to all the flies and the blood and guts of being around dead buffalo, Harry Fallon sold his Sharps in Dodge City. He ran into Josh Ryker at a faro layout, and the two had a run of luck. One of the losers mentioned that two cowhands that lucky ought to head to Fort Smith.

"Where's Fort Smith?" Fallon asked.

"Arkansas. Just across the border from the Indian Territory."

"What's in Fort Smith?" Ryker asked.

"Well, for one thing, there's a high-stakes poker game in the back room of the Cherokee Saloon."

The next morning, Ryker and Fallon rode east.

Fort Smith, Arkansas, was a bit more civilized than Newton, Wichita, Adobe Walls, or Dodge City. For one thing, it was older. A bunch of the streets were cobblestone, while most of the buildings were brick. The river turned things humid, but the town had an icehouse, a bunch of factories, warehouses, eating places, gambling halls, dance halls, boardinghouses, saloons, and plenty of places where a young boy could find a lady, if you weren't too particular on how you described a lady. They ranged from two bits to twenty dollars.

Fort Smith also had a federal court, which the fellow back in the Varieties Saloon of Dodge City had failed to mention.

At the Cherokee Saloon, in that fabled back room, Josh Ryker and Harry Fallon learned there was a big difference between playing faro in Dodge City and playing poker in Fort Smith. They lost their stake on the first night. They had to sell the pack mule they had bought for the trail to Arkansas. They moved out of the fancy hotel to sleep in a wagon yard. Then they did what seemed logical to a couple of kids with six dollars and fifteen cents between them.

They got drunk.

The streetlamps in Fort Smith made inviting targets, too, and they were making their way down Third Street when a man driving a buggy stopped and gave them a hard stare.

"Demon rum will land you in front of me one day, lads," he said.

He wasn't an old fellow. Kind of handsome, Fallon guessed, and dressed like a Baptist preacher, with black trousers, black vest, black frock coat, and black string tie over a white shirt of a fine silk. His hat, a derby, was likewise black. He sported a well-groomed mustache and beard, and his eyes were firm.

"Wasn't rum," Fallon said as he shucked the empties from his .45 onto the boardwalk. "Rye . . ." He paused. "I think."

Ryker didn't find the man in black's intrusion humorous. "Who are you, mister? God?"

Those eyes saddened. "Not God, lads. Just a concerned citizen."

Ryker had holstered his Colt, but now he drew it, thumbed back the hammer, and pointed the long barrel at the man in the buggy.

"You're interrupting our game, mister, and we might just change targets from streetlamps to preachers who stick their Bibles and their fat noses in where they don't belong."

The rye whiskey no longer felt so warm in Fallon's belly. He tried to swallow, but found no spit in his mouth. Eventually, he swallowed down the bile and found enough in him to say, "Josh." He wanted to say more but didn't have the strength, or spit. If he opened his mouth, he figured he'd probably just vomit.

"What?" Josh Ryker turned, but at least he had lowered his .45. "You don't think I got gumption enough to pull a trigger?"

Fallon shook his head.

"One thing I hate, Hank, is preachers who stick their noses in my business." There was something else about Josh Ryker, Fallon, even in his drunkenness, noticed. The eyes were wild, crazy, and his face had turned ugly. He was a man, Fallon felt, who wanted to kill. Anyone. It didn't matter if it was this man in black, or Harry Fallon.

Fallon thought a little humor might ease things up. "He's too close, Josh. Wouldn't be fair. And he don't flicker like the candle in a streetlamp."

"Our lamps are gas, boys," the man in black said. Fallon wished that man would've kept his big mouth shut.

They now looked at the man in the buggy. Fallon became aware of something else. The man in the buggy had no fear.

Yet he smiled. "We are getting civilized in Fort Smith, lads." He let out a little sigh. "If only such were the case across the river in the Indian Nations."

"Maybe then," said Ryker, who still held his pistol but no longer pointed at the driver of the buggy, "we'll just cross that river."

"There are some rivers," the man said, "that you should not cross." He was speaking to Fallon, though, for his hard eyes locked on Fallon's until Fallon could not hold the cold stare. He looked at his boots.

"You're about to cross the Jordan, preacher," Ryker said.

Fallon felt his hand gripping his own Colt. He tried to think about what he could do. What he should do.

He didn't have to think. He didn't have to do anything except raise his hands high over his head.

Because a city policeman had managed to sneak up behind Josh Ryker. Fallon hadn't even seen the lawman, but then he had been busy staring at the man in the buggy and his pard, Josh Ryker. The lawman carried a double-barreled shotgun, sawed off to the grip. He didn't pull the triggers, though, just raised the Damascus barrels over Ryker's head and brought down the steel like an ax. The Colt hit the ground before Ryker, but, though still cocked, at least it did not go off. Ryker landed hard. And just like that, the lawman pointed the twin barrels in Fallon's direction.

Once Fallon's hands were raised, the lawman said, "With your left hand, unbuckle your rig and let it fall. Your hand comes close to that hogleg in the holster, you'll be having double-ought buckshot for your midnight snack."

Fallon did as he was told. He found himself sweating.

"Leave the piece," the lawman said, "and come over here."

Fallon obeyed again.

The lawman lowered the shotgun and looked at the man in the buggy.

"What do you want me to do with these two skunks, Your Honor?"

Fallon stared at the man in black. *Your Honor? You mean this fellow wasn't a sky pilot but a judge?*

"They aren't a federal problem, Andy," the man said as he released the brake and gathered the lines to the buggy. "At least for the time being. They are the city's problem. But I'd recommend leniency, though it's up to Judge Walker and a jury, if needed. I've often felt like shooting out these infernal streetlamps myself sometimes."

Judge Walker was less inclined for mercy. They spent the night in the city jail, sleeping it off with about five or six other drunks, and appeared in court the following afternoon. The fine, once the arresting officer mentioned the presence of Judge Isaac Parker, was levied at fifty dollars. Ryker had to sell his saddle and his blue roan gelding to get them both out of jail. Fifty dollars. Or fifty days. They got seventy-five dollars for the horse and saddle. Ryker lost twenty of it shooting craps that night at the Arkansas Gambling Parlor. But at least the man gambling with them was free with his whiskey.

This time, they did not try to shoot out any streetlamps. In fact, they might have made it all the way back, no matter how roostered they were on that gent's whiskey, to the wagon yard to sleep it off there. But McAllister's Saddle Shop happened to be on the way.

Ryker stopped so short, Fallon almost ran into him. The tall Texan lunged toward the big plateglass window and looked with intense purpose at the saddle sitting on a sawhorse.

"Look at that, Hank," Ryker said. "Ain't she a beaut?"

Pretty drunk, very drunk, but Fallon could see the workmanship that went into the saddle. He also knew something else.

"You ain't gonna get that saddle for five bucks when this fellow opens up, Josh," Fallon said. "And you ain't got a horse to set it on even if you could afford it."

Ryker drew his revolver before Fallon could even think. Ryker turned the butt around and quickly smashed the glass.

"Josh!" Fallon yelled. "What the hell are you doing?" Which was a stupid thing to ask. Fallon knew exactly what his pard was doing. More glass shards rained onto the inside of the shop and on the boardwalk as Ryker swung the Colt again.

Holstering the .45, Ryker spun around, pushed Fallon aside, and stared down the darkened street.

"Nothing," Ryker said. "We got it. Help me get this thing out."

"I'm not doing any such thing." Fallon had done a lot of

things in his life, caused a lot of trouble, but he had never stolen anything. He didn't even care to ride the grub line.

Ryker didn't hear. He was too busy reaching through the busted window and dragging the saddle out.

Fallon moved toward him, trying to stop his pard. A saddle like that would cost a lot of money. If they got caught, they'd be looking at a bigger fine and sentence than anything they'd gotten for getting a little roostered and trying to sow their oats, raise a little hell, but all in fun.

Fallon had a choice to make.

CHAPTER FIVE

He made it.

Fallon grabbed Ryker's shoulders, tried to pull him away from the busted window and the hand-tooled saddle. The saddle fell among the glass. Ryker turned, cutting the top of his left hand on sharp glass. He almost tripped on the saddle.

"This ain't right . . ." Fallon started.

Ryker didn't let him finish. His fist came up and landed in Fallon's stomach. Air whooshed out of his lungs. He almost emptied his stomach of the free pretzels and whiskey he had consumed at the gambling hall. The next blow caught him just over the temple. He dropped to his knees on the boardwalk, feeling glass cutting through his threadbare trousers and into his knees. Then he felt himself being lifted, kicked, and hurled into the alley between the saddle shop and a millinery. He landed against a trash barrel, knocked it over, and rolled off into the dust. A cat screeched and ran. Ryker cursed.

Fallon lay on his back. He blinked. He stared at the stars. A roach crawled across his face. He wondered if he should close his eyes. That's what he wanted to do. But something told him, commanded him, to get up.

Get up, damn you. Get the hell up.

"Hold it!"

Fallon groaned. He mouthed, "Hold what?"

He made himself sit up, then leaned to his side and braced himself. Blood leaked from his nose and lips. He thought he would throw up, but somehow managed to avoid that. He shook his head to clear it. That didn't help.

"Step up. Hands up."

Fallon gripped the overturned trash barrel. He stared out of the alley at the street. A man stood there, dressed in brown pants, a tan vest, and a flat-crowned dun-colored hat. He held a short-barreled pistol.

"You heard me, buster. Do what I say or I bust you good, boy."

It struck Fallon that the man with the pistol wasn't talking to him. He certainly wasn't looking in Fallon's direction. Slowly, Fallon understood that the man was talking to Josh Ryker.

The man walked out of Fallon's line of vision.

"You dumb waddie," the voice said from the boardwalk in front of the saddle shop.

It wasn't the same policeman who had arrested Fallon and Ryker that night with the federal judge. That much Fallon could tell. Then this weird notion came to Fallon. The whiskey brought it on, he figured later. But there it was. *Maybe I can explain?* Later, he wondered, *Explain what?* Later, he thought, *I should have just stayed where I was. I could've even slept here, even with the roaches and that cat.*

But this was a night of choices. He made another. He found his feet, shook his head, and weaved this way and that, somehow making his way to the street. It took all of his effort just to reach the edge of the alley. He leaned against the side of the millinery's shop, tried to clear his head. He tried to remember what it was that he was supposed to be doing.

The voices reminded him.

"Attempted burglary. Destruction of private property. Drunkenness. Don't touch the butt of that pistol, boy, or you'll make everything a whole lot worse than what you're looking at now."

Fallon hadn't moved.

"Gun him down, Hank!" Ryker yelled.

The thing was, Fallon knew, Josh Ryker couldn't see him. Nor could the lawman.

"I've been lawing for a long time," the man said. "You ain't pulling the wool over my eyes."

Fallon wanted to explain. What, he didn't exactly know. He stepped out of the alley and saw the lawman's back. He was big, bigger than Fallon expected, with pants stuck inside tall, black, stovepipe boots. The tails of his frock coat had been pushed back, giving him an easy reach of the two revolvers he wore, one butt forward, the other, on his right hip, rear-facing. Of course, the shotgun was all he needed right now.

In the weeks, months, and years to come, Harry Fallon would remember the first lesson he learned about being a deputy marshal—or being even just an innocent bystander: never, never, never step behind a man who has a cocked, double-barreled shotgun while he's trying to make an arrest. And never, never, never clear your throat.

That's what he did though. He was just a fool kid, green behind the ears. And he was drunk.

The lawman whirled, bracing the butt of the sawed-off scattergun against his hip.

Everything that happened after that seemed to move incredibly slowly. All these years later, Fallon could remember it perfectly. Every detail, to the drops of sweat, the pounding of his heart, and the desperate breaths.

"No!" Fallon screamed, and leaped aside. He felt the rush of buckshot tear past him, burning his side, two chunks splintering the butt of his Colt, still holstered. He could even hear the shot tearing into the side of the building.

The lawman had rushed his shot and squeezed both triggers.

How he had missed, Fallon couldn't fathom. But now he saw the man pitching the empty twelve-gauge to the boardwalk and drawing the revolver on his right hip.

"Don't!" Fallon tried again.

The lawman didn't listen. Perhaps he couldn't hear. Harry Fallon barely heard anything except the ringing of the shotgun blast. He also saw Josh Ryker, palming his own Colt—the one he had refused to drop. A wicked grin stretched across Ryker's face.

What Fallon couldn't remember was drawing his own Colt. But the weapon was in his right hand, the hammer cocked, and he squeezed the trigger.

Screaming, the lawman dropped to his knees as his Colt spun into the center of the dark, empty street. He grabbed for his bleeding right wrist, cursed, and then made a move with his left hand for the other pistol.

Fallon felt himself thumbing back the hammer in the weapon that warmed his clammy right hand.

"Don't," he said for the third time.

And he saw the cocked Colt in Josh Ryker's right hand.

Fallon fired first. The shot sliced through the left collar on the lawman's coat, causing him to fall to his right. That allowed the bullet that Josh Ryker just fired to dig up sod in the street a few feet in front of the lawman.

The peace officer turned, but he had dropped his gun. He saw Ryker, the smoking Colt, and that look on Ryker's face. Desperately, he reached for the nearest Colt with his good hand. Ryker tried to cock his weapon, but the Colt had jammed. He ran forward, cutting loose with a Johnny Reb battle cry, and brought the barrel down hard on the lawman's head.

The lawman dropped, faceup, in the ground.

Fallon's ears rang even louder now. But somehow he could hear shouts coming from all directions. Dogs barked. He could see lights turning up through curtained windows. And he could see Josh Ryker.

His pard had pitched his jammed Colt into the street. Now he bent over and picked up one of the revolvers the lawman had dropped. Smiling again, Ryker brought the Colt up, cocked it, and pointed it just inches from the peace officer's face.

"This is better," Ryker said in a voice Fallon hardly recognized—which wasn't because of the ringing in Fallon's ears. "I'd rather you see this than gun you down from behind, you lowdown cur."

This time, Fallon didn't yell *Don't.* He called out Ryker's name. And he raised the .45 in his own hand.

"Stay out of this, Hank!" Ryker cried. "He's mine."

A second later, Ryker realized what Fallon meant. He swung the Colt in Fallon's direction, and the gun bucked and roared in Fallon's hand.

Left arm pulsing blood, Ryker spun around, landing on his knees beside the lawman. He hadn't dropped his weapon, though, and tried to bring it up with his good arm. Fallon wasn't standing still, however. As soon as he had fired, he had started running. He stepped inside Ryker's outstretched right arm, raised that smoking .45, and brought the butt down against Ryker's hat.

Ryker groaned, and dropped hard, unconscious. Fallon didn't like the look of his pard's arm, but he had sense enough to holster his Colt and jerk the weapon from Ryker's grip. The Colt he pitched aside, and then he squatted beside the lawman.

The man wore a six-point badge pinned to the lapel of his vest.

A slight curse came out as a sigh from Fallon's mouth. The badge read:

DEPUTY
U.S.
MARSHAL

The man gripped his bleeding wrist. He blinked. He was still conscious. Fallon heard hoofbeats now and footsteps pounding the boardwalk. Dogs still barked. Somewhere a bell rang.

Part of him wanted to stand up and run out of here. Run like hell. Maybe even run back to his folks' place in Gads Hill, Missouri. A body could hide a long, long time in that rough country.

Instead, he let out a sigh, and asked, "How bad you hurt, mister?"

If the lawman answered, Fallon never heard it.

There were steps behind him, a curse, and then something caught Harry Fallon on the back of his head. He saw orange, red, purple, white. Then he saw nothing at all.

He woke, not in the city jail, but a dark, damp dungeon. He found himself in a pit with men—white, black, Indian,

Mexican, even a couple of Chinese—some in rags, most in chains. He woke with a man emptying Fallon's pockets.

His knee came up and caught the man in his groin. When the man sat back, and grabbed his crotch, Fallon came up and belted the man across the jaw. The man went down, cried, gagged, vomited, and crawled away. Fallon would've gone after him, but his head hurt, and he became dizzy.

The men watching him just laughed.

One day later, two big black men in blue uniforms with badges came through the locked doors. One called his name. Fallon slowly rose and walked toward them. The silent one shoved him through the door. They led him out of the dungeon and into the courthouse. Outside of an office, the first one knocked on the door. A voice said something from the inside. The man opened the door, stepped back, and held the door open.

"Judge Parker'll see you now," the man said, and Harry Fallon walked in.

First, he recognized the man sitting in the leather-lined chair in front of the big desk. It was the lawman who had tried to arrest Josh Ryker, the one who had almost blown Fallon in half with a shotgun. His right wrist was bandaged, and another stretched across his head, but he seemed to be in good spirits for a man who had come this close to getting killed. He was smoking a good cigar. And he smiled at Harry Fallon.

The second man. Well, Fallon wasn't so sure he wanted to see Judge Isaac Parker. He remembered him from that night, what seemed a lifetime earlier.

"I told you, Mister"—the judge glanced at a sheet of paper on his desk—"Fallon . . . that demon rum would land you in front of me one day. And here you are."

Fallon studied his boots. "Yes, sir."

"Breaking and entering. Attempted burglary. Unlawful discharge of a firearm in the city limits. The state would have fun with you. But shooting an officer of the federal court, that puts you in my bailiwick. Resisting a deputy marshal is a year in prison. But shooting one. The solicitor says he thinks he should try you and"—he looked at the paper again—"your partner, one Joshua Ryker, with attempted murder. You won't swing. This time. But after a year in Leavenworth or Joliet, you'll wish you had."

The judge glanced at the wounded lawman. "What do you think, Bob?"

"He'll do," the lawman said.

That caused Fallon to lift his head.

The judge grinned. He tossed a six-pointed badge at Fallon. It landed at his feet. Fallon swallowed, looked at it, then the judge, and then the deputy marshal covered with bandages.

"It's not a gift," Judge Parker said. "And some people, many of whom I respect, might advise you that a ten-year sentence in some federal prison would be better than what you would likely procure if you pick up that badge, young man. The choice, however, is yours."

CHAPTER SIX

He made his choice. He lived with it. Mostly, it had been good. Not always, of course. Only a crazy person would think that having men try to fill you full of bullet holes was a good way to make a living. Fallon had been knifed, he had been hit with wagon spokes, chairs, brooms, ax handles, hammers, pistol barrels, shotgun barrels, rifle barrels, barrel staves, bottles of all sorts and sizes, and even a singletree. He had been shot twice. He had been in so many brawls, he couldn't count them all—certainly he didn't want to remember most of them. He had been bitten, clawed, scratched, urinated on, slapped, gouged, vomited on, and choked. He had been kicked by men, women, children, horses, mules, and asses. All in five years. Oh, for five glorious years, he had ridden for Judge Parker and his court with jurisdiction over the Western District of Arkansas, which included lawless Indian Territory. Fallon had sent men to federal prisons, and to the gallows. He had shot down nine men in self-defense.

For the past ten years, however, he had been in prison,

proving all those predictions from his parents, preachers, teachers, and friends correct.

He had been imprisoned. He was innocent, of course, but none of that mattered. Parker had sentenced him. Parker, feeling betrayed, had thrown the book at Fallon. The book? And half the damned library.

Harry Fallon didn't blame him. Considering the lies sworn under oath, the framed evidence, well, Fallon would have likely done the same thing Parker had.

The guards came to him while he was emptying bedpans from the prison hospital. The two burly men, newcomers—transferred from another prison, the turnkeys said—tapped their sticks against their thighs.

"Fallon," the one with the black front teeth said. "You're to come with us. Warden's orders."

Fallon held the two pots toward the guard, but kept his eyes on the dirt in front of him. "What about these?"

"Leave them," the one with the mustache said.

Fallon shrugged. "If you insist." He set the pots on the ground, wiped his hands on his trousers, and waited.

"To your cell," Black Teeth said.

When Fallon turned, Black Teeth stopped him. "Not that way." He pointed his stick. Fallon looked at that, questioning the newcomer, but not saying a thing. He walked toward his old prison block, to the cell he had lived in before the riot.

The block remained practically empty. Carpenters, hired from the outside world, busied themselves white-washing the bloodstains. Others worked on the doors or repaired the bunks. Hammers echoed in the cavernous building. Yet the smell of sweating men, of tobacco, paint, and sawdust, could not rid the block of the odor of burned flesh, or of splattered brains and human intestines.

He stopped in front of his cell and looked between the iron bars.

It was, he found to his surprise, relatively intact. A few papers had been thrown on the floor. The bunk even looked as it had when Fallon had left for his work assignment that day. The bunks of his cell mates looked no worse for wear either.

He tried to understand what the men had been thinking. Why they might leave one cell alone. His cell was easy enough to figure out. He had been in the laundry. The Mormon kid had been in the hospital with an intestinal complaint. The other two were on latrine duty. But the cell next to his was being painted. The rioters had found the keys, opened it, and tossed a bucket of coal oil onto the man who had killed a seven-year-old girl. Then they had shattered a burning lantern on the floor, slammed the door shut, and locked it.

The place still stank of death.

It always would.

So the men moved from cell to cell, killing some— turnkeys, mostly—releasing a few, ignoring many. Then they had moved on, to the lower floors, and outside to kill and be killed, before they had reached the laundry—and Harry Fallon.

Keys rattled in Black Teeth's hand as he stepped in front of Fallon and guessed which key would work. It took him four guesses, but at last, the door slid open. Fallon stepped inside. He waited for the door to close. Maybe this was the warden's idea of punishment. Make Fallon wait in his cell with nothing to do but smell the stink of a child killer who had been burned alive.

The door remained open.

"Get your stuff, Fallon," Black Teeth said.

"My stuff?" He did not look back.

"Whatever you got that you want. Hurry up, man, this place makes my skin crawl. And that smell . . . just get what you want, damn it, and let's get out of this horrible place."

Fallon tried to guess what all this meant. It didn't take him long. They had been transferring guards from other prisons to here, and they had been moving prisoners to other prisons, at least, until this would become inhabitable. Fallon might be considered a hard-timer, but his record was, compared to most inmates at Joliet, clean. A couple of fights, but those had been with prisoners, not guards. And while his attitude might not please wardens, chaplains, or guards, he had never struck any of those. Quite a few times, of course, that had taken remarkable restraint.

He moved to his bunk, reached under the pillow, and found the worn tintype. He didn't look at the images of the woman and girl, and quickly slid that in his pocket. Then he reached for the bedpost. He twisted the top, pulled it open, and reached inside the hole he had hollowed out. He found the tin star and tried to put that in his other pocket.

"What's that?" the mustachioed guard asked.

Fallon let his fingers open.

"You hid that to get out of here?" Black Teeth asked. "Figured you'd use it to walk right through these gates."

"Our guards aren't that stupid," Fallon said. This time, he looked Black Teeth right into his rheumy eyes. "At least, they haven't been."

"Deputy marshal," Mustache said.

"Deputy U.S. Marshal," said Black Teeth with a snort. His head cocked. "You mean to tell me you once was a lawman."

"I don't remember." Fallon held the badge toward Black Teeth. "It's contraband. Take it, if you want. Write me up."

Black Teeth started, but stopped, pulling his free hand

back and clutching the stick tighter. He must have thought Fallon was trying to trap him in something. Planning some escape.

"Hell, Gary," Mustache said, "let him keep the damned thing. What can he do other than stick someone with the pin on the back?"

That caused Black Teeth to snort and smile.

"That all you got?" he asked.

Fallon slid the badge into his other pocket.

"That's all." He looked again at the cell floor, giving the guards the respect they wanted. Or what they took for respect.

"Out," Black Teeth said, and Fallon stepped onto the walkway. He looked over the edge at the lower floor. The door clanged shut.

"To the warden's office," Black Teeth said.

Fallon walked.

Warden Jethro Amadeus Cain sat behind his mahogany desk, decorated with crystal lamps, a silver ashtray, a Bible, likely never opened. A portrait of Napoleon hung on the wall behind his head. He was a fat man, with white hair, a fat nose, puffy cheeks, and he spoke with a lisp.

"You ttthiink yer sssmartttt," he said when Fallon stepped inside the office.

Fallon said nothing, but he glanced to his right to find Captain Daggett sitting in another chair. Daggett shuffled through some papers, placing them on the desk as he read, or at least pretended to read, each one.

"Assskk me, you planned ttthat riottt," Cain said. "We jjjussst can'tttt ppprove ittt."

Fallon waited. If they were going to send him to another prison, he wished they would hurry up.

"Uunnderssstttand tthhhaat I had nnnnotthingggg to do with thhhisssss." Cain bit off the end of his cigar, stuck it in his mouth, and picked up a yellow telegram. He started to light the cigar, thought better of it, and set it in the polished silver ashtray.

He waved the paper in the air.

"Thhheee governor hasss given you a pppparole."

Fallon looked thunderstruck. He straightened, turned his head, and wondered if he had heard that clearly. Paroled?

"Issss evverythhhhhing in order, Caaaptain?" the warden asked Daggett.

Daggett placed the last page on the desk. "Appears to be in order, sir."

Picking up the cigar, Cain found a match and struck it, put the cigar in his teeth, and lit it. Once he had the cigar smoking, he removed it and waved it in Daggett's direction. That must have been his way of ordering the captain of the guards to speak. Fallon didn't care much for Daggett, but at least the pig didn't speak with an annoying lisp.

"The parole requires you to be employed within the state of Illinois," Daggett said. "This is not a pardon. It is a parole. Violation of the parole will land you back in this prison, or any prison, immediately for the duration of your sentence. You are required to attend church services, of your religious preference, on Sundays, and the minister will report your presence. Failure to attend church will mean this parole is revoked and you will be returned immediately to this prison or another to complete the duration of your sentence. You are not to drink intoxicating spirits. You are not to gamble in public or private. You must not associate with known gamblers or anyone who has been convicted of a felony in Illinois or any state or territory. Failure to comply with this requirement will result in the immediate revocation of this parole and you will be returned to this facility or another for completion of your original sentence. You will be employed. You must have a job. You will start employment on Monday at Werner's Wheelwright in Chicago. Lodging has been arranged for you at Missus Ketchum's Boarding House near Lake Michigan. Your first month's rent has been paid from the money you have earned while in prison. One word of negative nature about your conduct from Herr Werner or Missus Ketchum will lead to the immediate revocation of this parole and you will be returned to this prison or a similar facility for the completion of your original sentence. These are the terms, non-negotiable, of this parole. Do you have any questions?"

Before Fallon could open his mouth, the warden was sliding a few slips of paper in Fallon's direction. He removed his cigar, and said, "Thhhheesseee are thhee addressssssessss of your landlorrrrd and yourrr employeeeerrr." He found another paper. "Thisssss isss a copy of terrmmms of yourrrr parrolllle."

Daggett continued. "You must report to an agent of the court in the city of Chicago once a month, or whenever he requests you to visit. He will meet you at the wheelwright office on Monday." He slid one of the papers he had put on the warden's desk. "Sign here. Or back to your cell."

CHAPTER SEVEN

He understood then. He was walking out. Not free. Just paroled. But that meant something. He just couldn't quite believe it was happening. This fast.

"Ffffallonnn," the warden said. He grinned. "You'llll be baccckkk heeere. Rreeall sssoooonnn."

Fallon took the pen and signed the bottom of the paper. He slid the paper toward Captain Daggett, who looked up at him, nodded, and the guard's lips mouthed a silent *Thank you.* But the captain's eyes showed no kindness. Instead, Fallon figured that Daggett meant to warn him: *I got you paroled; I can put you back in the sweatbox too.*

Still, this was Captain Daggett's doing. The captain had lived up to his word. He had done something for Harry Fallon. Well, more than likely, he had wanted Fallon out of Joliet before he might start talking about what had really happened in the laundry during the riot.

Fallon didn't care.

"There's a suit of clothes in the warden's secretary's office," Daggett said. "You'll also be given the money due you, less the rent we sent to the boardinghouse in Chicago.

Transportation is on you, Fallon. You have to be in Chicago by eight o'clock Monday."

The suit felt worse than his prison garb. The wool was bristly and itchy, almost as bad as the socks. The straw porkpie hat didn't fit. The shirt he could tolerate, as long as no one asked him to button on a paper collar. He'd choke.

They gave him a small suitcase, not that Fallon had anything to carry in it. But he might, so he accepted it, and the money they handed him in a tan envelope, tied together with a string.

Once he stepped outside, he waited, eager to hear the gates close behind him. It sounded different than it had when he had first arrived at Joliet, when the door slammed shut, telling him loudly that he wouldn't be going anywhere for a long, long time. That noise had chilled and sickened him. "Nothin' like that sound," an inmate told him later, "to put the fear of God in a body."

This time, Fallon smiled. He stared at the sun, and he filled his lungs with fresh air. Free air. Some convicts had said they'd dance around the prison the day they got out. A few said they'd do something else on Joliet's walls. All Harry Fallon wanted to do was get away from this hellhole and purge it from his memory.

Even as he started to cross Collins Street, Fallon saw the dust.

"They must really want me gone," Fallon heard himself saying. Even his voice sounded different.

The hack arrived, and Fallon stepped inside.

"To the depot," he told the driver, and leaned back to enjoy the view from a buggy.

* * *

Having missed the last train to Chicago, Fallon slept on the bench at the station. The bench was hard, but Fallon could sleep where and when he felt like it. Other railroad workers and a few gamblers waited in the station, some bound for Chicago, others bound for wherever. None spoke to Fallon, and even the city policeman who walked through to check the station ignored the man on the bench.

The next morning, he crossed the street to the café and ordered a breakfast of ham, eggs, and coffee. The burly man behind the counter, his teeth clamped on a soggy, well-chewed cigar, glowered.

Fallon made himself look up at the big cuss. He wasn't used to looking men in the eyes. The man crossed his arms. The arms were huge.

Suddenly, Fallon laughed, and he reached inside his wooly coat's pocket and found the envelope.

"How much?" he asked.

"Dime," the man with the cigar said.

Fallon paid him. In prison, he never had to pay for his meals. This would take some getting used to.

So he finished his food, had a second and third cup of coffee, visited the privy, and returned to the depot. He thought about buying the morning newspaper—the ones he had read in the prison library were usually at least a couple of weeks old, and often, read and held so many times, most of the ink had smudged until the copy was undecipherable. He had grimaced at paying the driver for the cab ride from the prison. Now his envelope felt ten more cents lighter, so reading a newspaper would have to wait until he got his first pay. Unless Chicago had a good public library.

At 7:42 a.m., he stepped aboard the coach, found a seat by the window, and settled in. When the train pulled away from the station, he looked at his wrists, and then at the seat empty next to him. That hadn't been the case when he had left Fort Smith for Joliet ten years back. A federal deputy had been right beside him, hardly saying a word during the entire trip even though he had ridden often with Fallon into the Nations. And iron manacles had rubbed Fallon's wrists raw.

He stared out the window, watched the city pass, then the fields of grain and corn, then more towns. This wasn't the West, not the Indian Territory or Arkansas where towns could be few and far between. This was civilization. The outskirts of Chicago roared past him, then he found himself in a jungle of tall buildings, more people than he had seen in one place at one time than he could remember. It had been a quick trip. Fallon grabbed his grip, tried to get his hat on a little tighter, and left the train, then the depot, and found another hack.

"Where to?" the driver asked in a thick Irish brogue.

Fallon found the paper with the address and name of the boardinghouse. His mouth opened, and he grinned. "Lake Michigan."

He might as well see the lake. He had heard so much about it, he figured he wanted to see it.

"It's a big lake, mate," the hack said. "Any particular point?"

"It's your city," Fallon said. "You choose."

The boardinghouse was supposed to be near the lake, and Harry Fallon was in no hurry.

Once he paid that driver, Fallon read the address to the boardinghouse.

"You want to go there now, mate?" the Irishman asked. "You haven't even seen the lake."

"I want to know if I can walk there from here," Fallon said.

The driver shrugged and sighed. He reached under the seat and pulled out a map.

"It's a big city, mate," he said. "Never heard of the street. Ye say it's a boardinghouse?"

"That's right."

"Ye just get into town?"

"Yes."

"And ye want to see Lake Michigan before ye see anything else?"

"That's why I'm here."

"Well, I would have opted for Flannery's Saloon, or Molly's House of Purity."

"Maybe later," Fallon said.

"Here it is." The driver's stubby finger stopped at a point. "It's a fine stretch of the legs from here." He snorted. "A bloody long stretch of the legs from just about anywhere. Ye want me to wait?"

"Wait?"

"Sure. No charge for me waiting, mate. Come to think on it, I've never really looked at Lake Michigan me ownself. But ye strikes me as a lad who wants to be alone. So I'll go that way, ye go the other. Unless ye prefer the other way around."

Fallon stepped away from the wagon. "Meet you here in fifteen minutes."

"That's not a bloody long time, mate."

"But it's free time," Fallon said.

The driver just stared. Fallon nodded, and walked to the shore.

He had heard about the wind coming off Lake Michigan. Now he felt it. It blew his straw hat off. Fallon made a grab for it, but the hat was already rolling across the shoreline. He took a couple of steps, figuring to chase it down, but stopped. He laughed, leaned back, and watched it roll a few more yards before the breeze picked it up and lofted it high in the air. It rose like a balloon, started to fall, found another draft, and sailed out over the massive lake.

Fallon turned to face the wind, to feel all of this air— this free air—massaging his face, cooling his hair. He was a kid again. Mostly, he was free. Well, paroled. He was miles from the Illinois State Penitentiary.

The wind didn't die down, but it relaxed, and Fallon turned to look at the boats, boats of all sizes and shapes, at the docks and in the water. He turned to look at the towering buildings. He glanced this way and that, wanting to see if anybody else came here simply to admire and appreciate the view.

He was alone, except for the driver of the hack, who hadn't walked too far away from his cab.

Fallon started to sit down, to take off his shoes, but, heck, he was on parole. And stepping into Lake Michigan with his lousy shoes on would not violate the conditions of his parole resulting in his return to Joliet or a similar facility for the completion of his original sentence.

The water was cold. He wiggled his toes in his terrible socks and uncomfortable shoes. He moved a little deeper, but not even halfway to his knees. A gull flew overhead. Fallon watched it fly until it disappeared in the skyline of the city. He turned, trying to find any ducks, or geese, but saw only empty bottles and assorted trash. For some reason, that saddened him.

At length, he waded out of the lake and stepped onto the grass. Another urge struck him, so he sat on the grass, unlaced the shoes, and pulled them off. The water-soaked socks came off with them. Then Fallon stepped away from the shoes and let his feet settle in the grass. He wiggled his toes. He laughed.

The driver was walking back to the cab. Fallon figured close to fifteen minutes had passed, and he wanted to be a man of his word. He bent down, wrung out the socks, and stuck them in the wet shoes, which he picked up in his left hand. His right took the grip he had carried with him—just in case the Irish cab driver decided not to wait for the passenger—and moved back to the cab.

"Ye be an odd man," the driver said as he held open the door. "That's fer sure."

"I'm alive," Fallon said. *For the first time in ten years*, he thought, *I actually feel alive.*

"That be grand, me boy. Grand indeed. Shall I take ye to yer boardinghouse?"

"Remember the address?" Fallon asked.

"Indeed."

"Thank you, kind sir." Fallon stepped into the coach, heard the door shut, and set his wet socks–stuffed shoes on the floor alongside his grip. The wagon dipped as the heavy coachman climbed into the box. The brake was released, the quirt snapped, the driver cursed, and the wagon wheels rolled across the street of cobblestone. He saw the watchtower, or whatever it was, that had gone up after the big fire in the early seventies. He saw people of all sizes and shapes. He leaned back, enjoying the rhythm of the wheels. He wondered if he would make a halfway decent wheelwright, and he thought about seeing wheels that he had made on the axles of wagons. Maybe even this coach.

The scents of the lakeside faded. Other aromas assaulted his nostrils. Baked bread. Roasting peppers. Potatoes frying. Foods he could not place but made his mouth water.

He listened to languages he had never heard, vastly different from the guttural voices of the Cherokee, Choctaw, Creek, and Chickasaw, or the sing-song voice of the Kiowa or the fierce vocals of the Comanche. He heard laughter of children. A stick connected against a baseball. Pots clanged together. Hammers pounded. Hooves clopped.

No sound escaped his ears. Including that of the Irishman in the driver's box. The cab began to slow and came to a quick stop.

"What be the bloody meaning of this?" the Irishman asked.

Boots sounded on the cobblestone.

"Oh." The driver's voice lost its threatening tone. "Is there a problem, Officer?"

"Just drive on, you lousy little mick, once we get in." He gave an address that might have been in Chicago and might have been in San Francisco for all Fallon knew.

The doors opened on both sides of the cab, and big men climbed into the coach, closing the door behind them. One held a Remington .44 in his right hand. The other had a nightstick, which he tapped against the door.

They sat across from Fallon. They did not smile.

The coach pulled forward.

Both men had badges pinned to the lapels of their checkered vests.

CHAPTER EIGHT

"Remember me, Fallon?" the one on Fallon's right asked with a grin that held no mirth. He flipped the nightstick, caught it, and started tapping the seat with one end.

He was a big man, solid, nothing to him except muscles, scars, and a thick brown mustache and beard. The hair underneath his bowler was short cropped. His knuckles were crooked, and the tip of the pointer finger on his right hand was missing. The nightstick kept right on tapping, but Fallon saw the bulge under his left armpit. There was a shoulder holster underneath the Prince Albert coat. And from the way the big man sat on the bench, Fallon figured he had another hideaway weapon stuck near the small of his back.

The shield front badge was thin, brass, tarnished. Fallon studied it briefly, and saw that it was the same kind as the one the other man had on his ugly checkered vest. Engraved on the thickest part of the badge were the words

AMERICAN
DETECTIVE
AGENCY

Harry Fallon had never heard of it. As a federal lawman, he had worked with agents from Wells Fargo and Pinkerton's men, and some small-time operations out of Texas and St. Louis. But American Detective Agency? Well, he didn't care much for it. That much was sure.

"Holderman," Fallon said. He shot the one on his left a quick look. Not as big as Aaron Holderman, not as ugly, and no beard, just a twisted mustache of black, with streaks of gray in the twisted corners and on his sideburns. Fallon didn't know him. At least, he didn't recognize him.

But Holderman?

You don't forget a brute like Aaron Holderman.

"Been a long time, Hank." Holderman stopped tapping the nightstick, which he shifted to his left hand. His right thumb hooked into the pocket on his vest. Closer to the pistol in that shoulder holster, Fallon figured.

Fallon kept his mouth shut.

"Ain't you gonna say it's good to see me, Hank? Ask how I've been?"

Fallon had plenty of questions to ask, but he wasn't about to give Aaron Holderman the pleasure. He kept his eyes on the man he had put in prison for resisting arrest and running whiskey in the Cherokee Nation. So what kind of detective agency would hire a convicted felon? And what would the American Detective Agency want with Harry Fallon?

That's not what really bothered Fallon though. The coach turned around in the middle of the street and started going back—away from Fallon's new landlord's boardinghouse. What would two detectives want with Fallon? *Detectives.* He had trouble accepting that. Aaron Holderman was a lot of things, but he wasn't a detective. Or any kind of peace officer.

Fallon was out of Joliet on parole. Maybe a private

operative would be assigned to check on him. Yet the obvious place for that to have happened would have been at the boardinghouse. Or the wheelwright's shop. Yet Holderman and the other mass of muscle had found Fallon near Lake Michigan. Which meant they had followed Fallon as soon as he got off the train in Chicago. Which meant someone had to have been at the Joliet depot to let Holderman and his associate know when he would be arriving in Chicago.

No. Fallon wanted to dismiss that theory. Probably this was just happenstance. Fate. Holderman was passing by, recognized Fallon, and decided to have some fun.

Fallon quickly dismissed that theory. Holderman hadn't seen Fallon since Fallon had sent him to prison thirteen years ago. For a two-year sentence. Fallon remembered Holderman, but Fallon remembered most faces. That was a talent that helped you stay alive as a federal marshal. Holderman was a two-bit crook, a small-time whiskey runner and drunk whose only talent was in his fists.

Which would be the only reason anyone would hire Aaron Holderman.

So now his question was: What does the American Detective Agency want with me?

He refused to ask Holderman. Fallon would find out soon enough.

But Aaron Holderman would not shut up.

"You like this badge, Hank?" He rubbed his tie across the shield. "I think it's funny. Don't you? You once wore a badge too. Now I got one. You know what's even funnier? To me. Maybe to you too." He glanced at the other brute. "Timmons, me and Hank go back a long time. Here's the funny thing though. He has . . . had . . . this reputation for being honest. Honest as the day's long. Honest as ol' Abe Lincoln. But he's spent more time in prison than I did. Two years for me here in Illinois. Eight months in Cañon City, Colorado. Three years in Louisiana. At Angola. That's less than six years, all told. Fallon? He done ten years. In Joliet too. Ten hard years."

The coach turned again.

Holderman kept talking. Fallon kept thinking.

They followed me. You need to learn not to relax. Think just like you had to think in Joliet. In the Nations. Watch your back. Look for sign. Keep your senses sharp. Do that . . . to stay alive.

Holderman was still talking. Fallon again looked out the window, trying to figure out where he was, but this Chicago was new territory for him. He'd have to learn it.

"Man, Hank. I haven't heard nothin' from you. You gotta forgive me, pal. I've been talking this whole time. Hogging the conversation. So let's hear what you've been up to." He nodded, grinned, and poked the nightstick under Fallon's chin.

"Here's something you can answer for me. How's the wife and the kid?"

It happened before Fallon realized what he was doing. Reflexes took over. Reflexes . . . memories . . . pure hatred.

His right hand shot up, ripped the stick from the surprised Holderman's hand. The other brute, the one called Timmons, lunged across the coach, bringing his fist up. Fallon saw the flash and realized that the man wore a pair of brass knuckles.

Timmons didn't get a chance to use them. Fallon kept the stick moving, and heard it slam against the side of the man's face. The fist with the knuckles barely scraped Fallon's ear. Timmons dropped onto his knees, tried to shake his head clear, but Fallon brought his left fist up. He didn't have much room to land a solid blow, but it was enough to send Timmons back onto his buttocks, his back against the seat.

By then, Aaron Holderman had jerked the pistol from his shoulder holster. A pocket Smith & Wesson, Fallon noticed, which looked like a toy in Holderman's big hand. The hand didn't hold the weapon for long.

The nightstick came down, and Fallon heard the sharp crack of the leather-wrapped club on Holderman's wrist. The big man yelped in pain, and the little .32 dropped onto the floor. Holderman reached for his wrist with his left hand, thought better of it, and used it to grab for the nightstick. When he did, Fallon sent a wide haymaker with his left fist that caught the big man's ear. He hit the door hard. Fallon tried to open the door, and push Holderman into the street, but Timmons had recovered, and, on his knees, wrapped his arms around Fallon's torso.

The man squeezed. Fallon sucked in his breath, trying to make himself smaller. He saw Holderman shaking his head, seeing the Smith & Wesson and picking it up.

"Don't shoot him, you damned fool!" Timmons said in a tight voice. "MacGregor wants him alive."

Holderman shifted the gun, brought it up to bring the butt down on Fallon's skull.

Fallon lifted his legs, bending the knees and kicking both his bare feet into Holderman's big gut. The man grunted and fell back against the door, his bladder releasing. At the same time, Fallon rammed his head back. He felt the smashing of Timmons's nose and teeth, and the looseness of his grip. Fallon managed to jam an elbow into Timmons's ribs and broke free.

Holderman was getting up. Fallon belted him in the forehead. Down went Holderman again. Fallon grabbed one of his shoes. He turned sideways and swung the shoe at Timmons. The heel caught the man in his ear, and down he went. Fallon slammed the shoe harder against the back of Timmons's skull. He spun back to Holderman, who was reaching for the .32. The shoe nailed his fingers underneath the pistol. Fallon's left fist slammed into the pulp that was Holderman's nose. The detective hit the door. Fallon hit him again. Again. Again.

He went to hit him again only to realize that Aaron Holderman wasn't in the coach anymore. He had gone out the door. Fallon grabbed the .32.

He knew something else. The coach wasn't moving. The driver had stopped.

Another man appeared outside, one hand holding the door, the other a short-barreled .45 Colt that was cocked and pointed at Fallon's chest.

"Let's not make the mick's hack even bloodier," the man said. "Just drop the popgun in your pocket. That's right. You can keep it. For now. But we don't want to keep Mr. MacGregor waiting."

This new man, in a tan jacket and straw hat, wasn't like Holderman and Timmons. A tall gent, he was slender, clean-shaven, with gray eyes and an easy voice. The .45 he held did not waver, though, and Fallon guessed that he knew how to use it, and had used it many times before.

"Slap Timmons across the face a few times, if you'd be so kind," the man said. "See if he comes around." Once Fallon had slipped the .32 into his coat pocket, he moved to the unconscious detective. He slapped Timmons across the cheeks a couple of times, maybe a little harder than necessary, but the man's eyes opened, began to focus, and he started up, ready to charge. Fallon shoved him hard against the floor of the coach.

"How many times do you want to get your arse kicked, Timmons?" the newcomer said. "Just lie still for a minute, let Mr. Fallon come outside, and then you can crawl out of the coach and clean yourself up."

Releasing his hold on Timmons, Fallon turned to see the newcomer moving away from the coach. Fallon grabbed his shoes, socks, and grip, and stepped onto the paved street in his bare feet.

The newcomer was handing Aaron Holderman a handkerchief.

"You know how much Mr. MacGregor frowns upon having someone bleed on his rugs," the slender man said, and he turned to the Irish driver.

"Here's money for the fare." Fallon saw the gold coin spin as it sailed smoothly from the man's slender hand into the hack's big palm. Another coin followed. "Something for the trouble." And yet one more gold piece. "And something for your memory."

The hack understood. "I don't remember a bloody thing, mate."

"You're a good man. Carry on."

As the coach pulled away, the man walked to Fallon. He held out his right hand.

"I'm Dan MacGregor, Mr. Fallon. A pleasure to meet you. Come on inside. My father is eager to meet you."

CHAPTER NINE

A little man in an extremely large office.

Such was Harry Fallon's first impression of Sean MacGregor. He sat in a green leather chair behind a desk the size of a small ship. He wore a brown suit with a tan vest and red tie, smoking a potent cigar. Sean MacGregor, president of this American Detective Agency, had eyes of green, a dull green, nowhere near the color of the leather seat. His hair, thinning and streaked with silver, remained an ugly orange. He looked nothing like his thin, handsome son, but he did look like a man who enjoyed power and demanded respect that Fallon figured he did not deserve.

The office was on the top floor of the building. You had to take an elevator to make it all the way up. The paneling was dark brown. The rugs were dark brown. The ceiling was dark brown. It was a dark room. With no paintings, maps, or photographs hanging on the wall, and very few books on the shelves. But you could find newspapers scattered across the tables—also brown—that lined the walls on one side of the office, and wanted posters and yellow telegraphs atop brown filing cabinets that lined two others. Nothing except a window was on the wall behind

MacGregor's office. The curtain, brown, was closed. The only light came from the green-domed lamps on the sprawling desk and in the center of the three walls.

The cigar came out of MacGregor's mouth and found a place in a gaudy silver ashtray.

"Harry Fallon," MacGregor said. "Six-feet-one-inch tall, one hundred ninety pounds, brown hair, brown eyes, bullet scars on left arm, right thigh, other scars on back, right forearm, left side, right calf. Age thirty-three."

MacGregor spoke with a thick Scottish brogue, another difference he had with his son, who spoke without any accent at all. He wasn't reading this from papers. No papers covered his desk. It came from memory.

The detective kept on.

"Born Gads Hill, Missouri. One sister, still in Gads Hill. Mother dead, six years ago. Father employed at railroad station there. Previous employment as itinerant cowhand, temporary jobs, hunted buffalo. Five years as a deputy federal marshal for the Western District of Arkansas with jurisdiction in the Indian Nations. Past ten years at the Illinois State Penitentiary on a charge of bank robbery, resisting arrest, attempted murder of federal and tribal peace officers. Joliet appears to be taking federal prisoners as well as state cons. Out on parole. Wife, Renee, and daughter, Rachel—"

"I'm who you want," Fallon said sharply.

Sean MacGregor tried to stare down Fallon, but quickly relented, glanced at his cigar, didn't pick it up, and studied the other men in the room, including his son.

"You have secured employment with a wheelwright named Werner." MacGregor did not try to hide his contempt as he pronounced the wheelwright's name. "Lodging at a boardinghouse run by a woman named Ketchum. Have you ever been to Chicago, Fallon?"

He shook his head.

"I am a former attorney at law. Vocal responses if you don't mind. Or even if you do."

"No."

"Your record shows little sign of your having any experience as a wheelwright. Is this a hobby or did our checking of your background miss one of the odd jobs you had during your, shall we say, wilder days?"

"A man does what he has to do," Fallon said.

"Indeed. Especially when he has been convicted of a number of felonies."

MacGregor found his cigar. It was a good cigar, Fallon knew, because he had to nod as his son, who, looking thoroughly insulted, crossed the dark room, found the matches, and relit the cigar in his father's mouth. After Dan MacGregor returned to his place in the line of men standing beside Fallon, the elder MacGregor puffed his cigar for a few moments and said, "What would you say if I could find employment for a man of your, say, talents?"

"I have a job."

Removing the cigar, Sean MacGregor grinned. "That pays a dollar a day. You got that cowboying, I suppose, and a whole lot more marshaling. And you lived in Fort Smith and—"

"Van Buren," Fallon corrected.

Those green eyes burned with a fury that made Fallon smile. MacGregor was not a man who liked to be corrected.

"You are a detective," Fallon said. "Figured you want to get all your facts straight."

The punch caught him in the solar plexus.

Fallon saw Dan MacGregor stepping quickly to his left. Ready, he turned, and Aaron Holderman rushed to Fallon's right. By then, Timmons had grabbed both of his arms, and MacGregor landed the blow.

The thin man knew where to punch and how to hit hard.

Doubled over, one arm wrapped around the bottom of his ribs, the other keeping him from falling onto that ugly brown rug, Fallon struggled to catch his breath. So, he learned something about the younger MacGregor: he'd be the one to watch closely in a fight.

"Sit down on the rug, Fallon. I like pluck. I dislike insolence."

The stench from MacGregor's cigar made Fallon fear he might vomit. He managed to lift his head, found Sean MacGregor smiling, standing over him . . . the only way the dwarf could tower over Fallon, and then two hands grabbed him and jerked him back. He landed on his buttocks, still clutching his ribs, still trying to breathe, and spread out his legs. He stared at the president of the detective agency.

"You feel like listening to me now, Fallon?" MacGregor said.

Fallon nodded, but MacGregor wagged his cigar. "Unh-unh-unh. Vocal responses." He grinned. The Scot's teeth were as brown as his office. "Remember."

"I hear you." He could breathe a little better now.

"All right. Do you want to be a wheelwright's apprentice, or do you want a better-paying job that you're damned good at?"

Fallon's head shook. The man was going to offer him a job, but if this man hired men like Aaron Holderman, Fallon figured he'd be better off learning a new trade at a dollar a day.

"I like to pick my own bosses," Fallon said.

The little head on the little man bobbed a few times.

"Noble. Commendable. But since you want to keep the facts straight, you had no say in who was appointed federal marshal for your district. That was up to the whims of the people, who they put in the White House, and who paid enough money to get the nomination with the confirmation from the United States Senate. You didn't pick your boss."

"I could've always quit," Fallon pointed out.

"*Touché.* Point taken. But we don't always get to work for bosses we like and respect." Grinning, he found his son. "Isn't that right, Danny boy?" He laughed, shook his head, and said to Fallon, "Come to work for me, Fallon."

There. It was out now.

Fallon nodded at Holderman. "According to my parole, I'm not to associate with convicted felons and ignorant sons of bitches."

He expected the fist to slam the top of his head, so that didn't hurt as much as Dan MacGregor's savage punch.

"You've already associated with him. My son even found you armed with a revolver. That's against Chicago's city ordinance. It's also another violation of your parole. Which could land you back in Joliet . . ."

Fallon picked it up as if by rote. ". . . or another facility for completion of my original sentence. All right. You've had your fun. Send me back."

"For five more years?" MacGregor puffed his cigar.

"After ten, what's five more?"

MacGregor removed the cigar, tilted his head back, and laughed. "By God, I've known men hardened by the walls and bars, but you take first place, Fallon. Yes, you are indeed the man I need."

"Go to hell," Fallon said. No one hit him. And Sean MacGregor didn't look annoyed, angry, or insulted.

"Joliet's worse than hell, Fallon. And I plan to send you

to a place worse than Joliet. But you will be well paid. Very well paid."

Fallon could breathe now. He looked up, waiting.

"Before your arrest, trial, and incarceration your reputation in Arkansas and the Indian Nations was exemplary." MacGregor was walking back to his desk, putting his cigar back in the ashtray, and opening a drawer. He pulled out a wad of greenbacks, counted out several, and returned to the center of the room. This time he knelt and counted off twenty bills, letting them land between Fallon's legs.

"In a few years, I plan to be America's and the world's foremost detective agency." His face seemed to flush, matching the redness of his hair. "And put that idiot Pinkerton back where he belongs, in New York's Fifth Ward, fighting gangs to stay alive."

He sighed, regained his composure, and said, "I read that two officers of the United States cavalry, one solicitor, and two deputy marshals served as character witnesses at your trial. Yet Judge Parker gave you the maximum sentence. You must hate him."

Fallon's head shook. "He did what he thought was right. He's an honorable man. Unlike some I've met."

"Careful. Dan would love to practice the pugilistic skills he learned at Purdue."

MacGregor stared at the ceiling, pondering whatever went through his sick brain, and, satisfied, found Fallon's eyes again. "Two hundred dollars a month, not including expenses, to be deposited in a bank of your choice. Plus a bonus."

Fallon shook his head again. "The warden . . ."

This time, MacGregor interrupted him. "The warden has his hands full, especially since he has a riot that left several dead and will cost taxpayers a small fortune. And he relies on my agency to keep track of the parolees who are in this entire state. Joliet's a short distance from Chicago, but to Warden Cain Chicago might as well be in Canada's Yukon. Joliet is one of our accounts."

So, at least Fallon now knew how Holderman had found him at Lake Michigan.

"This German named Werner. He doesn't need an apprentice. He's hiring one because his boy is doing five years at Southern Illinois Penitentiary down in Chester. Three to go. Mrs. Ketchum's boardinghouse, you'll be happy to know, is also where Mr. Holderman resides. Don't worry. His room is in the attic. Yours is by the front door. And in Joliet, Warden Cain will be receiving wonderful reports as to your work ethic, following the conditions of your parole. That is, as long as you're working, and doing a job well done, for the American Detective Agency. What do you say?"

"Send a telegraph to Joliet. Tell Cain I'm coming back."

To Fallon's surprise, the little Scot grinned.

"Yes. You're tough. Just what I need." He drew in a deep breath, exhaled slowly, and said, "I need to know one thing from you, Fallon. Were you guilty of any of the charges that got you sent to Joliet for the hardest time imaginable?"

Fallon shrugged. "What does it matter?"

He felt the hand chop onto his left shoulder. That hurt not as bad as the punch that took his breath away, but it still hurt. "Answer the question!" Dan MacGregor snapped.

Through tight-set lips, Fallon said, "I can't deny that I resisted arrest," he said.

The little MacGregor laughed again. "Yes. Wouldn't we all? I know you were innocent, Fallon. What's more, I know who set you up."

Fallon looked up. MacGregor stepped back, and Fallon heard the cocking of revolvers all across the room.

"One thing I'm good at, Fallon," MacGregor said after

a retreat of fifteen feet. "I can read men. And I just read something in you that I don't like. You were thinking that you could get to me and beat out the information you want to hear. And you'd do it no matter how many bullets they put into you. As I said before, spirit is one thing. Insolence is another. And insanity only leaves you dead."

He started making his way back.

"Now, maybe we can have a conversation and leave distrust and animosity in our back pockets for the time being."

CHAPTER TEN

He found himself alone in the big office with the little man with a massive ego and too much ambition. Even Dan MacGregor had been asked to leave. Fallon came to the impression that neither father nor son trusted one another. He wanted to keep that in mind.

"Whiskey?" Sean MacGregor had settled into the green-leather chair.

Fallon shook his head. He hadn't tasted any spirits in ten years. He hadn't even tried the home-brewed beer or rotgut in all that time.

"It's Scotch." MacGregor poured himself a tall one. "Single malt. The best you can get in Chicago."

"No. Thank you."

MacGregor smiled. "*Quid pro quo*. You are familiar with the Latin phrase?"

"More or less."

"I give. You give." He laughed. "No, I mean the other way around. You give. I give. In short, if you do a few jobs for me, I'll give you something that you want."

"A few jobs?"

"Let's say three." The Scot drank some more whiskey.

"For starters, the man who made it so you spent ten years in one of the worst prisons in America for something you didn't do." He grinned again. "Except for that resisting arrest part." More whiskey. He refilled his glass and sipped some more. The little man could hold a lot of Scotch. Another thing to remember. He didn't appear to get drunk.

"So I'm supposed to trust you?" Fallon said.

Now, Sean MacGregor did not smile. He set his glass of Scotch on the table and stared hard. "Fallon, you're out of Joliet. Remember that. I got you out."

"The governor . . ."

"Listens to what I tell him. Remember that too."

"I'll remember."

"Good. Then here are the terms. You do the jobs for me. I give you information, indeed the name, of the man you want. I give you proof. After you've done those jobs."

Fallon said. "So you give me the man who put me in prison. With proof."

"Proof that will get him sent to prison. Not hearsay. Solid proof. Evidence that cannot be refuted. I am a detective."

With a reputation that smells like a dead skunk, Fallon thought, but said merely: "Whom I'm supposed to trust."

"Whom you have no choice but to trust."

"For one job?"

"Well. Three jobs. Three crimes. One man is responsible for all three, you understand."

Fallon was starting to sweat. He felt sick. He wanted to reach for that Scotch, but he made himself sit still. "What were the other two crimes?"

"You know what they were," MacGregor said. "And you couldn't be convicted of those because you were in prison when your wife and kid—"

"All right." His voice thundered in the room, so sharp,

so violent, MacGregor slid his chair back and spilled some of his precious Scotch whiskey.

The man recovered, slightly, though his voice faulted. "So by your declaration of 'all right,' you agree to the terms?"

"I want the terms in writing," Fallon said.

"Not a chance. I am . . ." He grinned, then replaced the Scotch he had spilled from his glass.

"In writing. I walk out of here with those in my pocket, or I walk back to Joliet."

"You can't be serious. You can go home, your name cleared."

"I am serious. I lost my wife and daughter. What the hell do I have to go home to?"

MacGregor sipped again and tried a different approach. "I can also arrange so that you are killed in Joliet. Not that I started that horrible riot. But I have convicts and guards who do my bidding. The riot, by the way, was unfortunate, but fortunate for me. Because of what you did, I was able to persuade officials, including Warden Cain and the governor and those on the board of parole, that . . ."

"In writing."

MacGregor tried to stare him down again, couldn't, and sighed, shaking his head.

"I can call your bluff. I have regular operatives in my employ. I can send one of them, as many as it takes, to help this agency earn the respect and power that the idiot Pinkerton enjoys now. While you'll be in Joliet. With what?"

"Three hots and a cot," Fallon said. "What else does a man need?"

For ten minutes, they stared at each other. No talking. No backing down. But one had to give, and Fallon knew that he was not bluffing. Eventually, Sean MacGregor came to the same realization.

Still, he did not speak, but he opened a drawer and

pulled out paper. After dipping the pen in an inkwell, he began scribbling. He wrote. Fallon waited. Still, neither talked until MacGregor dropped the pen in its holder and slid the document toward Fallon. Then the Scot said, "Why don't you blow it dry?"

Not responding, Fallon carefully turned the paper around with his fingers and read. He read it twice before sliding it back to MacGregor.

"You left out a number of important details. Try again. Be specific. Evidence that cannot be refuted."

The paper was wadded up, tossed in the trash. MacGregor slid another in front of him and grabbed the pen.

"Write neatly," Fallon said.

"Go to hell," MacGregor responded.

Minutes later, the paper was slid again before Fallon. Again, he turned it around and read.

"You forgot to sign it. And date it."

The man stiffened. "And I suppose you want it to be witnessed by a bloody priest, nun, schoolmarm, and Mrs. O'Leary's cow, for Christ's sake."

"Just your signature. And today's date."

When that was done, Fallon asked for an envelope.

"Remember what I said about insolence, Fallon."

He waved the paper off to the side, folded it evenly, stuck it into the envelope, which he folded and slid in his back pocket.

"Do we have a deal?" MacGregor asked.

"Yes."

"Shall we shake?" He held out his hand.

"Isn't our word good enough?"

"Very well. Allow me to bring in my son and my most reliable operatives." MacGregor rose, moved across the dark room, and Fallon stood, watching, quickly dipping into the trash and pulling out the first draft of the "arrangement," which he shoved into the same pocket. He walked to the window, pulled back the curtain, and stared down on the city of Chicago. It was, he decided, most impressive.

"Remember, Fallon," MacGregor said, "screw up, fail me, and you're back in Joliet. Violation of the terms of your parole. And anything else I might decide to add. And that riot will look like a picnic compared to what I'll see you go through. And if you double-cross me, or try to, or even think about it . . . you're dead. Dead, dead, dead."

Fallon turned to see Timmons, Dan MacGregor, and Aaron Holderman back in the office. They gathered around the old man's desk, and Fallon walked over to join them.

This time, Dan MacGregor took the lead.

"Fallon, have you ever heard of Monk Quinn?"

"I think I've read the name in a week- or month-old newspaper," Fallon said.

"He's a cold-blooded butcher. He's also a murderer and has broken all of the Ten Commandments at least once, most of them at least twenty times."

"All right."

"Six years ago," Dan MacGregor continued, and slid an old wanted dodger with Monk Quinn's likeness sketched on it for Fallon to examine. "Quinn pulled off a giant score. Robbed a Southern Pacific train hauling two hundred thousand dollars in gold bullion."

Fallon memorized the poster.

"You want me to find Quinn, or the gold?"

"Some of Pinkerton's men found Quinn," Dan MacGregor said, and Fallon looked up to catch the irritation on the older MacGregor's face. "He has been in Yuma for the past four years."

"And the gold?"

"That's where Pinkerton and his fools screwed up," the elder MacGregor bellowed. "They got the snake but not the snake's eggs. There's that much gold and Pinkerton can't find it. He's even given up. The mines in Nevada and the Southern Pacific aren't happy. I want to make them happy . . . with me."

Dan MacGregor hadn't looked up during his father's tirade. Now that the bellowing stopped, the young man said, "We believe it is buried just below the border in Mexico."

Fallon tapped the poster. "This says Quinn led the party of six men in the holdup. What happened to the other five?"

"If you believe Quinn, he killed them below the border," Dan MacGregor answered.

"Do you believe him?"

"It fits him to a T."

The small Scotsman drank more whiskey and said, "The railroad has offered a twenty-five-thousand-dollar reward for the return of the bullion. Or ten percent of the amount found and returned. If you recover the gold or any part of it, I will pay you two percent."

"Two?" Fallon grinned.

"You don't care about gold. And you have a signed contract in your pocket that does not mention gold."

Fallon nodded.

"The poster also says the robbery of the train was pulled off near the California border. So I assume Quinn is serving his sentence in Yuma."

Everyone answered with a nod.

"Six years isn't much of a sentence for robbing the railroad of that much money."

"The pettifoggers in Arizona couldn't convict him of that robbery," Sean MacGregor said. "They convicted him of assault with intent to kill when a deputy sheriff around Nogales tried to arrest him."

"So what do you want me to do? Go to Yuma and question him, see if I can't sweet-talk him into telling me where he hid the gold? Or go to Nogales, see if I can somehow find out where he buried it on the Mexican side of the border? Or just ride across the border till I stumble across the bones of his partners that he killed? And why in hell did he bury the gold to begin with?"

"Ask him yourself," Dan MacGregor said.

Fallon sighed. "So I am supposed to go to Yuma and question him."

"No." The old man grinned. "But you are to go to Yuma."

Fallon started to catch on.

"Last year," Dan MacGregor began, "we arranged to have one of our operatives arrive in Yuma, pretending to be a prisoner. We had the warden's full cooperation. And our agent reported back some of what we have told you. About Mexico. About murdering his partners."

"But Valdez wasn't good enough," the older MacGregor interrupted. "That's what I get for listening to my son and hiring a greaser to be one of the American Detective Agency's operatives." He snorted, swore, and headed back to his bottle of Scotch, which was almost empty by now, and the man was still standing, not weaving, not slurring his words.

"What happened to Valdez?" Fallon asked. He had an idea, but he didn't expect Dan MacGregor's answer.

"He got bitten by a half-dozen or so rattlesnakes that

found their way into Valdez's cell while he was in solitary confinement."

"You think I can manage any better than Valdez?" Fallon asked.

"The mistake we . . ." Dan MacGregor stopped suddenly, looked away from his father, and corrected himself. "The mistake Valdez made was trusting the warden and the guards. They knew he wasn't a train robber. We think one of the guards tipped off Quinn. Quinn arranged, maybe with help from the guards, to have Valdez killed."

"I've thought of something better for you, Fallon," Sean MacGregor said, and drank a healthy swallow of his Scotch.

"Mr. Holderman will accompany you to Tucson, Arizona Territory. You will rob a store, a bank, or a stagecoach. That is to be left up to you. Mr. Holderman will arrest you. Trust me on one thing, Fallon. Justice in Arizona is swift. You'll be tried, convicted, and sentenced to Yuma. The rest is up to you."

Fallon shook his head.

"Valdez did report one thing to us before he died," Dan MacGregor said. "Quinn's planning to crash out of Yuma. We don't know how. But he has some other felons with him. Most likely, he has lured them with the promise of some of that bullion he stole."

"So I somehow join this prison break?"

"Exactly."

Fallon nodded. He laughed. He said to himself: *No wonder the American Detective Agency isn't as well known as Pinkerton's.*

CHAPTER ELEVEN

"You mind telling me what you're doing with my grip?" Aaron Holderman snapped the luggage shut and turned just as Harry Fallon shoved him into the seat as the train rumbled along the rails in the night.

"Sorry," Fallon said with a smile as a few passengers looked at him and his traveling companion. "Train's rocking more than I expected." He held out his hand toward the detective and grinned at him, too, saying, "Slipped. That's what happened. No hard feelings, pard."

As Holderman took the proffered hand, Fallon sat beside him. He did not let go. He tightened the grip. Holderman grimaced.

The closest passengers were four seats back and on the opposite side of the aisle. Ahead of him, six seats up, a cavalry trooper and a drummer of farming implements snored loudly. A married couple sat ahead of them, but a two-year-old redheaded boy occupied their time. The conductor had gone on toward the smoking car.

"You think all I did in prison was wash laundry?" Fallon said in a hoarse whisper. "You want all the bones in your hand broken, or do you want to answer me?"

Tears welled in the brute's eyes. "I'll . . . tell."

"Then tell."

"Let . . . go . . . first."

Fallon tightened the grip.

"Makin' sure . . . you ain't . . . got . . . no . . . gun."

It was a lie, but Fallon had made his point. He released the hold. He didn't like touching any part of the ruffian, anyway, and he had nothing to wipe his right hand on. "All right," he said. Holderman began shaking his hand, trying to get the blood flowing again. Fallon figured the American Detective Agency operative was trying to find the contract, or explanation, Sean MacGregor had reluctantly written back in Chicago.

Fallon felt better. He looked better. Gone were the duds he had been given upon his release from Joliet. The American Detective Agency had bought Fallon black boots, gray-striped britches, black suspenders, a clean bib-front blue shirt, a red bandanna, gray vest, and black hat with a pinched crown. He had a change of clothes, extra pair of socks, change of underwear, and twenty-five dollars in spending money.

"So," Fallon asked, "when do I get my gun?"

"Right before you do your job," Holderman said. He now could rub his hand. "Not one second before."

"A second." Fallon smiled. "Be careful, Detective, or you might get arrested as my accomplice."

That seemed to put the fear of God, or of Arizona law, in the fat man's belly.

He had never been this far west, and had never seen Arizona.

When he stepped off the train in the early afternoon, he sucked in a deep breath and stepped toward the crowds.

"Huh." Holderman spit on the dusty deck. "Figured they'd all be takin' their *siestas* this time of day."

Apparently, Aaron Holderman had never been in Arizona either.

Oh, Tucson was definitely Mexican. Dark-skinned, dark-haired men and women lined the streets, outnumbering the Americans by at least three-to-one. Fallon smelled scents of food that made his mouth water and his eyes burn. The town was practically all earth tones, adobe, the streets dusty, the buildings dusty, but the air was clean, crisp. He saw a saguaro cactus, which looked exactly like the drawings he had seen in magazines. Women in colorful dresses walked the streets. Horses of all kinds frolicked in a livery's corral.

"Where to?" Fallon asked.

The big idiot shrugged. "I don't know. Hotel I reckon."

"Separate rooms," Fallon said.

The man stared and shook his head.

"Do you really want to go to Yuma with me?"

The detective considered that.

"We're the only two who got off the train here. So when I come to trial, no one will likely think to track down the conductor or crew or find some passengers and ask if they saw us. In fact, I can say I arrived on a stage. Or walked or rode in. Walked in after my horse was stolen. But we can't be seen together. Right?"

Eventually, Holderman nodded.

"So . . . I'm going to walk down this boardwalk. You walk down the other side of the street. When I find a hotel I like, I'll walk in and get a room. You wait. Then come in after I've walked outside. We'll manage to have a few conversations like this. Not looking at one another. Pretending we don't even know each other. You can leave your room unlocked, and I can sneak in, say, one in the morning. We'll chat then."

"No. You leave your room unlocked."

"All right." Fallon walked away.

As he suspected, the brute followed . . . on the same side of the street. But at least he did keep a discreet distance.

Seeing the church, Fallon got an idea. He stepped onto the street, let a burro hauling wood go by, and then walked to the gate, which he pushed open, stepping into the courtyard. A few minutes later, before he walked inside the church, he looked across the street. Aaron Holderman stood in front of a business, looking completely out of sorts.

Fallon held up a hand, spreading out his fingers and thumb. He flashed this three times. He mouthed the words, "Fifteen minutes."

All Aaron Holderman did was blink.

Fallon went inside the church.

He saw, and smelled, the candles, and stopped to admire the crucifix and the paintings on the adobe wall. A woman with her hair covered sat on the front pew. Another knelt by the altar.

Fallon looked around until he found something that had to be where he needed to go. He moved to the back of the room and stepped into the box. He sat in the dark, waiting.

Eventually, something slid across from him. Fallon tried to figure out what he had to say.

"*¿Español o Ingles?*" the voice in the dark said.

"English."

A long silence followed.

"Well." The voice across from him was Spanish, old, but the tone did not sound impatient.

"Father," Fallon said, "I need to ask you . . ."

"You do not ask me, my son, but to God, through Jesus, through his blessed mother."

Fallon pressed his lips together.

"Well . . ."

He waited.

"Son, you are here to confess your sins and to ask what you must do for penance? Aren't you?"

Maybe this wasn't such a good idea. But at least, he had a priest who understood English.

"Father, I'm not Catholic."

Another silence. He expected the slide to shut, or some nuns to come and drag him out and toss him into the street. Eventually, though, the priest asked, "What are you?"

Fallon had to think. "Methodist," he answered.

This time, the priest wasted no time.

"Then say fifty Hail Marys, try to live better, and all will be forgiven." The priest started to go.

"I need a favor. It's a matter of life or death."

"Perhaps," the priest said, "you should see the local sheriff."

"My name's Harry Fallon. Most people call me Hank. I'm a former deputy United States marshal out of Arkansas. But for the past ten years, I've been in prison."

He could hear the priest's breathing. "Yuma is an unholy place."

"I wasn't in Yuma, Father, but I'm about to go there."

The priest must have leaned forward. "You are not Catholic, but I must tell you that whatever you plan on doing, you must not do. If you wind up in Yuma, you will regret it for the rest of your life."

"I have to go in, Father. To find a man. To get some information from him. It's my job."

"Your job?"

"Can I tell you? And can you not tell anyone until . . . until you have to?"

More silence. This time, Fallon thought the priest had slipped away and was seeking out some town law to get this crazy man out of his parish.

"My son," the voice then said, "do all Methodists beat around the bush as much as you do?"

Fallon laughed. The priest said, "Tell me."

Which Fallon did.

"There must be another way," the priest said.

"I'm sure there is, but this is the hand that was dealt me."

"Then fold."

"The pot's too big. The hand's too important."

"You are a gambler as well as a peace officer?"

"Being a peace officer is the biggest gamble there is."

"Amen. So what do you need of me?"

Fallon sucked in a deep breath. "That Scot I told you about. The man who runs the detective agency."

"Most Scots are Presbyterian. Most Presbyterians I've met are not bad souls."

"I don't think he's anything but rotten."

"From what you've told me, I must agree. But I have not met the man."

"You don't have to do what I'm about to ask you, Father," Fallon said.

"And if I do not like what you ask me to do, I will send you on your way."

"Fair enough." Fallon breathed in deeply, exhaled. "I have that letter I made MacGregor write for me. Signed and dated. MacGregor knows this could land him in big trouble. He'll want it back."

"I understand."

"I'd like you to take the letter. Keep it. Hide it. Show it to no one. I have another letter MacGregor wrote, the first draft. I made him redo it. So with luck, I can make this idiot they sent with me think he got the letter and destroyed it. But there's no guarantee."

"So I take the letter. Then what?"

"Keep it. Do you read the newspapers?"

"Yes, my son. And many of our parishioners read too. And almost everyone who comes to this church talks. Between the newspapers and the gossip, I know much of what is going on in Tucson and the territory."

"That's good. So if you hear that a man got killed in Yuma who was sentenced to prison for robbery . . ."

The priest asked, "And if that man's name is Harry Fallon?"

"No. The name I'll be using is Hank Fulton. But there's a decent chance Harry Fallon's name will eventually come out. Especially if Sean MacGregor has any say in it."

"Who do I send the letter to?" the priest asked.

He was a smart one.

"Isaac Parker, federal judge, Fort Smith, Arkansas. The judge will know what to do from there."

"Slide the envelope through here."

Fallon did. He wasn't sure how he felt. Relief? Not yet. Regret for getting this old man involved? Hell, Fallon didn't even know if the priest was old. He could be in his twenties.

"I will remember you in Mass till I hear from you again, Harry." The use of the name made Fallon relax. "Is this all you have?"

"That's it," Fallon said. "It's not much."

"What else can I do for you?"

Fallon started to shake his head, but he remembered something. "I'm not Catholic. My . . . wife . . . she was.

Very Catholic, except for the part of her marrying a backsliding Methodist like me. Could you remember her in Mass? And my daughter?" He felt a wetness in his eyes. "And pray for their souls?"

"Tell me their names."

Fallon did.

"They are with God, my son. Remember this. Never forget it."

"Thank you, Father. I'd better get going. The idiot outside won't wait forever."

The hand came through the opening. A black robe covered the arm, but Fallon, even in the darkness, could make out the hand. It was old, covered with spots, the hand of a poor man. But the hand of a good man.

"I would like to wish you luck, Marshal Fallon."

They shook. The priest, whose name Harry Fallon did not know, did not want to know, had a strong, hard grip.

"Now we must pray for you, too, Marshal."

"I'm not much of a praying man, Father. And I told you already that I'm not Catholic."

"Just remember to say the Hail Marys for the latter. As far as the first, not praying much, you're going to Yuma Territorial Prison. You had damned well better pray . . . before you get there. I don't think people pray in hell."

CHAPTER TWELVE

"You was in that church a damned long time," Aaron Holderman said, a bit too loud, but no one on the street paid any attention.

"Ten years in Joliet," Fallon whispered as he stopped to clean from one of his boots those horse apples he had purposely stepped in. "Lots of things to get off my chest, my soul." He kept scraping the boot, and eventually he saw the private detective's eyes widen. Finally, he had spotted the envelope barely peeking above the top of the boot.

Bringing the boot down into the street, Fallon wiped the bottom in the dust. He looked up and down the street.

"I'll find us a hotel," he said. "Remember what I said."

"I already found us a place to stay," the brute said.

Fallon shot him a cold stare, and, when he realized this side of the street was empty for a few blocks, he let the stare harden. "What?"

"Over yonder." He pointed.

Fallon frowned. "A wagon yard?"

The brute's head bobbed. "See. Nobody in a wagon yard pokes his nose in anybody's business. Nobody remembers who was talkin' to who. And it only costs a dime a body."

Fallon shrugged. "All right. I'll get a place first. You wait and—"

"Already got my place. So you go ahead and get yourself a spot. But don't you go nowhere till I'm leanin' ag'in that corral fence yonder so I can keep my eye on you."

Fallon shrugged, and watched the cad amble across the street to the wagon yard. It wasn't even much of a wagon yard.

"Fresh out of prison," he said to himself, "and I've slept on a depot bench, on a train, and now in a wagon yard. I guess a downy bed just isn't in my future."

As many men as crowded into the yard by evening, Harry Fallon began to wonder if any hotel in Tucson had a vacancy. Several fires were going, but the men surrounding them seemed cognizant not to let the fires get too big. They watched them carefully. Hay, straw, and fire never made a very good combination. Fallon rolled out his bedroll in a corner that had not gotten too crowded. He removed his hat, positioned his grip so that it made a decent pillow, took off his boots and stuck the envelope deep into the foot, and interlocked his fingers as he rested his head against his hands and the piece of luggage.

He listened to the sounds he had not heard in ages.

The clopping of hooves on dirt and sand. The wind blowing through the scrub that passed for trees in this country. He heard the tinny sound of a piano banging away in some saloon, and beyond that what sounded to be a trumpet or some type of horn. Sounds carried far in the desert, even in a city the size of Tucson. Chickens cackled, and a rooster, perhaps unaware of the actual time of day, crowed. He could catch snippets of conversation as men and women passed down the boardwalk across the street.

"How is Alice faring?" "Can you believe what that butcher charges? This is Tucson, Margaret, not Denver or San Francisco." "What time is the hoss race supposed to start on Saturday?" "Mr. Cassidy says that he expects that he should have that bolt of calico from the Sears, Roebuck and Company in two days. Then, Mother will make that new shirt for me, and I can wear it to the church social." "Oh, won't Tommy be proud!" "When is the last time it has rained?" "Jasper Tanner. The schoolmaster told me that you brought a rattlesnake into school today and scared all of the girls, and that is why he gave you a good paddling, but trust me, young man, your father will tan your hide tonight." "But, Ma, it wasn't nothin' but an old bull snake. It couldn't hurt nobody."

He could listen, he thought, to such mindless banter forever. You never heard talk like that in Joliet.

But he frowned, sighed, and tried not to listen. Listening to sounds like that didn't help a man, especially when that man would be in another prison soon . . . if everything went according to plan. Listening to sounds of decency, or humanity, of common everyday lives, only tortured a man who was bound for Yuma.

The nearby church bells began to ring. He counted. Then his eyes closed and he was asleep.

He almost opened his eyes at the sound, but remembered where he was and what he was doing just in time, so he rolled over, muttered something that made no sense, and steadied his breathing.

For a few seconds, he heard nothing else but the popping of wood in the nearest fire. He could smell the smoke, and even with his eyes closed, he knew exactly where the fire was. The moon would be up by now, and it had to be near full. Had Holderman even part of a brain, he would have waited. Still, Fallon began to think that Aaron Holderman had done him a favor. The wagon yard would be a much better place. Much, much better.

He waited.

Holderman's big, clumsy feet trod closer. His knee joints popped as he knelt over Fallon's boots. He even farted. Paper rustled. The man might have even wakened the dead in the cemetery behind the nearby church. Then a new noise reached Fallon's ears. Men laughing, swearing, and the gate to the yard opening. Some of the residents for the night were coming in from a night on the town.

Which made the timing perfect.

His eyes shot open. There squatted Aaron Holderman, oblivious that Fallon was awake. The American Detective Agency operative held the envelope in his left hand by the ground, while his right hand held the first draft of Sean MacGregor's deal with Harry Fallon. The man's lips moved as he read.

At least, thought Fallon, *he can read.*

"What the hell are you doing?"

Turning suddenly, Holderman lost his balance and fell onto his buttocks. Fallon was coming up, and the big man dropped the envelope and tried to stand. Fallon had to time himself, slow himself down.

"You little sneak thief!" Fallon shouted. He saw the men, likely drunk as the devil, stop between the largest fire and one that had turned into embers. He saw the moon, guessed the time, and he saw Holderman's terrified face. The big man shoved the paper into his coat pocket and tried to stand.

"Give me that!"

Fallon came to his feet, and drove a right fist that caught a glancing blow against Holderman's face. He went down, but managed to stand. Fallon let him. Then he threw a wicked left into the man's gut.

Holderman gagged, bending over but not falling to his knees.

Don't hit him too hard, Fallon reminded himself.

The men standing about thirty feet away began pointing. One yelled, "Fight!"

Another cried out, "Hot dang!"

They shouted loud enough to wake some of the other nighttime patrons of the yard.

Holderman was up, shooting quick glances at places where he might retreat. Fallon swung high, and Holderman ducked underneath the blow. The big man backed up. Fallon threw another punch that glanced off the man's shoulder.

He came in again, let the operative block a punch, then sidestep another. Fallon was having fun.

Then Aaron Holderman landed a crushing blow that sent Fallon back against his grip and bedroll. His eyes blurred. He had to shake his head. Blood dripped from his upper lip and onto his tongue.

Don't get too cocky, Fallon warned himself. *There's one reason MacGregor has this blowhard on his payroll. He can hit. He will kill.*

The punch had, on the other hand, made Aaron Holderman think that he was top dog again. Instead of retreating with the prize that he had pulled out of Fallon's boot, he brought his own boot up in a savage kick. Fallon rolled underneath it and came up in a crouch, waiting.

He feinted. Holderman swung and missed. Fallon jabbed him in the back, three punches, a little softer this time but with still enough force to cause the brute to cough and swear.

Holderman turned, swinging wildly, and Fallon ducked

underneath it. He was breathing hard, and he wiped the blood from his lip, spit again, and made an uppercut, then a left, followed by a couple more jabs. Holderman deflected and dodged them all.

Behind the two brawlers, the guests of the wagon yard were making bets. Most were taking the big man. Holderman seemed encouraged by the cheers, but now Fallon felt his plan going the wrong way. The men had made a circle around the two fighters. That's not what Fallon wanted, or needed. So he let Holderman throw a fist that rang his ears. He propelled himself into the men, but these were strong men. Muleskinners, perhaps even freighters. They tossed, almost without effort, Fallon back into the center. He landed on his knees, saw the kick Holderman aimed at his head at the last instant, and leaped back out of the way. He sprang up, and the two circled one another.

"That's boring, boys," one of the admirers shouted.

Holderman swung, and Fallon let his momentum carry the big cur past. Instantly, Fallon turned, lowered his shoulder, and put every ounce of strength into his legs and arms as he propelled himself into Holderman's broad back, churning his legs, wrapping his arms around the man's ample torso, and driving, driving, driving Holderman toward the ring of men.

The ring quickly disintegrated as the drunks and half-awake ruffians dived out of the way. No one wanted to be trampled by a leviathan like Aaron Holderman. No one wanted the fat tub of scum falling on him.

He saw the fire, wanted to keep pushing Holderman in that direction, but the big man tripped, and down both men went. Fallon released his hold, moved to the left of the crashing man, who fell with a groan and rolled over. Fallon rolled, too, but came up, wiping the dirt and sweat out of his eyes. He could just make out other sleeping men rising out of their bedrolls, some cursing, a few still too groggy to do anything but try to find the source of the disturbance.

He was up, chest heaving. His vision became blurred, and something kept ringing in his left ear. He spit blood and sand, and ran his tongue over his teeth, surprised to find none loose—yet—and all that had been there still intact.

Holderman rose, surprisingly quickly and deftly for a man his size. It took a few seconds, but he soon found Fallon and moved toward him. The crowd had learned a lesson. Nobody tried to form a circle. They kept their distance while lowering their voices but increasing their bets.

He let the big man come. Fallon backed up. He threw one punch, deliberately missing, and then glanced behind him. He felt the heat. The orange flames hurt his eyes, but he had made it this far. Now . . .

He sprang forward, lifting both legs and driving them in a powerful kick that caught the man's gut. Down they went, and Fallon came to his knees and leaped on the man. He slapped Holderman rapidly—once, twice, four more times—and brought a knee into the man's groin.

Holderman groaned, and Fallon reached inside the pocket and pulled out the paper.

"Nooooo!" Holderman responded with a left Fallon never saw. He landed hard on the ground, tried to get up, but felt Holderman's boot catch him in the chest. He went up, then down, landing near the fire on his back.

If he lived to be a thousand years old, Fallon knew he would never understand how Aaron Holderman had managed to get up before he could.

Somehow, he saw the operative coming for him, diving, screaming. Fallon rolled, but could go no farther. The flames and hot coals already singed his face, his hair. Holderman's giant paw clasped Fallon's right wrist. Fallon elbowed the man with his left. That gave him enough time to turn his face away from the fire.

Then Holderman knelt on Fallon's chest, crushing him. He groaned, spit, coughed, and felt the man's massive hand gripping Fallon's wrist. Fallon slipped, somehow, to avoid his ribs from being splintered. He felt intense heat, turned his head just enough to see Holderman bringing the arm, the hand, the paper Sean MacGregor had written.

"Noooo!" Fallon managed to say, but the heat proved too intense for both men.

Crying out in pain, Holderman released his grip and fell back away from the fire. Not expecting that move, Fallon felt his arm and hand rush downward, slamming into the burning fuel and coals. He screamed, let go of the paper, and rolled away from the flames.

The paper Sean MacGregor had written erupted into flames.

Fallon came up, on his knees, alternately clutching his right wrist and hand, then shaking it. The sleeve smoldered, and welts and burn marks already started appearing on the back of his hand, but he had been hurt worse. He watched the paper turn into black ash, then nothing.

A second later, Aaron Holderman drove a fist into the back of Fallon's head. He fell down, rolled over, and closed his eyes.

"That'll teach you," Holderman said, spit, and staggered back toward his bedroll.

The men who had watched paid off their bets, or complained, or decided to go find a saloon and talk about what all they had seen.

When all had turned quiet, Harry Fallon opened his eyes. Someone had added fuel to the fire, and the blaze leaped higher. He tested his burned hand. He tested everywhere that hurt.

The letter, the paper, the first draft Sean MacGregor had written, was no more.

Just as Harry Fallon wanted. If he had not hurt so badly everywhere on his body, he might have even laughed. Or tried to smile.

Instead, Harry Fallon closed his eyes and slept in the dirt.

CHAPTER THIRTEEN

"I could've kilt you," Aaron Holderman said that morning. "The boss would've liked that."

Fallon rubbed butter on his hand. "I don't think MacGregor had you bring me all the way to Tucson to kill me."

"Yeah, well you ain't got nothin' no more. That note. That paper. It's gone."

"Then I can only hope Sean MacGregor's a man of his word."

The big man grunted. Fallon liked the bruises and cuts that covered Holderman.

"He is," Holderman said. "When it suits him."

"All right. So when do we do the robbery?"

"Today."

The revolver Aaron Holderman handed Fallon was covered with rust. A cap-and-ball Manhattan .36, Fallon somehow managed to turn the loose cylinder without having the entire relic crumble into dust. Eventually, he lowered the hammer, and adjusted the cylinder so the hammer fell into its proper place.

You didn't see many cap-and-balls anywhere these days. Those types of guns had gone the way of tubs of boiling oil and catapults. Guns like that had been great technology when Sam Colt had first patented his revolver. The hammer struck the percussion cap, which ignited the black powder, which sent the lead ball toward its target. A good weapon, as long as you kept your powder dry, and the cap actually fired, and the powder really ignited, and the gun didn't blow your hand off. Cap-and-balls had been converted so that they could take brass cartridges, which kept the powder—usually—dry, and could be used without the need of percussion caps.

"Just one cap," Fallon said, meaning that Holderman had put one percussion cap on one nipple, effectively turning the six-shooter into a single-shot weapon.

"That's all you need to get charged with armed burglary."

"Robbery," Fallon corrected. "And you know what you're doing?"

"Uh-huh."

Fallon inhaled, held the breath, and slowly let it out. The detective sure had a way of inspiring his colleague.

"Where's the bank?"

The man's big head jutted across the street.

Fallon studied the adobe building. "That's a store."

"Bank too. Not a real bank, maybe, but he takes money from them boys who ride into town and want to get good and drunk, but don't want to ride out of town flat broke. Holds it for them until they get out of jail or sober up or finish whatever they come to Tucson to get done. Then he charges them a little bit for the trouble. They ride out with some coins, and he gets a coin or two or a bill for his trouble."

Fallon wet his lips and put his hands on his hips, suddenly impressed. "That's brilliant. American ingenuity at its finest."

"And nobody never thinks to rob him."

"Till today." Fallon shook his head.

"You best get to it." Holderman stepped away from the trash barrel and looked into the window of the store he stood in front of. Fallon wondered if the idiot thought he would look inconspicuous staring at a lacey yellow hat in the display window at Natalie Delisa's Millinery & Women's Fashions.

After slipping the small pistol into his back pocket, Fallon stepped off the boardwalk, let a freight wagon go past, and walked in no particular hurry to the dry goods store catty-corner from the millinery.

He held the door open for a young woman carrying a handful of packages wrapped in brown paper, even tipped his hat, and waited until she was well down the boardwalk.

Inside, the man snapped, "You're letting flies in, buster, and flies don't buy a damned thing."

Fallon lost all of his respect for this capitalist. He walked inside and let the door close behind him. The bell chimed.

The man frowned and turned to assist an elderly woman asking about the difference in two cans of peaches.

Fallon studied the rest of the store. It was empty. He walked to the counter, away from the woman and the man with the sleeve garters and bifocals, and studied the various jars of candies. He didn't like candy, not even peppermint sticks or licorice. Eventually, the man convinced the woman that the brand that cost two cents more was the one she should buy. She paid him, then walked out with the can and her other purchases in a wicker basket. The door opened, quickly closed to keep any more flies from joining the others, and the man put the money in the register and moved down the counter toward Fallon.

"Can I help you?" he asked.

"Cain Warden," Fallon said, "a guy I worked for, he says that you'll hold a man's valuables for him." He grinned. "Let me explain. I just got into town last night, too late to do much of anything, and I want to make sure I got enough money when I leave Tucson to give to my sister." He jutted his hand toward the door. "She lives up in Globe."

He didn't know where Globe was, but heard the mining town mentioned by a few of the men in the wagon yard.

"I charge one percent of the money you leave with me for safekeeping," the man said.

"You got a vault in this place?" Fallon looked around.

The man disappeared and brought up a strongbox. A Smith & Wesson lay atop the box, which he laid on the counter. "This," the man said, as he held up the short-barreled revolver, waving it underneath Fallon's nose, "is all the vault I need."

Aaron Holderman had not mentioned the Smith & Wesson.

"I reckon not." Fallon made himself smile, and watched the man shove the pistol into his waistband. "You accept the terms. One percent. Per night. So if you'll have an extended stay . . ."

Meaning, *If you wind up in jail . . .*

"Should get everything I need done in one night. I'll be back tomorrow sometime."

The man glanced at the clock. "Twenty-four hours. It's nearly eleven thirty in the a.m. At eleven thirty tomorrow morning, you will be charged two percent."

Fallon nodded.

The man pulled out a receipt pad and fished the pencil off the top of his ear. "Name." It was not a question.

"Hank Fulton."

The man scribbled.

"And how much will you be leaving with me?"

"Oh, I got about a hundred, hundred fifty."

The man smiled with greed. He pulled a key out of his pants pocket and fitted it into the padlock. The lock opened, and the box opened. Fallon was reaching into his front pockets but stopped to stare.

"Man. You must be real busy."

"Payday was last week." He grinned. "Some of the boys are still in jail."

"Lucky you."

"You're damned straight."

He waited. The eyes narrowed behind the bifocals. "Your cash, sir."

"Oh." Fallon tried to look embarrassed. He put his hand into his pocket and came out. He began dropping pennies on the counter.

"One . . . two . . . three . . . four . . . five . . ."

The lid to the box slammed shut. "Is this some kind of joke, buster?"

Fallon stepped back. "Why, no, sir. I got about a hundred and twenty, maybe forty, could be fifty pennies in my pocket." He had, actually, maybe four more.

The man put his hands on the strongbox.

"Get out of here, you jackass. I'm not weighing down this box with a dollar and fifty cents in pennies for a three-cent payoff."

"Penny and a half," Fallon said, and shoved the Manhattan into the greedy man's face.

The man's eyes closed beneath the bifocals, his face turned ashen, and his hands reached for the ceiling made of punched tin.

Fallon shut the lid to the strongbox and reached across the counter and jerked the Smith & Wesson from the man's pants. The greedy man's eyelids squeezed tighter.

"You have a storeroom in this place?"

The man's head bobbed, but then Fallon saw something better. A cherrywood armoire stood in the corner, its long doors open, key in the lock and price tag as greedy as this fellow was; he never would try to bust the lock and have to pay for repairs. Besides, Aaron Holderman should be walking in at any minute to stop this act of crime.

"Never mind. Come around the counter."

What, he thought with bitterness, *is taking Holderman so long?*

He slid the Smith & Wesson down the counter, and it went off the edge and skidded across the floor.

"Move!" Fallon yelled, and prodded the barrel of the rusty relic between the man's shoulder blades. They made it to the corner. "Open your eyes and climb in."

The man timidly obeyed, and turned around. With one hand holding the Manhattan and the strongbox tucked underneath his left arm, Fallon kicked one of the doors shut. "I'm locking you in here," Fallon told him. "You make one peep before I'm gone and I'll fill this box full of holes."

If, he thought, *the .36 doesn't blow up in my hand.*

The bell above the door sang out its obnoxious chime, and Fallon let out a breath of relief. He turned, and felt the color leaving his own face. It wasn't the fat private detective coming into the store, but three men who looked like railroaders just coming off a six-night run followed by a two-night bender.

"Hey!" one of them yelled. "What the hell's going on here?"

Fallon couldn't tell if the men were armed or not. It didn't look like it, but he didn't want to risk getting shot, so he did what he wished so many outlaws back in Arkansas and the Indian Nations would have done all those years ago. He dropped the .36-caliber cap-and-ball revolver on the floor, raised his right toward the gaudy ceiling, and sang out as loud as he could:

"I surrender!"

His left hand kept the strongbox secured against his side.

Until the weasel in the armoire kicked him in the back.

The strongbox fell heavily, crashing on the wood, spilling out gold and silver coins, receipts, and paper money. Fallon fell on his knees, and then toppled like a drunken thespian on the opera house boards and lay on his back.

The shoes of the railroaders sounded like stampeding elephants as they raced toward him. The bell above the door did not chime, so Fallon thought that the weasel that owned this joint would soon curse them for letting the flies in.

The weasel had something else on his mind. He had picked up the .36, and started to cock it.

"What are you doing, Mr. Primm?" one of the railroaders yelled.

"Killing this thief," the man said, and aimed the pistol at Fallon's head.

Fallon brought his right leg up, the toe of his boot slamming into the miser's groin. Mr. Primm lost what little color had returned to his face, turned, collapsed into the armoire, and touched the trigger.

The little gun exploded, and the man cried out in pain. He

was on his knees now, shaking his hand, which gunpowder had blackened. Fallon counted the fingers. They were still all intact. It wasn't much of a gun, and hadn't been much of an explosion, but the sound must have trebled inside the confines of the cherrywood piece of furniture.

A boot thudded into Fallon's side, just between his ribs and the hipbone. He groaned, and rolled over.

"You all right, Mr. Primm?" another voice called out.

"My hand," the man wailed, "my hand, my hand. Where's my Smith and Wesson?"

Fallon felt himself jerked to his feet. Two men held his arms tightly. The third man found some silk scarves and wrapped the man's hand. The old man blinked, then pulled away from the man trying to help him, fell to his knees, and began gathering the items that had spilled out of the strongbox. At least, Fallon decided, the fool's greed would prevent him from searching for that Smith & Wesson.

His ears stopped ringing, but Fallon heard something different. So did the men, and even the skinflint of an owner turned to the sound. An amber liquid was spewing from a hole in the bottom out onto the floor. Fallon realized that the Manhattan had fired after all, sending its one bullet into the keg.

"My bourbon!" the man cried. "Pennsylvania bourbon!"

"That ain't right," one of the railroaders said, but no one made a move to save what bourbon they could.

"Was he tryin' to rob you?" the one not holding Fallon asked.

"Not me," the man said. "Not my one percent. He was robbing you!" He watched the bourbon spew from the puncture, still too stunned to put bowls and pots and glasses under the hole to salvage what he could.

The big railroad man turned and put a fist against Fallon's jaw.

"I say," the man said to his partners, "that we lynch this thief."

Fallon was bent over as far as his captors would allow. He couldn't see their faces to make a guess as to what they were thinking.

The bourbon kept splattering on the floor, vanishing into the cracks.

"Or find my pistol," the greedy man said as he slammed shut the lid to the strongbox. "I'll put a bullet between his eyes and we can say he died trying to rob me." He looked at his scarf-wrapped hand. "If I can hold the .32 in my hand, that is."

"Hold it!" Fallon shook his head at the voice from the doorway. The bell chimed, and heavy boots sounded. "Let him go, boys. I'll take this outlaw off your hands."

"And who in blazes might you be?" the owner demanded.

Fallon relaxed, though he couldn't say he was happy.

"Holderman," the fat brute said. "Aaron Holderman. Special operative for the American Detective Agency out of Chicago."

The man walked to the keg of bourbon, emptied a small candy jar he had picked off a shelf, and set it underneath the hole.

"Well, Hank Fulton, I reckon I've caught you at last."

CHAPTER FOURTEEN

Harry Fallon, alias Hank Fulton, could say one thing about the legal process in the Territory of Arizona: it was swift.

He sat for just two days in the crowded Tucson cell. On the morning of the third day, a deputy called his name, opened the cell, shackled the manacles on his wrists, and prodded him into the town marshal's office. The marshal, a man of Mexican heritage, twisted his mustache, propped his boots on his desk, and said:

"You are Hank Fulton, *si*?"

"I'm called that," Fallon answered.

"Do you have a lawyer?"

"Never needed one before."

"My brother-in-law is a fine attorney. He will help you."

"How much?"

"You had twelve dollars and thirty cents when you arrived. That will be sufficient."

"Fine with me."

"Your trial is tomorrow."

Fallon nodded. "So when do I meet with your brother-in-law?"

The deputy was already leading Fallon back to the cells. "He will be here after he has his breakfast. My sister is a very good cook. Miguel will speak to you then."

Miguel was a walking advertisement for how good his wife cooked. He was fatter than Aaron Holderman. He asked Fallon three questions between the jail and the court-house.

"Do you like honey on your tortillas?" "How would you like to plead?" "Have you ever been in trouble with the law before the misunderstanding at Señor Primm's establishment four days ago?"

The circuit judge did not look like he had eaten in weeks. He was thin, definitely American, with eyes set close together behind a Roman nose. His beard was thick and well past his chin, more white now than black, and his hair was slicked back and neatly parted in the middle. He looked to be in his fifties, and he wore a black suit that still wore the dust he had not had time to brush off. He kept checking the silver watch that was in one of his vest pockets as if he had a pressing engagement soon or a train to catch. His black ribbon tie hung askew.

"How does your client plead, Señor Perez?"

"Not guilty, Your Honor, and for the record Mr. Fulton has never had any trouble with the law . . ."

"I know, Perez, 'before the misunderstanding at such-and-such's place on such-and-such date.'" He slammed the gavel and pushed his chair back from the bench. "Let's get on with it. The charge is robbery at gunpoint and assault and battery and kidnapping. Mr. Solicitor, call your first witness."

Primm was the first witness. He testified pretty much truthfully, although his right hand now was in a sling, and bandaged so much that he must have had to order several new bolts of muslin from his supplier. He even had a bandage over his head, which had not been injured during the holdup. This had to be Primm's first time in a courthouse, or what served as a courthouse in Tucson, and if that wasn't quite the case, Fallon knew the man had never been on a witness stand before. He testified like a terrible actor in a stupid melodrama.

But he got the judge's attention.

"How much money was in that strongbox, Mr. Primm?" the judge asked.

The prosecutor and Señor Perez stared at each other. Having a judge ask questions was new to them. Fallon had to smile. They had never been in a court with Isaac Parker.

"Well, sir, ummm, well, it would be . . ."

One of the miners called out from the back seats, "Three hundred and thirty-three of it was ours, Your Honor. That's how much me and my pards give him."

The judge did not bang his gavel, but nodded. "How much, Primm?"

The miser sighed. "Four hundred and fifteen dollars and six bits."

"More than half of that came from these railroaders?" the judge asked.

"They just got paid, and just got to town, sir."

The judge took a peppermint candy and popped it in his mouth.

The examination continued. Primm had been shoved into the armoire. That was the kidnapping charge. He had been brutalized, threatened with death. He was just a poor, honest businessman.

"At one percent interest daily, not per annum, I don't think you're poor, sir," the judge said, "and I might even question, if not your honesty, at least your ethics."

"I am also out of a lot of valuable merchandise," Primm said.

Fallon leaned forward and whispered into Perez's ear. "Yeah, all the cloth he had to use to bandage himself."

Perez grinned and whispered for Fallon to please be quiet, that he was listening so he would know how to handle his cross-examination.

"A gun detonated itself in my hand." Primm nodded at his bandaged hand in the sling. "A gun like that would cost fifteen dollars anywhere on the frontier."

"Wasn't that the defendant's gun?" the judge asked.

"I cannot remember," Primm said. "My hand. My poor, poor, mangled, ruined, crippled hand."

"What else?" the prosecutor asked. He, too, was growing tired of the thespian performance, or at least he could see how angry the judge was getting.

"A keg of bourbon."

The judge leaned forward. "Bourbon?"

"Yes. The fiend shot a hole in the bottom of the keg. Just for spite. Shipped all the way from Pennsylvania, Mr. Judge, all that way, to get ants and beetles drunk."

Miguel Perez had no questions for the witness.

The railroaders testified. They were a lot more honest than Primm. Well, they didn't stretch the truth and when they didn't know the answer to one of the questions, they said they did not know. When they had not seen something, they admitted that they had not seen it. But they did identify Hank Fulton as the man who had attempted to rob the strongbox at Primm's Dry Goods and Sundries on the southwestern edge of Tucson.

Aaron Holderman took the stand. He said he had been

on the trail of this Hank Fulton since Albuquerque. That Hank Fulton was a scoundrel known far and wide. Perez did not bother to object. And that, sure, while there were no charges against Hank Fulton in New Mexico or Arizona territories, that he, Aaron Holderman, special detective for the American Detective Agency out of Chicago, Illinois, knew if he would just keep his eye on the miscreant, he would catch Fallon red-handed.

"Fallon?" the judge asked. "Who's Fallon?"

"Umm. Fulton. Fallon's another felon I've got my eye on. Sorry, Your Honor."

The judge sighed.

"And," the prosecutor asked for his final question, "did you catch this Hank Fulton red-handed?"

"Yes, sir." The prosecutor had coached Holderman very well. "Caught him before he could do harm to any more good citizens. Of course"—he nodded at the railroaders—"I had some mighty fine help. Good lads. Couldn't have brought this bad man to justice if not for their able assistance."

The territory rested its case. Miguel Perez asked Fallon if he wanted to testify, that he did not have to, that he probably shouldn't, but he could if it was his desire.

Fallon shrugged. "Why bother?" he said.

"Indeed," Perez said.

The defense rested.

The judge found another piece of candy. "You have forgone a trial by jury and left this in my hands. The charges are kidnapping, but I find no evidence of kidnapping. That charge is dismissed. Attempting to hold a man in a cheap pine box that has been painted a cherry color and being sold as cherrywood is a preposterous place to hold a kidnapped victim. The charge of assault is also dismissed. You fired a weapon yourself, Mr. Primm, and if I believe what

I have heard, you fired it at an unarmed man. You got what you deserved, and I don't mean the one percent per diem you charge."

The judge stared at Fallon, who began to wonder if he might get off and walk out and have to find another way to land in Yuma.

"But there is also the charge of robbery. Robbery with a loaded firearm. And you did threaten Primm with bodily harm." He found the gavel. "So you leave me little recourse under the laws of our nation and the territory of Arizona. It is, therefore, that I sentence you, Hank Fulton, to the territorial prison in Yuma for a sentence of six months for attempted robbery, and I tack on a sentence of eighteen months in the same prison, to be served consecutively, for the destruction of a damned fine keg of Pennsylvania bourbon."

The gavel slammed.

"Next case."

CHAPTER FIFTEEN

If Yuma wasn't the end of the earth, it was close to it.

Gone were the sloping hills, the saguaro cacti, the junipers, and the distant, rugged mountains. The country was flat, sandy, with a few scrubs popping up here and there, though few and far between. The Colorado River ran wide and blue; California lay on the other side, but it looked no greener, no wetter, and no less desolate. The sun shown with brutality, and the wind either blistered you with its heat or scarred you with sand.

The town of Yuma looked much like the desert itself, flat, wide, unimpressive, and almost uninhabitable. Few buildings topped one story. Adobe walls needed patching or simply to be rebuilt. There were few stone buildings, and nothing made completely of wood. A few tents served as roofs for itinerant businesses. More people lived in miserable *jacales* than adobes. No dogs trotted down the streets. No chickens pecked for food. Even the people appeared motionless. It was too hot to move.

Yet amid all this Spartan landscape rose one of the most impressive, yet terrifying, structures in the American Southwest. The high walls dwarfed the buildings of the town, and the brown color offered a wide contrast to the paleness of the desert that surrounded it. The massive, thick iron gate swung open as the wagon stopped outside.

Two lawmen shoved Harry Fallon, alias Hank Fulton, out of the back and into the sand. The first thing Fallon saw was a scorpion that looked ready to sting before it scurried underneath a cactus. The second thing Fallon spotted, when he lifted his head, was the words chiseled into the adobe above the iron-barred gate:

YUMA TERRITORIAL PRISON

"You're home, Fulton," one of the lawmen said. "Ain't it what you always dreamed of?"

They made him bathe first, in scalding water with lye soap that felt like shaved iron. The barber cut his hair, almost shaving it down to his skull, and the striped uniform he was given felt worse than the clothes he had been forced to wear at Joliet. But the colors were different: yellow and black stripes instead of black and white. They gave him a hat to wear, to protect him from the sun, but the piece of wool had no brim and the wool just made the top of his head hotter. His extra clothes consisted of two handkerchiefs, another pair of socks, trousers, and a jacket. Fallon didn't think in a furnace like Yuma he would ever need a jacket. They also gave him two towels, though one seemed to have more holes than cotton.

They also gave him a number: 1776. Patriotic, Fallon figured.

Fallon's next stop was the warden's office. There were no windows. Adobe was supposed to be cool, but Collin Gruber, superintendent of Yuma Territorial Prison, sat at his desk sweating. He studied the paper, handed one of the lawmen who had escorted Fallon from Tucson a receipt, and said:

"Two years. Robber of a mercantile? Oh my, what a hard-nosed lawbreaker they've sent me this time. We shall not have any trouble with you, will we, Mr. Fulton?"

Before he could answer, he felt a blow to his kidneys. He collapsed against the desk, tried to catch his breath.

"Answer the boss man," the rough voice behind him said.

He didn't reply quick enough. Another blow bounced off his head, knocking the woolen cap onto the floor.

"Now, you piece of filth. Answer the boss man."

"No . . ." Fallon managed ". . . trouble."

He put his hands on the top of the desk to help himself stand. As he was rising, a stick came up rapidly, catching his arms just below the wrists, forcing him to lose his hold on the desk, and he went to the floor again. Hard.

"You keep your hands off the boss man's desk, you piece of filth."

Fallon rolled over. Sweat dripped into his eyes, burning them and making it harder to see, but he could make out the guard before him. He held a stick, but not a billy club or nightstick. It was more like a pole, four feet long. No, it was a staff—like something an artist would have put in Moses's hands in a painting of the Ten Commandments, challenging the pharaoh or parting the Red Sea. The man even looked like Moses, with a wild mane of gray hair and a darker, thick, long mustache and beard.

The man raised the staff as though to bring it down against Fallon's skull, but a shadow covered him, and Fallon saw a man wearing a striped woolen uniform kneeling beside him, taking him under the right shoulder and lifting him to his feet.

"Easy, there, tenderfoot. Easy. Let ol' Pinky help you up. There. There. You'll be fine. Just fine. Here. I'll get your cap."

Fallon felt himself leaning against Gruber's desk, so he pulled away and somehow managed to keep his feet while the prisoner named Pinky bent to grab the woolen cap.

Pinky was a small, frail man. His hair was long, white, and flowing, and a few days of stubble brightened his face. He looked to be more bones than flesh, and his fingers were the longest Fallon could ever remember seeing on a man. The man's back was to the guard with the staff, and the staff was up again, but this time the figure straight out of the Old Testament had changed the direction. He was going to crush the puny old-timer with the wooden rod.

Fallon's mouth opened, but the voice that sounded was not his:

"Mr. Allan, please mind your manners."

The guard stopped, frowned somewhere underneath the beard, and lowered the long piece of wood, butting it on the floor as the frail inmate turned and looked at the warden. Not speaking, Pinky rose and placed the woolen cap in Fallon's left hand.

Fallon's escorts took their receipt and left Fallon standing in the sweltering room. The warden handed an envelope to the big, brutal guard named Allan and said, "Make sure that none of this is contraband, Allan." He gave a waxy smile at Fallon.

"Mr. Fulton, this is Pinky. He's a friend to us and a friend to his fellow inmates. If you have a question, you go to Pinky. Don't ask a guard. Don't ask a guard anything. Don't even look at a guard. Don't speak to a guard. Don't touch a guard. If you need to see me about anything, ask Pinky. If you need to find the privy, ask Pinky. If you need to find the library for prisoners, ask Pinky. If you need to empty your bladder or bowels, ask Pinky. Do this, and your sentence will breeze by. Make one mistake, and Mr. Allan will introduce you to pain you have never even imagined."

Still smiling like a snake-oil salesman, Gruber looked back at the big, burly, biblical Allan. "Well?"

The guard sniggered and tossed a badge on the warden's desk.

"It says," Allan sniggered, "Deputy U.S. Marshal."

"My, oh my." Gruber fingered the badge and cocked his head. "Why would a deputy marshal resort to robbing a tiny store in Tucson?" The badge spun in an arc and landed in a trash can in the corner of the office. "But I'm afraid, Mister . . ." He had to glance at the paper before him. "Mr. Fulton. Yes, yes, Fulton. So why would you have a marshal's badge. Did you forget which side of the law you were on?"

"I was hungry," Fallon said.

"Well, you shall not go hungry here, Mr. Fulton. You have beans and potatoes every day. With bread too. For supper. Gruel for breakfast. More beans and potatoes for your dinner, sometimes even with a bit of meat." He looked back at the guard. "Anything else, Mr. Allan?"

The man held the old photograph in his massive fingers. He stared, grinned, and waved the small print under Fallon's nose. "I don't think you can have this, you piece of filth. No. Not at all. Looking at a petticoat that looks this good, why, it would give you some real bad thoughts. Not good. No, not good at all. Now, me, now I could have an image of this fine thing. And give that kid a few years and, well, maybe I wouldn't even have to give her any years at all before . . ."

Fallon hit him. He moved so fast, the big guard had not even looked away from the photo of Fallon's wife and daughter. No one had expected it. From the corner of his eye, Fallon saw the warden putting both hands on the desktop as though trying to push himself out of his seat. Fallon didn't even look at Pinky, the skinny little trusty. He saw only the face of Moses. He felt nothing but blinding fury.

Allan had a couple of inches and sixty pounds on Fallon, but none of that mattered. The man's bearded face turned with the punches, this way, and that, then drove back against the adobe wall. The staff rattled on the floor. The man could not even move, never even brought his arms or hands up to defend himself. Fallon punched, and punched, and punched. All he saw was the photo, slipping out of Allan's fingers and drifting away, toward Pinky. He thought he saw the trusty catch the old print. Then he went to work on Allan's stomach and ribs.

Something rang in his ears. For a moment, he thought it was the sound of blood, rushing to his head. Then he realized that it was a whistle. The superintendent of Yuma was blowing a whistle. Gruber remained in his seat, but Pinky was moving. He quickly pulled open the door.

Gruber's voice reached Fallon. The man was screaming in terror, but Fallon did not understand the words. All he understood was the sound of his fists driving the behemoth Allan to his knees. Blood spurted from the man's nostrils, and his lips.

A moment later, Fallon knew he was on the ground, and his head was throbbing. He didn't see Allan anymore, or Pinky, or Gruber. He saw flashes of white and red and lavender, and felt his head throbbing. Excited curses and shouts bounced in his eardrums. Someone kicked him in his side, and he gasped for air.

At last, as he lay on the hot floor, he managed to make out Gruber's now sharp voice.

"Stay where you are, Allan. You brought that on yourself and . . ." The warden—superintendent, whatever he wanted to call himself, even God—chuckled. "And I must say, I really enjoyed it. A big man like you, getting the hell beat out of you by a man who robs a puny little store, and doesn't even get out of the business before he gets caught. You're a fine guard, Allan. Sit there. Sit there and quit bleeding on my dust."

Gruber sighed, and his voice went back to the placating, sarcastic tone he had been using earlier. "But, well, we can't allow this, Mr. Fulton. No, sir, we cannot allow our residents acting like this, beating up a big man like Ezekiel Allan. I'm afraid I'll have to put my foot down, before my strongest guard decides to shove that long stick of his up your . . . throw the bastard in the Dark Cell, gentlemen."

Fallon felt himself being lifted up.

The warden spoke again as Fallon was dragged out of the superintendent's office.

"And if you ever try a stunt like that again, we'll bury you just beyond the walls, my boy."

CHAPTER SIXTEEN

It felt much cooler in the Dark Cell. Cooler than anywhere Fallon had felt in a long, long time. He lay still on the floor, his head propped up against the iron wall. He raised his hand over his head, turned it this way and that, and brought it down to a few inches above his eyes. At least, he thought he had. He couldn't see a damned thing.

Blackness. A blackness of which he had never experienced. Darker than he remembered one night with his father back in Gads Hill. A new moon, and his father had blown out a candle as they walked home together, and Fallon remembered coming to an abrupt stop, sucking in a deep breath, and feeling terrified of the instant darkness. His father had chuckled, but put a reassuring hand on the boy's shoulder. Fallon could not have been older than seven or eight.

"There's nothing to fear in the dark, Hank," he could remember his father saying. "Remember that. Dark's just dark. That's all it is."

But this was a different kind of darkness.

Not only was the blackness so permanently deep, there was no sound. He knew he remained in prison. He had opened his eyes outside to see the chambers on either side of him as they dragged him to this cell. He remembered them opening another barred door, and then he saw the emptiness, the murkiness that soon turned into a gloom. When the door had been shut behind the guards, that darkness turned into an awful gloom.

They called this the Dark Cell. It had been dug into the caliche hill, a ten-by-ten-foot solitary cell in which they had put in an iron cage. Light—and precious air—came from the ventilation hole in the ceiling.

There was no light, of course, at night. There was only darkness now.

Yet when he lowered his arm, and tucked his hands underneath his head, he did not feel the gloom. When a man closed his eyes, it did not matter if it was day or night. He could see, or at least imagine, what he wanted to see.

This time, Harry Fallon saw Renee. And he saw Rachel.

His wife's family, her grandparents, at least, had left France for America. New Orleans, first, followed by Memphis, and then St. Louis. Renee DeSmet had left St. Louis for Fort Smith to work for a watchmaker. The watchmaker, a Swiss man whose name Fallon never could remember, was getting old, and his eyes kept failing him, and his hands trembled. So he told Renee what to do.

Fallon watched the process once. The man sitting in a chair in his shop, hands on his knees, listening, and Renee, black-haired with stunningly blue eyes, at the table, holding the tools like surgical instruments. The man would say something, often in French, and she would bend closer or look through the magnifying lens. Fallon had never seen anything like it.

Nor had he ever seen a woman like Renee DeSmet.

They roomed in a boardinghouse in Van Buren, just

down the road and river from Fort Smith. Rents were cheaper in Van Buren, and the town did not have all the drunken railroaders, the drunken deputy marshals, the commotion and bustle, and the hangings like Fort Smith. It was, for the most part, fairly peaceful.

Her room was three down from Fallon's. The widow Rita Talley ran the boardinghouse, and served decent food—an extra fifteen cents for boarders, or twenty-five cents for guests—that usually consisted of chicken and dumplings or fried catfish. Her tea was especially sweet. She did wonderful things with onions and carrots.

Since they both worked in Fort Smith, he volunteered to escort Renee to the watchmaker's shop. For a month, they did this, barely speaking to each other for the first four days. She didn't like his gun, but he loved everything about her.

By the second month, she had grown used to him. After the third month, they were engaged. Six weeks later, they moved out of the boardinghouse into a rented room still in Van Buren but closer to Fort Smith.

He had been riding for Judge Isaac Parker's court for a little more than a year and a half.

Renee didn't care much for the life of a federal lawman. Waiting for her husband to come back home, worrying every day that he walked out the door if she would see him alive again. But the job paid well. A nice salary. Even expenses. And when court was in session, Fallon got to spend a good bit of time in Van Buren and Fort Smith. He got to take his wife out to supper, or swing by the watchmaker's shop and marvel over how she managed to do the old Swiss man's work for him.

Those long, dull hours in the courtroom made Fallon a little more interested in the other side of the legal system.

He watched the attorneys—those for the federal court and those defending the men brought before Judge Parker. One evening, Fallon found himself waiting outside the courthouse when Judge Parker stepped out. They walked to the corner where the omnibus stopped and they talked. Parker suggested that Fallon read law, maybe pass the state bar and get an appointment. A lawyer could go anywhere. So could a lawman, but a lawyer had a better chance of living to see his fortieth birthday. Parker even suggested a pretty decent lawyer who could help Fallon study, so Fallon began spending a lot of time in the office and home of Chris Ehrlander.

Renee liked that a lot. She even liked Ehrlander. Then she had a baby, and when Fallon held the tiny, pink-skinned six-pound loaf wrapped in swaddling cloth, Fallon felt his life change.

In the darkness of the solitary cell, Fallon could still see the baby—the baby he and Renee had made—in his arms. He feared he would drop her. No one had ever told him how to hold a baby. He didn't know what to do. Horses? He knew about them. And dogs too. At least some dogs. But a six-pound bundle with eyes that barely opened and a set of lungs that could make Fallon's ears split and unnerve him worse that a .44-40 slug tearing a hole through the crown of his hat.

Then, his world unraveled. He found himself charged with robbery. It could have been worse. A deputy marshal had been killed, but the solicitor said he didn't have enough evidence to convict former deputy U.S. marshal Harry Fallon on that charge, and Judge Parker had, reluctantly, agreed. Oh, Renee stuck by Fallon all the way. So did Chris Ehrlander, his lawyer friend and mentor. Even a few deputies refused to believe that Harry Fallon would ever turn his back on the law. Rachel was too young to know what was going on, or why her father couldn't rock her to sleep or tell her stories or let her sit on his belly and pretend that she was riding a horse.

He remembered Renee's gasp and instant sobs when the verdict had been announced. He remembered her face, how pale, how dead it had appeared after Judge Parker, Fallon's longtime ally, had delivered the sentence. And he remembered Chris Ehrlander and Renee, holding little Rachel in her arms while tears streamed down her face, promising that they would fight, fight, fight and not sleep until Fallon's name had been cleared, the jury's verdict overturned, and Parker's sentence set aside.

Rachel was two years old when federal lawmen escorted Harry Fallon out of the dungeon that served as Fort Smith's jail and put him on the northbound train for the federal hellhole in Joliet, Illinois.

Renee had told him that she'd wait, that she'd visit. He told her not to. He didn't want her to have to travel to Illinois. He didn't want to have to explain to Rachel all that had happened, and why her father was being treated like a . . . a . . . a . . . criminal.

Ten years. Ten long, inhumane, miserable years in Joliet. He had finally gotten out, with nothing to return to. Ten years, without ever seeing Renee's face. Without ever seeing his daughter.

The photo had been taken in Van Buren when Rachel was six. Fallon had been in Joliet for four years. Renee mailed him the picture, and he had kept it with him or in his cell, looking at it when he needed to, when he had to. A few men in Joliet that he trusted had warned him not to do it, that family just meant heartaches for prisoners. They had reminded him of just how long the law had put him behind bars.

She was eight years old. Eight years old.

Eight years old. Renee would have been twenty-eight. Too young.

To be dead.

He remembered Warden Cain summoning him to his office. He remembered hearing the words as the warden read the telegram. It was a cruel joke. Only it wasn't a joke.

They said that Renee had killed her daughter. Distraught, the newspapers said. Heartbroken that her husband turned out to be nothing but a lowdown criminal. She couldn't bear the shame of it all, the looks her neighbors gave her, and since the old Swiss watchmaker and repairer had died, she had no income. No way to make a living, even though Chris Ehrlander, the attorney, kept paying her rent and begging her to take a job in his office. She didn't want pity. She abhorred charity.

She didn't want to live.

So she had killed her daughter in her sleep. Then she had taken her husband's revolver and shot herself in the heart.

As what the newspapers called a "lapsed" Catholic and a suicide, she was buried in Fort Smith's potters' field. Buried alongside the men who died in Judge Parker's dungeon, or died at the hands of federal lawmen with no one to claim their bodies. The baby, sweet, young, pure Rachel was buried with her. Chris Ehrlander paid the expenses.

He had written a brief note to Fallon, but it had arrived after Cain read the telegram. It had arrived after Harry Fallon had died too.

He couldn't really remember the two years that had passed since the deaths of his wife and child. He had hardened. His heart had never healed, never would heal. He had gone from an outstanding prisoner and turned into a hardcase. He acted like a man with nothing to live for.

Because, Harry Fallon had figured, he had nothing to live for.

And yet sometimes he could see Renee's face, and hear her voice, and something told him that Renee was not the type who could take her own life. Something told him that his wife had not committed suicide. But he was locked up in Joliet. Too far away to do anything.

Until Warden Cain had given him a parole. He knew he was supposed to stay in Illinois, and then Sean MacGregor had given him a way out. With a promise that Fallon's name could be cleared. He didn't care about the ten years of his life that had been ruined, but he could make everyone pay for Renee, for Rachel.

If he did a job or two for Sean MacGregor.

Was it worth it?

Fallon didn't know. Did he care if he died right now? Sure. Because he had decided that someone had murdered his kid, his wife, and he wanted to make sure that son of a bitch or all of those bastards paid for it.

He tried not to think of that. He wanted to think of Rachel, of Renee, how beautiful both were. He wanted to remember how they sounded, their voices. He would try to guess at how Rachel had looked. Was she more like her mother? He sure hoped so. He wouldn't want anyone saddled with his looks. Did she talk like a wild child from southern Missouri, or a French aristocrat? He would never know.

He blocked both his wife and his child out of his mind. He focused on the blackness. He tried to think about the job he had to do.

A sniggering voice echoed from above. "Company for you, Fulton." Tensing, Fallon could not recognize the distorted voice until he realized that it came from above, bouncing down the shaft with the air. Footsteps moved away from the barred window at the top of the cell that allowed air to keep the prisoners confined in solitary alive. He knew who had shouted at him.

Then he heard the sound that put the fear of God into just about anyone.

An intense rattling, and he knew one thing. No Western man ever mistook the sound of a rattlesnake.

There was something else Fallon remembered. The Dark Cell had another nickname: the Snake Den.

Fallon stiffened. He did not move. He barely breathed. He heard something else, and then he knew for sure.

There were two rattlesnakes in the pitch-blackness with him.

CHAPTER SEVENTEEN

Fallon thought, Can snakes see in the dark?

The rattling, amplified in the cramped cage of iron, sounded like both snakes had been dropped in from the air hole off to Fallon's right. They were shaking their tails in annoyance, not because they felt threatened, not because they were about to strike.

Keep telling yourself that, Hank.

He never considered himself scared of snakes. A kid exploring the woods near his house in Gads Hill got used to rattlesnakes. They didn't bite out of aggression, except maybe when they were just coming out of that long winter's nap or in September or October when they were about to go into hibernation. In a hot place like Yuma, rattlesnakes likely had no need to hibernate.

Fallon recalled the time that dog-and-pony circus came rolling into Van Buren. It was before he had married Renee, when they were courting, and she had wanted to go. Fallon had never cared much about circuses, and this one looked incredibly cheap, but he had paid the fifty cents admission and they had visited the man whose arms were crisscrossed with scars from snakebites.

He remembered everything so vividly.

The so-called snake doctor was willing to make side bets on a contest of bravery. He had two large jars, the bottoms filled with sand, a rattlesnake in each one.

"Put your hand against the glass, my brave friend," the doctor had said. "If you can keep your hand against the glass when that Mojave strikes, then you'll get your two bits back. If not, well, then I'll be eating a steak supper tonight on your generosity."

The muleskinner ahead of Fallon and Renee had taken the bet. The rattles sang out their warning, the snake raised its head high in anger, and, like a bullet coming out of a Colt's barrel, struck. The wiry skinner's bronzed hand recoiled and the man even let out a little cry.

"No shame, my good man," the snake doctor said. "I've been eating steak dinners for a long, long time. But here . . . I'll make this bet a little cheaper. Five cents. If you can keep your hand on this jar. Shouldn't be any contest at all. Notice the snake's head?"

Fallon and Renee had moved closer, curious, and the skinner had laughed. "Five cents? Why not fifty?"

The snake doctor had stepped back and pushed up his gray derby. "You mean double or nothing?"

"Or make it sporting," the skinner said as he pulled out a Morgan dollar.

"Well, that's a bit steep, sir. I mean, this snake's blindfolded."

Which was true. Renee had looked at Fallon, hoping he could explain, but Fallon had shrugged. A black band was wrapped across the snake's eyes.

Fallon had whispered to Renee, "That's how that doc has gotten bitten so many times. Putting blindfolds on rattlesnakes' eyes."

She had elbowed and *shushed* him.

"That a real blindfold?" the skinner asked, suddenly skeptical.

As proof, the snake doctor moved his hand up and down in front of the jar. The snake appeared not to notice.

"But a dollar?" the scarred man said. "That's a lot of money. Fifty cents, perhaps?"

The skinner had laughed. "Where's your sporting blood, mister?"

So the bet was confirmed at a dollar. The skinner put his hand against the glass, and grinned. The snake rattled. The head turned. The skinner's face paled.

"I promise you, sir, that this Mojave rattler cannot see."

The snake struck, its head bouncing off the glass, and the rattler coiled up again, threatening another strike, but the skinner's hand was high over his head. The skinner looked at the hand in disbelief, then at the doc, and then his hand went for a knife sheathed in his boot top.

"Leave it be," Fallon had said, and pushed back his jacket to reveal the six-point star on his vest.

"That ain't no real blindfold," the skinner protested.

"Take off the lid, then," Fallon had said. "Take the blindfold off. Let's see."

The skinner had stopped his curse, tipped his hat at Renee, and stormed out of the tent. He left his money by the jar.

"I swear on a stack of Bibles, Marshal," the snake doctor said, "that the snake is blindfolded. He cannot see a thing."

* * *

Now, Fallon exhaled and slowly sat up. His hands raised to grab hold of the iron bars and, even slower, pulled himself to his feet. The rattlers still sang their warnings a good distance from him. He started inching his way from the nerve-numbing whirring, and he remembered what the snake doctor had told him all those years ago.

The snake in the second jar was indeed blindfolded, but snakes, the old doc had learned or at least made a good guess, didn't see very well to begin with. Their secret sense, as cold-blooded critters, was detecting heat. Heat from warm-blooded animals like rats and rabbits and human beings. The Mojave had detected the heat from the muleskinner's hand. That's why the ugly-looking blindfolded serpent had struck.

He could see nothing, and would be as blind as those snakes until dawn began to creep in through the hole in the ceiling. The problem was: those rattlesnakes could detect his heat, and he couldn't sense their coldness. He could only hear their warning.

He inched his way, feeling, trying to remember the layout of the ten-by-ten cell when he could see.

That snake doctor from the Amazing Sebastian J.C.C. Culpepper's Traveling Exposition of Amazing Wonders and Freaks of Nature had told Fallon something else about rattlesnakes.

"There are different species of genera *Crotalus* and *Sistrurus*, part of the subfamily called *Crotalinae*. Eleven, all told, in our United States and territories, and I have been bitten by six of those. The timber, diamondbacks— both Eastern and Western—and, well, let's just say that the meanest and the deadliest is this baby here that I have to blindfold every few days. Yes, Marshal, you never, ever want to be bitten by a Mojave rattlesnake."

Fallon couldn't see, of course, if the snakes the guards,

most likely, had dropped into his cell were Mojaves of that muted green coloring or just your everyday Western diamondback variety. Right now, Fallon didn't really care. He just wanted to get through this night without looking like the arms of that snake doctor, Horatio K. Jakes, from the Amazing Sebastian J.C.C. Culpepper's Traveling Exposition of Amazing Wonders and Freaks of Nature.

The rattling stopped. Fallon drew in a deep breath. He imagined the snakes crawling across the hard floor, separating, slithering down the opposite walls, and hoping to catch Fallon in a venomous crossfire. A breeze reached him, and he raised his hands, finding the iron bars. He gripped as hard as he could, and pulled himself up.

Grimacing, drawing in a deep breath, he managed to swing his legs up, and then bent his knees and braced them against the hard bars. His muscles already strained. This, he decided, would be the most uncomfortable night he ever spent. But being struck repeatedly by a couple of rattlesnakes would feel worse than strained muscles and chaffed hands.

Every few minutes, Fallon unbent his knees and allowed his legs to dangle a foot or foot and a half off the cold, hard floor. He moved his hands to the other bar, just to keep his muscles from locking up. Mostly, he ground his teeth and breathed regularly, straining, aching, but refusing to drop to the ground.

He half-expected the brutal guard named Allan—Fallon had recognized the voice when the demon announced the present he was dropping into the cell—to return, to step on Fallon's fingers until they broke, and send Fallon to join the reptiles waiting for him somewhere on the dark floor.

But Fallon was alone. He peered up into the darkness

but saw nothing. It was like looking up a chimney. You saw only blackness.

He had no conception of how long he had hung from the bars, but gray light filtered down the shaft. Dawn came quickly to this desert, but not in the Snake Den. Yet there was just enough sunlight making its way into the Dark Cell for Fallon to find the two snakes. One lay still near the door. The other, awake, slid this way and that along the wall's edge. Fallon kept his bleary eyes locked on the snake, which had to be a good two feet long. He couldn't tell if it was a Mojave or any other species. Hell, he had never even known rattlers came in various kinds until that dog-and-pony show back in Arkansas.

As he slowly lowered his legs again, Fallon held his breath. The snake slithered. Fallon waited. He wondered if a snake would understand what it was passing under if it sensed heat of a mammal above him. He gnawed on his lower lip. His throat turned dryer than the sand in his cell. And Fallon released his hold on the bars.

He dropped, slamming his right boot heel onto the rattlesnake's head. His knees buckled from the impact, from the pain of the night's torment, and he almost toppled over. His left hand, however, reached out and slammed against the wall, and his fingers clasped on a bar. His right arm swung wildly and Harry Fallon kept his balance. The snake's tail whipped frantically. Maybe it was dead. Fallon couldn't tell. He remembered his father telling him at least a dozen times: "A snake don't die till sundown. Don't never get close to one. Known many a man to die from gettin' bit by a dead rattler."

Fallon turned, grabbed the tail just below the rattles with his right hand. He didn't count how many. He slid his boot carefully a couple of inches below the snake's triangular head, gripping it with his left hand.

Groaning, he made himself stand, then stepped and swung, releasing the snake's head with his right hand but holding the tail with his left. The head smashed against the iron bars, and Fallon dropped the snake. It twitched from nerves, but Fallon saw the tear in the serpent's head and neck. It was dead.

The other rattlesnake, however, was awake.

Fallon moved in a wide circle. The light sneaking down the shaft began to fade. It would be black again soon as the sun moved away from the hole in the ceiling. He picked up the dead snake and tossed it against the wall, watching it land near the living reptile, which reacted quickly, coming into a coil, and letting its tail sing another warning.

Fallon moved faster than the rattler, faster than he had ever moved. He pinned the snake's head with his boot, crushing, driving, twisting against the iron floor as Fallon held his breath. Finally, he dispatched the snake against the metal just as he had killed the first one.

His heartbeat slowly steadied. He checked his hands and fingers to make sure no fang had punctured his skin. He thought about removing his prison shoes and prison socks to make sure he had not been bitten there either.

Darkness descended again as voices and footsteps sounded down the caliche tunnel that led to the Dark Cell, and Harry Fallon heard the grinding of the key in the lock of the outer door.

CHAPTER EIGHTEEN

When the outside door opened, the sunlight caused
Fallon's eyes to squeeze even tighter. He heard footsteps,
and as he sat against the far wall of the cell, legs stretched
out in front of him, hands holding the snakes on either side
of his body, he made out the guard named Allan's laughter.

A key ground into the lock of the iron cage, and when
the door squeaked open, Fallon's eyes opened.

The light still caused him to squint, but he heard the
gasps from the two younger guards, one Mexican, the other
blond and wearing a black patch over his right eye, who
flanked Allan.

Allan came to a stop and straightened, his eyes register-
ing surprise. "How in the hell . . ." he started, but Fallon
was raising both hands, the long tails of the serpents dangling in the air. And before any of the guards could react,
two dead snakes were flying across the tiny cell.

"Want these back, Allan?" Fallon asked as the guards
scattered and screamed.

* * *

They dragged Harry Fallon, known in Yuma as Hank Fulton, out of the Snake Den and into the prison yard, bleeding from his head, nose, lips, but smiling all the while. It had been worth it, and, though groggy from the beating and the bruises and the stiffness of muscles and a sleepless night hanging like a piece of drying beef, Fallon was aware of the inmates staring at him and Allan. He could imagine their whispers.

"Captain Allan!" a voice bellowed. "What is the meaning of this?"

"It's that son of a bitch from Tucson, Mr. Gruber." So, Allan was a captain of the guards. Yuma, Fallon decided, was really hard up for men. Allan's voice remained an octave or two higher since he had ducked underneath a dead snake.

Of course, Fallon had reminded the three men when they realized the snakes were dead: "My pa has known many a man who died after being bitten by a dead rattle-snake."

The prison superintendent called out, "Allan, I don't want to have to explain why a prisoner died from multiple rattlesnake bites again, or answer to some Red Cross lady about certain bruises and broken bones. Get back to your post. Pinky, take Fulton to see the 'Killing Sawbones.'"

Fallon remembered Pinky. The bony little cuss with the flowing white hair knelt and slowly raised Fallon, who let out a slight chuckle that held little mirth.

"You all right, boss?" the old man asked.

Running his fingers across his hands, Fallon said, "I think so."

"Well," Pinky said, "Pinky had best get you to the

hospital. Mr. Gruber said so. So Pinky's gonna help you up. If you start hurtin' bad, you just let ol' Pinky know."

"You can put your shirt back on, Fulton."

Stiffly, Harry Fallon obeyed the doctor's orders. He sat on a hard table, his legs dangling over the side in the spartan quarters that served as Yuma's prison infirmary. In a prison the size of the territorial pen, Fulton expected to see several inmates filling sick bay, some with good reasons, others just being the typical shirkers, but the only men inside were Fallon, Pinky, and the coughing, silver-headed doctor with the pasty skin and bloodshot eyes.

With trembling hands, the doctor rolled a cigarette. His fingernails looked rotted, and he coughed again like a man suffering from consumption. He wore gray pants, black boots, and a dirty white shirt. Beard stubble covered his face. The man lit his cigarette with a candle, and lifted a bottle of clear liquid.

The label read ALCOHOL.

The doctor drank from it, coughed, and stuck the cigarette back in his mouth.

"Allan's getting better . . ." Another savage round of hacking interrupted the doctor's comment. He flicked ash, caught his breath, and smiled at Fallon, who had his shirt back on but did not slide off the table yet.

"Better at what?" Fallon asked.

The man took another drink. "Not beating a man to death."

Fallon shrugged. "Is that how most people die in Yuma, Doc?" he asked.

The deathly looking physician smiled and shook his head. "I, my good man, have kept studious notes of those who have died here. Shot while trying to escape is not as common as you might think. Suicide is fairly popular. Pleurisy of effusion might be the least known way out of the Hell Hole. Heart failure, which might have been caused by a sound beating. Typhoid. Phthisis. Bronchitis even. Diarrhea. Watch what you eat, my good man. Acute catarrh. Dropsy. Cholera. We have, if you can believe this, very good water at the prison, but the town of Yuma . . . well . . . just thank whomever you pray to that you don't have to eat and drink and work in that blight on our fine territory.

"Let's see. Where was I? Oh yes. Well, there's paralysis of the heart. Cancer. Remittent fever. One poor soul had the misfortune of being crushed to death by a cave-in while digging in the caliche hills. Remittent fever. Oh, wait, I've already said that. Drowning. They made it to the river but the river is quite wide and deep. Bright's disease. Stomach ulcers. Pneumonia. Paralysis of the brain. Heat prostration. Can you imagine that, in a frigid winter wonderland such as Yuma, Arizona? An aorta aneurysm. Heart attack. One even came to us already a corpse. I wasn't sure how to record his death, so I simply marked him, 'Received dead at prison.' But the most common way out of Yuma is . . ." He coughed savagely, and wiped the flecks of blood from his lips onto his sleeve.

The doctor did not need to explain. Fallon figured consumption, or tuberculosis, killed more men in Yuma than the guard with the staff.

"Mind if I ask you a question?" Fallon asked.

The doctor drew another long pull on the cigarette, and shrugged as he blew white smoke toward the ceiling.

"How long have you been here?"

The doc grinned. "I figured you'd ask how I got my nickname. Most of my patients . . ." Again, the spell of coughing doubled him over, and this time he dropped the cigarette to the floor and staggered back to a shelf filled with bottles. This time, he drank from the bottle of dark liquid. Its label revealed that it was some brand of Scotch.

Pinky went over and crushed out the cigarette that was smoldering on a Navajo rug.

The doctor wheezed. Fallon slid from the table and found his hat. He nodded at Pinky, then at the doctor, and moved toward the door.

"Aren't you . . . curious?" the doctor called out to Fallon's back.

Fallon opened the door and turned back. "Why they call you the 'Killing Sawbones'?" His head shook. "That's obvious, Doc. You're killing yourself."

Doctor Jerome Fowler raised the Scotch in salute.

"Not fast enough," he said, and sank into a chair in the corner, the bottle of whiskey clutched in a sweating, trembling left hand.

Fallon turned but before he could exit the infirmary, he had to back up and let another inmate inside.

The prisoner came through so fast, Fallon couldn't make out any features. He saw the back as the convict stopped in front of the Killing Sawbones and said, "Doc . . . Doc . . . Doc . . ."

The rough hat came off, and long black hair fell to the shoulders as the prisoner turned.

Harry Fallon straightened and stupidly removed his own hat. They taught young boys to do that back in Gads Hill, Missouri. You always remove your hat in the presence of a lady.

A crow's wing might not have been as dark as this woman's hair. Likewise, her eyes appeared as black as midnight, and her face had been tanned deeply, which one would expect in Yuma. She wore the same uniform as the men in the prison, but her breasts pushed against the rough material. The breasts were big. Her waist was small, her nose delicate.

"Don't take your hat off to me, buster," the woman said with a snarl. "I'll break your neck."

"Easy, Gloria," Pinky told her. "Allan done tried that and got nowhere."

The woman shot Pinky a glance, then looked back at Fallon.

"So you're the fresh fish, eh?" Now, she looked Fallon up and down, this way and that, and looked back at Pinky. "What's his name?"

Pinky answered, "Hank Fulton."

"This the one who tried to feed Allan some rattlesnake for breakfast?"

"Two," Pinky answered. "But ol' Pinky ain't figured out how Fulton here managed to kill two rattlers in the Dark Cell in the middle of the night."

She looked back at Fallon. This time, she did not look away. "Maybe he's an owl."

"He ain't that wise," Pinky said. "Else he wouldn't have gotten caught and come to stay with us."

"Maybe." She had not looked away.

Fallon wondered how she managed to keep her hair so shiny, so clean. Her clothes wore the dust and dirt, but her hair had been freshly washed. Fallon studied her small hands. She had the long fingers of a piano player, and even her fingernails were clean. He guessed her height to be around five-foot-seven. Tall for a woman. And even wearing a striped uniform meant for a man, a much smaller man, she would take most men's breath away. She was a haunting woman, stunningly beautiful, yet mysterious.

And cold. Very, very cold.

"What's he in for?" the woman asked.

She was younger than Fallon. Younger, he remembered, than Renee. Their eyes held, and he refused to break, but Pinky gave her the reason to look away when he began answering her inquiry.

"He robbed a store or something like that down in Tucson."

"A store?" She snickered.

"Store had a strongbox," Pinky said, "holding a lot of money. They gave him two years."

"A store thief." Her head shook.

"He didn't just break in. He had a gun. And from what ol' Pinky has learned, that owner was heeled, too, till this *hombre* took the gun away from him."

"Penny ante," the woman said.

"Maybe. But he has gotten the better of Allan. Twice. You should've seen the beating he put on that horse's arse—and that was in Gruber's office. He ain't no fresh fish. Pinky'll swear to that. Might be his first visit to Yuma, Gloria, but I'll swear that this *hombre* has done some time before. Hard time. In a hard, hard place."

"Miss Adler," Doctor Jerome Fowler said at last. "Your attention to Yuma's latest guest is making me jealous."

Her face softened. Maybe, Fallon thought, even saddened. She turned away from Fallon and Pinky and looked at the sickly prison doctor.

"How much have you had, Doc?" Gloria Adler asked.

He lifted the bottle of Scotch and smiled. "My first of the day."

"Most prisoners haven't even finished breakfast yet," she told him.

He laughed. "And I'm still working on mine." He pulled hard on the Scotch, but another coughing spell sent whiskey and saliva spraying the dusty floor.

The Killing Sawbones fell to his knees, and Fallon and Gloria Adler were by the doctor. Fallon saw the flecks of blood on the man's lips and realized that he had been right. This wasn't the cough of a man with pneumonia or some cold.

It was the rasping, lethal cough of a man suffering from tuberculosis. The doctor was dying of consumption, if the whiskey and the cigarettes did not claim him first.

Fowler turned his head and coughed and gagged. Globs of mucus and blood splattered on the floor. His breathing turned ragged, short.

What Harry Fallon smelled was not the stink of the doctor, the whiskey, the sweat, the sourness, the sickness, the dying breath of a man who was taking a damned long time to die. He smelled the scent of a woman. Gloria Adler had washed recently, her body, and her hair. He had almost forgotten what a woman smelled like.

"Help me get him up," Gloria Adler said.

They lifted him. Doc Fowler weighed next to nothing. They looked around the empty room, and Fallon nodded at the examining table.

"No," Gloria Adler said. Her chin jutted out toward a closed door.

"All right," Fallon said. "Let go. I'll take him."

She listened, and moved to the door. Fallon followed with the gasping doctor in his arms. Pinky trailed Fallon. The woman opened the door, revealing other beds, also empty of patients. She pulled back the sheets on the closest bed, and Fallon lay the man atop. Fowler started to bring the bottle of Scotch back to his lips, but Gloria Adler snatched it from his weak hand. The bottle came out easily and she tossed it onto another bed.

"You are . . . no . . . fun . . ." the doctor wheezed.

"Shut up," she said. "Close your eyes and go to sleep."

"I'll never sleep, my darling," Fowler said, "till I'm dead."

"Shut up," she told him, and brought up the covers. She wiped his lips with a handkerchief she pulled out of Fowler's breast pocket, ignoring the bloodstains. She ran her fingers through his sweat-soaked hair, before placing the back of her hand on his forehead.

"That's cool," Doc Fowler whispered in a faraway voice. "That's so cool. So pleasant." His eyes were closed, and Gloria Adler kept the hand there.

She stared at him, and now her dark features softened. She was tough. Hard. Bitter. But only when she had to be. Only to survive this hell on earth called Yuma Territorial Prison. But she had some feelings. Yuma had not robbed her of everything she had been taught growing up. She had not lost all of her humanity. She cared for at least Doctor Jerome Fowler, the "Killing Sawbones."

"Get out of here," she said without looking at Pinky or Fallon. "I'll take care of him."

"You always do, Gloria," Pinky said.

"Get out," she repeated.

CHAPTER NINETEEN

"Doc Fowler's all right." Pinky had caught up with Fallon as he stood in the center of the compound, looking at the convicts milling around, the guards in the towers, others walking around the interior escorting some inmates to the giant sally port secured into the thick adobe walls.

"I don't mean his health. He's a sick, sick man. But a good man."

"How about the woman?" Fallon asked.

"Well . . ." The thin, ancient man grinned. "She ain't sick. Ain't sick at all. No, sir. Ol' Pinky would say she's as healthy and as fine and as . . ." He turned and winked.

"Gloria Adler. Come in six months ago. Ol' Pinky, he don't know that much about her, but she killed her husband or her beau or something along those lines. Put in for manslaughter. Ten years. But don't you get no fancy notions about her. She takes care of Doc. And Monk Quinn. Well, he takes care of Gloria Adler. Last fella to get bit real bad by rattlers in the Dark Cell? He'd been seen talking real cozy-like to that fine figure of a petticoat. Seen by Monk Quinn."

"Monk Quinn?" Fallon pretended that he had never heard of the bandit.

"That's all Pinky's gonna say about Monk Quinn."

They kept walking. Pinky had more to say.

"He's the big man here. Bigger than Gruber. Bigger than Allan and his big arse staff. You don't get on Monk Quinn's bad side."

"Maybe I have already."

The old man stopped walking and turned to stare at Fallon. "What you mean?"

"I had two rattlesnakes visit me last night."

Pinky smiled again. "The last fella in the Dark Cell to get bit . . . he had six. But Monk ain't one to touch no snake. Pinky ain't neither."

Pinky's thoughts about Monk Quinn and rattlesnakes did not interest Fallon. What Fallon could guess, though, was that dead man most likely had to be the Mexican operative for the American Detective Agency that Dan MacGregor had mentioned back in Chicago. Valdez. But had he been murdered by Monk Quinn or the guard with the biblical staff named Allan?

Pinky started walking again. "Monk Quinn don't know Hank Fulton. Those snakes that you kilt was Allan's idear. Don't have to even ask Monk Quinn about that. You had two rattlesnakes, not even big ones, although Monk Quinn had a couple of babies put in there with that greaser."

Which confirmed to Fallon that the dead man had been the operative named Valdez.

"Baby rattlers. They'll bite you just as bad as a big one. Anyway. You got two snakes, the greaser got six or so. That's the difference between Monk Quinn and Allan. Allan, he ain't scared of no snakes. Monk is. But it'd be Allan who dropped the bag of rattlers into the Dark Cell. But only because Monk Quinn made that bastard do it."

They took a few more steps before Pinky continued. "But you start sidlin' up to Gloria Adler and you won't finish your two years here. You'll be out yonder." He pointed toward the wall.

Fallon started to ask—"What's out there?"—although he already knew. He had seen it when the deputies had escorted him from the train depot to the prison's main sally port. But he decided to let Pinky know that Fallon wasn't blind, and wasn't stupid.

"The boneyard," Fallon said.

Pinky stopped to reconsider the bruised, bloodied fresh fish. Fallon stared right back into the old man's eyes and grinned. "I'm not stupid. I'm not blind. And I'm not spending two years in this adobe hell."

Pinky wet his lips with his tongue. "Man who thinks like that gets hisself kilt."

"Or he gets out." He nodded south. "Mexico's just a hop and a skip away."

"You know Mexico?"

"A little."

Pinky shook his head. "Don't get notions. Notions get men kilt."

"Don't you ever get notions, Pinky?"

The old man grinned. "All the time. But Pinky . . ." He waved off the suggestion.

They kept walking to the long rectangle building that had to be the mess hall. Inmates were slowly filing out.

"It's Sunday," Pinky said. "Free day for most of the boys, 'ceptin' those that gets hit up for outside work or latrine duty or gardenin'. Gardenin'?" He laughed. "In this furnace. It ain't the best grub you'll ever have inside your belly, but it'll fill you up." His head bobbed at a thought he just got. "We should bring Doc a plate after we've et our fill."

"What's the story about Doc Fowler?" Fallon asked.

"He's been here forever," Pinky said. "No, longer than

that. He come right after they opened this hellhole. Too long for one man to have to patch up wounds, drain snakebites, and make sure the dead is really dead."

Fallon looked at the old-timer. "I asked the Killing Sawbones," Fallon said. "He didn't tell me anything. You know a lot."

Pinky grinned. "You remember what Mr. Gruber told you. 'If you have a question, you go to Pinky.' You asked about Doc Fowler. Doc, now he's a bit close-lipped. Which is fine to ol' Pinky. Don't really want a lunger breathin' on Pinky all the time. But you're fresh here, Fulton. You'll learn that you gots to ask Pinky."

Fallon smiled. The grin hurt his face, and he rubbed his jaw. "How long has Pinky been here?" he asked once his jaw stopped hurting for the time being.

The old man shook his head. "Pinky's been here so long he don't remember. Feels like that, anyhow." The rail-thin man straightened. "The first of July," he said as his eyes brightened, "in the Year of Our Lord Eighteen Hundred and Seventy-six."

Fallon remembered that year. He had started riding with Judge Parker in 1876. Fifteen years ago.

"That's when ol' Pinky came here. Yep, ol' Pinky and six others." His head bobbed with satisfaction. "Pinky helped build this place."

Fallon nodded. "You did a damned fine job."

The main guard tower had been built atop of the water supply, just beyond the whitewashed wall, in the northeast corner. Fallon could see the guard with the rifle, staring at the yard, enjoying the shade the roof provided. The guard had a rifle in his arms, and Fallon remembered the guard sitting in the booth in front of the sally port when Fallon first arrived at Yuma. He, too, was armed with a repeater, a .44-40 Winchester.

There were other towers, including one that must have been connected to the main one by a small walkway. The guard in that corner tower carried a Sharps rifle with a long brass telescopic scope. A man like that with a gun like that could see and shoot for a far distance. He saw the other corner posts atop the whitewashed walls, and even a few guards walking along the tops of the walls. More guards here than there had been at Joliet.

Moving to the wall nearest him, Fallon studied the southeast guard tower across the compound. Moving to the wall closest him, he studied the guard there. And the gun. This was a little different. The guard didn't have a Winchester or a Sharps. It was something else.

Finally, Fallon realized what it was.

"Gatling gun," he said to himself, but Pinky had heard.

"Not exactly," Pinky said. "It's what they call a Lowell battery gun. Better, we're told, than 'em ol' Gatlin's."

Fallon laughed. He had read all about the Lowell in some military journal that wound up in the Joliet library. The Lowell, if he remembered correctly, could fire six hundred rounds in a minute. Accuracy almost perfect up to one thousand feet. With a horizontal sweep of ninety feet.

If there was a blind spot at Yuma Territorial Prison, Harry Fallon couldn't find it.

He lifted his boot to scrape the heel on the wall.

"It ain't adobe," Pinky told him.

Fallon lowered his foot and looked at the old man.

"Solid rock," the prisoner who had helped build this prison said. "At least on the foundation. After that, it's adobe bricks all the way up."

Fallon looked up. Eighteen feet high, he guessed. Nothing to grip.

"How thick?" he asked.

"Close to eight down here," Pinky said. "Up top . . ." The old-timer shrugged. "Five or around there."

He heard the lonesome whistle of a train, and watched the black smoke rising above the high adobe wall off to the west. He could even hear the *clickety-clack* of the iron wheels on iron rails. The tracks of the Southern Pacific ran close to the outer walls, but Fallon knew that already. His escorts from Tucson had led him off the train, into a wagon, and just around the corner to the prison.

"So don't get no notions 'bout gettin' out of Yuma, sonny," Pinky said. "We built it good."

Fallon chuckled. "Yeah, you did a fine job, Pinky."

"Too fine." Pinky let out a sigh. "Ol' Pinky did too fine a job buildin' this prison." The old man pointed at the smoke as the train moved toward the nearby Colorado River. "I think they put the tracks this close just to torture everyone in here."

Fallon rubbed his jaw. "Allan does enough torturing," he said.

Pinky laughed. "Ain't that the truth!"

"How about the guards?" Fallon asked.

"What about 'em?" Pinky said with a good bit of suspicion. "You've met the worst of the lot."

Meaning, Fallon figured, the man with the staff and the iron fists, Allan.

"How much money do they make?"

"Good wages," Pinky said. "Seventy-five a month. Lots of folks want the job just for that reason. Jobs that pay that kind of money ain't common in this patch of Hades."

"So bribing them's not much of an option."

Pinky shrugged. "Depends on the guard. Most of 'em be honest. Then you get the bad apples. Thing is, you can't trust the bad apples."

Like Allan, Fallon knew.

"All right. What else can you show me that I need to know about Yuma?"

They walked around the compound.

The hospital was new, five, six, no more than seven years old. Fallon knew the superintendent was trying to get funds from the territorial government to build cells for the women prisoners, and there was talk about adding a library for inmates one of these years.

Fallon figured, from what he had determined from Superintendent Gruber, that if the territory turned funds over to Gruber for women's cells and a library, well, they might get another cell dug into the caliche hill and maybe a few newspapers and a Bible for prisoners to read in the hospital. The rest of the money would line Gruber's pockets.

The breeze blew off the Colorado River, up over what the residents of Yuma called Prison Hill, and over the whitewashed walls.

Pinky laughed. "The story goes that the breeze from the river is always cool. Makes life almost pleasant here in prison."

Fallon looked at the old man. "That wind's cool?" he asked sarcastically.

"That's the story," Pinky said. "You've seen enough?"

"For now," Fallon replied. "I'm hungry."

"Good. So am I. Let's eat. Then we'll have to report for work detail. After that, I'm sure Allan will figure out where you're bunking for the next two years."

"What work?" Fallon asked.

Pinky shrugged. "Cooking. Digging at the quarry. The good ones might get out to make shoes or canes, stuff like that."

"What do you do?" Fallon asked.

"Me?" Pinky grinned. "I try to stay alive. In Yuma, that can be a hard, hard job."

CHAPTER TWENTY

The guard opened the door to the cell, and grinned at Fallon. "Welcome home," Allan said as his smile turned into a sneer.

Fallon stopped at the iron-barred door. "No snakes?" he said.

"I wouldn't say that," Allan answered. "Get in."

Fallon slid through the narrow opening and stepped to his right as Pinky followed. The door slammed shut, and Allan locked the door, laughed, and walked away.

The first thing Fallon did was crush a black widow with the toe of his boot. It was, he figured, better than a couple of rattlesnakes.

The slop bucket in the corner was filled to the point that one more bowel or bladder movement would have the contents seeping over the top. Narrow bunks crisscrossed the room in pairs, and Pinky had already taken the top one nearest the door. A cell this size could hold two prisoners in what no one would call comfortable but at least they'd be tolerable. This one had beds for six. Two bunks were empty, however.

He saw a few beetles—no cockroaches like they had to

feed the rats at Joliet—but no more spiders. He didn't see any scorpions either.

"Here's your bunk, Fulton," Pinky said, and pointed to the bedding to Fallon's right. Bed? Well, there was one sheet over some straw on the floor. Bedbugs? Fallon figured he'd learn if he had any of those paying rent when he woke up the next morning.

Pinky and the two other top bunks at least had a mattress, which might have been stuffed with straw but at least the canvas would keep the straw from spreading, or being covered with human excrement.

"Boys," Pinky said, "meet the fresh fish, our new bunkie."

No one paid any attention.

"He's the fish who tried to make Allan eat the rattlers he tossed into the Dark Cell last night."

Now, the men—all but one—raised their heads.

Pinky made the introductions.

"Hank Fulton, this be the Preacher."

Preacher Lang needed no introduction. Fallon had seen the wanted posters on him in Arkansas, in Kansas, in Texas. He must have been captured in Arizona while Fallon was serving his sentence in Joliet. The long dark hair was gone, cropped short, but the mustache and beard remained thick, brown with some white streaks showing up. His nose was long and crooked, and a deep scar ran from his left eyebrow and across his cheek to the ear. His eyes were blacker than Miss Adler's hair, though probably not as black as Preacher Lang's soul.

If you believed the wanted posters Fallon had seen many years ago, Preacher Lang—first name unknown— had killed twelve women and fifteen men. Fallon wondered who was worse, and who was crazier, the Preacher . . . or the Deacon from Joliet? Well, the Deacon was now dead so . . .

"He's doin' fifteen years for manslaughter."

"Woman-slaughter," said the Mexican in the bottom bunk next to Fallon.

"She was no woman," the Preacher said. "She was a demon, a sorceress, the left hand of Satan."

"Left?" the Mexican asked, and laughed.

"Yes. For I am the right. The right hand of our God Jehovah. The right hand of Lucifer as well."

Preacher Lang, Fallon decided, was as crazy as all those wanted posters said.

"New Mexico Territory wants the Preacher too," Pinky said. "So does six or seven other states. But Arizona got him first, and they ain't doin' no extraditin' till he finishes his sentence here."

"That'll be the day," Preacher Lang said.

"Shut up!" the Mexican said.

Preacher Lang let out a muffled chuckle, nodded at Fallon, and lowered his head while lifting the Bible he held with long fingers, the nails unsightly and desperately needing a trim.

Pinky looked down at the Mexican, who grinned and made a mocking wave of his right hand at Fallon. "*Señor*, I am Yaqui Mendoza. At your service. For a price that you might not be able to afford." He read no book. He just sank his head on the clasped hands and stared at the ceiling. Fallon glanced to see what held the man's fascination, but saw only the brownish dirt and stone.

"Mendoza has only thirty days left," Pinky said. "Then he gets out."

"Lucky."

The fourth man laughed. Mendoza cursed and turned

his head away from the ceiling. "You laugh again, *señor*, and you will awaken to find a tarantula in your mouth tonight."

"Is that supposed to scare me, Mex?" The man laughed again.

"He gets out," Pinky explained, "when they hang him for killing two men in Flagstaff."

"They were not men," Mendoza said. "They were pigs."

Fallon waited for Pinky to introduce the last of the inmates, but instead the old man nodded at the bunk and said, "Might as well lie down and rest. You gots to be sore after the beatin' you took, and I doubt if you slept real good last night in the Dark Cell."

Fallon waited, and studied the last man.

"No need to get to know me, boy," the man said in a rich Southern drawl. "They hang me in six days."

Pinky and the Mexican snored. The Preacher talked fire and brimstone in his sleep. The doomed man whose name Fallon did not know twisted and turned and kicked, raining straw and dust down toward the floor. Somewhere beyond the walls, coyotes sang.

A train whistle blew in the night, and Fallon agreed. The railroad must have laid its tracks close to the prison walls to torture the inmates.

He heard the footsteps and smelled the cigar smoke before the door to the cell rattled and swung open. Fallon felt the coolness of the desert night reach him. A man coughed and said, "Up, Fulton. The boss man wants to see you."

Fallon opened his eyes and sat up. He knew Pinky and the other inmates were awake, even though the Preacher pretended to be snoring. He knew none would say a word, or even lift their heads off what passed for pillows. Fallon saw the lantern that Allan held at his side.

It had to be two in the morning. Fallon did not think Superintendent Gruber wanted to see anyone at this hour.

"Either you come, bucko, or I drag you out. Fact is, I'd rather drag you. So give me a reason."

Fallon pulled on his shoes and found his hat. He rose, dodging the other bunks and arms, and careful not to come close to the slop bucket, slid through the open door, which slammed shut and was locked by the guard named Allan.

"This way," Allan said, and nodded.

The superintendent's home was, naturally, outside the whitewashed walls, through the sally port and close to the Colorado River. Fallon had seen that on his way inside the Hell Hole. Allan was leading him the opposite direction, to the south wall. *Back to the Snake Den?* Fallon wondered, but the guard behind him with the lantern grunted, "Right." Fallon moved east, between the wall and the line of other rock-walled cells. Fallon glanced at the guard towers. He saw no signs of movement, no glows from cigarettes. There could be guards up there, watching, but Fallon didn't think so. Allan had likely arranged that both guards take a break for a spell.

Yellow light shone through the cell at the end of this block. Fallon walked, listening, staring at the shadows that danced on the ground just outside of the cell with light. On the far wall stood the hill of caliche.

Something else was coming out of that cell at the end of the block. Music. Fallon tried to remember when he had heard music inside a prison except during Sunday church services or when visitors were brought in to serenade some of the less vicious convicts on Easter, Christmas, or Thanksgiving. No one was singing, though over the wind Fallon thought he heard someone humming inside the cell.

Allan said, "Stop."

Fallon stood in front of the light-filled cell. Not only light, but music—bells and tines—playing some tune from a cylinder music box. The song slowed, died, but the light kept flaring. The door to the cell opened.

"Inside, Fulton," Allan ordered.

Fallon saw the figure of a man in prison clothes bending over a table, fumbling with the cylinder while puffing on a fat cigar. Fallon saw the greasy black hair, long, past the shirt's collar. His shoes were not what any of the other prisoners wore, but fancy, hand-tooled black boots, gleaming from wax, with long mule-ear pulls that were inlaid with red and gold crosses. The man gave up on the box and turned around. He removed the cigar and studied Fallon up and down, and then he spoke to Allan.

"Wait here. This won't take long."

Behind Fallon, the guard grunted.

The prisoner asked, "Do you know who I am?"

CHAPTER TWENTY-ONE

Monk Quinn almost looked like a Mexican with that long dark hair and a face bronzed a deep brown, yet his accent revealed more than a touch of Ireland and his eyes were a deep, dark green, practically jade in color. His shirt and pants were Yuma Territorial Prison regulation, only his, like many other inmates Fallon had seen, featured gray and white stripes rather than yellow and black. As far as Fallon could tell, there was no rhyme or reason as to who got what color. It was probably just random.

"You're the Boss Man," Fallon said, and hooked his thumb back at Allan. "At least, that's what he calls you."

The man had no reaction. Slowly, he removed his cigar and pitched it into the slop bucket in the corner. His bucket, from the looks of things, got emptied on a regular basis. "I'm Moses Quinn," the man said. He pointed at Fallon and grinned. "Call me Monk. And you're the man who isn't afraid of rattlesnakes."

Fallon wet his lips, trying to figure out why he was here. Sure, he wanted to get in close with Quinn. That's why he had come to Yuma, but this seemed to be happening too fast, and he couldn't figure out why he would be brought to Quinn's cell in the middle of the night after being in Yuma for all of two days.

"How do you figure I'm not afraid of snakes?" he asked.

"You killed two."

Quinn, Fallon thought, looked sort of like a serpent himself. Long, lean, his hair slicked with grease, and he even spoke with a lisp.

With a shrug, Fallon said, "It seemed like the thing to do."

"It was. Otherwise you'd be with the Killing Sawbones getting patched up or, more than likely, you'd be on your way beyond these walls"—his smile even reminded Fallon of a serpent—"to spend eternity in a shabby box in the hard ground with a bunch of rocks piled over your hole to keep the coyotes from getting at you."

"Maybe I got lucky."

"Maybe. But to kill two rattlesnakes in the Snake Den tells me that you know how to handle yourself with snakes."

Suddenly, Fallon knew. Monk Quinn was scared of rattlesnakes. From what all Fallon had learned about the hardcase, Monk Quinn feared nothing, but that was a façade. Now Fallon knew how to play this game, this cat-and-mouse session.

"When a body gets sent to Yuma Territorial Prison," Fallon said, "he has to do a few things like staying alive. I've killed snakes before. I'll kill them again. I'm not afraid of rattlesnakes."

"Nor am I," Quinn sang out, too loudly, too boastful. Yes, this man was frightened to death of rattlesnakes, and the desert around here—and into Mexico—was filled with rattlers. Fallon had to guess that Monk Quinn had deposited that stolen gold in a den of rattlesnakes. Which was a pretty safe place to leave a fortune.

"There's nothing to fear as long as you respect them, and know that they can kill you if you don't kill them first."

"Like most people I know," Quinn said.

"I killed those two snakes," Fallon said, "because I want to get out of the Hell Hole."

"Don't we all?" Quinn turned back to the music box. "But how did you manage it? In the dark? In the Snake Den?"

"Killing snakes," Fallon said, "is my specialty."

"Take him away," Quinn said without looking back at Fallon.

Fallon turned to go, but Quinn called out to him, still looking at the music box. "Is Hank Fulton your real name?"

"It's a name," Fallon said with his hand on the flat-iron-barred door.

"Ever been in Arizona before?"

"First time." That wasn't a lie either.

Quinn was sitting now, so Fallon stepped through the door, and let Allan close the door and lock it.

"Lights go out in ten minutes, Monk," the guard told the prisoner. "They'll be back from the breaks by then." Meaning, Fallon guessed, the sentries at the two closest guard towers.

As Fallon started back down the corridor toward the cell he shared with other men, Quinn called out his name once more from inside the cell he had to himself. Fallon stopped but did not turn back.

"You want to see how men get out of Yuma? Be near the sally port around noon on Thursday. Sleep well, *amigo*. And watch for snakes."

* * *

Thursday, Fallon thought. Three days from now. Was that an invitation to take part in Quinn's crashout? Or was it an invitation to get shot dead?

He was thinking about that at breakfast the next morning, and all through his work detail at making adobe bricks for prison repairs. He thought about it over supper, and considered it till he made himself sleep in his bunk. Yet something had changed. The slop bucket was emptied and the cell cleaned and fumigated. He even found all the beddings replaced for all of Fallon's cell mates. That, Fallon thought, could have been due to the upcoming execution of the man in the cell whose name Fallon still had not learned. But Fallon's photograph had also been returned, so, no, this had to be Monk Quinn's doings, because Monk Quinn truly was the boss man inside Yuma's walls.

The next morning, Fallon figured he would be back making more adobe bricks, but this time he was sent to the caliche hills with a pickax. To his surprise, he found Moses Quinn sitting in a chair in the shade. Two other inmates held shovels, but none was digging.

One man had his back to Fallon. The other had his foot on the spade while he rolled a cigarette.

Fallon stopped. The guard assigned to this duty, Allan, did not order the men to begin work. Moses Quinn nodded at Fallon and pointed at the man with the smoke.

"This is Percy Marshall," Quinn said.

He knew the type. The kid had long, stringy blond hair, and his face was pitted with pockmarks. His eyes were dead; he was slender, pale, with yellowed teeth and jaundiced eyes. Fallon did not know what crime Percy Marshall had committed to be sent to Yuma, but he had seen this type for years in Arkansas and the Indian Nations. He was a punk. A young punk.

"Percy," Quinn said without taking his eyes off Fallon. "I'd like you to meet Hank . . . Fallon. Isn't that right, Morgan?"

Fallon. So Quinn knew, and as the other inmate, the only one wearing yellow-and-black stripes like Fallon turned, Harry Fallon knew how Quinn had learned Fallon's real name.

Morgan Maynard grinned his crooked smile and pushed back the sorry cap on his head.

"Hank," the gunfighter said. "Been a long time, Hank. Or should I say, Deputy Marshal Hank . . . I mean, Harry . . . Fallon."

Morgan Maynard had aged some. His hair, once long and flowing and black, was close-cropped like all of the convicts in prison except Pinky and Moses Quinn. His face bore stretch marks, wrinkles, and blotches from bad sunburns over the years. Two fingers on his left hand were missing, and there was a hole in the top of the lobe of the right ear, which was blackened by gunpowder. All of these, Fallon knew, were occupational hazards for a hired gun like Morgan Maynard.

Fallon had arrested him for murder in 1878. Maynard had been acquitted—the witnesses, most likely, had either been intimidated or bought off, but Judge Parker had made it clear to Maynard that he had best leave the judge's territory at a high lope. Apparently, Morgan Maynard had taken that advice and wound up in Arizona Territory, where he had not been able to frighten or pay witnesses to forget that someone got goaded into a gunfight he couldn't possibly win, or had been shot in the back.

"Here," Fallon said, "I'm called Hank Fulton."

"I call you a lawdog." This came from Percy Marshall.

Fallon did not even glance at the kid. He said, "I don't recall inviting you into this conversation . . . punk."

The punk dropped his cigarette and grabbed the handle of his spade.

"You come at me with that shovel, boy," Fallon said, still not taking his eyes off Maynard, "and they'll use it to bury you."

"Marshall," Quinn said. "Make yourself another smoke." He looked at Fallon. "You are Fallon?"

"It's the name I was born with."

"Federal marshal." Quinn cackled. "Interesting. Last man the government sent was a detective. Not a Pinkerton, but some small-time operative. Too bad, Fallon. You know snakes. But, well . . ."

"Listen to me, Quinn," Fallon said. He could tell Moses Quinn did not like being interrupted, but he kept right on talking. "Here, my name is Fulton. You got that. It's Hank Fulton. You tell your ugly, slow as Easter gunman here, that too. Because if I hear anyone calling me Fallon, I'll be killing your bigmouthed blowhard."

Maynard laughed a hollow laugh, and Moses Quinn grinned.

"Morgan Maynard had quite the reputation riding with the cowboys down in Tombstone, Fallon. He's fast too. Greased-lightning fast."

Fallon shook his head. "Ask him who put that hole in his ear back in '78."

Maynard stiffened and stepped toward Fallon, who brought up the pickax.

"Fallon," the gunman said icily.

"You call me that again and I'll kill you," Fallon said.

"Why?" Quinn asked, suddenly curious.

"You got ears outside these walls," Fallon said. "Your boy remembers a deputy marshal from years back. Why don't you find out what happened to Marshal Harry Fallon? And then you sons of bitches can leave Hank Fulton alone. Now . . ." He turned to face Allan. "Are we digging? Or what?"

That night, the guard named Allan unlocked the door to the cell and said, "Get up." He didn't use any name, not Fulton, not Fallon, but Fallon rolled out of his bunk, pulled on his shoes, found his cap, and walked into the night.

"Keep your voice low," Allan said. "And remember this: You can see snakes in the dark. I can see you. One false move, and your body will look like a sieve. Got that?"

Fallon didn't answer.

He knew the way to Quinn's cell, but this time there was no light shining in the darkness. "Stop," Allan whispered, and Fallon obeyed.

No music sounded from inside Monk Quinn's cell, but the man had to be standing against the hard stones next to the iron door. Fallon heard the whisper.

"Holdups do not seem to suit you . . . ummm . . . Hank Fulton. A bank in the Indian Nations. A store in Tucson. You were much more successful as a lawman. Why the change in careers?"

"You know how long most marshals in Judge Parker's court live?"

Quinn laughed.

"Was it worth it?"

"What are you in for?" Fallon asked.

"Robbery," Quinn answered. "But they only caught me. I have money waiting for me beyond these walls."

"Was it worth it?" Fallon asked.

"If I can get out to spend it." Quinn chuckled.

"You were paroled," Quinn said, changing the subject. "Yet you are in Arizona Territory. How come?"

"It's a long way from Joliet. I don't want to go back."

"I've never been in Joliet."

"Ain't no place to be."

"Nor is Yuma." Quinn let out a long breath. "Two years in Yuma. Maybe you're out in eighteen months. After ten years in Joliet, I would think you can do eighteen months or even the full twenty-four with no problem."

"Except I have a much bigger problem thanks to your pal Maynard. He lets the warden know my real name, I serve my time here, and then they extradite me back to Illinois to finish my sentence there. And like I've said, Joliet ain't no place to be."

A long silence held till the guard Allan spoke. "Best hurry, Quinn."

"Very well. I told you a few days ago that if you want to see how to get out of Yuma, you should be near the sally port tomorrow afternoon, when you've finished your work detail and before supper. Make sure you're there."

Fallon said, "All right."

"Let's go." Allan prodded Fallon's back with the curved edge of the staff. As Fallon turned, Quinn called out his name, the Fulton name.

"One thing to remember, though. If I were you, I wouldn't leave the way these men will be leaving. I have a better way in mind."

CHAPTER TWENTY-TWO

The footsteps of Fallon and Allan made little sound as they walked near the whitewashed wall.

"You were a lawman," Allan whispered.

"Five years," Fallon said.

"Nothin' sickens me more than a lawman gone bad."

Fallon reached the end of the block of cells and turned left to head to his own new home.

"Felt the same way when I wore a badge," Fallon said. "But after a month in Joliet, my tune changed."

"How so?"

"These days, nothing sickens me more than a prison guard who violates his oath."

He expected to feel Allan's staff to slam against one of his shoulders, but the guard merely said, "You try to live off seventy-five bucks a month."

Fallon caught his breath. "That's more than I made as a deputy."

"You didn't have to deal with the scum of the earth like I do."

"I do now," Fallon said, and this time he felt the staff. It didn't come down hard. Instead, Allan must have reached the long rod forward. In the darkness, Fallon didn't see it, and the crooked hook caught his left leg. Allan pulled hard, and Fallon hit the hard earth with a thud. The shinbone ached so fiercely that for a moment Fallon thought it might be broken, yet he rolled over and tried to sit up, but now the staff was against his throat. Allan was right, Fallon thought. He must be able to see in the dark.

"I don't like you, Fallon," the guard said, but lowered the staff. "When we get out, I'm going to kill you."

When we get out . . .

Fallon felt the heavy staff pull away from his throat. He rubbed his shin, tested his leg, and realized that he would likely just have a bad bruise on his leg, and some cuts and scrapes from the fall.

"Get up."

When we get out . . . So Allan was in on this jailbreak too. He had to be. The prisoners would likely need an inside man, and Allan already had been bought off. *When we get out . . .* So Monk Quinn had decided to bring Fallon into the crashout too. But when? And what was tomorrow supposed to be about?

A match flared in Allan's hand, and Fallon came to his feet and watched the guard move to the cell. He leaned the staff against the wall and found the key. Fallon limped over and saw the burning match, the features of the brutish guard, and the cell door as it started to swing open.

Then Allan looked inside the cell, and the match dropped and went out.

In the darkness, Fallon heard the guard's muffled curse.

Fallon stood still. The cell door squeaked. Another match flared, and Allan held the match toward the door. He cursed again, backed up, and turned to Fallon.

"Stay where you are!"

Fallon froze.

The guard turned toward the closest tower and yelled, "Sergeant of the guard! Cell number twenty-four! Sergeant of the guard! Cell number twenty-four! All guards to cell number twenty-four! All guards to cell number twenty-four!"

The match went out again, but darkness lasted but a few seconds. A spotlight swept down from two of the guard towers, bathing Fallon and Allan and the open cell door in yellow light.

That told Fallon something else about the prison. Over breakfast, he had heard some inmate mention something called the Dynamo. He had paid no attention, but now he recalled reading an article in a magazine in Joliet. Most of it had been like reading Greek, but he remembered the principles about rotating wire coils, and magnetic fields, and the rotation somehow converting into power. Dynamo. A Dynamo generator. Yuma Territorial Prison might be in the middle of nowhere, but it had electrical power. Now Fallon remembered the wires that were strung overhead. He had thought that they might be telegraph lines, but that made little sense. Telegraph lines outside the prison maybe. But inside? No. The prison had electrical lights, and those lights were bright. Fallon shielded his eyes and stood still.

Footsteps pounded and Fallon saw guards racing from the sally port. He lowered his hands, then decided to raise them high over his head. He was a prisoner in stripes, and outside of his cell in the middle of the night. But other prisoners slowly left his cell too.

Pinky . . . Preacher Lang . . . Yaqui Mendoza all stepped away from Allan, who stood in front of the cell door. They lined up beside Fallon, their hands reaching skyward, too, as the armed guards quickly formed a semicircle around them, covering them with their .44-40 Winchesters, cocked and ready.

One man had not come out of the cell. The man who was awaiting his execution.

From other cells, shouts, grunts, and curses rang into the eerie light.

"What the hell is goin' on?" "Can't a man get any sleep?" "It's supposed to be lights out!" "Escape? Did somebody crash out?"

The sergeant of the guard, a tall man with a well-groomed mustache, came jogging over. The sergeant stopped in front of Allan, whose head nodded inside the cell. The sergeant looked, sighed, and cursed.

"What happened, Captain?" the guard asked.

"Just found him, Dickinson," Allan answered.

Pinky stood next to Fallon, who whispered, "What happened?"

"Roach hung hisself," the old man said.

Which is what Fallon figured had happened. The nearest guard pointing his rifle at the inmates in cell number twenty-four said, "Shut up. No talking."

Fallon wet his lips. He ignored the guard and yelled at Dickinson and Allan, "He might still be alive!"

"Shut up!" the guard with the Winchester said.

"At least check on him!" Fallon yelled.

Two other guards adjusted their aim on Fallon's head. The sergeant and the captain stared at each other. None looked inside the cell where the condemned man named Roach—Fallon had just learned his name—likely still hung from the bars at the top of the cell.

"Should we wake Mr. Gruber?" Dickinson asked.

An electrical alarm rang out in the night.

"I'm sure he's awake now, Sergeant!" Allan yelled over the deafening racket.

* * *

Mr. Gruber, superintendent of Yuma Territorial Prison, stood with a black Prince Albert over his plaid nightshirt. He wore bedroom slippers—probably not wise in a land filled with scorpions, centipedes, and rattlesnakes— and looked as if he had just been pulled out of bed.

Two other guards stood at his side. The alarm had been turned off, but the spotlights still shone down, bathing this part of the prison in light. The guards kept their Winchesters trained on the surviving residents of cell number twenty-four. No one had set foot into that cell to check on inmate Roach.

"What were you doing here, Captain Allan?" Gruber asked the guard again.

"I make it a habit," the captain lied, "to enter the prison at night, making sure no one has found a way out, that there is no contraband, nothing . . . peculiar . . . happening with our residents."

"Commendable," Gruber said, "but dangerous."

"Comes with the job, sir."

"In the future, Captain, you will let the guards know when you are doing one of these secret missions. And I would like to know it too. You could have been killed by accident."

"I'll remember that, sir."

Fallon sighed, and held back from shouting. The hanged man had to be dead by now. If he wasn't, he might as well be.

"So what made you check this particular cell?" Gruber asked.

There was no denying the fact that Captain Allan thought fast on his feet. "The new convict, Ha—" Allan stopped himself. He had almost said Harry Fallon. "Hank Fulton.

Yes. Fulton. He has been put here. I always make a habit of keeping a special eye on the fresh fish, sir. So as I came around here, I heard something. I struck a match and looked inside. It was the convict, Roach. His boot must have banged against one of the bunks. I opened the cell, and, as Fal— Fulton was starting to sit up in his bunk, I ordered him out. Then I sang out for assistance."

Gruber turned and studied Fallon. "He was the only one awake?" the warden asked without looking away from Fallon.

"It appeared so, sir." He quickly added, "Just waking up, sir. Likely he heard the same noise that I did."

"I see."

Gruber walked over beside the guards with their rifles still aimed at the inmates outside.

"You just woke up?" Gruber asked Fallon.

"I was awakened by something," Fallon said. That wasn't a lie, but sort of a fabrication of the truth.

"And you heard nothing?"

"No, sir."

Gruber considered that, and asked, "Did Roach give you any indication that he planned to take his own life?"

Fallon shook his head. "Warden, he never even told me his name."

"Louis Roach," Gruber said. "He was supposed to be transferred to Cochise County in two days to be executed there for murder. Instead, Cochise County will be saved the expense of a burial—although I am sure the gallows have already been built—and we will get to bury this man at the prison's expense."

Gruber sighed, shook his head, and looked at Fallon long and hard before he turned to the Mexican.

"You heard nothing?"

"*No sabe*," Yaqui Mendoza said.

"Don't tell me you don't know, Mendoza," the warden fired back. "You understand English. I'll ask you again, and you might consider your answer before you open your mouth. Because I can put you in the Dark Cell." He looked at the other inmates out in the yard, and even turned back to Fallon. "I can put every single one of you in that cell. For two days. Even three. Now, Yaqui, what did you hear?"

The Mexican grinned. "I hear the ringing of bells. I hear *el capitán* yelling. I see the blinding light in the middle of darkness. And I see poor Roach. He swings. Till I wake, I hear nothing."

"Nothing?"

"*Sí.* I sleep *muy grande* after a day of hard labor."

"And you?" The warden frowned at Preacher Lang.

Lifting his hands and spreading them out, the homicidal fiend began his sermon. "Poor Brother Louis should have awakened me, but we do not question the ways of the Lord, who deafened me to the sounds of that poor, tormented soul as he fashioned the noose, that instrument of death, around his throat and secured the other end to the iron bars. Oh why, oh why, oh why?"

The killer shook his head, and looked into the lights shining from not heaven, but one of the guard towers. Fallon looked at Lang's hands.

"I shall pray for Roach, who has taken God's greatest gift. I shall try to remember him as he was in the months I have shared my Bible with him. I shall picture him in better times, knowing that I will never see the poor man again. For someday I will walk the Streets of Gold with my Lord and savior. But Brother Louis . . . ?" Lang shook his head and lowered his hands to his side. "He took his own life, and it is written that the man who does that will never see the kingdom of heaven. Brother Louis will spend his eternity"—he grinned, and then even chuckled—"with his kinfolk, the roaches . . . Amen."

"So you didn't see or hear a thing?" the warden asked.

Lang dabbed the corner of his eyes with the cuff of his right sleeve. "No, Brother Gruber. I heard nothing."

Gruber studied Pinky.

"And I suppose, Pinky, that you'll tell me that all your hard work left you sleeping soundly. That a man in a crowded cell could hang himself without waking you or anybody else up."

"Ol' Pinky's an old man, sir. He don't hear good even when he's awake."

The superintendent spit in the dirt. "Write up your report, Captain Allan, and have it on my desk in the morning. Pinky." He looked at the inmates outside and likely had no other choice. "You and Fulton cut Roach's body down, take him to Doctor Fowler who can confirm the cause of death and give me a death certificate. I'll have to send that to Cochise County to satisfy the officials that Louis Roach is dead. Then we'll need a burial detail tomorrow afternoon."

"Tomorrow afternoon, sir?" Allan blurted out.

"It's summer, Captain. Corpses ripen quickly in Yuma."

"I'll make out the detail, sir."

"You'll be busy writing your report, Captain. No haphazard job. Every detail explained. We've robbed the residents of Cochise County the chance to watch a hanging. We've robbed the family and friends of the man Roach murdered of the chance to see justice served. Your report shall be spotless, Captain, because the attorney general, the governor of the territory, and most likely the editor of the Yuma newspapers and about fifty others in this territory are going to demand some answers."

CHAPTER TWENTY-THREE

The sky to the east was lightening, black becoming gray, by the time Pinky and Fallon got the body of Louis Roach into the prison hospital. They laid the corpse on a cot, and Pinky muttered, "I'll see if I can wake up the Killing Sawbones." He shook his head, then pointed at the stove. "It might take a while. Why don't you heat up the coffee?"

Fallon looked at the stove as Pinky turned up the lights in the office.

"You sure there's coffee in the pot?" Fallon asked.

"Doc? He don't drink much . . . coffee."

Fallon had the fire going again in the stove, and the coffee boiling. He found the other lights, turned some switches, and realized that the spotlights in the guardhouse were not the only things powered by a Dynamo generator. He glanced at the doctor's quarters, saw little signs of life, but still heard Pinky's pleading voice, so Fallon walked to the body of Louis Roach.

A few minutes later, the front door opened. Fallon

turned to see more daylight shining outside, as two guards led Gloria Adler into the hospital. One of the guards was Captain Allan, who dismissed the other and escorted the woman prisoner to the corpse.

"Where's Doc Fowler?" Allan asked.

Fallon nodded at the door. "Pinky's trying to get him up."

The guard cursed. "Get in there, woman. He'll do whatever you tell him to do."

Gloria Adler crossed the room without argument.

Allan said, "Mr. Gates will be waiting outside. Autopsies make him sick. When you, that petticoat, and Pinky have been dismissed by the doctor, Mr. Gates will escort you to your cells. You're lucky. No work details for you two, or that wench, today."

Gloria Adler had stepped inside the doctor's quarters.

Allan's voice turned into a whisper. "No need to be in front of the sally port today. Roach's death has caused a delay. And I have to write a damned report that won't have a bunch of know-nothings butting into our business. Be there instead tomorrow afternoon. Don't disappoint Monk Quinn."

He spun on his heel and stormed out of the building, slamming the door behind him and leaving the youthful, pimply guard named Gates leaning against the wall near the door, a Winchester .44-40 cradled in his arms.

Doc Fowler used his teeth to pull the cork out of the bottle of clear alcohol. He spit the cork into his left hand, brought the bottle to his mouth with his right, and guzzled. Even before drinking, Fallon had smelled the alcohol on the drunkard's breath. Fowler did at least use the rest of the alcohol to dump over his hands, which he dried off on the legs of his pajama bottoms before he staggered over to the table on which lay the remains of Louis Roach.

"Gloria," the doctor said, stifled a cough, and supported himself by bracing his arms on the bunk. "My darling, take notes for me if you would be so kind."

Obviously, Gloria Adler had done this before. She held a pad in her left hand and pencil in her right. She stood just a few feet behind the doctor as Fowler glanced at the clock and the wall and noted the time. He had to ask the date, but the guard by the door gave him that. Gloria Adler wrote it down. Fowler described the clothes the dead man wore, his lack of shoes and socks, that the man was white.

Fowler managed to raise one hand and close the dead man's eyes. "Gloria, please note that conjunctiva of the eyes has been observed by me."

Her pencil went to work.

"Primary flaccidity has already occurred in the deceased's eyelids," the doctor said, and paused as Adler scribbled on the page. Fowler tested Roach's jaw, and tried to turn the head. "As well as the jaw and neck. Rigor mortis has set in. Given the condition of the body and taking into consideration the cooler temperatures of the night, I would put the time of death as three o'clock this morning."

To Fallon, that sounded just about right.

Fowler estimated the dead man's weight and height, both of which were within reason. He noted the "India ink marks" on the back of the dead man's right hand, a type of Gaelic cross. He recorded the missing tip of the index finger on Roach's left hand. He pried open the jaw and offered remarks on the teeth that were missing, the teeth that remained, the rotted molar, and the chipped incisor. He said, "The age of this man appears to be around twenty-six."

Twenty-six hard years, Fallon thought, but that would have been Fallon's guess, as well.

Even drunk, the Killing Sawbones seemed to know exactly what he was doing.

"Write that the deceased is positively identified by me, surgeon at the territorial prison, as Louis Roach. No middle name. No middle initial. Convicted of murder in Cochise County, Territory of Arizona, and awaiting the sentence of death by hanging."

He moved along the body and came to the man's throat.

"A red ligature circles the neck. It is dark." He found tweezers and removed the fibers from the rope Pinky had removed. "Pieces of hemp line this wound. The mark continues across the anterior midline of the neck and is positioned an inch below the laryngeal prominence. I detect petechial hemorrhaging." The tweezers worked for three minutes. "More hemp has been removed, suggesting that a rope was used. There are several other evidences of asphyxiation."

He dropped the tweezers and moved to the shelves, found another bottle, and drank.

"It is the ruling of the surgeon examining the body that the deceased, Louis Roach, died from strangulation as the result of hanging."

Which is what Harry Fallon already knew.

"Suicide," Fowler said, and drank greedily.

When the surgeon rested the bottle on the shelf, and moved toward the dead man, Gloria Adler brought the pad to him. He took the pencil from her hands and signed at the bottom. He patted Gloria Adler's arm, turned to Pinky, and said, "Thank you."

Pinky shrugged.

He turned to Fallon and started to thank him, but Fallon spoke first.

"You sure about that, Doc?" Fallon asked.

The man blinked. Gloria Adler turned to stare hard. Pinky shuffled his feet and held his breath.

After a long pause, Fowler chuckled. "What would you say?"

"I wouldn't call it suicide."

The doctor frowned. Gloria lowered the pad the Killing Sawbones had returned to her. She did not take her eyes off Fallon.

After a quick glance at the bottle he had left on the shelf, Doc Fowler wet his lips and turned again to Fallon.

"An accident?"

Fallon's head shook. "Murder."

Pinky let out his breath.

The doctor laughed. "Well, Fallon, let's hear your theory."

Fallon stepped to the corpse, turned the head, and bent back the top of an earlobe.

"A contusion and laceration," the doctor said.

"Fancy talk for a bruise and a cut," Fallon said.

"Which likely happened when he struck his head against the post."

Fallon's head shook. "Skin would not have bruised had Roach hit something after he was dead. But if someone knocked him out before he was hanged . . ." He stopped and studied the Killing Sawbones.

The doctor grinned, but Gloria Adler frowned hard. Fallon did not look back to see Pinky's reaction. "Since the drop did not snap the deceased's neck, he was still alive and strangled on the rope. You suggest that someone hit him from behind, knocked him out, put the rope over him, and hanged him by the neck till he was dead, dead, dead." He nodded and bowed. "A fine theory. But, Fallon, just a theory. He was strangling when he hit his noggin."

Fallon touched the ear. "The rope was here," he said.

"And it was a big rope. Don't see how he could have hit his head. The rope would have protected it."

"Well, sir, when you are out of the Hell Hole in two years, I invite you to read for the bar. You have a theory, but nothing to support it."

"Ever been strangled to death, Doc?" Fallon asked.

The doctor laughed.

"Ever seen a man strangle when a hangman botched the job?"

The laughter stopped.

"I have," Fallon said, and he turned to Pinky. "More than once. More than a half-dozen times. They try to cry out, but they can't. Mostly, they gag, if they can even manage that. But what they can do is kick, kick, and dance on the air that keeps them off the ground, the air—the space—that prevents them from living. They kick their shoes off." He pointed behind him at the dead man's feet. "We sleep with our shoes on in Yuma, Doc. Don't want to get bitten by a bug or spider or step in something when we have to use the privy. They kick until they're unconscious or dead." His eyes did not blink.

Pinky stared at his own feet, but Fallon did not turn around.

"So tell me, Doc, if a man's strangling from a bad hanging, kicking the veritable life out of him, how can anyone just a foot or two away from him not wake up?"

The doctor took the report from Gloria Adler's hands. He nodded at the guard and spoke loudly:

"Mr. Gates, I have no further need of assistance from our guests. Please escort Miss Adler to her cell, and then our doctor and his bunk mate to cell number twenty-four. I must take this report over to Superintendent Gruber. I appreciate your theory," he told Fallon, "but you have nothing but a guess." He waved the pad of paper. "I have an official report, which is legal and which will help the relatives of the deceased—as well as the relatives of the man Louis Roach butchered on the other side of Arizona Territory—come to terms and maybe let both men rest in peace. May God save their souls."

The guard motioned with his Winchester repeater. Pinky led the way, followed by Fallon and Gloria Adler. Doc Fowler, the "Killing Sawbones," headed for the bottle on the shelf.

CHAPTER TWENTY-FOUR

They were left alone in cell number twenty-four. Preacher Lang and Yaqui Mendoza were on whatever work detail they had been assigned to. The bunk of Louis Roach had been stripped, and what few personal items he had owned—a collection of Homer, a newspaper clipping, and a tintype of a woman sitting in a chair—had been taken away. The rope that had strangled Roach to death had been removed. Even the chamber pot had been emptied and the floor swept and mopped.

The guard named Gates closed the door, turned the lock, and walked away.

Pinky waited a few seconds, found his bunk, and said, "You talk too much."

"I could've said more." Fallon sat down and found the photograph of his dead wife and daughter.

"Like what?" Pinky asked.

"Like the rope burns on Lang's hand."

Pinky sucked in a deep breath, and held it.

Fallon kept talking. "So Allan gets me out of the cell in the middle of the night. Takes me over to talk to Monk Quinn. We talk . . . about absolutely nothing. Quinn got you, Lang, and Mendoza to murder Roach. The man's going to hang in less than a week, so what's the point in killing a man doomed to die? That's what I can't understand."

"You don't have to understand. Just listen to Pinky. Pinky knows."

"Pinky knows how to kill."

The man jumped down from his bunk and crept closer to Fallon. "Yeah, Pinky knows how to kill. Why do you think he's been in the Hell Hole for all this time? Pinky knows something else, though, and that's how to stay alive. If Monk Quinn says that Roach has to die, he dies."

"So you knocked him out, fixed the rope, and strung him up." Fallon tucked away the photograph and turned to Pinky. "Lang put the rope on Roach's throat. Choked him to death before you boys ever got him swinging. That's how the rope burn got on Lang's hand. That meant Mendoza had to haul him up, tie the knot, make sure it looked good. Lang isn't strong enough to do that. You certainly couldn't have done it."

Pinky just stared.

"Which means you had to knock him out, Pinky. All three of you have to take part in a murder. Monk Quinn could have it no other way. Otherwise one of you could sell out the other two in a trial."

Pinky fell back and sat on the—by Yuma standards— relatively clean floor. His head dropped.

"So why Roach? Why not me?" Fallon asked.

Pinky's head shook.

"They say if you need to know anything about what's going on in Yuma, you ask ol' Pinky. All right, Pinky . . . I'm asking."

The white-haired old-timer let out another sigh. His head shook. He looked at his fingernails, and turned to stare out the cell door and admired the view of the whitewashed wall. Pinky shook his head again.

"Roach was supposed to go with us. His lawyer said he would get the conviction overturned, force a new trial. That didn't happen. And then the sentence is confirmed. So Roach is supposed to leave tomorrow to be held in the county jail before he goes to the gallows. Monk Quinn decides that's too risky. Wouldn't be unlike Roach, a Southern gentleman, to go to Gruber and make a deal. He says what Quinn's planning to do. Gruber gets the judge to change Roach's sentence. At least call off his hangin'."

Fallon tried to comprehend this. He said, "So Monk Quinn plays God."

"You best be glad he is playin', and that he decided he needed you." Pinky nodded. "Ol' Pinky knows things. He knows that Monk Quinn decided you could replace Roach. That's another reason we had to get rid of Roach. You said you wanted out. Well, Pinky can tell you *that* you'll be gettin' out. With Pinky and some others." He grinned.

"Monk's got a fortune in gold buried in Mexico. Pinky's gonna get his share. You'll get yours too. With some others Monk figures he needs."

Fallon felt his stomach, which was empty, turn into knots that pulled and twisted and tightened. They had killed Louis Roach because they wanted Fallon instead. Fallon had wanted to get in on the break, but not this way. He couldn't figure out why. Why would a murdering rogue like Monk Quinn want a former deputy United States marshal tagging along with him, over the prison walls, and into the desert south of the border? For a chance at two hundred thousand dollars in gold bullion?

"Who all's coming with us?" Fallon asked.

"That," Pinky said as he pulled himself to his feet, "be a thing Pinky might know but Pinky can't say. Because

Pinky don't want to find himself hangin' from the ceilin' and on his way to get covered with rocks in our little ol' boneyard. No, sir. Pinky won't tell you nothin' more. And"—his voice turned from stern to hopeful—"you won't tell Monk Quinn nothin' that Pinky's tol' you. Will you?"

"No," Fallon said. "Because I might need you when we're out of the Hell Hole."

Pinky grinned, and almost instantly his face saddened. "Don't look like we'll be gettin' our breakfast this morn. Might not get no dinner or supper neither."

Fallon barely listened, but lay back in his bunk and tried to make a few guesses. Who was in on the plan with Quinn, other than Pinky, Preacher Lang, and Yaqui Mendoza?

Morgan Maynard and punk kid Percy Marshall? Probably. Seven men. That seemed a lot, unless, considering the spotlights and the Lowell battery gun, Quinn figured a few of the men wouldn't make it as far as Mexico, and likely not even a thousand yards beyond Yuma's walls.

The guard with the shepherd's staff, Captain Allan. He had to be part of it, had to think he would collect whatever Quinn promised him or whatever he could get after he killed Quinn. The woman? Gloria Adler? Fallon couldn't figure her out, but he knew the doctor, the "Killing Sawbones" named Jerome Fowler, was in on the deal.

In the hospital this morning, Fowler had called Fallon by his real name, not Hank Fulton.

Anyone else?

The guard named Gates came by and let Fallon and Pinky out early that afternoon and led them to the mess hall. It was late to be eating dinner, and most of the convicts had already cycled through in their shifts. Fallon fell into line behind Pinky, grabbed his plate, and had it filled with potatoes and something green. Roasted prickly pear cactus, Fallon figured. He poured brown gravy over both, took a tin cup of coffee, and moved to an empty table by himself. Pinky had been summoned over to talk to some other prisoners.

Fallon spooned in some potatoes. The food was tasteless. He made himself eat, and tried not to look around at the others in the facility, the guards, the servers, and the convicts. The coffee was bitter, but strong, and not bad at all. When he had finished his cup, he remembered the routine that had been drilled into his head.

If you want more coffee, you are to raise your left hand, fingers toward the ceiling, nothing in your hand.

He did that, and held the hand high until he heard the footsteps. Without turning around, he sat straight, elbows bent, waiting for the cup to be filled.

A slender arm held the once blue coffeepot, which had long ago been burned black. Steaming brown liquid poured out of the spout and filled the cup.

The voice of the holder said in a whisper, "Who are you?"

Fallon knew Gloria Adler stood behind him. The coffeepot disappeared, but Fallon felt its warmth at his shoulders. He wondered if she might dump the pot's contents over his head. The hat he wore would offer no protection from scalding coffee.

"I call myself Hank Fulton," he answered.

"Jerome says you are Harry Fallon."

"I have called myself that too."

"Drink your coffee. Then raise your hand to ask for more.

"What are you in for?" she asked as she refilled his cup.

"Destroying bourbon," he said. "I was innocent."

"Don't get smart."

"I tried to rob the wrong place in Tucson. You heard that before. You know all about me."

"Before that you were a deputy marshal?"

"I'm not the first outlaw to pin on a badge, and not the first lawman to decide the other side pays better."

"Does this pay better?"

"Two hundred thousand dollars." He picked up the cup and sipped.

"Hold up your right hand with your fork. No one drinks more than two cups of this swill."

"No one eats more than one helping of this . . ." He left off the curse and sighed. Gloria Adler was walking away. He made himself finish the undercooked potatoes and the over-salted gravy. The prickly pear might have been tasty if it did not have the texture of boiled rubber.

A handful of potatoes bounced on his plate. At least they were small potatoes. The guards did not let anyone leave the mess hall who did not finish their plates. Fallon speared a potato and waited before he put it in his mouth.

"You're not a bad man," she said.

He was about to pull the spud off the fork with his teeth. He paused. "How would you know?"

"Your eyes."

"All right. I'm not a bad man. I've done bad things."

"Haven't we all? Why are you here? Don't answer. Raise your left hand with your fork."

"Make sure the prickly pear you bring is small."

She stifled a laugh. "The needles," she said as she walked away, "will be big if I don't like your answer."

He had to think as he ate the potatoes, saving some of the coffee to wash down the prickly pear.

Her footsteps sounded. He wanted to look at her but that would bring guards pounding him with their sticks and hauling him to the Snake Den—and he had an appointment tomorrow afternoon near the sally port. He sat erect, waiting, and saw a giant piece of prickly pear land on the remnants of potatoes and gravy.

"I am here," he said, "because I made mistakes."

"Monk Quinn is a mistake," she said.

"Louis Roach told me that when he died. I think I knew that before."

"Yet you are here. And alive."

"I plan to stay alive."

"That's hard to do when you partner with Monk Quinn."

"Maybe you should tell that to the Killing Sawbones."

He could feel her stiffen. "His name," she said, "is Jerome."

"Everybody makes mistakes," he said.

"What does that mean?"

"You fell in love with the wrong man."

She started to walk away, but stopped. "Finish your cactus. Then raise your hand for more coffee."

"But nobody ever drinks three cups of this swill."

"Everybody should have a full stomach when he dies."

She was gone. He thought about her, then looked at the massive but thin strip of cactus. He used the fork—prisoners were not allowed knives—to spear it, and tore off a mouthful with his teeth. He chewed, and chewed, and chewed, and swallowed. Pinky was already walking out the door when Fallon managed to choke down his last bite of green cactus. His hand went up and he waited, eagerly, because he needed that third cup of coffee to push down the rest of the cactus and potatoes that felt as though they were in a logjam halfway to his belly.

She was back then, filling the cup.

"Do you know what an adler is?"

His head shook.

"It's a very poisonous snake in parts of the Orient

and much of Europe. And an Adler is standing right behind you."

He gripped his cup, sipped the coffee, and grinned. "That snake is called an adder. Not an adler."

He felt her stiffen. "You know a lot."

Fallon shook his head. "Not enough."

"Well here's something you should learn. From me. You can't help who you fall in love with."

He spilled coffee and sucked in a deep breath. She was starting to walk away, and he turned toward her, ignoring the rules of the mess hall and said, "I know that lesson already, Gloria Adler."

She turned back to him. Their eyes locked.

She was beautiful. Somehow, Gloria Adler reminded Fallon of Renee. She looked nothing like his dead wife, but there was an honesty to her, about her, and she carried herself as Renee had, with pride but not arrogance, with a toughness that might have been a façade. It was for Renee. Had been for Renee. He found himself hoping that Gloria Adler was not as hard as she made herself out to be. He hoped that she was smart enough not to make that mistake and become part of Monk Quinn's scheme to crash out of Yuma.

"I wish," he said and almost choked on the words, "that she never fell in love with me."

Gloria Adler hurried away. Fallon drained his coffee, brought the plate and empty cup to the guard at the washbasin for inspection. The guard nodded, and Fallon dropped the dishes into the tub.

"Get enough to eat, boy?" the guard said, and snorted.

Fallon shrugged, and walked out of the mess hall with a bloated belly.

CHAPTER TWENTY-FIVE

The monsoon shower that afternoon cooled the desert off considerably. The thunderstorm had lasted only five or ten minutes, dumping water onto the sand that almost immediately was sucked below. Yet with the brief moisture, the desert seemed to turn alive, and prisoners caught outside in the storm looked up and let the cold, hard rain pound their faces. It felt cleansing and refreshing, and the fragrances of the cactus plants and the trees made Harry Fallon think that there was more to this country than just heat, sand, scorpions, and rattlesnakes.

Now he sat on a bench where he had a good view of the sally port. This time of day, too early for supper but with most of the work details over, was free time for the prisoners. Some tossed baseballs over toward the south wall. Most just dragged their tired, bedraggled bodies to their cells to wait until the bells began to sound for dinner.

Fallon kept his head bent and every few minutes turned a page of the book he held in his lap. The prison library, for the time being, consisted of a corner table in the mess hall. Ladies from Yuma's few churches donated copies of books for prisoners. Fallon held a copy of *The Count of Monte Cristo* by Alexandre Dumas. The front cover had been torn off, and pages two hundred and eleven to two hundred and fifty-six were missing, but he had always enjoyed Dumas, had never read this particular novel, and, in prison, *The Count of Monte Cristo* seemed like the best novel a convict could read. Too bad this version was in French. Fallon could not read French, but he wasn't interested in reading. He watched what was going on near the prison's main gate.

The gate was closed. Fallon could make out the wiry man in the building just outside the gate, the man with the Winchester .44-40 who made sure everyone who came in or left was supposed to be entering or leaving. Every now and then, he would lift his head, stretch his arms, yawn, and study the guard towers nearest him: the ones on the north corners, and the big one housed over the walled water reservoir outside the wall. Behind him, he knew that the Lowell battery gun was on the southeastern wall, but that seemed to be primed for prisoners racing across Prison Hill toward Yuma, or the Southern Pacific tracks. The sally port led to the barracks for the guards, the superintendent's residence, and the Colorado River.

The gate opened, and Fallon returned to his lesson in French.

Into this den of thieves walked Superintendent Gruber. He carried no weapon, not even a nightstick or staff. The gate closed behind him, and Gruber began walking to the mess hall. He held a notebook in his hand, and stopped every once in a while to jot down something with a pencil in the pad, or speak for a few minutes to one of the inmates. Gruber did not stop to ask Fallon anything. He did not even glance at the book Fallon was pretending to read. Gruber ignored Fallon and soon disappeared around the corner.

Fallon waited and read words he could not pronounce

or translate into English. Monk Quinn was nowhere around. But Captain Allan was on duty in the nearest guard tower. He held the Sharps rifle with the telescopic sight in his arms, causing Fallon to wonder: *Is this just a setup to get me killed?*

He saw none of the women prisoners. Where was Gloria Adler? he wondered. Preacher Lang? Morgan Maynard? Percy Marshall? They were nowhere to be found. A few minutes earlier, he had seen Yaqui Mendoza walking around, speaking to a few of the many Mexican prisoners housed in Yuma, but Mendoza had moved south. Even Pinky, who was practically everywhere at once, had disappeared from Fallon's view.

This time of day, he thought, *is siesta time south of the border—maybe even just a few hundred yards south of the walls*. The time during the heat of the afternoon, the hottest part of the day, when men and women left their jobs or their chores or whatever they were supposed to be doing to take a nap. Sleep. Refresh their bodies for the rest of the day. Maybe, he decided, that *siesta* time had passed, and now people were waking from their naps, heading back to finish a good day's work.

How the hell would Fallon know? He had never been to Mexico, had barely spent time in Texas. What was he doing in Yuma, trying to find a way to finagle himself into Monk Quinn's acceptance and good graces? To help a carpetbagging scoundrel like Sean MacGregor, and his equally unlikable son, climb a few notches toward the Pinkerton National Detective Agency.

Suddenly, he found himself thinking again of Gloria Adler. He made himself stop dreaming in the afternoon about the raven-haired, deeply tanned woman. He thought of Burton Wren and a few minutes outside of the dungeon in Fort Smith, Arkansas.

* * *

"Who'd you bring to the gallows, Marshal Hank?" Burton Wren asked casually as the gates to the dungeon closed and Fallon breathed fresh Arkansas air again.

"Unless the judge gets a little ornery, I don't think anyone," Fallon said. He extended his right hand as he smiled and felt the big Negro guard's firm grip. They shook, quickly, released their grips, and Burton offered Fallon some of his plug tobacco.

Fallon accepted, tore off a mouthful with his teeth, and began working on softening the chewing tobacco.

"Cured with apples, Marshal," Burton said.

"I can taste them," Fallon said.

"No one to test the hangman's skill?"

Fallon grinned. "Three whiskey runners, one horse thief. Not a good one either. The piebald he wandered off with is blind in both eyes. An agent riding with the KATY railroad who tried to get across the Red River with three thousand dollars and change. And Slim Fenady."

"Slim? He beat up somebody again?"

"Deputy Marshal Barney Drexel."

The guard spit. "Likely, Mister Barney deserved it and he got it."

"I only wish I could have seen it myself."

The big-boned, silver-haired black man grinned, spit, and wiped his lips.

"You home for a while?" Burton Wren asked.

Fallon shrugged. "Hope so."

"Seen that little baby of yourn?"

"That's where I'm off to now."

Burton Wren nodded and stuck out his big right hand. "Well, don't let me keep you no longer, Marshal. You's a daddy now. And daddy's got lots of responsibilities. More important than any lawman's duties, even one that rides for the federal court with jurisdiction over this part of the country."

The black guard had an intense grip. Somehow, the bones in Fallon's hand survived the ordeal. He said with a smile, "Even Judge Parker's court, Burton?"

"Even his." They were about to separate, Burton Wren to start making his rounds, and Harry Fallon to find his horse at the hitching rail a few blocks away and ride to his home and see Renee and Rachel.

"But there's one question I been meanin' to axe you, Marshal Harry."

"What's that?" Fallon asked.

The birds appeared to stop singing at that moment, and the wind stopped blowing. Fallon felt he could hear everything from the Arkansas River to the Carden Bottoms over in Yell County around Dardanelle.

"Man alive and Lord have mercy," the old guard said in an urgent whisper. "It ain't never a good sign when all goes quiet like this."

The quiet ended with an explosion.

Burton Wren was already running toward the iron gates by the time Fallon knew what was happening. He saw the gate flying open, the smoke pouring out of the hole, and guards rushing from their stations to the gate. A primal scream erupted out of the throats of several prisoners.

Fallon drew his revolver and stepped toward the dungeon.

He saw little. He remembered even less. A giant white man picked up one jailer and slammed him repeatedly against the wall. Another hurled the heavy ball that he had somehow gotten off the chain secured around his ankle into the chest of a charging guard. One of the filthy prisoners picked up the guard's rifle while the one with the chain worked desperately to pull the Remington from the man's holster.

Gunfire erupted. Men screamed. Fallon smelled the acrid odor of burned powder and his eyes stung. His right hand felt warmth, and he later understood that the heat came from the .45 he kept shooting.

And just as quickly as the violence had erupted it was over. Army soldiers stormed onto the scene and formed a cordon around the blown-apart gate. Federal deputy marshals like Harry Fallon and city policemen surrounded the area. Prisoners fell to their knees. Many covered their heads. More sent their hands reaching for the heaven. Men groaned. A few cried out, "Don't kill me, lawdog. Don't kill me!"

One boy groaned and wailed and pleaded, "For the love of my mother, kill me. Kill me. I'm dying, dear God, and don't let my mother see me suffer. Kill me. Have mercy on a sinner."

Fallon holstered his revolver. Hours later, he would realize the weapon was empty. He knelt by a prisoner lying facedown in the grass, and gently rolled the body over. Blood oozed out of a half-dozen bullet holes in the man's chest. Fallon looked into the gray eyes that saw nothing on this earth, and he recognized the face.

Billy Parker, twenty-two years old, arrested for grand larceny, his first offense, and had a lawyer that Judge Parker held in good graces. Most likely, at least according to the word going around the district court, the youngster would be given a reduced sentence. Six months, reduced to four with good behavior and time served. And here lay Billy Parker, shot to death, twenty yards from the gate of the dungeon.

A few yards later, Fallon found Burton Wren. The top of his head had been cleaved off with an ax that giant of a man Fallon had spotted through the smoke had found. Fallon felt his chest tighten. He knelt beside the guard and saw the giant being pinned down by two army corporals and a city policeman named Blocker. The giant found Fallon and laughed.

He would hang six months later, but Fallon never felt satisfied. He just remembered Burton Wren lying dead with his brains and blood soaking into the grass, and for years he would wonder:

Burton, poor Burton, what the hell did you want to ask me that morning?

He slammed the battered copy of Alexandre Dumas's novel shut and set it at his side. Fallon's body tensed. He was aware of the sudden stillness in the afternoon. He felt the chill, the numbing silence, and he waited for the death that he knew would follow.

CHAPTER TWENTY-SIX

Two convicts Fallon did not know had found a spot near the sally port and appeared to be shooting marbles. The clouds from the monsoon had passed on, and the sun shone hot and bright as it dipped toward the prison walls. Warden Gruber rounded the corner and headed toward the sally port when one of the marble players rose, removed his hat, and said in a respectful voice, "Mr. Gruber, might I have a word with you, sir?"

"About what, McMahon?"

"Well, sir, I have five more years before I'm out, and I was wondering about getting a position in the shoe factory in town."

"You want to be a cobbler?" Gruber shifted his notepad under his arm and against his side.

"It's a trade. I thought I could set up a store in Wickenburg when I get out."

"Commendable, McMahon. What experience do you have in the shoe business?"

"None, sir. But a man can learn a lot in five years if he puts his mind to it."

"Also commendable." Gruber looked at the other marble

player, who was just beginning to stand and pocket the marbles. "You could learn a lot from McMahon, Lopez, other than how to play marbles."

"Putting shoes on another man's feet won't do me no good, Gruber," the Mexican said in an acid voice. "I'm in the Hell Hole for life."

McMahon shuffled his feet and asked, "So I know that shoe factory in town has only a few openings for prisoners. How do I go about getting in it, sir?"

Gruber shrugged. "I will talk to Mr. Sandoval when next I visit Yuma, McMahon."

McMahon smiled. "Thank you, sir. Thank you, kindly."

Gruber gave Lopez a hard stare, and turned toward the gate. That's when McMahon and Lopez rushed alongside him, each grabbing one of the prison superintendent's arms and jerking him back. Almost simultaneously, two other convicts charged toward him. One, a skinny man with a pale face, had a knife he had manufactured, and he put the blade against the warden's throat. The other, a burly Mexican with India ink marks covering his arms, held what appeared to be a railroad spike, its edges filed down, and he jammed the spike into the gut of a prison guard—the one named Gates—as he rushed to assist the warden. The big Mexican held Gates upright, using him as a shield, and turned toward the guard tower from which Captain Allan aimed the Sharps rifle.

"Open the damned gate," McMahon shouted, "or we cut the warden in half."

"And Señor Gates will die soon eef you no do as we say," the burly Mexican demanded.

Fallon saw the blood gushing out of the vicious wound the railroad spike had made.

Prisoners hurried to the scene, forming a semicircle around the four prisoners and their two hostages. They kept a lot of ground, however, between them and the men trying to crash out of Yuma. From the rear, Preacher Lang began a prayer for the deliverance of everyone. Fallon figured that the killer did not mean Gates or Gruber.

McMahon saw Fallon and warned, "Just go back to reading your book, bucko."

Fallon nodded and opened up the battered copy of *The Count of Monte Cristo.*

"Open the damned gate!" McMahon yelled.

"For God's sake, Charles!" Gruber cried out. "Do as he says."

Fallon felt as though he were back in Joliet, hearing Captain Daggett's screams.

"That's right, Gruber!" McMahon said. "And tell your boys with their rifles and that damned machine gun that one shot gets your throat sliced from ear to ear."

"Hold your fire! Hold your fire! Hold your fire!" Gruber was sweating. Fallon could see that from here, but he did not blame the superintendent. Fallon was sweating himself.

He tried to figure out what McMahon's plan was. Once the gate was opened, where could they go? To the barracks or Gruber's home and find more weapons? They'd be surrounded instantly. To the river? Unless some boats were waiting, they'd have a long swim. And on most boats, they would be sitting ducks. To town? Unless someone was waiting for them outside, Fallon figured they had no chance whatsoever of getting far before they would be cut down. The Lowell battery gun would cut them to pieces before they made it past the railroad tracks. And Fallon saw no smoke and heard no locomotive on the rails. This was an act of desperation. McMahon and his followers had no chance. Then again, he didn't hold out much hope for Gruber living much longer. And Gates? He was already dead.

"Charles, for the love of God, man, get that damned gate open!" Gruber wailed.

"I'm working on it, sir!" Metal clinked. The gate swung open just a bit.

"Hold it!" McMahon shouted at the gatekeeper named Charles. "Step inside . . . with your Winchester and sidearm."

The guard hesitated.

"Do it, man!" Gruber yelled, his voice high-pitched. "We have to get Gates to a doctor quickly. The man's bleeding to death."

Gruber couldn't see Gates's body slumped against the burly Mexican, the guard's arms hanging limp, and his feet being dragged as the Mexican backed up.

The gate opened wider and the gatekeeper named Charles slipped inside, the Winchester rifle shaking in his trembling hands. The inmate named Lopez rushed toward Charles, while the skinny, pale convict moved around, but kept the homemade knife against the warden's throat.

The guard stopped, his face dripping with sweat, and Lopez jerked the rifle from the man's grasp and tossed it to McMahon, who released the warden's arm, caught the Winchester, and swung the barrel up to aim at Captain Allan.

"Lower that long gun, Cap'n. And stick your hands up high."

Fallon didn't watch to see if the big brute obeyed. He watched Lopez jerk a Remington .44 out of the guard's holster and viciously slam the barrel against the man's skull. The gatekeeper fell hard to the ground and did not move.

"Open the gate wider!" McMahon shouted. "And let's get out of the Hell Hole now!"

"*Vamanos!*" yelled the big Mexican, as he dropped the dead body of Gates, pitched the bloody spike toward McMahon and the pale man with the blade against the warden's throat, and ran to pull open the gate. Fallon glanced at the closest guard tower. Captain Allan had dropped back out of sight. Fallon could not tell if the big brute still held the Sharps, but he gave odds that Allan had not followed McMahon's directive.

The big Mexican in the prison uniform of gray and white stripes dragged the gate open. He stepped into the entrance and came erect. "*Mi Díos*," he said, his words barely audible.

Bullets drove him back, spun him around and to his knees, sending geysers of blood in all directions. More rounds drilled him into the back, knocking him into the dust. White smoke poured from behind the bars.

The prisoner named Lopez snapped three shots from the .44. One sent sparks off the hard iron, and another ricocheted off and wined over the heads of the spectators to Fallon's right. They dropped into a heap, while a few others laughed as though they were watching Buffalo Bill Cody's Wild West Show or some other outdoor melodrama.

Lopez hurried away from the gate, yelling in rapid Spanish. He tried to fire another round from the Remington as he ran, but more gunfire erupted. Now Fallon could see barrels of repeating rifles sticking through the holes in the iron. The impact of several bullets lifted Lopez into the air and he flew forward a few yards, the Remington sailing out of his hand, hitting the dust, and skidding about ten feet in front of Fallon, who was now taking shelter behind the bench he had overturned.

Fallon flattened his body on the hard earth. Bullets thudded into the walls near him. He inched forward and saw

Lopez lying in the dirt, a pool of blood already forming around his twitching corpse.

McMahon worked the Winchester, firing into the gate. Sparks flew off the dark iron, and the bullets whined. By now, most of the prisoners who had been watching were running for the safety behind some of the buildings. Others lay flat and played possum. Over the roar of gunfire and ricochets, Fallon heard several prayers in Spanish and English.

He bit his bottom lip.

"Kill Gruber!" McMahon roared as he levered the Winchester and kept firing.

The pale man with the makeshift knife stood frozen by fear. All he had to do was drag the blade over Gruber's throat.

McMahon jacked another cartridge into the Winchester and whirled around. "Kill him, damn you!"

Fallon saw motion above him. He looked to find Captain Allan aiming through the telescope on the Sharps rifle. The massive weapon roared, and both the pale man and the prison superintendent slammed into the ground.

The pale man did not move. A few feet away, Gruber dragged himself no more than a few inches, and rolled onto his back. The bullet from Allan's weapon had gone through the pale man's body, struck the superintendent in the lower part of his back and exited just above his hip. Somehow, miraculously, the pale man's knife had not even nicked Gruber's throat.

The warden's mouth moved, but nothing audible reached Fallon's ears.

McMahon swung around and snapped a quick round at Allan, but the captain of guards had dived back behind the wooden structure and the .44-40 slug just splintered a corner post. McMahon jacked another round into the rifle and dropped to a knee, aiming the rifle at Gruber's head.

"I swear to God, I'll kill him. I'll kill him, you double-crossing sons of bitches!" He looked toward the scattering prisoners. "Quinn! Quinn! Quinn! Where the hell are you?"

The echoes of gunfire bounced around the prison.

Another shot roared from the guard tower on the southwest corner. A large chunk of adobe blew out of the wall behind McMahon, who squeezed the trigger as he ducked. The bullet carved a gash across the top of the warden's head. McMahon scrambled to his feet, snapped a shot at the guard, and backed toward the wall. He levered another round into the chamber.

That's when Fallon decided he had to make a play.

He came to his knees and lunged toward the Remington the dead prisoner named Lopez had dropped. McMahon was aiming the Winchester at the warden, now unconscious, but when he saw Fallon, he brought the rifle up and at him. The bullet McMahon fired sliced the coarse fabric of the back of Fallon's shirt. He crashed to the ground, found the Remington in his right hand, and rolled onto his left side, lifting his arm—and the .44—as he moved.

McMahon had the rifle ready. The Remington in Fallon's hand spoke first. Blood spurted between two orange stripes in the center of McMahon's chest—about the same time two bullets dug up the earth on either side of Fallon. The guards thought he was taking a hand in the escape, and shooting at Gruber.

He moved, onto his knees, diving as more bullets chewed up the earth where he had been.

"Don't shoot him!" came a cry from the tower Captain Allan occupied. "He's working for us. Kill McMahon! Kill McMahon before he gets Gruber!"

Fallon already had the Remington cocked. He squeezed the trigger and saw more blood fly out of McMahon's body, this one higher up and to Fallon's right, catching the killer in the shoulder and spinning him around. The Winchester flew out of McMahon's hands and slammed against the wall. McMahon dropped to his knees, but forced himself up, then fell. His arms reached out to stop his fall. He came up with the railroad spike that had been dropped. After pushing himself to his knees, he lunged toward the warden. Fallon shot McMahon in the belly.

McMahon did not fall. He spit up blood and dragged himself toward the warden, not moving, bleeding profusely, an inviting target for a bloodstained, sharpened piece of metal that could serve as a snake. Fallon knew the Remington was empty. Lopez had fired three times. So had Fallon, who raised the gun over his head and behind his back, and hurled it.

It caught the crazed inmate in the face, breaking the nose, and driving him off his feet. The momentum also sent Fallon to the ground and dust. He lifted his head to see McMahon push himself back to his feet. He still held the railroad spike.

He raised it again to drive it into the unconscious Fallon's chest.

CHAPTER TWENTY-SEVEN

A .50-caliber Sharps bullet tore the top of McMahon's head off. He dropped the spike and his body collapsed in a heap.

"Inside! Inside! Inside!" Captain Allan yelled from the tower as he lowered his Sharps and hurried toward the ladder.

The gate at the sally port swung wide open. Fallon was sitting up, but now he raised his hands skyward. Four guards rushed to him, covering him with their rifles. Fallon held his breath. The other guards, numbering somewhere between eight and a full dozen, came to the other prisoners lying in bloody heaps. A few cut loose with a few rounds before Allan reached the gate.

"Stop it!" he yelled. "Stop it!"

He offered only a glance at Fallon, and took full charge. "O'Brien, Hernandez. How is Gates?"

Two guards came over, but had no need to check the man's pulse. "He's dead, Captain," the dark-skinned one said.

"Gruber?"

Another guard was plugging the hole above Gruber's hip with a rag. "Bad shape, sir," he said.

"Donovan," Allan yelled. "Hitch up a wagon. We have to get Mr. Gruber to Doctor Roybal in Yuma."

"In town, sir? But—" He was pointing in the direction of the prison hospital.

"Are you crazy, Donovan?" Allan roared. "You're going to put Gruber's life in the hands of the Killing Sawbones? Not on my watch, man. Not hardly. And I'm in charge until the assistant superintendent gets back from Phoenix. Hurry, man. Some of you boys lift Charles. Be careful. He got hit hard on the head. We'll take him to Roybal's office."

"Do we want to send a telegraph to . . . ?"

"No, no, no, damn it!" Allan cut the guard off. "We'll have newspaper reporters and lawmen rushing over here. Posses too. And putting citizens from here to Ajo in a panic."

Allan managed to catch his breath.

"How are all the rioters?"

"Dead, sir. All dead."

The guard nodded, and he walked among the bodies, and finally walked back to Fallon.

"You hit?"

Fallon's head shook. "I don't think so."

"Lucky." The big brute grinned. "You might have saved Gruber's life. That'll be in my report."

He stopped by McMahon's body, grinned at his handiwork, and drove the toe of his boot into the dead man's ribs. Fallon heard bones crack.

"All right. Get these stinking killers to the hospital . . . the prison hospital. We'll have Fowler write his death papers on these scum. Then we'll bury them. Bury them and Roach immediately. Right now. Before the sun sets. Find Pinky. Find Pinky and . . ." He whirled, his wild eyes stopping at Fallon. "No. We'll use this one. Fulton. All the other prisoners are to be locked in their cells. If they are not there, heads will roll. Find Pinky. Never mind, here he is."

Pinky ran his fingers through his white hair and swallowed. "Yes, Cap'n."

"Get some men. Haul these carcasses to Fowler. I want death certificates done immediately. And I want the bodies buried by nightfall. I'll go with you to read over the graves. That's Mr. Gruber's job, but he won't be reading anything for a while."

"Captain," a young guard said. "We're supposed to hold the bodies of inmates on ice in case the families want to . . ."

"Who in hell would claim these vermin?" Allan roared. "They just tried to kill Mr. Gruber and break out of Yuma and raise hell from here till their deaths. We're not holding anyone any longer. I'll take responsibility. Full responsibility. If some mama wants to dig up her scum of a son, she's welcome to have him. But I want these dead men out of here. Pronto!"

He stormed away.

The weapons trained on Fallon were lowered, and one guard even held out his free hand and pulled Fallon to his feet. Fallon breathed in deeply, wiped his hands on his trousers, and stepped toward the superintendent. To his surprise, he found Gloria Adler kneeling beside him, wrapping a bandage around the warden's bloodied head.

"He's in bad shape," Gloria said.

Fallon nodded. He thought, *What kind of shape is Doc Fowler in? Maybe Allan has a point in getting the warden to one of Yuma's town doctors.*

Captain Allan had returned. "I don't want Gates's body with McMahon and those other villains. Take his body to the greaser doc in Yuma too. He can make out the death certificate, and he can fill Gates's veins with that juice to keep him in decent shape till his family comes to take him back to Camp Verde."

The big man's eyes found Gloria Adler, and he grinned. "You, Adler. You go with Fallon. Get the hospital—morgue, rather—ready for when Pinky and his crew bring in the dead. Then both of you help the doctor make out these death certificates and load the coffins for burial. Hurry."

"I'd rather go with him." She nodded at the warden.

Guards were already backing a wagon toward the gate at the sally port.

"What on earth for?" Allan demanded.

"He needs help," Gloria Adler said, and she nodded at the warden. "The others don't."

"You're not stepping through that gate, missy. Do it. To Fowler or to the Snake Den for ten days. I'm in charge now."

When Gloria Adler and Fallon walked into the hospital, they found five coffins on the floor. Every one was empty, and Doctor Jerome Fowler was leaning a lid against the wall. He whirled around, sending the coffin lid he had been struggling with tumbling. It bounced off the edge of a bed and slammed onto the floor.

"Get in and close that damned door," the doctor said.

Fallon nodded at Gloria, who stepped inside, as did Fallon. He pulled the door shut. Things started to make sense.

"You expecting an epidemic?" Fallon asked. He watched the doctor find a nearby bottle, but kept Gloria Adler in his vision. She seemed surprised by the coffins as did Fallon.

"I heard the shots." The doctor took a heavy pull on the clear liquid.

Fallon looked around. The shutters were all closed. The electrical lights had been turned low.

"Jerome?" Gloria asked. Her voice was confused. So was her face.

"We're getting out of this hellhole," Fowler said. He smiled. "Trust me."

The door opened, and Fallon stepped away as Pinky and Percy Marshall brought in the body of the pale man who had held the makeshift knife. They lugged the body toward the nearest coffin, but Fowler snapped, "Not there, you damned fools. In the icehouse." He pointed.

They started for the back door.

"Someone will see you," Fallon said, and shook his head at the incompetence of the drunken doctor. "Monk Quinn won't like that."

Morgan Maynard and Preacher Lang brought in the body of Lopez.

"In my room," Doc Fowler said quickly. "In the armoire. Both of you. They'll fit."

Gloria Adler drew in a deep breath, slowly realizing what was going on.

Yaqui Mendoza arrived, hauling the body of the big Mexican over his shoulder. "Where does *mi amigo* get to rest his weary soul?"

"Storeroom." Fowler pointed.

Monk Quinn came in dragging McMahon's body, which left a grisly trail of blood and gore.

"Storeroom," Fowler said, but this time he went to grab McMahon's arms and lift the upper half of the dead man's body off the floor.

That caused Quinn to laugh. "You want to keep the floor clean for your replacement, Doctor? That is a fine, fine thing to do." Fowler strained, and Fallon sighed, and stopped the doctor and Quinn. He took McMahon's arms and helped Quinn deposit the body, unceremoniously, on top of the corpse Yaqui Mendoza had left on the dust-covered floor.

When everyone was back in the main room, Fowler asked, "Where is Captain Allan?"

"Getting things in order," Quinn said. He pressed the toe of his boot against one of the coffins, and turned to Fallon.

"Do you know what this is for?" Quinn said.

Fallon had his own question in mind. He asked, "Where's Louis Roach?"

Monk Quinn laughed. "Poor Louis needs no coffin. He . . ." Then the man understood, and his face hardened as he whirled toward the doctor. "Where did you put the body of Roach?"

The doctor took a step back, his face paling, and pointed at a table. "He's still there. I couldn't get him to the icehouse by myself."

"The icehouse? You fool. You would put a dead man who is supposed to be buried in the icehouse? In the middle of the summer? Do you not think guards and trusties come to that house to keep themselves cool?" He spun away from the cowering drunkard and saw the sheets covering the body of Louis Roach.

"And you leave him there. What if someone comes in and sees a corpse when all of the dead are supposed to be six feet under." Quinn's fingers snapped. "Yaqui, Lang, get that body out of sight. In the storeroom. Then lock the storeroom."

While the two killers crossed the floor to retrieve the body, Quinn kicked the coffin again.

"Is that for me?" Fallon asked.

Quinn's head shook. "Not yet, my friend. You have to bury us. Remember? But I would like to climb out of this coffin in a few hours." He pulled up his shirt to reveal the butt of a revolver. "If I grow suspicious, I shall open up with this. I might not hit anyone, but the guards will be upon you immediately. And then, if you are still alive, you will wish you were dead long before your heart stops beating."

"You are a trusting partner," Fallon said.

Quinn laughed and climbed into the coffin. "I trust everyone," he said.

"Like McMahon trusted you?"

The killer was beginning to squat in the coffin. He studied Fallon for a moment, and shrugged his shoulders. "McMahon was necessary. If he and his fools did not die, we would not have enough coffins for all of us to get out. I might have even had to kill you."

"Your explanation is acceptable by me, and I applaud your generalship."

Monk Quinn laughed deeply and stretched out his legs and lay down in the coffin. As he made himself comfortable, he told Fowler, "Make sure you have your death certificates all neat and in order for Allan to leave on the desk."

"I'm working on them now," the doctor said, and began scribbling on some papers.

Lang, Mendoza, Percy Marshall, and Morgan Maynard climbed into the other coffins.

"Ahhh," Quinn said, his voice muffled by the pine box. "This is a comfortable place to rest."

"I don't like it," Percy Marshall said. "Don't like this at all."

"Relax," Mendoza said. "Your lid isn't even nailed on yet."

"How long do we have to wait in this thing?" asked Morgan Maynard.

"An hour," Fowler said. "Maybe a little more. Get those lids nailed on, Fallon."

"Wait a danged minute!" The kid sat up in his coffin. "There ain't no call to have us nailed tighter than a fight girl's corset."

"Lie down, you fool," Quinn said. "Fallon. Get all the lids on. We don't want some guard or even a trusty coming in here and seeing the five of us in coffins and not the dead. Lids on, Fallon. Now. But don't forget that I have a pistol."

Fallon found the hammer on the floor and nailed down the lids, loosely. It wouldn't take much for even slender Percy Marshall to bust out of this coffin, and there were enough gaps in the wood so that suffocation would not be a risk at all.

He tossed the hammer underneath one of the hospital beds and moved toward the coffeepot on the stove. Gloria Adler was already there, and when she saw Fallon, she set her cup down and found another. She poured.

"You can have more than three cups of this swill," she said, and forced a smile.

He took the cup, nodded, but did not have enough in him to return the smile. He turned to watch Pinky drinking from Doc Fowler's bottle while the prison's doctor wrote death certificates for four inmates, two dumped into the doctor's armoire in his quarters, two others lying in the floor of the storeroom. Killed, murdered, by Monk Quinn. Oh, Quinn had not pulled a trigger, but he had ordered their deaths. Just as he had ordered the death of Louis Roach, who also now rested in the storeroom.

Yet, Fallon had to concede, Quinn's plan had a genius to it. Brilliant. But even more so, the plan was utterly . . . revolting.

Behind him, Gloria Adler sighed. Fallon turned. She

was staring at Jerome Fowler as he slid the death certificates on the top of a desk and snatched the bottle of liquor from Pinky's trembling hand.

"Like I said," Gloria Adler whispered, "we can't always choose who we fall in love with."

CHAPTER TWENTY-EIGHT

Once the sun had set, Gloria Adler turned the switch to the electrical lights. Nothing happened. She tried again, and Fowler told her to fire up the kerosene lamp and light a few candles. This part of the crashout, Fallon thought, had been well-planned, too, but there was something else he wanted to know. He turned to Pinky, who sat on Monk Quinn's coffin while chewing tobacco and spitting into a lard can.

"What happens when a guard checks on our cell and finds it empty?"

Pinky spit without answering, but Monk Quinn laughed inside the coffin. "Do you think, my friend, that any yellow-livered guard would enter the prison at night, with the only light from torch, candle, or match? After all that happened today?"

Fallon shrugged.

"But there are bundles underneath the bedrolls. That should suffice until the head count at breakfast. And Captain Allan, if he does his job, will sign off that all prisoners are present and accounted for."

"If he does his job," Fallon said softly.

"If he does not, he will be dead. This I have sworn to him."

A half-hour later, Captain Allan entered the hospital without knocking, flanked by a half-dozen guards. Sitting on the coffin that contained Preacher Lang, Fallon looked up without comment and sipped some more coffee.

It was dark outside, Fallon noticed, and the moon offered just a sliver of light. Torches lit a path toward the sally port, and lanterns glowed on the driver's seat of the buckboard parked outside.

"Something wrong with that Dynamo generator?" Fallon asked.

"Yes. We'll get it fixed though," Allan answered, and searched with his eyes until he found Doctor Fowler. "Is all the paperwork in order?"

"Yes, indeed." The doctor slurred the words.

"Take it to the warden's office. The assistant superintendent will read over that when he arrives by train tomorrow evening. We will pick you up on our way to the cemetery."

Fowler nodded, grabbed a grip, and started to walk out. A few guards studied the doctor and the large satchel he held. Captain Allan did not notice, but Fallon did.

"Hey, Doc?" he said, and set his coffee cup on the coffin lid.

The drunkard stopped. Fallon nodded at the bag. "What's in the carpetbag? Going somewhere?"

The doc looked at the gaudy bag as if he had never seen it before. He recovered and sighed. "After we have buried the deceased, I am taking the train to San Diego. The prison owes me some time, and I aim to take it."

"Before you take it," Fallon said, and nodded at the countertop, "you might want to take those papers the captain wants you to put in the assistant warden's office."

"Oh yeah, thanks."

Fallon grinned at the guards. They did not return the look.

"All right," Allan said once Doc Fowler was out of the building with both his luggage and the fraudulent death certificates. He cleared his throat and pointed a thick finger at Pinky first, and then at Fallon.

"You two pigs are my gravediggers."

"Captain," said one of the guards, "we can help with that."

"Not a chance, Scott," Allan said. "You boys. All of you. You went through hell today. These pigs can dig the graves."

"Sir," the timid guard said softly, "that will take them till dawn."

"Good."

"But this one . . ." Scott nodded at Fallon. "He saved Superintendent Gruber's life."

"If Gruber lives." Allan pointed. "Get off that box, you miserable cur dog, and you and Pinky get that box loaded on the back of the buckboard outside. Get all five coffins on that wagon. Now!"

Pinky strained to get Lang's coffin into the wagon bed. He could barely handle Percy Marshall's. Fallon had to do most of the work, and Gloria Adler came over to help with the second.

"Captain . . ." the guard named Scott pleaded.

"All right," Allan said. "You keep an eye on these cur dogs. I'll help these lazy convicts who ain't good for nothin'."

Fallon was glad to have Allan's help. Even with Gloria Adler assisting Pinky, they never would have been able to lift the coffins of Yaqui Mendoza or Monk Quinn. He

wasn't even sure they could have managed the one holding
Morgan Maynard.

When the coffins were loaded, next to the shovels, pick-
axes and five wooden crosses that would not last in this
harsh climate more than a season, Allan ordered Pinky to
drive the wagon and Fallon to sit beside him.

"I'll be right here," he said as he crawled into the bed of
the wagon and leaned his back against one of the coffins.
"You try something, we'll bury you too."

"Captain," the guard named Scott said again, "I think
we should have more guards with you. Or at least wait till
morning."

"These swine ain't fit to stay inside these walls no
more. Don't you fret no more, Scott. Just keep an eye on
the walls. Inside the prison. Not enough lights so we'll
need to be extra careful. I'll handle the buryin'."

The guard said, "We can send some guards to do
random checks throughout the night."

"You'll do no such thing, Scott. You want to risk putting
us in another situation like the one we faced this afternoon?" Allan's big head shook violently. "Not on my
watch. And I have to think the prisoners are wetting their
britches they're so scared after they saw what we did to
fish that try to swim out of the sally port. Get some rest.
But when any guard is on the walls, he had damned well
better keep his eyes open and looking inside. I hear about
any fool caught sleeping on duty and he'll find himself
spread-eagled next to an ant hill."

"Yes sir, Captain," Scott said.

"I'll see you boys at breakfast." Allan grinned. "Oh, one
more thing. Miss Adler. Why don't you join us?"

Fallon turned around to see the woman prisoner stiffen.

"You've got a sweet voice. These fiends don't deserve
no sendoff from an angel like you but, well, I'll never let

anybody say that I lack a kind heart. Crawl up between them two bad boys on the wagon seat. We'll pick up the doc on the way out the gate."

Fallon waited until Gloria Adler sat down. He released the brake, grabbed the leather reins, and slapped them hard, grunting something. The mules moved forward, and Fallon kept them moving slowly, before he reined them in. The doctor tossed his grip over the side, and it rattled against the gravediggers' tools. He smiled at Gloria and moved to the back of the wagon.

"Make sure the gate's locked when we're out of here. Good job, boys," Allan called out. "Good luck tonight, and don't worry about me. I can take care of myself. Mitchell."

Another guard ran from the office outside the gate. He handed the captain of the guards a repeating rifle and a belt that had two holstered revolvers.

"We're ready, you thieves and killers. Let's go bury some thieves and killers."

The prison cemetery was about as ugly a place as Fallon had ever seen. No trees. Not even a lot of cactus. Almost all of the crosses had disappeared, so there was no way any next of kin could figure out who was buried where. Mounds of rocks covered the graves. Fallon figured he would be here more than one night, even with Pinky, Doc Fowler, and Gloria Adler helping, to get five graves filled. He didn't think Allan would offer any help.

So, Fallon decided, that meant one thing. They would not be digging any graves.

"That's far enough," Allan called out from the back of the wagon. He had to yell louder than he wanted to because of the blowing wind. It blew like a gale on this open plain of miserable rocks.

Fallon stopped the mules, set the brake, and wrapped the reins around the lever. After climbing down, he helped Gloria to the ground. She smelled again like yucca soap and shampoo. The wind whipped her hair into his face.

"Thank you," she said, her words just able to reach him, and moved around the wagon to be with Jerome Fowler, where she began asking him questions rapidly.

"Quiet," Allan barked. "And start singing, wench."

"Why did you bring her along?" the drunken doctor asked.

"To keep you in line." Allan levered a round into the Winchester. "That goes for you, too, Marshal." He laughed. "I mean it, Adler. Sing loud and long. 'Rock of ages, cleft for me.' You sing. That'll give them fools back at the prison something to hear. And it'll cover what us men have to talk about. Sing!"

The wind whistled between the spokes of the wagon wheels. Fallon's hat blew off and into the darkness. He didn't think he would miss it, even when the sun rose over the harsh desert heading toward Mexico.

If Allan or Monk Quinn had not already killed him by then.

"All right, Fallon. Get up in the back of the wagon and start prying the lids off these coffins. Pinky. Dig."

"Dig?" the old man asked.

"Dig. Give the night a sound of graves bein' dug. Sound travels far out in this country. I want the boys back on guard duty to think we're workin' hard. Just for a spell."

"Why don't you let me dig?" Fallon suggested. "Pinky can get the coffins opened."

"No way, Marshal." Allan laughed. "I ain't trustin' you with no pickax or shovel on a night as dark as midnight like this one is."

The only light came from the lanterns on the side of the driver's seat.

Fallon reached over the wagon's side and found a pickax. He watched Allan train the rifle barrel in his direction, and he handed the tool to Pinky, who sighed and walked toward the graves. Fallon walked to the back of the wagon. Allan waved the rifle barrel at another tool, and brought his aim back onto Fallon's middle.

"You trust me with a crowbar?" Fallon said.

"Use it wrong, and this is where you get buried."

The lids came off easily. Like five men named Lazarus, the dead rose out of the coffins.

Almost immediately, as soon as they got out of their coffins, they rushed to the ugly carpetbag Doc Fowler had brought along.

The wind wailed. At least it was a cool wind.

Preacher Lang was first, and he pulled out one gunbelt and holster, tossed it aside, and found a derringer that must have been more to his liking. He hefted the hideaway Remington and grinned, but the grin died when he pushed the over-and-under barrels down.

"Bullets?" His eyes sought out Monk Quinn, who reached into the bag and pulled out a box of shells. "These are .44 caliber," he said, and grinned. "Yours is a .41. Sorry, Preacher. Please forgive me."

Gloria Adler began singing. Fallon could not tell what hymn because of the wind.

CHAPTER TWENTY-NINE

Over the furious whipping of the wind, Quinn also withdrew a haversack from the grip, and he dropped the box of shells into it and walked away. Angrily, Preacher Lang moved back to the doctor's luggage, only to be shoved away by Morgan Maynard, who buckled the gun rig the killing parson had shunned and withdrew the long-barreled Colt Peacemaker. He thumbed open the loading gate, pulled the hammer to half-cock, and rotated the cylinder. His eyes hardened. He looked across the wagon at Monk Quinn.

"And yours is a .45, Maynard. My bullets won't work in your gun neither."

Maynard spit, and reached into the bag, only to find Yaqui Mendoza's strong hands had grabbed both of Maynard's arms. The gunfighter showed intense pain.

"You have had your choice, my friend," Mendoza said. "Now let me get my weapon." He withdrew a machete, found the sheath and belt, and waved at Quinn. "I think my caliber is just right. Would you not agree?"

"You chose wisely," Quinn said.

The wind suddenly died down. Gloria stopped singing.

"No," Allan said. "Keep singing. Now they'll especially hear you back in the prison."

Monk Quinn laughed. "Sing away, pretty lady."

She sang. She had the voice of a chorus of angels.

Percy Marshall found a .38-caliber Colt Lightning. Naturally, he had no bullets for his gun either.

Pinky, apparently, had no gun. He kept working the pick, grunting with each swing.

Marshall stifled a cough and turned the bag over. Only dust fell out, reflecting the light from the lanterns.

"You and him have the only ammunition?" Marshall pointed at Captain Allan. "You trust a prison guard more than you trust us?"

"I don't trust any of you more than I'd trust a dead snake." Quinn shrugged, cocked his head, and smiled as Gloria Adler sang. "I don't even trust her, but damn, what a voice." He turned to face Captain Allan, and Quinn smiled. "No, I don't trust him. But I need him. And, well, he knows as well as I do that I can shoot faster and straighter than he could in a month of Sundays."

The wind kicked up again, not as wild and hard, but strong and steady.

"We can't fight off those guards with empty weapons, Quinn," Morgan Maynard said.

"You'll find your bullets when we get to the horses," Quinn said, and spun the revolver on his finger before sliding it into the holster that was slick with grease for a faster draw and to keep the barrel clean.

"Horses?" Mendoza asked.

"Well, I don't think these two mules will get us to all that gold." Quinn patted the rump of the nearest mule.

Mendoza looked around. "Where are the horses?"

"Not here."

"They're not here?" Percy Marshall asked.

"Keep your voices down, gentlemen," Quinn said. "As I've already said. Sound travels far. The hooves of a bunch of horses riding south would attract the attention of Scott, Mitchell, and all those other idiots back at the prison."

"How far away are the horses?" Mendoza asked.

"Five miles."

"Five miles?" Maynard exploded.

Quinn brought a finger to his lips. "Shhhhhhhhh. Remember . . ." he whispered mockingly. "Sound . . ."

"Over this wind?" Maynard said.

The gunman stiffened. Allan had jammed his spine with the barrel of the rifle he held. "Be smart, Maynard," the guard said. "Which way is the wind blowing, you damned fool?"

Maynard said nothing. The wind kept blowing. Fallon could just make out Gloria's voice and the unsteady, uneven sounds of Pinky's pickax striking sunbaked, rock-hard dirt that covered this part of Prison Hill.

"We can't walk five miles," Marshall said. "That won't give us enough time."

"We're not walking. And we're not burying anybody." He nodded at the wagon. "Keep the lanterns going, but turn them down. The coffins can stay where they are. Fallon, you go first."

"Where?"

The killer drew the .44 and waved to the edge of the hill that overlooked the Colorado River.

"To the river," Quinn ordered. "That way if a rattlesnake is out hunting, it will strike you first."

"Are the horses at the river?" Marshall asked.

"Tell them, Captain," Quinn ordered, suddenly annoyed.

"Boy," Captain Allan said, "you've been in prison long enough to know that the Colorado River isn't five miles from those damned ugly walls I've been staring at forever."

"But . . ."

"If my fellow guards or some fisherman or some ship's captain found a bunch of horses staked this close to prison, we wouldn't be walking. We'd be deader than McMahon and his idiots. They're five miles downstream. At a place I know, and held by a man I trust. That's where we're going."

"I can't swim," Marshall said.

"You don't have to. There's a flatboat in the rocks. Hidden and covered with brush. We float downstream. The current's running fast so we'll make good time. Then we find our horses and ride to Mexico."

"All of us?" Doc Fowler had spoken.

"Well, Doctor Fowler," Quinn said. "I'm sure you wouldn't like being left alone with no one to care for you, to tuck you in after you've passed out blind drunk. And, as I've said, that fine-looking woman will help keep us all in line."

"Why do we need him?" Maynard pointed at Fallon.

"We need him," Quinn said. "But if you don't like his company, you're free to go."

"And the doctor?" the kid Marshall asked.

"In case someone gets sick," Quinn said.

"And him?" Mendoza pointed at Pinky.

"We never could have gotten as far as we have without a good trusty. And we needed our fine, strong, fearless captain too. Boys, boys, boys. We are really still too close to the walls of Yuma to be debating anything. Let's get down to the banks of the river. Shall we?"

* * *

They walked to the edge, away from the light of the lanterns, away from the empty coffins and the sleeping mules. Fallon tried to figure out how far down they had to climb to the banks. He sought out a trail, but in the darkness, that proved hard.

"There's a trail down to where the boats dock by Gruber's home," Quinn said, his voice laced with sarcasm. "Maybe you'd like to use that one."

"This'll do," Fallon said. "Watch your footing. Go slow."

"Not too slow," Quinn urged.

Fallon sat down and slid over loose rocks but mostly dirt a few feet. He stopped at a ridge, and found a switchback just wide enough that even the biggest of this bunch—Yaqui Mendoza—could make it with ease. Fallon couldn't tell how far the switchback went though.

At least the ridge above blocked the wind. It felt calm here. But just as dangerous.

He moved away and, hugging the wall, slid along the path. The guard came down next, followed by Gloria Adler, Pinky, and Doc Fowler, who almost toppled over but somehow righted himself.

Fallon breathed again. He whispered to Captain Allan. "Better watch the doc and the girl. It might not be a fatal drop from here, but it'll bang them up a bit."

"I'd prefer it killed them," Allan said. His breath stank of gin. "More of that money for us."

"And if they scream on their way down . . ."

Allan shrugged, considered the suggestion, and swore. He moved back toward the doctor, the old convict, and the woman, but stopped and looked back at Fallon.

"You try something, I kill you."

"All I'm trying," Fallon said to the shadow a few feet before him, "is to get down this hill in one piece."

When the switchback ended, Fallon waited till the others had made it. No one was missing; even Pinky had made it. Fallon wiped his hands on his trousers. He could hear the river now, even see its outline in the darkness. At least the stars shone, and the sliver of the moon. Not much light, but enough to make out a path.

"Keep close to the wall," he said. "The sides are nothing but loose stones. Step on one, and you're likely bouncing your way down."

He started again, sweating now, despite the coolness. He cursed for allowing himself to be hornswoggled into this stupid plan by Sean MacGregor of the American Detective Agency. His boot knocked a stone and it rattled as it bounced its way down.

Five minutes later, he had reached the end.

Allan came down a moment later, gasping for breath. He stepped toward Fallon and asked, "Is this it?"

"Not quite." Fallon nodded below.

The captain of the prison guards swore.

Quinn moved past the others, knocking stones into the darkness. He moved between Allan and the wall and said, his voice seething, "What is it?"

"We either jump," Fallon said, "or we climb back up and try another way down."

The killer whirled and shoved the .44's barrel underneath Allan's chin. "This is what you do? You don't bother to figure out how we get down in the middle of the night? Do you really think that's worth even one bar of gold?"

"If you're going to kill him, I'd do it now," Fallon said. He pointed downstream. A ship was heading up the river.

The killer swore and holstered his gun. "Jump," he told Fallon. "Now."

Fallon never hesitated. He leaped into the darkness, feeling the wind and the back of the rocky wall rush past him. He hit, his knees buckled, pushed upward, and he tumbled down sand and stones. Instantly he came to his feet. He cupped one hand over his mouth and said, "Twenty feet or thereabouts. Just get enough distance away from the wall."

Allan landed, and almost took Fallon down a few feet with him. The guard sat up, shaking his head.

"You all right?" Fallon asked. He could care less.

"I'm alive. And I still got my rifle and Colts."

"Good for you. Get down to that rock. Keep one eye on the boat coming upstream and the other eye on the path that leads to Gruber's place. If the ship's stopping, someone will be waiting for it up there."

"You don't give me no orders, Marshal."

There was no time to argue. From above, Monk Quinn said, "Here comes the girl."

Gloria Adler landed gracefully—at least from what Fallon could tell in the dark. He picked her up and pointed to a rocky partition. "Get down there. Hide."

She ran, but Allan had found his feet, and he grabbed her by the arm and jerked her hard. She fell in the dirt and cried out in pain.

"We'll hide till the ship passes."

"Better hope it ain't stayin' overnight," Captain Allan said. "Because if that's the case, we're all going back to the Snake Den for a mighty long time."

CHAPTER THIRTY

He remembered steamboats, side-wheelers and stern-wheelers, chugging up and down the Arkansas River. Larger ones, of course, he had watched whenever his job as deputy marshal took him to Jefferson City and the state prison there in Missouri. When he was just in his teens, he had ridden out of Gads Hill, Missouri, with a couple of boyhood pals just to soak their boots in the Mississippi River. They had watched in awe two stern-wheelers churning in practically utter silence downstream, bound for New Orleans or some other foreign place that the kids had dreamed of seeing. Later, he had dipped his boots again in the river—with his new bride by his side, giggling as she did the same—in St. Louis. That had been on their honeymoon.

Fallon tried to block that memory from his mind. He focused on the steamboat coming up the Colorado River. All those times, all those years, all those boats, big and small, that he had watched with awe and amazement . . . and he never realized just how infernally slow they were.

Little wonder people preferred trains these days.

The boat's lights reflected off the water. He could

make out the voices of passengers and crewmembers wandering on the various decks. He saw the red glows of men with their cigars. The sound of the steam organ glided across the night.

Fallon turned to look up at Prison Hill. He could see the lights near the decking and the stairs and trail that led to the docking point for boats. In Missouri's state penitentiary, he remembered some of the guards saying that, when the intimidating structure had first been built, the only way prisoners could be brought to the penitentiary was by boat.

No one could be seen at the top of the hill. The good news was that the superintendent, most likely, was still in the doctor's office in Yuma—and Gruber had no wife, no children, no family, just a Mexican maid who cleaned house and cooked for him. She'd be in Yuma, too, either home with her own family or in some church praying for her employer.

"This is what you do, Captain Allan?" Monk Quinn whispered in the darkness. "This is your idea of planning?"

"I checked the schedule in the *Yuma Clarion*," Allan said. "There's no steamboats scheduled to dock tonight. Not even tomorrow. Hell, we haven't had a boat stop here in two weeks."

Quinn spit.

"If that boat stops, we're doomed," Quinn said. "Deader than McMahon and his party. You understand that, Allan?"

"It won't stop," Allan answered. Fallon could almost taste the big guard's fear.

"If it does, you'll be the first to die."

"It's not stopping," Allan said, but Fallon could detect the captain's mouth moving as if in silent prayer.

The boat kept creeping in the river.

"Keep quiet," Monk Quinn said as he turned toward the

men and one woman with him. "Not a sound. Don't move. Don't even breathe."

"Just pray, brothers and sisters," Preacher Lang said. "Just pray."

"Shut up."

"A silent prayer," Lang said, and chuckled.

Monk Quinn swore.

Fallon inched over to Quinn. "She won't stop," he whispered.

"You better hope not."

"She won't." Fallon pointed. "She's still in the middle of the river. If she were docking, she'd have to be turning by now."

Quinn remained silent for a full minute, watching the steamboat continue its course. He nodded, let out a sigh of relief, and turned to Fallon. "We still have to wait till she's gone."

Fallon shook his head. "Why?"

"They'll see us."

Fallon shrugged. "Maybe. But it's not like they'll be hollering or shooting off Roman candles. They'll think we're fishing from the banks, or a bunch of drunks holding a gathering."

"Maybe," Preacher Lang said, "a gathering at the river. A good ol' head-dunkin' baptismal service." He laughed again.

Allan voiced his objection. "And if some of the guards are up there taking in the show to watch the boat pass?"

"You put the fear of God in your boys, Captain," Fallon said. "They're all in the prison, worried sick that something will go wrong tonight what with the Dynamo not working, a warden shot, and four prisoners dead."

"I say we wait," Allan argued.

"We wait," Fallon said, "and chances are we get caught. If one of your guards came down to watch a damned steamboat pass, he would have noticed that the lanterns were burning at the cemetery but that he couldn't see any shadows, anything, anyone actually digging one grave. We'd be seeing torches burning and hearing whistles and dogs barking."

"He's right," Monk Quinn said. The killer looked at the captain of the guards. "Where did you hide the raft?"

They moved down the riverbank, not bothering to crouch or duck or stay hidden. Allan led the way toward the hiding place, and Monk Quinn hurried along beside him. Suddenly, Quinn stopped. He sucked in a deep breath. Fallon stopped, too, uncertain, trying to figure out why the leader had stopped. There was nothing on the top of Prison Hill. Nothing looked strange on the passing steamboat. Ahead, Allan stopped and turned.

"What's the matter?" the crooked guard asked.

Quinn whispered the answer, but that was directed at Fallon.

"Is that a snake?"

Fallon moved closer, inching his way along. A rattlesnake would be singing its warning now, but there were other snakes in the desert, Fallon figured. He came along Quinn's side.

"Where?"

Quinn just pointed a finger. A cloud passed over the moon, but only briefly, and then Fallon studied the ground. It took a while for him to spot what the killer feared was a rattlesnake.

He said, "No. It's a stick, Quinn. A dried out cactus spine."

"You tell anyone," Quinn said, "and I'll kill you."

Fallon said, "I've been fooled by sticks, even shadows too."

"Fooled. But not scared."

"We best get going, Quinn."

They kept close to the hill until they came to the flatboat. The convicts pulled away the brush that Allan had piled up against the boat, and then they hauled it toward the river. Monk Quinn kept his rifle aimed at the top of Prison Hill. Captain Allan kept his pointed at the riverboat, which was now past the docking point at Yuma and steaming into the night.

Fallon could smell the smoke from the ship's twin stacks. Now, he could only make out the silhouette of the boat. Yaqui Mendoza carried an anchor. Pinky, Doc Fowler, and Gloria Adler brought the oars.

"An anchor?" Morgan Maynard said, and laughed while shaking his head.

"Quinn said to bring one," Captain Allan said. "And you'll find a couple of torches leaning over yonder. Dipped in pitch. All we should have to do is light a match to them."

"Well," Quinn said. "Let's not light that yet, but definitely let's put those aboard our U.S.S. *Constitution*. Old Ironsides." He laughed.

Moses Quinn lowered his rifle, no longer worried about someone seeing them on the river's edge. "Anchors come in handy," he said.

"Yeah," Percy Marshall said, and coughed. "In a desert. Real handy."

Preacher Lang bowed his head and said, "'Which hope we have as an anchor of the soul, both sure and stedfast, and which entereth into that within the veil.' Hebrews. Chapter six. Alas, I cannot remember the verse."

"Nineteen," Monk Quinn said.

"Amen, Brother Monk. Amen." Preacher Lang laughed, and said, "'They that go down to the sea in ships, that do business in great waters; These see the works of the Lord, and his wonders in the deep.' Psalms, Brother Monk, and I need no assistance this time. Twenty-three and twenty-four."

"Just get the damned flatboat in the river and let's get out of here," Quinn said.

Flatboat. Well, that was one name for it. Raft was another. But what it looked like, in the darkness, was a bunch of leftover boards from a sawmill or a woodworker's shop laced together and topped with planks to form a deck. The oars were, at least, real oars.

Yaqui Mendoza lowered the anchor onto the edge of the raft. Fallon wet his lips. There was no rope attached to the anchor, and Quinn did not appear to notice. Or if he noticed, he did not care.

"Maybe," Maynard said, "it would be faster if we walked those five miles."

"I can't swim," Percy Marshall said.

"I can't either," Pinky said.

"You won't have to," Monk Quinn said, and put his arm around Pinky. "But you sit by me, Pinky. If you fall in, I'll save you."

They moved to the river, Pinky and Percy Marshall climbing onto the makeshift raft first. Fallon and the others kept going deeper, to their knees. That's when Gloria Adler, Doc Fowler, and Preacher Lang got in.

The boat, or whatever you wanted to call it, did appear to be floating, even with the weight of the passengers and anchor. At least they did not have to worry about luggage—unless you counted Monk Quinn's haversack and the doc's grip. And the two torches.

Quinn climbed aboard, and put his arm around Pinky. Allan and Mendoza came in next. That left Maynard and Fallon. They were up to their waists. Fallon nodded at the gunman, and both climbed up from opposite sides. Their legs kicked and they pulled themselves up. No one offered to help. Gloria might have, but she was busy holding Doc Fowler close. He seemed to be trembling, from the rotgut in his body or maybe fear.

The boat rocked, but soon stabilized. The current took them downstream.

"This reminds me of *Huckleberry Finn*," Moses Quinn said. "We're bound for adventure. I always wanted to be a pirate."

Fallon studied the killer. He never would have guessed that a man like Monk Quinn had read anything, least of all *The Adventures of Huckleberry Finn* by Mark Twain. None of the others reacted to the comment. Quinn also knew about the U.S.S. *Constitution*, and could name the verse from a part of the Scripture that Fallon never recalled hearing—and Judge Parker quoted a lot of Bible verses during his sentencing. That meant Monk Quinn was a smart man. At least, Fallon figured, he was smarter than the men he had picked to accompany him. And that likely included Harry Fallon.

"Let's see," Quinn said. "Maynard, you take the oar and work that side." His head tilted. "Fallon. You work there. Port or starboard. I never knew which one was left and which one meant right. And there's no reason to learn now because we'll only be on this vessel for five miles." He gestured toward the rear. "But keep on the back of the boat. That's stern. Isn't it?" He laughed. "Steady as she goes. Don't rock us too much."

The boat tipped a bit, but never precariously.

"Captain Allan," Monk Quinn said, "I must admit that I thought earlier that I never should have trusted you. But the steamboat did not stop, and you did a fine job of picking a raft."

"I know what I'm doin'," Allan said.

Fallon found his oar. He gripped it with both hands, spread out his legs to keep his balance, and began pushing, silently, steering the flat barge down the river.

"Which side?" Maynard asked.

"How's that?" Quinn asked.

"Which side will the horses be on?"

"Captain Allan?" Quinn asked.

"East. Left-hand side," Allan said.

"We ought to push this hodgepodge of wood closer to that bank," Maynard said.

"Keep her in the center of the river," Quinn said.

"Can we light that torch you have?" Percy Marshall asked.

"Not yet," Quinn said. "Let's get a little farther away from Yuma."

They kept floating downstream.

The torches had been lit and posted at the front of the boat. They needed the light now, because the middle of the Colorado River was dotted with islands. Most of these were more sandbars than actual islands, barren of any type of growth, but now it was, as Monk Quinn ordered, "All hands on deck and poles in hands."

Allan took over what passed for a rudder on the barge, while Fallon and Maynard continued with the oars. The others found long sticks that they sometimes had to use to push the bow of the boat away from an island.

They moved on, carefully, around one large chunk of earth in the middle of the Colorado, then up past where the land jutted out at a harsh angle, and the river turned sharply, through a narrow passage between Arizona Territory and the State of California. Eventually, the islands disappeared, and the river bent sharply south.

"We should be clear from here on out," Allan told Quinn, and the guard relaxed, letting out a breath of relief.

Despite the wind and the ripples of waves, the Colorado looked peaceful. Fallon worked the oars, and studied both sides of the banks as well as the river. He looked for any sign of snags or a sandbar.

"Monk," Allan called out. "I told you the anchor was a bad idea. It weighs fifty pounds. Pounds we don't need."

Quinn pitched a cigar he had been smoking into the river. "But what is a ship without an anchor? Be that as it may, First Mate, Mr. Mendoza. Would you be so kind as to weigh anchor?"

The big Mexican slid across the raft on his buttocks, causing the barge to tip a bit. Pinky grabbed hold tightly to the edge. Quinn reached over and took the old man's left hand. "Fear not, Pinky. Monk Quinn has you." With his other hand, he reached inside the haversack that hung over his shoulder.

It happened so fast Fallon did not realize what was going on until it was all over. Quinn brought out a pair of handcuffs. One bracelet was snapped tightly onto Pinky's wrist. The other locked onto the anchor as Yaqui Mendoza heaved.

CHAPTER THIRTY-ONE

"What . . . ?"

That was all Pinky had time to say, because the anchor splashed over the edge, jerking Pinky underneath. Fallon dropped the oar when he saw the handcuffs, but he had no time to prevent the murder. And as soon as the anchor left the boat, the raft tipped and turned violently, sending Fallon off balance and to his knees. Out of the corner of his eye, Fallon saw Maynard being hurled into the water.

Water splashed onto what served as decking on the raft. Fallon slipped. He heard screams. Another splash. The boat rocked and heaved, and above all of this, Monk Quinn laughed.

A wave of cold water slapped Fallon's face. The raft had become a seesaw, and Fallon rolled this way, then that way, but gradually the rocking stopped. He came to his knees to find the torches still glowing, Monk Quinn still laughing, and Gloria Adler missing.

Maynard had grabbed the ribbing that ran along the side of the boat. He spit out water and tried to climb back aboard. No one bothered to help him. Monk Quinn was too busy laughing. The others were coming to their knees, except the petrified Percy Marshall, whose fingers seemed to be digging into the wood to keep himself from being thrown into the dark water. Doc Fowler had been catapulted into the Colorado, as well, but he was pulling himself aboard on the opposite end of Morgan Maynard—which had to help the raft's balance.

Finally, after countless seconds, Fallon saw Gloria Adler about twenty yards behind the floating contraption. He dived into the cold waters, and heard the raft rocking again, causing men to curse or splash, and Monk Quinn to laugh even harder.

He came up, saw the woman convict closer. She could swim. She stopped, treaded water, and shook her head. "I'm all right. I can swim." She spit out some water. "Find Pinky. I have to help Jerome."

Fallon paused, letting the girl swim past him toward the boat. He tried to get his bearings in the dark. The ship was now thirty yards from him. He swam a few more yards toward the middle of the river, closer to where he figured they must have been when Monk Quinn did his dirty work for the night. He grabbed a lungful of air and went under.

He came up, filled his lungs, looked back toward the raft. It appeared to be turning around. He wasted no more time, and submerged again. His eyes opened. He saw nothing but the blackness of water. He had not touched bottom. Something swam past him. He went deeper, and still found no bottom. His lungs began tightening. He reached down, felt only coldness, and had to come back up.

Wrong place? Likely. His first dives had been only wild guesses. He saw the torches from the raft, and knew Quinn had managed to get his ship turned upstream. The lights from the torches hardly reached him, but he swam toward them, for about ten yards, and dived in again.

Nothing again. Still, he tried. Still, he found no sign of

the anchor, no sign of Pinky, no sign of anything but water that went on forever, and a darkness that stretched toward eternity.

He came up, gasping, tiring, and bitterly angry.

The voice called from the raft: "Give it up, my friend." It was Monk Quinn.

"No."

He went down again. Came up. He couldn't hold his breath as long now. His legs and arms ached. His chest heaved. The raft had made little progress toward him.

"Now, will you come back to my ship?" Quinn yelled out in the night.

He tried, and failed, again.

As soon as he broke the Colorado River's surface, Quinn called to him: "Do you think that old geezer could have held his breath for one minute? Not even fifteen seconds. He is gone. Even if you found him, what could you do? Without this?"

He heard a splash, faint, and he knew Monk Quinn had tossed the key to the handcuffs over the side of the raft.

"You waste precious time, my friend. Come to the raft. Come home, my brother."

When Fallon hesitated, he saw the orange flame, heard the shot, and felt the bullet splash in the darkness a few yards to his right.

"That is Captain Allan's warning shot," Monk Quinn said. "He sees very good in the dark, you know. And the captain only gives one warning shot. Swim toward us. It is too tiring to try to row against the current. Swim toward us. Or you will join your old friend at the bottom of this river."

He heard the metallic sound of a Winchester's lever being cocked. Fallon looked around, sighed, and whispered,

"I'm sorry, Pinky." He began swimming downstream toward the raft and the crew of killers.

Gloria Adler and Doc Fowler pulled him aboard. Fallon caught his breath. Someone tossed him a blanket, or maybe it was just a shirt. Either way, he dried off his face. He still shivered.

"Is that why you wanted an anchor?" He looked directly into Monk Quinn's eyes.

The killer shrugged. "I did not want his body to be found. That would tell Gruber's derelicts which way we are heading. So I thought, hearing the steamboat whistles when they docked down below our prison, I thought that if we were to journey downstream, an anchor. An anchor would do the job I needed. So I asked the fine and talented Captain Allan to find one for our journey. He thought I was crazy. He was not the first. But you see"—Quinn tapped his temple with a forefinger—"Monk Quinn has a brain. He thinks ahead. No one will find Pinky's body at the bottom of the Colorado River. And he would have no time to scream out a warning that might be heard, for, I think we have heard this enough: sound carries far in the desert night."

"You could have brought Pinky with us." That, to Fallon's surprise, came from Doc Fowler.

"That old man? He barely made it down Prison Hill to the river. He would not have lasted two days in the desert. I did him a favor."

"Did us all a favor," Yaqui Mendoza said. "One less man to get a share of our fortune."

"It was a despicable thing to do," Gloria Adler said. "He was harmless."

"Harmless, my dear?" Monk Quinn chuckled. "Harmless men . . . nor harmless women like you . . . do not spend any time behind the iron of Yuma Territorial Prison.

His wife didn't find Pinky harmless, especially when he had his hands around her neck and was strangling the life out of her so many, many years ago. That's why Pinky was in Yuma. He got us out. He got himself out so he could die a free man, more or less, and maybe go up to heaven and ask his wife, who has been feeding worms since '74, for forgiveness."

Quinn's head shook with bitter amusement. "He strangled her. Strangled." He showed off his own hands. "That's the only person he ever killed. And I do not need men who strangle. Stranglers will do us no good when we get closer to the gold I've buried. I need guns. Gunmen. Good men with guns."

Percy Marshall managed to find his voice: "Is Doc Fowler any good with a gun?"

"He'll be good at patching any of you up who turn out to be not as good with a gun as you said you are."

"And the *señorita*?" Yaqui Mendoza asked.

Quinn laughed. "She will make sure Doctor Fowler does his job. And I think she can handle a gun very well too. So does the man she shot to death."

"Where is it we'll be going?" Preacher Lang asked. "Where we will have need of our proficiency with firearms?"

"In good time. In good time. Again, I did what I had to do for Pinky. I even think I did him a favor."

"Is that the kind of favor you plan on doing to me?" Morgan Maynard asked. "I could've drowned too."

Quinn shrugged. "I did not anticipate how my wonderful, unsinkable ship would react once the anchor was weighed."

"Weighing an anchor," Fallon said, "is pulling it up. Not dropping it."

The killer grinned. "On my ship, it is whatever I say it

is. Pinky did what he was supposed to do for us. I did what I had to do for him. That's all we shall speak of this."

"No," Preacher Lang said as he removed his hat. "First, we must say farewell to the comrade we have buried at sea. Matthew, chapter fourteen, says, 'And in the fourth watch of the night Jesus went unto them, walking on the sea. And when the disciples saw him walking on the sea, they were troubled, saying, It is a spirit; and they cried out for fear. But straightway Jesus spake unto them, saying, Be of good cheer; it is I; be not afraid. And Peter answered him and said, Lord, if it be thou, bid me come unto thee on the water. And he said, Come. And when Peter was come down out of the ship, he walked on the water, to go to Jesus.' And if Pinky was Jesus, or Peter with Jesus with us, he would still be with us. Although nothing in the Good Book says Jesus could have walked on water handcuffed to an anchor. I'm sure Peter couldn't have done that miracle. And where in Poseidon's name did you find an anchor in this country? Amen."

He laughed, and returned the hat to his head.

"How much farther?" Quinn asked Allan.

The raft was turning around, moving downstream. The captain of the prison guards peered into the blackness and shrugged. "Hard to tell. I've never come down here by the river before."

Quinn let out a heavy sigh. "I'm beginning to see less in your usefulness than I saw in Pinky's, Captain. You had better find those horses."

"We'll find it, Quinn. Can't miss it. And if you try to chain me to an anchor, that anchor will get dropped and it'll be weighing you down."

Quinn clapped his hands. "A pun. The great captain of Yuma Territorial Prison has made a pun. Too bad he doesn't know what a pun means."

It would have made things easier, Fallon thought, if Captain Allan whirled around and shot Monk Quinn dead with the Winchester just as Monk Quinn put a bullet in Allan's heart. Yet things did not go easy for Harry Fallon.

The conversations stopped. Fallon shivered in the cold. Gloria Adler attended to Doc Fowler while Maynard and Yaqui Mendoza worked the oars and Percy Marshall clutched the ribbing tightly. Preacher Lang lay on his back and stared at the heavens. Captain Allan scanned the eastern banks of the river. Monk Quinn picked his teeth with the long nail of his right pointer finger. Harry Fallon kept shivering.

The raft kept floating down the Colorado—moving farther and farther away from the sunken body of a convict called Pinky.

CHAPTER THIRTY-TWO

"There it is." Allan turned and gave a nod in the direction where the river began to bend to the southwest. Fallon saw the yellow glow of a lantern.

"You said it was the southeast," Yaqui Mendoza said.

"That's right. So if you killed me, you'd never find it."

Monk Quinn was standing. "My first mate, he has a brain too. Let us dock and sink our wonderful boat."

The trading post on the Fort Yuma Indian Reservation, across the Arizona border in California, was nothing more than a *jacal*, a small hovel of dirt. The corral surrounding it was massive, and horses danced around, kicking up dust.

It was night. They were on the water. But the air remained dry, and that had helped dry Fallon's soaking clothes considerably. The front of the barge struck land, and Monk Quinn leaped off, turning quickly and pointing at Percy Marshall and Morgan Maynard.

"Chop the boat to pieces. Then meet us inside the post."

"There better be tequila there," the young lunger said.

"There better be bullets," Maynard said.

Quinn chuckled. "There better be both!"

* * *

There was tequila. There were bullets. And there was a skinny man in white cotton pants and shirt, a blue denim jacket, and a sugarloaf *sombrero* who called himself Diego, who kept his lecherous eye on Gloria Adler and his right hand on the butt of his Colt revolver.

The trader had a fire going in what passed for a fireplace, although it probably sucked more heat out of the tiny building than anything else.

"Where are the clothes?" Allan asked.

Diego, moving neither his hand nor his good eye, tilted his head toward a table against the crumbling wall.

"All right," Allan said. "I did my best guessing at your sizes, so help yourself. We can't go around Mexico looking like you just broke out of the Yuma prison."

The men seemed more interested in the tequila and the ammunition than in dressing. Monk Quinn had to warn them. "Boys, you know we are in California, not Mexico. Still part of our United States."

Reluctantly, the men and Gloria Adler went to the table. Someone passed Fallon a bottle of tequila. He set it on the table.

"I didn't know you were coming along, Fallon," the Yuma captain said. "So you don't have any duds. Well, there's Pinky's. But his won't fit you. I didn't know the girl was coming neither." He scowled at Quinn. "So there ain't nothin' fer her neither."

"Pinky's will fit her just fine," Quinn said. "Tight, maybe. But that would be all right. Get dressed, honey."

"Is there another room?" Gloria asked.

Diego grinned. "I hang a blanket over there." His head bobbed. "It is where I sleep." He wet his lips.

She took a pile of clothes and boots and moved toward the rough wool blanket, and slid behind it. Most of the men stared at the blanket. Doc Fowler helped himself to the tequila Fallon was not drinking.

Quinn took a pair of black leather pants, held them to his waist, studied the length of the legs, and asked the trader, "The Indians . . . they make this?"

"Most likely they jumped the reservation and took those britches off a Mexican they killed."

"They are nice pants." When he had dressed, in the black pants that he stuck inside his boots, a shirt of red silk, blue bandanna, black vest, and tan hat, he smiled.

"Now we look like men."

The men grumbled as they collected stuff from the pile of clothes.

"These boots don't match."

"You're not going to the church social."

"Ain't a hat here that comes close to fitting my head."

"At least the bullets fit your gun."

"If you didn't have such a hog head . . . Here. Wrap this bandanna over your noggin."

At the bar, Doc Fowler whispered to Fallon. "There was nothing you could do."

Fallon turned and stared at the man as he gulped down a shot of the clear liquor, and quickly refilled the glass with more tequila.

"About Pinky," the doctor said.

Fallon said nothing.

"Likely he drowned by the time he hit bottom. I'm told drowning is a peaceful way to die."

"There's nothing peaceful, Doc, about being handcuffed to fifty pounds of iron and thrown overboard like yesterday's garbage."

"Well. You did your best." He drank. Refilled again. Killed that shot as well. And tried to pour more tequila into the shot glass but spilled the rest of the liquid on the bar. Sighing, he studied the empty bottle, brought it up to his lips to suck out the last moisture, the last few drops. "There was nothing you could do."

"What about you?" Fallon asked.

The man turned, paling, and dropped the empty bottle that rolled back and forth across the uneven bar. "Me. What could I do?"

"I don't know," Fallon said. "Tell Gruber what was being planned? Let one of the guards you could trust know? Wire the United States marshal or the attorney general? What could you have done?"

"I did what I do best, Marshal. I drank."

Fallon shook his head.

The outlaws finished dressing.

To Fallon, they looked like murderers out of their prison uniforms and wearing cheap clothes—except for Monk Quinn's outfit.

Then, Gloria Adler stepped from behind what passed for a curtain.

Her pants were of Mexican denim, and she wore ankle-high moccasins of soft deerskin, decorated with beads of blue, green, white, yellow, black, and lavender. The boiled cotton shirt of yellow was too tight, and it did highlight her breasts. No vest. No bandanna. Just a flat-crowned straw hat secured around her throat by a stampede string.

"And, my friends"—Monk Quinn removed his hat and bowed at the dark-haired beauty—"here is another reason I dropped Pinky into the wine-dark river."

Gloria Adler spit onto the floor. Her eyes glowered with hatred. Quinn frowned, but only briefly, and he returned his hat and said, "The river is but a few yards away. Anyone can join Pinky and feed the fish."

Preacher Lang laughed and opened his mouth, but before he could speak, Quinn said, "That includes you, Parson, should you start another verse recitation right now." He clapped his hands. "The horses. Let us see what horses you have."

"They will carry you a long way," Diego said.

Quinn shrugged. "Indian ponies?"

"What else is there to be found on a federal reservation, *amigo*? But their blood comes from the Spaniards. They are fast. They are strong. And they know how to survive in the desert."

"And the mules?"

"Percherons. *Muy fuerte*. Very strong. Very strong."

"Saddle the best for me, Diego. Then meet me in your *cantina* and you shall be paid." He leaned back his head, laughed, and called to the men, "Choose your horses. There are plenty. Make sure they are game. Saddle them up, put packsaddles on four mules. Pick out a fine horse for *la señorita* and the man who swims like a fish and does not like me very much, although I do not know why. We do not want them to disappear in the night. And, please, find a good horse for our doctor. If we wait for him to catch up an Indian pony and get it saddled, we will be dead."

The bar was made of kegs stacked atop one another and lined in what wasn't close to a straight line. Diego stood behind it and poured a glass for Monk Quinn. Captain Allan stood on Quinn's left. Gloria Adler, Doc Fowler, and Fallon stood at the corner closest to the wall and the curtain that separated Diego's sleeping quarters. It was also on the opposite side of the door.

"Did the captain explain the financial arrangements?" Quinn asked the grinning man with the tequila bottle.

"A bar of gold bullion."

Quinn clinked his glass against Diego's. "That is true."

"Then the tequila is on the house." He splashed more liquid into the dirty cups held by Allan and Quinn.

"But we must get the gold first."

The bottle stopped pouring. The Mexican slammed it on the top of an empty keg. "This was not explained to me."

"We would like you to come with us."

"Into Apache country? Into Mexico where the Rurales want to put my head on a spike and parade it around the village?"

"But that's where the gold is."

"I do not allow credit. You pay. You pay me handsomely."

"A bar of gold bullion for a few horses, some mules, and clothes and ammunition would look handsome to me."

"It would look handsome to me, as well, if it were here."

"Two bars," Quinn said, and drained his tequila. "If you come with us. A bonus."

Diego shook his head. "No. My life would be worthless in Mexico."

"Do you know how much two bars of gold bullion are worth, my friend?"

"They are worth nothing to me if I am dead."

Quinn thought, sipped some tequila, and said, "Well, there must be something we can arrange." He looked at the centipede crawling up the wall behind the Mexican, and his face beamed with pleasure. "I have it!" he said, and spilled tequila on his hand. He cursed his clumsiness, lowered his hand, wiping it across his vest and onto his pants of black leather. His hand came up with a revolver in it. The gun roared. The white cotton of Diego's shirt burst into flames as he was slammed into more kegs behind him that served as the saloon's back bar. He stood there, his face in shock, blood seeping from the left corner of his face, a yellow stain emerging on the front of his trousers.

Beside Monk Quinn, Captain Allan looked as stunned as the gut-shot Diego. He blinked rapidly, and cried out, "You shouldn't have shot him, Quinn. There are Indians all around here at night!"

Quinn cocked the hammer and shot Diego again. This bullet caught him in the chest, and he was too far away for his clothes to catch fire from this powder flash. The bullet turned him around, and before he fell on his belly, putting out the fire in his shirt, Quinn stepped away from the bar and out of the white smoke from his .44. He flashed a grin at Allan and said, "How about that shot, Cap'n? Think the Injuns heard it? Or maybe this one!"

He cocked the pistol again, and took careful aim. He shot the centipede, and turned, leaning back against the bar.

And as calmly as if he were at a Thanksgiving turkey shoot in Gads Hill, Missouri, Monk Quinn shucked the empty cartridges from his smoking weapon, filled the chambers with fresh rounds, and waited for the men to come rushing in to learn what had happened.

Doc Fowler clucked his tongue.

The killer turned away from the door and studied the drunkard, and the man and the woman standing next to Fowler.

Fowler raised his glass and shook his head. "That was not very original," the doctor said, and sipped the tequila. "An anchor and handcuffs for poor Pinky. But just a couple of bullets for this man."

Quinn shrugged. "He was a greaser. He deserved nothing more. But you did not think my killing the centipede was original?" The insane murderer of men and insects looked back as Morgan Maynard and Yaqui Mendoza came through the door.

CHAPTER THIRTY-THREE

When the horses and the pack mules were saddled and waiting out front of the hovel, the escaped convicts helped themselves to whatever liquor bottles or jugs they could find, tobacco, the makings for cigarettes, and the stale tortillas. They ransacked the building, leaving it looking pretty much as it had when they had first entered. Percy Marshall and Yaqui Mendoza went through the pockets of the stiffening body of Diego. They found no extra ammunition, but Mendoza pulled the pistol shoved in the back waistband. Grinning, he showed the old cap-and-ball Manhattan .36 to Quinn and said, "In case, *amigo*, my machete loses its razor-sharp edge." He pushed the gun into the deep pockets of his pants.

"Do I need to remind you boys, and girl, that we still remain in the United States?" Monk Quinn said. "Or that Mexico is a fairly short ride away?"

The men started to file through the narrow opening. Fallon let Doc Fowler and Gloria Adler go out before him, and when he stepped into the opening, Monk Quinn, who leaned against the whiskey and beer kegs that formed what had been a bar, called out, "You did not find yourself a revolver or any bullets, my friend?"

Fallon looked back at the killer.

"So that you could take them off me?"

Quinn laughed, gave a mocking salute, and Fallon stepped into the night.

The clouds had moved west to east, and now the stars glowed with intensity. Fallon could make out the vastness and the misty white trail of the Milky Way and the sliver of moonlight. It was beautiful, this view, in the still, crisp, and cool desert evening. He had not seen night skies like this since riding across the Indian Nations, and even then it had never seen so vast, so wonderful. In that territory, forests and tree-dotted hills—which some people called mountains—blocked the view. In the desert, the hills seemed distant, and the big sky dwarfed the land.

Yet, Fallon thought with apprehension, something did not feel right.

He could see the reflection of the stars and the moon in the Colorado River. He could smell the residue of gunshots and the death from inside Diego's trading post. There was a stillness on this night. A foreboding. The sky above was beautiful. The river that he could hear sounded so peaceful. What was it that made him apprehensive?

He realized that when he stepped into the saddle of the bay mare he had been given.

He could hear the river. The Colorado was a hundred yards away. Certainly, sound carried far in the desert. How many times had he heard that saying? But it was too quiet.

The reins were in his hands, his feet had found the stir-rups, and Monk Quinn was smoking his cigarette, stepping out of the door to Diego's post when something whistled past Fallon's left ear. He heard the thud against the wall. His horse danced to the left. Another whistle thudded into the luggage strapped behind Doctor Fowler's saddle. His horse bucked. Fowler flew out of the saddle after only one jump and he landed hard on his left shoulder, as Gloria Adler leaped out of the saddle, calling out Fowler's first name.

At the doorway, his body silhouetted by the light from inside the *jacal*, Monk Quinn dropped to a knee. He spit out the cigarette and drew his .44.

Captain Allan leaped out of his saddle, wrapping the reins tightly around his left hand and working the lever of the Winchester with his right, the stock of the rifle braced against his thigh.

"I warned you, Quinn!" Allan bellowed in the darkness. "Told you Injuns were all around this place!"

The rifle roared, spitting out flame and smoke, and causing Allan's horse to rear and pull away. Allan was jerked to his knees, but did not fall. Swearing, he pulled hard on the reins and somehow managed to lever another shell into the chamber of the Winchester. An arrow whistled over his head. He fired again.

"Hold your fire till you can see something to shoot at!" Quinn barked.

The captain of the guards sent another bullet into the dark.

Arrows slapped into the sand, the building. One splintered the hitching rail as Fallon wrapped his bay's reins tightly and short around the juniper post. He wasn't sure if this would hold the horse, if that bay could just pull down the creaky, dried-out rail or merely snap the reins off and gallop. But Fallon wasn't going to make himself a target and fight a frightened horse and hostile Indians from the Fort Yuma Reservation the way Captain Allan was.

Let Allan get himself killed.

But it wasn't Allan who caught the first arrow.

Fallon was trying to make his way toward Gloria Adler and Doctor Fowler, both of whom he could just make out several yards ahead. The drunken doctor cowered behind a barrel set out to catch rain on the rare times rain actually fell here. Gloria Adler was on her knees, holding the reins to both her horse and Fowler's. The horses were dragging her knees in the dust, rocks, and cactus, about to jerk her facedown, but she refused to release her hold. Those animals might even drag her off to wherever the Indians were hiding.

That was going on to Fallon's left. To his right, he heard Yaqui Mendoza shout, "You fool Indians, we have left you plenty of tequila inside!" He switched to Spanish, probably shouting the same thing, Fallon guessed, or maybe just cursing the Indians.

Fallon rolled and ducked under the hooves of a rearing horse. An arrow slapped the ground between his left forefinger and thumb, spitting dirt into his mouth and bouncing off the ground, the feathered shaft popping him in the nose. He heard something else, like someone gargling, and a heavy thud. The horse that had been so close to him turned and galloped north.

Fallon saw Percy Marshall lying faceup, his mouth moving but no words coming out of it—just blood. He could see the arrow, the bloody barb protruding from his neck, the feathered shaft on the other side. The gunman lay there shivering, and, Fallon knew, dying.

He wasn't going to let that happen to Gloria Adler.

Fallon came up quickly. He ran in the dark, feeling another arrow part his hair. When he reached the girl, he grabbed the reins to both horses, ripping the leather from Adler's hands. She fell to the ground, stopping her fall with her forearms. She looked up as the horses pulled Fallon a few feet before he managed to stop their momentum.

Turning, he saw Gloria Adler come to her knees. "Get back!" he yelled. "Back. To the doc!"

Another arrow sliced the untucked end of his shirt. He started back, pulling the horses with him. They seemed to accept his dominance, or, perhaps, thought he was leading them out of the carnage.

"They're not shooting the horses!" Morgan Maynard called out from the darkness to Fallon's right.

"Of course not," Preacher Lang said. "They're heathen Indians! They want the horses for themselves. Or for supper."

Adler tumbled behind the water barrel. Another arrow thudded into the front of the big keg of oak. Fallon brought the horses over to the rail where his own horse remained tied. He wrapped the reins around the post tightly, and ducked beneath the animals just long enough to catch his breath.

"The army's going to be here soon!" Captain Allan called out. His Winchester spoke again with three rapid, loud reports.

"And if not the soldier boys, then more Injuns!" Preacher Lang yelled.

Fallon came into a crouch, and exploded forward, running low toward Percy Marshall, who lay spread-eagled, fingers twitching, his pale head like an island in a sea of dark, sticky blood that the desert sand was sucking up.

He glanced at the gunman's eyes, saw them beginning to glaze over, and quickly Fallon went to work. He did not bother trying to remove the arrow or stop the pouring blood. He reached for the Colt Lightning and jerked it out of the holster. There was no time to check the cylinder.

Another arrow slammed into the dying killer's groin. Fallon slipped the revolver into his waistband and snatched off the killer's hat. Another arrow quivered as it sank into Marshall's thigh. The lips kept moving. The eyes kept losing their focus.

"I hope you're praying, Marshall," Fallon whispered. He ran toward the rain barrel. Fallon was doing a little bit of praying himself.

He slid between Doc Fowler and Gloria, wiped the sweat off his brow, and tried to catch his breath.

Fowler saw the double-action Colt in Fallon's right hand. "If they rush us, sir," he said softly, "you will shoot me, I hope. And Miss Adler too. To save us from . . ."

"Shut up!" That came from Gloria Adler.

Fallon opened the cylinder. Six beans in the wheel. He couldn't have asked for more.

"No gunbelt?" Adler asked.

A quick shake of his head was Fallon's reply. He was busy now, removing the latigo string from Marshall's hat.

The Lightning had a barrel length of four and three-quarter inches, and it had a lanyard swivel attached to the bottom of the walnut grips. Fallon sent the rawhide string he had removed from Marshall's hat through the swivel and quickly retied a knot at the end of the loop. He stuck the small revolver inside his shirt, and dropped the latigo over his neck.

"You're hiding the gun?" Fowler blinked. "Confound it, man, why aren't you protecting us?"

"Shut up, Doc." This time Fallon spoke.

"Monk!" Fallon yelled. "Marshall's dead. And the rest of us will be joining him if we don't get out of here. Now!"

Fallon saw an orange ball coming at him through the night. It flew to his left and into the opening of the dead

Mexican's trading post. Another followed. And then two more.

"Flaming arrows," Gloria Adler said.

Fallon smelled smoke. He pulled the late Percy Marshall's hat on his head. The bloodstains smeared Fallon's fingers, and the hat was tight on his head even when pushed back. But it would do. For now.

"Monk!" Morgan Maynard shouted in the darkness. "They're torching the damned place!"

"*Vamanos.*"

Fallon saw Monk Quinn leaping into his saddle.

"Amen!" Preacher Lang said.

"Let's go." Fallon stood. He found Gloria Adler's horse, first, undid the reins, felt another arrow slam into the hovel. She took the reins, leaped into the saddle, and galloped into the night.

Good girl. Fallon boosted the doc onto the horse. Fowler just stood there. An arrow went between him and the horse's head.

"Ride, Doc. Get the hell out of here!"

Morgan Maynard thundered past, pulling the string of pack mules behind him.

But Doc Fowler had not budged when Fallon was on the bay. Another arrow creased the back of Fallon's neck. This one drew blood.

Fallon slapped the rump of Fowler's horse, and the horse bolted south. Fallon galloped beside him, leaning low in the saddle, watching Fowler keep looking back.

Then the damned fool reined up.

CHAPTER THIRTY-FOUR

The bay raced past the doctor, and Fallon swore underneath his breath, wheeled the horse around, and came back to the doctor, who was trying to turn the horse around and go back to the carnage and the Indians. The horse fought. It wanted to ride south after the others—for good reason.

"Damn it, Doc!" Fallon said.

"My bag!" The doctor pointed at the grip a few yards beyond the *jacal* and the rain barrel. Fallon could see it clearly now. The flaming arrows had done their job, and flames and smoke roared out of the opening of the post. The ground in front of the place was bathed in fiery light. Even from here, Fallon could see arrows slamming into the body of Percy Marshall. He looked like a porcupine.

"I need my bag!"

"You don't need any more whiskey, Doc." Fallon raised his hand to slap the horse's rump again.

"It's medicine, damn you! Medicine!"

Fallon lowered his hand. He looked at the doctor but could not see him well enough in the darkness to read his face, his eyes. "Ride, damn it," Fallon said. "I'll fetch your bag."

Kicking the bay's ribs, he leaned low in the saddle. The hooves thudded against the dirt. He could hear the Indians whooping, and feel arrows as they flew over his back. As the trading post, the grip, and Percy Marshall's gruesome corpse came closer, Fallon leaned low, to his left, away from the Indians and their arrows. He gripped reins and horn with his right hand, lowered his left. The piece of luggage appeared to be bouncing up and down and left and right, but Fallon knew that the carpetbag wasn't moving. What was moving was the bay and Fallon's body.

The ground rushed past him. He stretched his hand as far as he could. Fallon's fingers found the handle, closed around the leather instantly, the grip came up, and Fallon righted himself in the saddle.

The Indians no longer whooped. They didn't even fire any more arrows at him. They cheered. They cheered.

They cheered him as he turned the horse to the left and circled around the corrals, through the darkness, and made a wide loop around the burning *jacal* that had once been a trading post but now was a crematorium for a dishonest, dead man named Diego. He came out, back on what passed for a trail, and looked back once. He saw the Indians lifting what had to be Percy Marshall's body. They tossed it into the burning building too.

The Colt Lightning bounced painfully across his chest, but he couldn't do a thing about that. It was the only place where he could hide the weapon. Monk Quinn would be sure to see it if he stuck it in his waistband. And the moccasins he had scrounged from the trading post and put on were too short to hide the pistol there. The double-action .38 wasn't as big as a Peacemaker, but it wasn't the derringer that Preacher Lang carried. Too bad, Fallon thought, it had been the consumptive Marshall who had caught that arrow in the neck, and not Preacher Lang.

Fallon rode into the night, holding the grip in his left hand. Bottles rattled. Fallon sure hoped the doc had not been lying and that the carpetbag had medicine. Not liquor.

Although right about now, he thought, he could sure use a stiff drink.

He saw the horses on a little rise to the east, so Fallon slowed the bay to a trot and eventually reined in. He counted the animals first. A few short of the number, but Fallon figured that had to be Monk Quinn's bunch. The two missing horses could be out scouting . . . for Fallon, or Indians, or checking the trail ahead.

Fallon reached inside his shirt, and rearranged the Colt Lightning, making it harder to see. He felt his sternum. There would be a bruise there, but at least Fallon had a weapon. As long as Monk Quinn didn't find it. As long as Doctor Jerome Fowler didn't let the killer know. Fallon hefted the carpetbag and placed it on his lap. He kicked the bay's ribs with the heels of his moccasins and eased his way through the night toward the small hill.

"My friend," Monk Quinn said as Fallon stopped the bay and let it breathe. "You came back." Quinn's head shook.

Fallon saw Gloria Adler and Doc Fowler. He turned the horse and let the horse walk to them, where he swung the carpetbag over and handed it to the doctor.

"You owe me, Doc." His eyes bore through the drunk's.

"Yes." Fowler managed to clear his throat. He took the bag and turned in the saddle to secure it behind the cantle. "Thank you, Mr. Fallon. Thank you, kindly."

Monk Quinn repeated. "You came back."

Fallon turned the horse around, but he did not ride to Monk Quinn. He searched the hill and realized Captain Allan and Yaqui Mendoza were gone.

"Where could I go? Other than back to Yuma?"

Had he thought about riding north? Fallon had to ask himself. Or even turn west? He was in California. He could have disappeared in San Diego, maybe Los Angeles, or that gold town called Julian or something like that. Change his name. Disappear from Monk Quinn and Sean MacGregor. See if San Francisco was everything people said it was. No. It never even crossed his mind, and now he wondered why. His eyes landed on Gloria Adler, but just for a moment.

"That is true, my friend. Where is your hat?"

Fallon looked up and even brought his left hand to his head. The Lightning was under his right shoulder. He didn't want to move his arm too far from the pistol. He wore no hat.

"Blew off in the night," Fallon said. He was looking at Monk Quinn. "Didn't even realize it."

"You're having no luck with hats, my friend."

"Can't be lucky about everything." At least his neck had stopped bleeding.

"It is true. And Percy Marshall? Is he truly dead?"

"The Indians were throwing him into hell when I looked back," Fallon said.

"Shouldn't we be riding?" Morgan Maynard asked. "I can still see the flames from that greaser's tradin' post."

"We are in Mexico," Quinn told him.

"Those Injuns don't care nothin' 'bout no borders, Quinn. And they might be comin' after our scalps."

"I think they will be satisfied with Percy Marshall. And the army from Fort Yuma is likely there by now."

"We're still too close to the American border for me to be comfortable, Quinn," the preacher said.

"Snakes come out at night," Quinn said. "We will rest here for a while. Dawn is not far off."

"I hear that traveling through the desert is best done at night," the preacher said.

"I like to see where I'm going."

"I know where you're going, Quinn. That's to hell. Just like Percy Marshall."

"You are free to go, my friend. Ride out. Find your flock and preach to them."

Lang chuckled. His horse snorted. "I think I'll just wait with you, Quinn." The leather creaked as he swung out of the saddle and stretched his legs. "Besides, I'll need me some of that gold bullion to build me that church. A temple in the desert. Blessed be thy Lord God's name, and his name is . . . Matthew Ezekiel Lang."

So they would be here a while. Fallon stepped out of his saddle and walked the bay back toward Doc Fowler and Gloria. The doctor was drinking from a bottle, which he lowered when he saw Fallon.

"A bracer," the doctor explained sheepishly. He corked the bottle and slipped it into a pocket.

Fallon wrapped the bay's reins around a rock and walked to the horse.

"There is medicine in my grip," Doctor Fowler tried to explain.

"There won't be if you keep it tied like this." Fallon loosened the knots Fowler had made and retied the ugly piece of luggage. "What kind of medicine?" he asked, the question popping into his mind suddenly.

"My own invention," the drunk said, and straightened

in the saddle. "Bread and clay, mixed with ammonia and gunpowder. A poultice."

Fallon stepped away from the horses and studied the doctor. Bread and clay? That sounded new to him, but he knew about gunpowder, and he knew about ammonia. He turned and stared at Monk Quinn, but the killer was looking off toward the southeast.

Gunpowder had been the remedy back in Gads Hill. Fallon remembered when a rattlesnake had bitten little Jodie Reynolds when Fallon had been twelve years old. Fallon's father had been the first to get to the boy, and Fallon remembered his father breaking open a paper cartridge for a Navy Colt. He had sprinkled the powder on the two fang marks and quickly struck a match.

"That'll do it," his pa had reassured the sobbing youngster, and then went on to explain to Fallon. "That should burn the venom right out." He had nodded his reassurance.

Ammonia? Well, at least three deputy marshals that Fallon had ridden with in Arkansas and the Indian Nations carried small bottles of ammonia whenever they traveled. They all proclaimed that was the best way to treat snakebite. You just poured it over the bites. It certainly sounded less painful than burning gunpowder over the punctures.

On the other hand, Jodie Reynolds survived both the snakebite and the cure applied by Fallon's father, and was showing off the scar on his arm for years and years. Probably still showing it off, Fallon figured.

The ammonia? Fallon couldn't swear to it one way or the other. None of those lawmen had even been bitten by a snake, as far as Fallon remembered. That said, it had to be a better method than the only other he recalled.

Slicing an "X" across the punctures with a knife and sucking out the venom, and then spitting it out. He recalled a song, but couldn't remember the lyrics, about a girl being bitten by a snake and her lover coming to cut the wound and suck out the poison. The girl died anyway and her lover had a cavity that took in the rattlesnake's poison and wound up killing him too.

So Doc Fowler had combined the ammonia and the powder with a poultice. And Monk Quinn was deathly afraid of rattlesnakes.

Doc Fowler kept talking. "Some other medicines. Anchor brand laudanum. Kimball's white pine and tar cough syrup."

"Is that it?" Fallon asked.

"No." The doctor started to speak again, but Fallon cut him off.

"The snakebite stuff. That your idea?"

"You know whose idea it was, Fallon," the doctor said, but lowered his voice to a whisper. "That's why he brought me along. Or asked me to join him. He had seen me treat prisoners after they have been bitten by snakes. He had asked about my poultice. Then, later, he took me into his confidence. He is scared beyond reason of rattlesnakes."

"A lot of people are," Fallon said.

"Not like Quinn," Gloria Adler said.

"True," Fowler said. "Quite true. But if he had not this irrational fear of rattlesnakes, I would not be here. I would not have this opportunity to make a fortune.

Opportunity? Fallon shook his head. *Fortune? Quinn will kill us all when he's finished with us.*

But Fallon nodded as if he agreed with the drunk. "What else?" He gestured at the grip, and looked away to study Monk Quinn some more.

"Some alcohol," Fowler said. "And whiskey, of course. Plus my own small surgical kit. And bandages. Speaking of which . . ."

Fowler dismounted. When Fallon turned toward him, the doctor gently forced his head back toward the southeast. "Your neck, sir."

"It's nothing, Doc," Fallon said.

"Until it gets infected. Gloria. Bring me my grip."

The medicine burned, but Fallon gave Doc Fowler credit for an otherwise gentle touch. He cleaned the arrow wound thoroughly, then wrapped it and taped it, and even handed Fallon a tincture.

"For the pain," Fowler said.

"It doesn't hurt," Fallon said.

"Yes," Fowler said, "it does."

Fallon handed the tincture back. "Let's just say that I want to keep my mind clear."

The doctor shrugged, then slipped the tincture into his pocket. "I don't," he said, and grinned. "That's why I drink."

CHAPTER THIRTY-FIVE

Captain Allan returned first, riding in easily from the north.

"Well?" Monk Quinn asked.

"Indians scattered like birdshot. Army patrol galloped up, and the bucks headed back home. The soldier boys were busy putting out that fire. A few of them rode a bit south, trying to figure out what had happened, but they must've known we were well across the border, so they didn't do much more lookin'. Anyway, the Bluebellies won't come after us. I'm certain of that."

"And the Indians?" Quinn asked.

Allan shook his head. "They're back in their wickiups. Pretending that they never left their camps, that they don't know what happened at Diego's."

"And Percy Marshall?"

Allan chuckled. "Those Injuns done us all a favor. They must've tossed him into the burning buildin'. Now, that place wasn't nothin' more than mud and dirt, but from all the tequila spilt inside that hellhole, well, it burned hot and long and big. No way they'll be able to tell that was Percy

Marshall. Won't be able to tell him from the bones left of Diego's carcass. If that fire didn't burn the bones too. Is Mendoza back?"

"Not yet," Quinn said.

About ten minutes later, Mendoza rode in. He slugged down water from his canteen and smiled.

"The way to the trail is clear," he said. Reaching at his side, he patted the handle of the machete that stuck out of the sheath. "The farmers will give us no trouble. The dog will not even bark."

The big man reached inside his shirt and withdrew a mass of black hair and held it up, letting it dangle. Fallon realized that it was a scalp.

"If we go to Valle Verde, they still pay a bounty for the scalps of Apache." He chuckled, let the hair dance in the wind, before he returned it to the inside of his shirt.

"The thing is, it is hard to tell the difference between the scalp of an Apache and the scalp of a peon farmer."

Quinn nodded and looked at the graying sky. "Dawn is near. We should ride." Twisting in the saddle, he looked at the others. "Mount your horses. We ride to our gold. Nothing can stop us now, my friends. Nothing."

They rode in silence. Monk Quinn took the point. Captain Allan brought up the rear, riding just behind Fallon, who had been given the job of leading the pack mules. The Colt Lightning had found a more comfortable position under his right arm. It didn't bounce so much, especially since they kept their horses at a walk.

They were still walking when the sun peered over the horizon.

Heading southeast, they passed a silent farm. Buzzards

were already circling overhead, and Yaqui Mendoza chuckled with content and contempt as they passed his handiwork.

Nobody spoke. Fallon's stomach tightened. He wanted to spit, but thought if he did that he might just vomit. They had no reason to murder the family, or even the dog. Fallon looked at the sky and shook his head.

Yaqui Mendoza and Monk Quinn were idiots. They had butchered those poor people so they could not tell any Mexican authorities that a bunch of *norteamericanos* had ridden past. Yet the buzzards would bring someone here.

At mid-morning, they came to a stream, and formed a line to let the horses drink. Fallon led the mules a little farther downstream, then rode into the shallow water. His bay and the mules drank thirstily. So did the horses upstream of him, and the riders drank from their canteens.

Fallon's throat was parched, but he made no move for his canteen. He looked at the dust on the other side of the stream.

"Quinn." That was Captain Allan's voice. He had seen the dust too.

"I see it," Monk Quinn said.

The Rurales rode around the bend in a column of twos. Ten men, including a scout wearing a sugarloaf *sombrero* and a young lieutenant in a spotless uniform despite the dust. The eight soldiers wore dirty uniforms, mismatched, and carried old rifles. Fallon saw that the lieutenant had the flap closed over the revolver on his right hip. His saber clanked against his thigh and the saddle as he rode forward, raising his hand and calling out for the column to halt.

They drank water on their side of the stream. Monk

Quinn's group remained on the far banks. And in between, though out of the line of fire from both parties, in the middle of the stream, was Harry Fallon on his horse and holding the rope to four pack mules.

The lieutenant spoke in rapid Spanish to the scout, who returned with grunts. The scout either did not speak English or he said he was as close as he wanted to be to these men. The lieutenant spoke to his men, but all eight heads shook.

So the young Mexican sighed and kicked his horse into a trot. He glanced at Fallon, who wanted to warn the fool, but by this time it was too late. Fallon pressed his arm against the hidden Lightning. He twisted in the saddle and looked at Gloria Adler. To his surprise, she was staring at him.

He motioned with his hands for her to drop out of the saddle. He patted his canteen, and she understood. She removed the canteen and slipped out of the saddle. Her legs splashed in the water. She led the horse away a little bit and let it drink.

Monk Quinn and Yaqui Mendoza rode into the water to meet the young officer.

"*¿Hablas Español?*" the Rurale officer asked.

"*Sí,*" Yaqui Mendoza answered.

The officer sighed. "*Bueno.*" He grinned. He asked a question.

Mendoza translated. "He asks if we come from the north."

"Tell him yes," Quinn said. "Tell him we are meeting friends in Valle Verde."

Spanish resumed. Mendoza said, "He asks about the buzzards in the air near what would be the farm of Luis and Maria de la Rosa."

"Tell him we have seen no buzzards."

Mendoza grinned and turned to the Rurale. He answered.

The lieutenant frowned. He spoke in rapid Spanish, and pointed at the faint outline of the carrion birds that could just be made out in the blue sky.

"Oh," Quinn said. "Those. Tell him the ugly birds are waiting for him."

As soon as Yaqui Mendoza had finished, Monk Quinn blew the soldier out of the saddle.

That's when Fallon slipped from his horse, using the bay as a shield. He thought about pulling the revolver from out of his shirt, but knew better. There was nothing he could do. He wrapped the reins to the bay around his right hand and pulled hard on the lead rope that held the four mules. He looked back at Gloria Adler, and saw she was shielding herself with her horse.

Guns roared. Fallon saw Allan working the Winchester, shooting from the saddle, his face masked by the white smoke rising all around him.

Horses screamed. Fallon knelt, the water of the stream soaking his pants. He watched the slaughter.

Four horses were down. Two others galloped away, but Captain Allan's gun roared twice and those horses somersaulted and lay still. Bile crept into Fallon's throat. The captain was killing all of the horses, although Mendoza had shot the one in the middle of the stream, and it lay atop the dead body of the young lieutenant.

Killing the horses, Fallon knew, *so they would not ride back to the village.*

He spit the taste of gall out of his mouth.

Two soldiers had managed to get out of their saddles and find their weapons just before bullets from Allan's

Winchester killed their horses. One tried to work the bolt on his rifle, but two bullets from Morgan Maynard's gun dropped him to his knees and the rifle, unfired, fell into the wet sand. The man made the sign of the cross and fell face-down in the shallow water.

The other man fired a shot, but he rushed it, and Yaqui Mendoza put two rounds into his chest, twisting him to his knees and turning him around. A geyser of blood erupted from the center of his back, and the man fell on his face just a few yards from the other man.

A white horse splashed into the water. It was the scout, and he had drawn his revolver and put the reins into his teeth. His gun belched flame and smoke, but Monk Quinn casually drew his revolver and put a bullet between the man's eyes. The gun flew out of his hand and splashed in the water while he flipped over the back of the horse and landed in the stream. The horse kept galloping, but Quinn turned, using his other arm as a resting spot for his gun. The revolver blasted again, and the magnificent white horse screamed and fell into the water. Monk Quinn rode closer to it, ignoring the gunfire all around him, cocked his pistol, and shot the horse in the head. It shuddered and its bloody head sank beneath the frothy water.

Two others, their horses shot down, were running toward the bluff. Morgan Maynard spurred his mount and ran them down, shooting one in the back, and knocking the other into the dirt with his horse. He wheeled the horse around, but did not fire the pistol. He rode up and made his horse rear. The Mexican looked up and screamed as the hooves came down, crushing him. Maynard pulled hard on the reins. The horse reared again, came down. And again. And again.

Then Maynard cocked his revolver and shot the first man in the back of the head.

By then, the others were dead, or dying. Fallon rose and leaned against the saddle for support. He looked at Gloria, who was slowly standing, her face paling at the sight of this carnage, this slaughter, this massacre. Still in the saddle on the banks of the stream, Doc Fowler was desperately trying to get the bottle of liquor out of his pocket.

Preacher Lang had crossed the stream and was kneeling by a mortally wounded Rurale, who did not appear to be out of his middle teens.

"I don't know how to pray in Mex, boy," the killer said. "But I know that our Lord knows how to speak all languages. And so does this Remington." He laid the barrel of the derringer on the boy's nose and pulled the trigger. Then, Preacher Lang laughed.

"That should take care of the Rurales," Monk Quinn said. He waved the men over. "Cross the stream. Now."

When they had gathered on the other bank, Monk Quinn was on the ground. He found a *kepi* and tossed it to Fallon.

"See if this one will fit you, Fallon. You can't ride around in the desert without protecting your head. And this one will even protect your neck too."

Fallon reluctantly put the hat on. To his disgust, it fit perfectly.

"How about that?" Monk Quinn laughed. "I will deduct the price of the hat from your share of my gold." He turned. "Doctor Fowler, what on earth are you doing?"

"I thought . . ." The doctor had dismounted and was trying desperately to untie the grip behind his cantle. "I thought . . . I should . . . these men . . ."

"Are beyond need of our services, but that's most commendable. Here." He reached into his saddlebag and withdrew a small bottle of gin. "Maybe this will help you live up to your Hippocratic oath."

The bottle was flipped. Doc Fowler dropped it, but the glass did not break and the cork did not pop out. He bent quickly, snatched it up, and drank greedily.

"You . . ." Gloria Adler said, staring with malevolent eyes at Monk Quinn. "You . . ." She looked at Mendoza with eyes just as hateful. "You butchered that family back there. To bring out these poor soldiers. So you could kill them too."

"Yes, my sweet little thing," Quinn said, and he climbed back into the saddle. "That is exactly what I have done. And now there is nothing standing between me and my gold. *Vamanos.*"

CHAPTER THIRTY-SIX

They traveled hard and fast. The country turned rougher, drier, more brutal, and the *kepi* did its job, even though Fallon detested wearing it. The doctor kept drinking. No one spoke, and the coats of the horses soon slickened and shone with sweat.

In the heat of the day, they rested in what passed for shade.

"How far . . . ?" Preacher Lang paused to pour water into his parched throat from the canteen. "How far . . . to Valle Verde?"

"If we ride hard," Monk Quinn said, "tomorrow."

"Ride hard?" Lang drank again. "What in heaven's name do you think we've been doin'?"

"You are soft," Quinn said. "We have rested enough. We must move."

"Don't be a fool, Quinn!" Morgan Maynard shouted. "It's stupid to push these horses at this time of day. It's too hot. Nobody rides through the desert when the sun's like this."

"Exactly," Quinn said. "So no one will see us. *Vamanos.*"

* * *

That night, they made camp in an *arroyo*, more dip than a canyon, nothing more than a depression, but it dropped them below the skyline. No one would see them unless they fell on top of them.

"Loosen your saddles," Quinn said. "Do not take them off."

"These horses are almost played out," Maynard countered.

"And if someone by chance happens upon us, Indians or Rurales or scalp hunters? Do you want to take time to saddle your horse? Then, by all means, take off the saddle. Roll yourself in your blankets. Why don't you even light a fire and make it a big one? No wonder you were in Yuma. You must have been easy to catch."

"You were in Yuma, too, Quinn," the gunman said icily.

"Yes. But only after I killed one of the lawdogs who tried to arrest me." He laughed.

Morgan Maynard did not unsaddle his horse.

They ate jerky and hardtack, which they washed down with hot water from their canteens. They did not take off their boots. They did not roll out their bedrolls. They leaned against the sandy wall of the *arroyo* and listened to the coyotes yip and howl. The wind blew across the *arroyo*. The air turned cold.

Gloria Adler came from her horse and sat next to Fallon.

They sat in silence until Fallon asked, "How's Fowler?"

"Passed out," she said. "Sweating."

"Too much liquor," he said. "Dehydrated. He needs water."

Her response was a haggard cough.

"You could use some water too," he said.

"I had some."

"Not enough."

"Do you know how far it is to Valle Verde?" she asked.

"Just what Quinn told Maynard. Be there tomorrow, if we ride hard."

She turned to him, and he saw her face. It was a hard face, filled with years of hatred, abuse, and injustice.

"This is my first trip to Mexico," he said.

"And your last," she said.

He shrugged. "Maybe. Maybe not." Fallon found his canteen. The cork popped out.

"I would save your water," she told him. "We will not be at Valle Verde tomorrow. Maybe the day after, if God watches over us. Maybe two days. And there is no water between here and Valley Verde."

He looked at the canteen, his throat turning more parched the longer he stared at the opening. The cork was returned, and he slammed it in tighter with the palm of his hand.

"He wants to kill us," Gloria said. "Kill us in the desert."

Fallon shook his head. "No. He needs the mules to pack out that bullion. He just wants to wear us out. Break us a little. Once he has the gold, then he can kill us."

She studied him, and must have decided that he knew what he was saying. She looked over at the sleeping doctor. She started to spit, but then swallowed it instead.

"Why did he bring Fowler?" she asked.

His eyes found her again. Fowler, she had called him, this time. Not . . . Jerome.

"Snakes," Fallon answered.

Again, she looked at him.

Fallon explained. "He's scared to death of rattlesnakes. Doc's grip is filled with remedies and medicines. I'm not sure they all work, but that's most of what he's carrying— other than the booze he needs to get through each day."

Her head shook. "That seems like a lot of medicine for what few we have with us."

He nodded. "Could be." He crossed his legs at the ankles. "Or it could be a lot of snakes."

They listened to the coyotes howling now, their voices echoing across the desert, to be answered by others. It felt as though coyotes surrounded them.

"A pit," Gloria Adler said softly, thinking out loud.

"That would be my guess," Fallon said. "Drop the bullion into a snake den. No one would go exploring down there. It's like he has his own guards, only he doesn't have to pay them anything."

She said, "Quinn needs us to get the gold out."

Again, Fallon nodded. "He's too scared of the snakes to do that himself."

"That's why he brought you along."

He leaned his head back and laughed. "Because of nothing but luck. I happened to kill two rattlesnakes in the Dark Cell in Yuma. He decided that I must be some kind of snake charmer. A witch doctor. Something along those lines. I'm not exactly sure. He . . ." Fallon chuckled again.

It had been his job, his assignment for the American Detective Agency, to sidle up to Monk Quinn, get on his good side, get picked to take part in the crashout from Yuma Territorial Prison. And he had done it, done exactly what he was supposed to do, but not out of any skill, not because he was some exceptional undercover operative or detective. Because he had lucked his way out and managed to kill two rattlesnakes. Because all those years in Joliet had taught him how to be tough, hard, uncompromising.

Inhuman. Devoid of feeling.

"Fallon," she whispered.

He started to look at her, but made himself focus on the

night sky, so clear, so peaceful, so very far from this desert floor and these people with him.

"Hank," he said. "The name's Harry. Most folks call me Hank."

"Hank." She tested the word. He heard Renee's voice and he closed his eyes, still refusing to look at her. If he looked at her, he thought, he might become human again. At least whole. But for the job he had to do, if he let himself feel again, feel anything, that might get him—and Gloria Adler—killed.

The silence stretched on. Gloria, though, did not turn away from him. He heard her voice again.

"I wish I'd known you . . . a long time ago," she said.

He closed his eyes and let out a heavy sigh. Finally, his lips parted and through his parched throat and cracked lips he spoke to her.

"A long time ago," he said softly, "I was a different man."

To himself, he thought, *A long time ago, I was at least a man. A human being. And not an animal.*

When the sun appeared to be at about the ten-o'clock position and Quinn stopped to rest the horses, Fallon swung out of the saddle. He removed the *kepi*, wiped his head with his sleeve, and used the cotton cloth that protected his neck to wipe his face. Most people were drinking water, guzzling it, but Fallon made himself take only a quick sip. More than he had swallowed he poured into his *kepi*, and this he held under the horse's nose. The bay drank thirstily, and when the water was gone, Fallon donned the cap again and returned the canteen.

He bent to his knees and found a pebble, didn't like that one, tossed it away, and discovered another. He put it in his mouth, and picked up two more. These he brought to Gloria Adler.

She stared at the one he held between thumb and forefinger.

"Put it under your tongue," he told her. "It'll help make saliva. Keep your mouth wet. Moisture. You'll need it."

She took it, and when her fingers made contact with his skin, he felt an electrical spark. He tried to ignore that. She had the pebble, and her chapped lips parted as she stuck the piece of rock into her mouth. She said nothing. Speaking exhausted what little energy anyone had.

Fallon smiled, or tried to, and moved to the doctor.

"Doc?" His voice sounded raw, like the rattle of death in a dying man.

The doctor, his face an odd color, stared. He blinked. Maybe the doctor did not even recognize him. Fallon held up the pebble.

"Put this in your mouth."

"Is it a pill?" Fowler asked.

"Something like that, Doc. Just don't swallow it. Leave it in your mouth. It'll help with spit. Keep your throat moist. Keep you alive."

"Who cares to live?" The doc let out a raspy cough, but he did take the pebble. He put it in his mouth and made a face.

"It doesn't taste like bourbon." This time, Doc Fowler managed to laugh just slightly, but that laugh, that joke, brought a bit of life back into his face.

"Kind of like gin, Doc," Fallon said. He patted the man's thigh, pulled the *kepi* down, and walked back to his horse.

"How"—Preacher Lang rasped—"much farther . . . till . . . Valle . . . Verde?"

"Tomorrow," Monk Quinn said, "if we ride hard."

"You said . . ." Preacher weaved in the saddle, but grabbed the horn and somehow managed to stay on the back of the horse. "Said . . . said . . . that . . . yes- . . . yes- . . . yesterday."

Quinn was already riding. "The sun's getting to you, Preacher. You don't know what you're saying. Let's go. *Vamanos. Vamanos.* That gold's waiting for us all."

Through his cotton shirt, the sun seemed to bake the .38-caliber Colt Lightning so much that his right side burned from the metal. Yet as he looked around, Fallon realized the other men must have been in worse condition than he was. The pebble in his mouth helped, and, he had to admit, so did the dead Rurale's *kepi* that he now wore. His bay horse was holding out better than at least Preacher Lang's and Morgan Maynard's mounts. Lang appeared about ready to fall out of the saddle. Doctor Fowler looked even worse.

Across the desert, Fallon saw nothing that resembled a town, or even a village. Certainly nothing that would have made him suspect they were riding into a place called Valle Verde, or Green Valley. The only colors Fallon saw were shades of tan and brown and white and beige. Even the sky no longer looked blue, just white, and hot, and ugly.

When they camped that night, they were still in the desert. Lang's canteen was empty; Morgan Maynard had only a few drops left. Doc Fowler had consumed the last of his liquor and was trembling underneath his bedroll.

"This is . . . crazy . . ." Preacher Lang said, half-delirious. "We can't . . . go on . . . like . . . this . . ."

Monk Quinn was checking on the pack mules tied to the picket line. He walked back into camp and nodded at Fallon.

"You know mules, my friend. You have taken good care of them."

Fallon shrugged. "I'm from Missouri," he said. "We know mules."

The killer walked over and kicked Preacher Lang's boots. "Fear not, Reverend. You have made it. You have reached Valle Verde."

Lifting his weary head, Lang looked at the endless desert. He coughed, and his eyes finally found and focused again on Monk Quinn.

"You have . . . to be . . . kidding . . . me," he said.

"It is true." Quinn squatted beside the preacher and tipped back his hat. "I am kidding you!"

He laughed at the look that appeared on Lang's face, but then leaned and patted the man on his thigh.

"No, this is not Valle Verde. I play a joke on you. But we are close, and this I swear on the soul of my father, whoever he was. We are two miles or so from the valley, and the gold is just two miles beyond that."

Suspicious eyes glared.

"Ask him." Monk Quinn pointed at Yaqui Mendoza. "He knows this country better than anyone."

The brute shrugged. "*Es verdad*," he said. "Two miles. Maybe three. It is not much of a valley, but it has been used by travelers since ancient times. More of a canyon than a valley. And often a slaughterhouse."

"That's a fact," Quinn said. "My *compadres* were slaughtered in that valley."

"Slaughtered by you," Morgan Maynard said.

Quinn just laughed.

Everyone but the trembling, delirious doctor and Gloria Adler, who busied herself trying to break the physician's fever, came closer.

"You got . . . that much . . . gold this . . . far?" Preacher Lang asked.

Quinn shrugged. "You must remember that the robbery was not at Yuma. It was well to the east."

"You killed the men who helped you pull off that job," Maynard said, and touched the butt of his gun. "Maybe you'll try to kill us off too. In that canyon. Or maybe right here."

Quinn laughed. "I killed no man. I liked the story though. Do you want to know what really happened? I remember it as though it happened yesterday."

CHAPTER THIRTY-SEVEN

Six years earlier

The Southern Pacific train braked hard as it rounded the curve, sending sparks across the sandy floor of the desert. The engineer and the fireman in the locomotive gritted their teeth and leaned back as though it would stop the train before the cowcatcher reached the twisted iron and derailed the train.

The engineer and fireman were brave men. They could have leaped off the train and saved themselves, but they did their job. And the train stopped just a few inches from the ruined iron rails.

Those two fools should have jumped.

Pete O'Brien came out of the rocks and shot the engineer in the head. Then he shot the fireman twice in the back, driving him into the coal-burning boiler, causing his shirt to erupt in fire as he tumbled over the bloody body of the engineer and rolled off the metal steps onto the hot sand.

Luke Dundee hurried over and tossed sand on the burning clothes of the dead man. O'Brien moved down the train toward the express car.

Pedro Negro and Juan Baca moved along the other side of the track.

When the brakeman stepped out of the caboose, Monk Quinn shot him in the head. Then Quinn approached the express car along the same side as Dundee and O'Brien. Malcolm Conrad, who had tipped Quinn off about the gold shipment—for fifty percent of the take—walked down the same side as Negro and Baca. Conrad held a Henry rifle in his trembling hands. He was a bookkeeper for the Adams Express Company. He didn't know about rim-fire rifles or anything about robbing trains. He just wanted to be rich.

Conrad had told Quinn that the Adams Express Company and the Southern Pacific thought that the best way to ship that much money in gold bullion would be on a special run that only a few people between San Diego and El Paso would know about. The crew, the Baldwin locomotive, the tender, caboose, and express car. The express car would hold the money, two guards, and Howard Malone Jr.—Conrad's brother-in-law who drank too much and couldn't keep his mouth shut even when sober.

The bandits wasted no time. On the side of the express car with the door, Negro and Baca tied the two sticks of dynamite to the handle, and Baca struck the match and lit the fuse. Conrad climbed between the tinder and the express car and braced himself for the explosion, while the two Mexicans hurried down the grade and took cover behind the rocks. On the other side of the train, O'Brien and Dundee lay down on the ground and covered their heads. Down the grade a bit, Monk Quinn dropped to one knee and worked his repeating rifle, firing as quickly as he could jack the lever and squeeze the trigger. He aimed at the little window in that side of the car.

The deafening explosion knocked Conrad off his perch, and he landed hard and twisted his ankle. Smoke belched from the car, and splinters and chunks of wood—painted a horrible shade of yellow—rained down on the rocks. Once the shower of wood and hot embers died down, Baca and Negro came up and fired their rifles into the smoke-filled opening that once had been a door and part of the frame of the express car. When their rifles were empty, they pitched them to the ground and filled their hands with revolvers.

They kept walking, waiting for the express agent or the two guards to show their faces. They never did, and once they reached the car, both men leaned forward. One took the right side of the car, and the other took the left, and they emptied their revolvers into the smoking, burning mess.

Baca then crawled inside the car. By the time O'Brien, Dundee, and Monk Quinn had come to that side of the train, Baca was leaning out of the splintered opening in the car. He grinned.

"Wasted a lot of lead on three dead men," Baca said.

Conrad had turned the Henry rifle into a crutch and had limped over. His face paled.

"You mean . . ." He looked like he was about to lose his breakfast. "Howard's . . . dead?"

"Would you rather him being alive to testify in court that he told you about the plans to ship that gold?" Dundee asked.

Conrad blinked repeatedly, wiped his mouth with the back of his left hand, and asked, in a rather hopeful voice, "Did Howard suffer? Do you think?"

Baca laughed. "I can't tell which one was the express agent and which ones were the guards. They must've been leaning against the door when the dynamite went off. There's parts of them all over this place." He laughed, spit, and called out to Malcolm Conrad, the traitorous express agent, "You want to come in and see?"

The weak man sank to his knees.

O'Brien and Monk Quinn climbed into the express car and stood beside Baca. Quinn called out to Negro, "Get the wagon." To Dundee, Quinn said, "Bring the horses around. We'll make this fast."

They used the remaining stick of dynamite to blow open the safe. By the time the heavy freight wagon had been positioned underneath the still-smoking wreckage of the express car, they were ready to unload pound after pound, bar after bar of beautiful stamped gold bullion.

In the back of the wagon, Conrad and Negro divided the gold evenly into saddlebags.

Monk Quinn had figured everything out perfectly.

A bar of gold bullion weighed roughly twenty-seven pounds. With gold priced at just under twenty dollars an ounce, that meant one bar was worth five hundred and forty-seven dollars and fifty cents, or something around there. Two hundred thousand dollars meant three hundred and sixty-five bars. A pair of heavy-duty saddlebags could hold two hundred pounds. They had brought twenty saddlebags, just to be safe, and they had filled eighteen, just to be safe. The wagon, pulled by a team of four strong oxen, could carry six tons. Traveling at the crawling speed of ten miles a day, they would be across the Mexican border in two days.

Baca would drive the wagon. He knew mules and could get more out of them than anyone Monk Quinn had ever known. Conrad would ride in the wagon. That was about the only thing Conrad would be good for. O'Brien, Negro, Quinn, and Dundee would ride alongside the wagon or scout ahead. Before they rode out from the robbery site,

Dundee climbed up the telegraph pole and managed to send a wire to the next relay station.

EXPRESS DELAYED STOP PART OF TRACK
DERAILED STOP WORKING TO REPAIR STOP
SHOULD REACH STATION IN TWELVE
HOURS STOP ALERT WESTBOUND AND
EASTBOUND TRAINS STOP NO TROUBLE
OTHERWISE STOP
SIGNED MALONE
ADAMS EXPRESS

"Twelve hours is not much of a head start," O'Brien said. He was the type of man who worried a lot and did most of his worrying out loud. "Considering how long it'll take us to move this weight south of the border."

"Would you like to leave most of it behind?" Quinn asked, and grinned.

"Well . . ." O'Brien smiled a bit too. "I reckon not. I'm just saying . . ."

"In twelve hours we will be halfway to the border."

"But the tracks this wagon will leave hauling this much gold," O'Brien countered, "will be like following a trail left by a herd of buffalo."

"I've thought about that already, O'Brien," Quinn said.

The outlaw's eyebrows arched in curiosity.

"How so?"

"I'll show you," Quinn said. "In twelve hours."

It actually took them fourteen.

At Walnut Pass, the wagon crawled up a hard-rock surface to the top of a mesa where they found three other wagons, each one harnessed to four oxen.

"What the hell?" Dundee said as he stopped the oxen pulling the big wagon weighed down with gold.

Monk Quinn grinned. "This wagon goes to Nogales. This one toward California. And this one southwest for Yuma." Three skinny Mexican drivers came out of a Sibley tent. Monk Quinn nodded at them, grinned, and watched as they climbed into the fronts of the three other wagons.

"Conrad," Quinn said. "You'll find six gold bars in that sack under your seat. Give two bars each to our drivers." Quinn turned to the hired drivers and spoke to them in Spanish. With smiles on their faces, they hurried to the side of the freight wagon.

The Adams Express Company employee pulled out one shining gold bar, looked at it curiously, then seriously, and finally looked down at Quinn.

"Just give them the gold, Conrad," Quinn said, losing his patience. "We're two hours behind schedule already."

"I don't get this," Baca said.

Because you are an imbecile, Quinn thought but grinned. "The posse that is likely being formed now and coming after us will reach this spot," he said. "And won't know which wagon to pursue. These other three are weighed down with rocks."

He called out to the drivers he had hired, speaking again in Spanish, and reminding them that they should hide the gold bullion they were being paid so that when any lawmen caught up with them, they could not be held for the robbery as accomplices or anything stronger.

They thanked him profusely. He shook all their hands and they left at the same time. Quinn dismounted, drew the rifle from its scabbard, and slapped his horse across the rump with the hot barrel of his Winchester. The horse galloped in the general direction of Tucson.

"Send your horses in various directions," Quinn ordered. "And crawl into the wagon." He laughed. "The lawdogs will have to follow our empty saddles too."

Now one large freight wagon carried two hundred thousand dollars' worth of gold bullion and six men who were armed to the teeth. They kept going south as dawn faded into afternoon.

"That gold?" Adams Express Company employee Conrad said after swallowing water out of his canteen. "That you gave those drivers?"

"Yes?" Quinn wondered why it had taken Malcolm Conrad so long to bring this matter up.

"It wasn't stamped," Conrad said. "That didn't come from the shipment we took."

He laughed. All eyes were upon him in the freight wagon, and Monk Quinn loved an audience.

"Do you think I'd give any of my gold . . . our gold . . . to those ignorant greasers?" He leaned his head back and laughed heartily. "They are being paid in lead bars. That have been painted gold."

CHAPTER THIRTY-EIGHT

When they crossed the Arizona border and entered Mexico, they made their way to Anton Bonito, the sleepy little village that once had been on one of the major trails from Mexico City to San Diego. Few wagon trains or burro trains used the trail these days, but the town still had a few wagon yards and livery stables, and pack mules were waiting for Monk Quinn at Carlos Villanueva's livery.

The saddlebags filled with gold were transferred from the big freight wagon to the mules, and the wagon was then reloaded with gravel and sent to Puerto Rojo.

"You think of everything," Dundee told him.

"Not always," Quinn replied, fairly honestly. "But for this much money, one tries to plan ahead."

He liked the idea. Another mule train—led by an honest merchant Quinn did not know—had left for Tucson that morning. The lawmen in Arizona could not pursue Quinn and his men south of the border, but Pinkerton agents and bounty hunters could. The freight wagon and the mule train would make the trail just too damned confusing to follow.

"We will leave in opposite directions, guiding a few

mules at a time," Quinn explained to Baca, Negro, Conrad, O'Brien, and Dundee. "That way even if they bring back Apache scouts to follow our trail, it will be too difficult to follow. You will circle back, taking your time, being very careful, and we will meet at Furnace Flats in two days."

"Why not just split up the gold now?" O'Brien asked. "And go our separate ways."

"Because the mines and the railroads and the detectives will not let this much gold disappear without a valiant effort to find it and bring it back." Quinn made himself some coffee as he explained. "Because this is Mexico, where there is little law and bandits roam free and easy. One man leading a few mules would make an inviting target once that one man and his gold-laden mules are far enough from Anton Bonito."

When they had arrived in Anton Bonito, they had to let a funeral possession pass before they could continue on to the wagon yard. Baca had asked a local who had died, and Baca had told his comrades that the man being carted off to the dusty but sprawling cemetery south of town had been robbed and murdered by bandits. He had been hauling melons to sell in town.

"If they kill for melons," Quinn said, "think of what they would do for gold."

"So," Conrad asked, "when do we go our separate ways?"

"When we reach Vera Cruz," Quinn said.

"Vera Cruz!" Negro snapped. "That is a long way to travel."

"And as a port, you can pick any place you want to live," Quinn said. "Away from the American law. Away from Pinkerton agents. Away from bounty hunters."

"It's too damned far," Baca said.

"It is very far. But if we take the cutoff at Valle Verde, it will save us much time."

"Valle Verde?" Malcolm Conrad asked.

"A canyon," Quinn said, "that begins near the edge of a brutal patch of hell on earth. Desert. Hot, even during the coldest of winters—as if they actually have winter in this land."

"That is not much of a trail," Baca said. "It is a canyon, and during the rainy season, it is dangerous."

"It is also a trail used more by Apache than anyone else," Negro added.

Quinn laughed. "How many Apache are left in Mexico?" He shook his head. "Are you bandits? Or are you women?"

Reluctantly, they agreed to make the journey south and east to Vera Cruz on the Gulf of Mexico, but first Monk Quinn had to pay off Señor Villanueva for all of his help.

"My last partners were paid off in lead bars," Quinn said. "But you will get only lead." He drew his gun, and shot the man twice in the heart. Then, one at a time, they rode out of the wagon yard, leading mules behind them. Conrad would never have been able to lead one mule to the edge of town and back, so he went with Monk Quinn.

They rode south. To the furnace. And there, they waited.

"What makes you think the Mexicans or Dundee or O'Brien won't just keep riding?" Conrad asked as he slaked his thirst from the canteen.

"Because I picked those *hombres* for one reason." Quinn was cleaning his rifle.

"Which is?" Conrad corked the canteen.

Quinn looked up and grinned. "They are greedy."

The one-time employee of the Adams Express Company cocked his head. "Greedy?"

"Would you rather have thirty-three thousand dollars in gold? Or two hundred thousand?"

"That's too much gold to handle across the desert," Conrad said.

"But once we are in Vera Cruz?"

Conrad considered this, but shook his head. "Thirty thousand in gold is enough for me."

Setting the Winchester against a rock, Monk Quinn smiled. "Is it?" he asked.

After chewing on this for a full two minutes, Conrad shook his head. "I don't think they'll come," he told Quinn.

But they did. Baca arrived first. Then Dundee. Followed by O'Brien. And at last Negro.

They rode the trail that led to Valle Verde.

Everything that had been said about Valle Verde was correct, and maybe a little bit understated. It wasn't a valley. It was barely a canyon. It wasn't a trail. It was barely a path.

They moved through it slowly, carefully, and now they were glad they had sure-footed mules and not stubborn, clumsy oxen pulling a heavy freight wagon that could not have fit through some of the twisting turns or narrow passageways or gotten over rockslides or across fallen timbers.

At one point, the valley or the canyon or the narrow passage opened out into a real valley, a place of trees and shade and water, usually *playas* that filled in the rainy season, but also a natural spring, with shade. It was an oasis in Hades. It ran on like this for better than two hundred yards wide and six hundred yards across. After that, however, Valle Verde returned to its narrow path that eventually got smaller, deeper, and more treacherous as it shrank into a slot canyon before coming out on the main road to the Gulf of Mexico and—eventually—Vera Cruz.

They camped that night before entering the treacherous slot canyon of Valle Verde.

On that night, O'Brien killed a snake that boasted sixteen rattlers. And Negro killed another, a smaller one. Monk Quinn paled. He shivered. He checked his boots and climbed on top of a rock, thinking that snakes could not climb. He did not sleep for fear that he would dream of rattlesnakes.

That fear likely saved his life.

Because around midnight, the scalp-hunters attacked the camp.

Scalp-hunters were Mexican outlaws who butchered Apache Indians and took their scalps to the *alcades* of various villages. The Mexican government paid fine bounties for the scalps of Apache. One hundred *pesos* for men. Fifty for women. Twenty-five for children. But the Apache were becoming fewer and fewer and soon, word spread, the *yanqui* army of the *norteamericanos* would defeat the Apache and the bounties would dry up. So the scalp-hunters turned to doing what they had been doing before the government in Mexico City offered bounties for Apache scalps. They robbed. They killed. They plundered.

Baca had been on guard duty when they hit. They stabbed him in the back, but the blade missed the heart, and the Mexican pulled away, spitting up blood, but cursing and drawing his gun. He put two bullets into the belly of the man who had killed him.

The surprise was over. The gunfight began.

When it was all over, Monk Quinn had to guess that the scalp-hunters had been drunk when they attacked. The moon was full, and it bathed the canyon, the valley, and the opening in wan light. They charged drunkenly into the center of camp.

Quinn was awake, and on the rock high above the others, he worked his rifle and shot two of the charging bad men dead. Out of the corner of his eye, he saw Conrad running up the hill to the northeast. Well, Quinn thought, Conrad wouldn't be worth a damn in a fight like this anyway.

Dundee shot the second charger.

The sound of the gunshots and eerie echoes faded, to be answered with the howls of coyotes and wolves deep into the northern side of Valle Verde.

Hearing the sound of rocks tumbling, Quinn adjusted his aim and fired in the direction.

"Watch where you're shooting!" O'Brien yelled. "You'll hit one of our mules!"

Quinn worked the lever, and then he understood. "They're after the mules!" he yelled.

O'Brien stood up. The mules brayed. A bullet tore through O'Brien's forehead and blew the back of his head off.

"The mules!" Negro yelled and he ran to the picket line. Dundee followed, and Quinn climbed down from his rocky perch and took off after his two companions. By the time he reached the picket line, all he could hear were the echoes of all of those mules, and the mocking laughter of the scalp-hunters as they wound their way through the slot canyon portion of Valle Verde.

Dundee's chest heaved. He cursed, and slammed his empty rifle to the ground. Negro walked along the outskirts of the line counting the packsaddles, but mostly, counting the saddlebags. When he came back to the other two, he laughed.

"Fools. They got the mules. They did not take one saddlebag."

"Sò . . ." Dundee wet his lips. "All the gold . . . ?"

"Still there," Negro said. "As far as I can tell."

"And more for us to split," Quinn said. He pointed in the general direction of the bodies of Baca and O'Brien.

"What about the yellow one?" Dundee asked.

Quinn made a gesture toward the hilltop over his shoulder. "Conrad ran off in that direction."

"Conrad!" Dundee called out.

The answer was his echo.

"It's all over."

"Over . . . over . . . over . . . over" bounced across Valle Verde.

"At least," Negro said, "we are still rich."

"So you'll die rich," Quinn told him. He pointed at the picket line. "We have no horses. We have no mules. We have several saddlebags filled with gold bars. How do we get them out of here?"

"The scalp-hunters know that too," Dundee said. "They'll be back with more guns. Just to find what we've been using those mules to haul."

"Maybe we can hide the gold," Negro suggested.

"Where?" Quinn snapped.

They stood there in silence for a while, and Dundee began reloading his six-shooter. Negro grabbed a canteen off a saddle and began to drink.

That's when Monk Quinn drew his pistol and shot Dundee in the heart. He whirled around and put two bullets into Negro's belly.

Dundee hit the ground dead. Negro was on his knees, bleeding like a stuck pig and coughing up blood. After holstering his pistol, Quinn picked up the gun Dundee had just reloaded, thumbed back the hammer, and touched the trigger. The bullet slammed into the back of Negro's head, and the bandit fell facedown near a saddlebag.

The shots faded away in the night. Quinn saw a figure coming down the hill. Shoving Dundee's hot pistol into his waistband, Quinn cupped his hands over his mouth and called out, "Conrad. Hurry up. We have to hide the gold before the bandits return. We are rich. And the gold is all for you and all for me."

CHAPTER THIRTY-NINE

"You said you didn't kill anyone," Morgan Maynard told Monk Quinn.

The outlaw leader shrugged. "I said I killed no man. Those who rode with me? They were not men. They were no better than animals. Stupid animals too. I was the only smart one there."

"The bandits? The scalp-hunters? They did not come back?" Yaqui Mendoza asked.

"What about the gold?" Allan said. "What did you do with it?"

Monk Quinn's face brightened. He seemed to enjoy being the center of attention. Shrugging, he continued his story:

"It was like this. Conrad, the fool working for the express company, came down the hill. His face had lost all color, and he pointed up and said that he had almost fallen into a pit. When he looked into the pit, he saw that it was alive with serpents. Rattlesnakes."

The outlaw shivered. "I do not like snakes of any kind, but I despise rattlesnakes in particular."

Allan bellowed again, "What about the gold?"

With a sigh, Quinn shook his head and looked back at the corrupt prison guard. "I am telling you that, my friend. Be patient. There is not much left to my story."

After clearing his throat, Monk Quinn said, "I do not like snakes, but this time I got an idea. I turned to Conrad, demanding, 'Where is this den of rattlesnakes?' He pointed at the hill. Not really a hill, but a ledge. 'Hurry!' I demanded, and I ran to the packsaddle that was closest to me. Straining, I hefted one of the pairs of bags over my shoulder. 'Grab one!' I yelled. Conrad just stared. 'Grab a saddlebag!' I demanded. 'Or do you wish to lose the gold and your life?'"

Preacher Lang gasped. "You didn't?"

Quinn's whole body rocked with laughter. "Indeed, I did. What choice did I have? If we left the saddlebags there, or tried to bury the gold, the bandits would have returned and found it. I knew I could not make it to Vera Cruz with all this gold. I did not want to run away with just a few bars myself. So I stumbled and made it to the ledge. I had to sit down to catch my breath. I was sweating. My chest heaved and ached. And I was scared . . . yes, I, Monk Quinn, was quaking in my boots . . . for Conrad was right. I could hear the whirling of the rattles in that pit. So frightened was I that I shoved the bags I had carried into the pit. I could not look inside. I feared I would fall in. The leather dropped. I heard the loud thud and then what sounded like a hundred, nay, a thousand, rattles from inside that deep pit of death. They sang like the serpents of hell."

"Twenty saddlebags?" Allan sank down on his haunches. "You dropped twenty saddlebags full of gold bullion into a nest of rattlesnakes?"

Quinn shrugged again. "Only eighteen bags. Remember?"

"That," Maynard said, "weighed something close to two hundred pounds each."

"True. It was hard. It was more than hard. It was excruciating, for I had to do almost all of the work. A timid, puny, pathetic man like Conrad? What could he do? He dragged one bag up the slope, and that took him as long as it took me to bring up three more. Four times I went up and down and up and down and up and down . . . carrying my bags over my shoulder. Conrad? He dragged his. It left a trail anyone could follow. And when he got his up to the top, he did not have the nerve to push it into the den of snakes."

Quinn stopped here to drink some water. He gargled it, but did not spit it out. After swallowing, Quinn said. "I had to push it into the hole in the earth, and you know how much I detest snakes."

"How far?" Yaqui Mendoza asked.

"A hundred yards from where we were to where the slope begins. Forty or fifty yards up the slope to the edge. Twenty yards to the hole in the ground."

Preacher Lang's pale head shook. "That must have taken you a long time."

"It took forever," Quinn said.

Doc Fowler finally asked a question. "The robbers and killers? They did not come back?"

"They would have to get their plunder, the mules they had stolen, through the slot canyon first. That would take them a while. Then they would come back, but they likely thought there was no hurry. They figured that Conrad and myself, or anyone who survived, would be hightailing it for the border, for the nearest town, to get as far as we could from the killing fields as quickly as possible."

"The snakes didn't come out of the hole?" Mendoza asked.

"It was not the time of evening when rattlesnakes come out to hunt," Quinn said. "We could hear them snapping and hissing and even striking at one another. They were not used to having heavy bars of gold rain down upon them. I am sure we crushed many of those demons to death."

"And," Maynard said, "you got all that gold all the way up the hill and left it in the snake den?"

"Yes."

"But," Allan said, "you said it yourself. The gold that the express agent dragged, it left a trail. And even you, a big man such as yourself, carrying two hundred pounds of gold. That would have left an easy trail to follow too."

"Of course. We were not hiding our trail at that time. To do so would have been folly. Conrad?" Quinn let out a mirthless chuckle. "He sat on a rock a good twenty or thirty feet away from the opening of the pit. He said he had to catch his breath." Quinn shook his head and bellowed. "Like I did not have to catch my breath? Like my shoulders did not ache from the strain of lugging all that fortune all that distance, all the way up to the edge? But I had no time. And, eventually, Conrad came back down and tried to carry another of the bags. I had to help him. And to be honest, by the time we were bringing up the last of the bags, we had to do it together. My strength had begun to ebb. Sweat stung my eyes so much I felt practically blinded. Yet I was determined to get this gold out of sight.

"So I backed up. We moved slower than a crippled snail. Me holding one of the leather bags and Conrad straining to keep the other bag just inches off the ground. We did one of the pairs that way. It took forever. He had to rest every ten or twelve feet. Then it would take him two or three times, sometimes five or six, before he could even lift the bag just a few inches so we could move it. But he did it. We got that bag up, and I shoved it into the pit."

"That was the last bag?" Fowler asked.

Again, Monk Quinn laughed. "The last bag? Ha! No, my good doctor. Not at all. Maybe the tenth. That seems about right. Once again, Mr. Conrad was utterly exhausted. Played out. He sank again, wiping his sweaty face, groaning, moaning, whimpering like a sick dog. My muscles ached. I wanted to quit. I wanted to run. Run from the sound of the serpents in the hole. Run from the bandits that surely had to be out of the slot canyon by this time. Yet dark clouds passed overhead. We thought we could smell rain. And the temperature dropped. It was a sign from God."

"Amen," Preacher Lang said.

"Yes. Amen. Because that gave me the strength to return. I managed to get another pair of bags on my shoulder, and I stumbled. It took me three times as long as it had taken me to get the first couple of bags to that pit. My knees were bleeding from falling under the weight of the fortune I carried. It was hell. It was pure hell. My shoulders and neck were rubbed raw from the weight and the leather. I made it up. Again. And while Conrad just sat there, heaving, aching, complaining, down I went again. For yet another pair of saddlebags."

All eyes remained on the storyteller. Even Gloria Adler looked at the brutal killer. Fallon tried to read the others. Preacher Lang seemed to be half out of his head, and he listened with great attention. Fowler had this dreamy look about him, and Fallon couldn't tell if the doctor was drunk or suffering from sunstroke. Maynard had the look of the cocksure gunfighter he was. Allan seemed to be trying to think of how he could get all that gold out of a rattlesnake den. Yaqui Mendoza's face read something entirely different. He was, Fallon thought, trying to figure out exactly where this rattlesnake den could be.

"Conrad, the weakling, eventually came down. I will give him some credit. He passed me while I staggered up that slope with the crushing weight of the gold on my shoulders. He said nothing, but he was determined to bring up one more pair of bags. And, to my amazement, and likely to his . . . the fool did it. Dragged and pulled and somehow managed to bring up one more load of gold bullion."

Quinn had another swallow of water.

"Conrad was sitting on one of the saddlebags near the pit. Soaked through with sweat. Panting like a dying man. I brought up the last of the bullion, and heaved those bags into the pit. Then I helped Conrad to his feet, mainly so I could get the last of the bags into that hole. Then we could run as far as we could . . . but only after I had done something to wipe out that trail we had left."

He shook his head, and tossed the canteen to Preacher Lang.

"Then we heard the loudest roar we had ever heard. It sounded like the end of the world."

There was a long pause. No one dared to encourage Monk Quinn to finish the story.

"The sound, we realized, came from the slot canyon. Like the roaring of a train. I've heard that tornadoes sound like that, but I have never heard of a twister in the deserts of Mexico. Then . . ." He shook his head. "It was like we were in the heavens, Conrad and me, watching the great flood. Or maybe we were aboard the ark with Noah. Water—tons of water—almost to the top of the entrance, exploded out of that canyon, turning the bottom into a shallow lake."

Quinn again wet his lips. He even appeared to shudder. "Limbs and the carcasses of two of our pack mules and rocks and sand and stones and debris from who knows where . . . they all came out, spreading across the ground below us.

"It came out so suddenly, so violently, so shockingly, that Conrad screamed out and took a step back. He started to topple over into the pit with the rattlers, but I reached out and grabbed hold of his arm. I stopped him from falling. His face turned even the starkest, the most fearful, of whites. His eyes bulged. I started to pull him to safety."

Quinn laughed. "And then I realized something extraordinary. I let go of his arm. And he screamed and fell back, disappearing into the pit. He landed with a thud that I could barely hear because the water still poured out of that canyon.

"Then I walked to the edge, and watched the last of the water pour out. I did not go back to look into the den of snakes. I hurried down the hill. I found a canteen and filled it with water. I walked through the water—it was just past my ankles, but sinking into the desert very quickly. I walked out of that part of the Valle Verde and into the other canyon. I walked away. I left the gold . . . all two hundred thousand dollars of bullion—in the hole.

"That is where I am taking you."

CHAPTER FORTY

A silence hung over the camp like a thick fog.

The men and the woman had to let the story Monk Quinn had told them sink in. Eventually, Captain Allan cleared his throat and asked the most important question:

"What makes you think the gold is still in that snake den?"

Quinn moved to his horse and began tightening the cinch. Speaking with his back to the others, he said, "The floodwaters wiped out any sign Conrad and I left behind. And none of that gold bullion has ever shown up in Mexico or our United States as far as we know. The Pinkertons, as I've said, and other detectives, professional and amateurs, have been after that gold, after the reward. No one has claimed it. Most have forgotten it."

"What about the bandits?" Morgan Maynard asked.

Quinn tugged on the saddle, seemed satisfied, and stepped away from his horse. "When I saw the carcasses of two of our mules come out with that water, tossed about as though they were nothing but rag dolls, it struck me that most, and maybe all, of the bandits were caught in that terrible canyon. There might not have been any left alive."

"But you did not see for yourself," Maynard said.

"I was not about to set foot in that canyon. Not after what I had seen. For all I knew another thunderstorm had filled the canyon again, and I was not going to risk drowning."

"You didn't check on the express agent?" Preacher Lang asked.

"There was no need. When the sound of the flood ended, I heard no groaning, no moaning, no screams. The fall likely did not kill him. With luck, he was unconscious, though, and did not feel the fangs of the many, many rattlesnakes sinking into his flesh and veins."

"You are sick," Gloria Adler said. "Sick. You said you killed no men. But you are no man yourself. You are not even an animal. You are the devil himself."

He mockingly bowed at her and turned back to his horse. "We should ride," he said.

Yaqui Mendoza said, "I know of this place. Not the den of vipers, but where the canyon spreads out and begins again. I have been there. But not in many years."

"I have not been there in six years myself." Quinn had climbed into the saddle. "I would like to see it again. *Vamanos.*"

The wind blew the sand off the desert floor so violently that they had to pull bandannas over their mouths and noses and keep their eyes trained on the ground. The sand stung like millions of cactus needles pricking their skin. Yet Yaqui Mendoza saw the entrance to Valle Verde, and they found themselves in the shelter of the canyon.

The sun no longer baked them so harshly, and the sand stopped stinging them. But the moaning of the wind inside the canyon was haunting, and even unnerving.

Quinn rode his horse close to Preacher Lang and patted

the killer's thigh. "I told you, *Padre*," Quinn said, and laughed. "That we would be in Valle Verde soon. Aren't you glad to be out of the desert? You have delivered your people, Mr. Moses."

The sickly looking murderer did seem to be revived once he felt the shade of the canyon's walls. He wet his horribly cracked lips and tried to grin. His lips parted, but he said only in a hoarse whisper, "I can't seem to recall any Scripture about Moses . . . or . . . the desert . . . or . . ." He shook his head.

"How about this one, *Padre*?" Quinn called out. "It's from Exodus. 'And they shall take gold . . .'"

Preacher Lang chuckled. So did Quinn, Allan, Maynard, and Mendoza.

"I would like to scout ahead," Yaqui Mendoza said as he rode his horse up alongside Monk Quinn.

Quinn turned in the saddle and studied the big man long and hard. Next, he twisted the other way, and standing in the stirrups, looked back. Captain Allan rode immediately behind the two men at the point, followed by Doc Fowler and Gloria Adler, then Hank Fallon, with Preacher Lang dragging along a few yards behind them, and Maynard pulling the string of pack mules behind him at the rear.

"Very well," Quinn said as he looked ahead. "Be quiet. Be careful. And don't try to double-cross your *compadres*."

"*Bueno*," Mendoza said. "*Yo se*."

He kicked his horse into a trot and rode on ahead.

"And don't fall into any snake dens, my friend," Quinn called out, and laughed.

Mendoza laughed, too, and rounded one of the many twists and turns in the canyon.

* * *

Gloria Adler let her horse fall back to Fallon, and rode on his right.

"How's the doc?" Fallon asked.

She did not answer. Staring straight ahead, she asked, "What happens when they get the gold?"

Fallon kept his eyes trained on the rocky ledges above him, left and right. This was the trail frequented by scalp-hunters, chasing the bounties on Apache. Fallon had seen many arrowheads along the trail, which meant this canyon had been used for a long, long time by Indians. Yet most of the Apache were imprisoned on reservations across America these days. There were reportedly a few bands of Apache hiding in the mountains of Mexico, but not likely enough to interest scalp-hunters.

He looked ahead and on the canyon floor now. He watched Monk Quinn's back. The man rode with confidence. At length, he turned to find Gloria Adler's eyes.

"You know what happens," he said.

"But when does it happen?"

He shrugged. Fallon had decided that this part of the canyon would not be where any ambush would be made. Too many boulders along the floor offered too many hiding places. There were not enough rocks on the top to roll down to block one or even both openings to prevent escape, and the top offered very little cover. Once they rode out, into the clearing where the snake den—and the gold bullion—was, maybe the slot canyon would be different. Maybe if any bandits still frequented this area, that's where an ambush could be sprung.

But Fallon and Adler were not talking about an ambush by scalp-hunters or Mexican outlaws.

"That's anyone's guess," Fallon said. He nodded ahead at Monk Quinn. "Does he need us once he has the gold loaded? Or does he kill us then? Has he selected a partner to help him kill the rest? Or maybe two?" He looked at her. "Am I one of Quinn's partners?"

Her head shook. "You are honest."

He laughed. "You're talking to a convict who violated his parole."

She asked, "Am I one of Quinn's partners?"

He shook his head. "You are honest too."

Her laugh was short, and filled with bitterness.

"I killed my husband. Why do you think I was in Yuma?"

"You had your reasons," he said without looking at her.

"Is any reason enough to commit murder?"

He looked back at her. "You tell me."

"I thought so. He was coming at me with a knife. He was drunk. I had told him that he had beaten me for the last time. He should have listened to me. He slapped me, and I fell across the bed. Then he picked up a lantern in his hand that did not hold the knife. He said he would burn me, then kill me. He kept a pistol under his pillow, but he was too drunk to remember that. I grabbed the pistol, and I shot him. I shot him and I shot him and I shot him."

Her eyes were closed all this while, and Fallon thought she was revisiting that nightmarish scene.

"He fell. He dropped the knife and the lantern, which exploded and fire spread across the rug, onto the bed, over his body. But he was already dead. I think. I climbed out the window. I ran to our neighbor's place. I lost my mind for that night. We watched our home burn to the ground."

The eyes opened, and she turned back to look at the saddle. "Is that a good enough reason to kill the man you were once in love with?"

"Self-defense," Fallon said.

She laughed and spit on the ground. "Our neighbors did not think so. The judge did not think so. The jury did not think so. They knew my husband as the justice of the peace, an honorable man. They thought I was nothing but what the Spanish call a *puta*. You know what that means?"

He kept his eyes on the trail. "I know."

"So they sent me to Yuma. You know what prison . . . especially a place like the Hell Hole . . . does to a man."

Fallon only nodded. He felt his chest tighten and his teeth begin to grind at the memories of Joliet . . . of Yuma . . . of even being locked in the dungeon at Fort Smith.

"It is much worse on a woman."

He sighed. "Especially an innocent woman."

She did not look away from him, and he made himself turn to look into her eyes.

"Or an innocent man," she said.

They stared at each other, and Fallon made himself look back at the trail.

"I was innocent once," he said. "I'm not sure I can say that ever again."

"I know how you feel."

He shook his head. Fallon tried to think of something to say, but he could find nothing reassuring in his vocabulary. Besides, hooves were sounding up the canyon. A horse was running at a decent lope, and Monk Quinn was reining in his mount and bringing up his left hand. Signaling them to stop. His right hand reached for his revolver, and he drew it.

Fallon reined up, and heard those behind him and ahead of him do the same.

"Whenever it happens," Fallon whispered, "do whatever you have to do to stay alive."

"You do the same," she said, and rode up, stopping alongside Doc Fowler.

The rider rounding the bend was Yaqui Mendoza. He

slowed his horse once he saw the others and trotted up to Monk Quinn.

Preacher Lang called out, "Is it scalp-hunters?"

The last word echoed up and down the canyon, and Monk Quinn and Captain Allan whirled in their saddles. But Allan snapped and cursed first.

"Keep your voice down, you damned fool! You want everyone up or down this canyon to hear us? Shut up!"

Quinn looked back at Mendoza, but he did not holster his pistol. The big brute rode alongside Quinn and waited for the others to ride up close.

Mendoza's face was beaded with sweat.

"What is it?" Quinn asked.

"Trouble," Yaqui Mendoza said. "But it is not scalp-hunters. Not bandits. It is the kind of trouble you did not expect. Nor did I."

"What is it?" Quinn demanded.

Mendoza laughed. "You will see for yourself. Come. It is not far."

"An avalanche?" Allan asked. "The trail's blocked? It's a dead end?"

"No. Come. *Vamanos*. This is something you must see for yourself."

Monk Quinn cursed the big man, but kicked his horse into a trot. The others followed.

"Stay close," Fallon whispered to Gloria Adler as he eased his horse ahead of hers and Doctor Fowler's.

The drunken doctor said, "Gloria, dear, soon we'll be richer than God."

"Shut up," she snapped at him.

Two turns later, they saw the opening, where this part of

the canyon ended, to spread out into a wide valley, more or less, with the narrow canyon on the opposite end.

Monk Quinn dismounted, left the reins dragging the ground, and crept to a boulder. He peered over the side and looked out into the clearing.

He holstered his gun at last and uttered the vilest of oaths.

CHAPTER FORTY-ONE

The first thing Fallon noticed was the cornfield. Then he caught the scent of beans being cooked. A dog barked. A woman sang in Spanish. He saw the *horno*, the outdoor oven, and then the corral and lean-to. A Mexican man in a white cotton shirt and trousers walked along the edge of the cornfield, beyond which lay a field of cabbage, of potatoes, of carrots, and of beans.

Yaqui Mendoza laughed. "This is what two hundred thousand dollars in gold buys," he said, mocking Monk Quinn, who scowled at the big man and spit in the dirt.

"No. This is just some poor farmer. Too stupid, too frightened, to even look into a den of rattlesnakes."

"Like you were six years ago?"

Quinn's hand darted for the butt of his revolver. Mendoza reached for the hilt of his machete, but both men froze, though hatred remained etched into their faces.

"Why don't we be sociable?" Captain Allan said. "Pay a visit to these folks." He motioned at the path that led across the farm to the entrance to the far canyon. "See what has happened. And then maybe we can see if we've come a long way for nothing."

"At least we are out of the Hell Hole," Morgan Maynard said.

Monk Quinn did not remove his hand from his revolver until Yaqui Mendoza had nodded and had taken the reins to his horse in both hands. He turned the horse around, kneed it gently, and led the animal toward the farmer.

Behind him, Fallon heard Gloria Adler pray, "Please, God in heaven above, do not let this poor couple have any children. Please, God in heaven above, do not let this poor couple have any children. Please, God in heaven above . . ."

Hogs roamed the edges of the cornfield. Two large cats sat lazily in the shade of the canyon. Fallon saw the corral, with only a couple of burros standing contentedly near a water trough, and another bunch of piglets suckling from their fat mother. The dog stepped off the porch and barked a warning as the riders came out of the canyon. The farmer stepped away from the corn. His wife appeared in the doorway to the adobe and stone cabin, and wiped her hands on the apron.

Yaqui Mendoza kicked his horse into a trot and rode over to the farmer, who had walked over to his dog and now approached the men. The woman stepped off the porch. She looked to be between thirty and forty years old, Fallon thought, not exactly the prettiest woman he had ever seen, but not ugly. Behind him, Fallon heard Preacher Lang whispering to himself. Fallon moved his hand to the double-action revolver that remained under his shirt.

"Hold up here for a moment," Monk Quinn said, and he brought his horse to a stop. "Let's see how Mendoza plays out this hand." Still, Quinn gripped the butt of his revolver, but he had turned his horse at an angle so that neither the farmer nor his wife could see his movement.

Once the farmer was close to Mendoza, they began conversing in Spanish.

Doc Fowler moved his horse alongside Fallon's. The drunkard asked, "Can you make out what they're saying?"

Fallon shook his head. "My Spanish is limited. Very limited."

"They are making introductions," Quinn said in a voice just loud enough for the men and woman right behind him to hear. Captain Allan and Morgan Maynard kept their eyes trained on the hill just behind them and to their left. They could see the rocks, and the ledge, and they knew that somewhere up there was a hole that was filled with many rattlesnakes, the bones of a former Adams Express Company employee, and eighteen saddlebags holding a fortune in gold bullion.

Preacher Lang, Fallon saw, kept his eyes on the woman, who had moved to a well and began drawing a bucket.

Gloria Adler had stopped her prayers.

"His name is Ignacio," Quinn translated. "He and his wife have been here for two years." Quinn sighed bitterly and spit again. "The fool is giving Mendoza a history in farming in this desert."

The farmer turned and pointed to the clouds behind the far canyon, to the mouth of the canyon, to the crops.

Mendoza interrupted him and pointed at the shelf and the rocks. He asked something. The farmer laughed.

"He has never climbed that hill," Quinn translated. "It is not good soil to grow corn, and there are no rabbits up there or other game to hunt for meat."

"He must not eat rattlesnakes." Morgan Maynard chuckled.

"Why don't we kill them now?" Captain Allan asked.

"Let him finish," Quinn rebuked them, "and be quiet. I cannot hear when you all gab foolish nonsense."

"The trail is not used much anymore," Quinn translated. "No bandits have been cleaned out or have taken their trade south or north, where more people, where rich people live. The Apache are all but ghosts and long-forgotten nightmares."

Quinn shook his head. "This man loves to talk about farming. He . . . wait . . ." He leaned forward and listened with religious intensity.

"The cats, the dog, and, yes, even the pigs they have keep most of the snakes away. One dog was bitten by a rattlesnake when they first got here, and it died, but their new dog has never been struck. Yes, they see snakes, but not as often as they once did when they had chickens. They got rid of their chickens. It is hard not to have eggs for breakfast, but lard from the pigs is good to use in cooking. His wife cooks fine. Fine enough for him."

Quinn shook his head. He drew his revolver and thumbed back the hammer.

"They have no children."

"Thank God," Gloria Adler said.

"Yet," Quinn continued. "But if it is the wish of the Lord . . ." He shook his head and yelled to Mendoza in Spanish. Quinn spurred his horse and brought the pistol up.

Fallon was reaching for the revolver he had hidden underneath his shoulder, only to feel Doc Fowler dive off his horse, knocking them both to the ground. Their horses bolted. Gloria Adler shouted, "Look out!" Preacher Lang loped his horse toward the cabin.

Hitting the ground, Fallon felt the air rush out of his lungs. He saw Doc Fowler astride him, heard him whisper, "Don't be a damned fool. There's nothing you can do."

A gunshot rang across the valley.

Fallon pushed, but Doc Fowler found some strength from within and shoved him down.

The dog barked. A revolver spoke. Fallon heard the whimper and cry of a dog.

"Get off me!" Fallon roared, and shoved the doctor to the dirt. Coming up, Fallon slammed into the horse Captain Allan was on. The prison guard had his Winchester. The rifle roared, but Fallon had spooked the animal. Allan turned in the saddle, pulled the reins tight to get his mount under control, and looked down at Fallon, who was backing away while reaching again for the revolver hidden underneath his shirt. He saw the flash of the rifle, felt the hot barrel slam against his face, and down Fallon went.

He tasted blood on his lips. His nose was busted.

"For God's sake!" Doc Fowler was yelling, but not at Fallon now. He directed his plea to Captain Allan. "Kill that woman before Lang reaches her!"

Fallon rolled over. Underneath the belly of Allan's horse, he saw the woman. She had dropped the bucket of well water and was running back toward the house. Preacher Lang was riding toward her, leaning low in the saddle, reaching out to grab her by her long black hair.

The red splotch appeared on the back of her plain yellow dress almost as soon as Captain Allan's rifle roared. She fell to her knees, and Preacher Lang's hand just missed snatching more than a few strands of her hair. The horse raced by, and Lang turned the horse at a full gallop. The woman sat on her knees. The redness spread against her back. Captain Allan sent another round from his Winchester. This one struck her lower in the back and drove her facedown into the dirt.

The sounds of gunfire died down.

Fallon came to his knees. He felt Gloria Adler beside

him. Holding a silk scarf wadded into a ball, she dabbed at his bleeding nose and a wicked cut across his cheek. Fallon saw Quinn moving his horse to the body of the farmer, Ignacio, who lay spread-eagled across two rows of cabbage plants. The evil killer stopped, extended his pistol, which sent smoke and flame toward the man's head. The body shuddered, the act of a dead man.

Off to the left, the dog lay dead.

Fallon wondered if these sons of bitches had killed the two cats or the pigs too. He heard Preacher Lang's screams at Captain Allan. "Why'd you kill her, you miserable cur? Why'd you kill her? That was my job. I am the right hand of God. I kill all the wicked women. You robbed me of my glory."

Leaning forward, Fallon vomited. He wiped his mouth, and felt that insatiable rage roaring to his head. He whirled, found the doctor, and sent a haymaker to Fowler's jaw. The man fell, stunned, his top and bottom lips bleeding. Fallon went over to punch him again, but Gloria Adler stepped between them.

"What?" Fowler said through his busted mouth. "Get yourself killed? Is that what you wanted to do? Get her killed."

"Stop you from becoming richer than God?" Fallon fired back. "You're a doctor. You're supposed to save lives."

"And what about you?"

"Shut the hell up," Captain Allan said. "The both of you. Let's see if that gold's still in that hole."

First, they put the livestock in the corral with the burro. The cats paid no attention to their dead masters, the dead dog, or the newcomers. The burro tried to give the horses and mules a wide berth.

"What about the dead farmers?" Morgan Maynard asked.

"Why did you not let me save this woman's soul?" Preacher Lang wailed over the bloodied corpse.

"Let's look at that gold!" Captain Allan said.

Maynard and Mendoza hauled the bodies of the couple and the dog into the root cellar. After that, they followed Monk Quinn up the path.

Clouds had formed off to the southeast, but overhead in this rugged opening, the sun shone hot and long, directly overhead. Gloria Adler had to help Doc Fowler make the journey uphill, even though the grade was not steep at all. Preacher Lang kept stumbling. When he reached the ledge, Monk Quinn hesitated and drew his revolver. He had found a stick down below and kept this in his left hand.

"Where is that hole?" Captain Allan demanded.

Quinn nodded and carefully moved toward the wall that rose about six feet over the level part, then climbed up several more feet to form the canyon. He stopped, moved back, and then inched his way to the opening of the pit.

Having little fear of any snakes, Lang, Maynard, Mendoza, and Allan rushed to the edge. Even Doc Fowler found his strength and moved to the side nearest the rim, which he gripped for support.

"Fallon," Monk Quinn called.

Again, Harry Fallon had to choke down the bile and made himself step to the edge. Gloria Adler stepped up beside him. At the same time, they looked into the pit.

"My God . . ." Gloria Adler whispered.

CHAPTER FORTY-TWO

"It's still there!" Monk Quinn shouted with glee. "Heaven be praised, it's still there."

The pit was a half circle that started at the walled ledge, four feet wide, six feet across at the longest point, maybe fifteen feet deep.

"Could that be . . ." Preacher Lang even shivered. "That express agent?"

After six years, everyone expected to find the bones of what once had been a man named Malcolm Conrad, one-time employee of the Adams Express Company.

"The desert has its own peculiar ways," Yaqui Mendoza said.

The dead man remained intact. His clothes had faded from the sun whenever it shined directly into the pit, and from the elements, while rats had nibbled off much of the shirtsleeves and the trousers. His shoes remained intact. So did the gunbelt he had strapped on, the butt of the pistol halfway out of the holster.

But the body? The body was not mere bones bleached with age. It was intact. His eyes and mouth remained open, terror and agony locked for eternity, one hand clutching his throat where a rattlesnake must have struck, the other hand locked at the elbow, pointing toward the opening . . . like he was reaching out to Monk Quinn for help, or for mercy. Only this was no longer the body of a man. The skin had shriveled and tightened across his skeleton, and darkened into a grisly brown and yellow hue.

"He has mummified," Doctor Fowler explained. "The lack of humidity, away from carrion. I have heard of such things, but this is the first time I have ever seen anything like this."

"Well," Quinn said, and chuckled, "maybe when you get back north, you can write something for the *Journal of the Royal Society of Medicine.*"

Monk Quinn seemed pleased with the looks practically everyone gave him. "Maynard," Quinn said. "Go fetch some ropes."

The gunman nodded and took off down the hill for the pack mules.

"I don't see any rattlesnakes," Preacher Lang said.

"They're down there," Quinn said. "Millions of them. Well, hundreds anyway. The floor was crawling with them six years ago."

"It's the heat of the day," Captain Allan offered. "Likely resting in the shade. Sleeping."

"Means you might get out of this affair alive," Quinn said, and he looked into Fallon's eyes. "With maybe just two or three rattler bites." The leader turned to Doc Fowler. "Best get your valise, Doc. I got a feelin' that ol' Hank Fallon will need some of those rattlesnake cures you've brung with you."

Gloria Adler went down the hill for the Yuma doctor's grip. Fallon wet his lips. He tried to think of just how he could get out of this mess alive. Grab his revolver and start shooting? Gloria Adler was out of the line of fire, but

Morgan Maynard was down there, near Gloria, and out of range for most pistols.

He glanced into the pit one more time. He couldn't tell how far back it went. Maybe it had another opening. He could get down there, avoid all of those snakes, find another way out. He spit into the hole, disgusted. That would still leave all this gold to the outlaws. Worse, it would still leave Gloria Adler with those cutthroats.

There had to be another way. But he would need to come up with something soon.

The girl came up first, heaving from the exertion, and sat the doctor's ugly carpetbag by Doc Fowler's feet. Morgan Maynard was right behind her, lugging three coiled lariats.

Monk Quinn took command. "Maynard. Take the stoutest rope. Tie one end around that rock over there. Make it tight. It has to support two hundred pounds. Allan, take the other rope. You and Preacher . . . no . . . you and Mendoza will use it to lower Fallon into the pit. Fallon, go ahead and slip the loop over your chest and under your shoulders. When you get down, you'll tie the stout rope to the center of one of the bags. We'll heft that bag up, and then toss it back down." Quinn laughed. "All you have to do is get all of those saddlebags out of that hole. Without getting bitten to death by a thousand rattlesnakes."

A thousand snakes. A million. A hundred. The number kept changing, but numbers really did not matter. All it would take was one bite, although Fallon had known many men, a few kids, two women, several horses, and maybe a dozen dogs that had survived snakebites. On the other hand, he had been to more than one funeral for folks that were not so lucky.

"Before you go though," Quinn said, and he drew his

revolver and cocked it. "I'll take that Lightning you've been hiding under your shoulder."

Preacher Lang reached for his derringer. Captain Allan whirled, his face showing surprise. Morgan Maynard looked up from where he was securing the heavy rope around that boulder. Yaqui Mendoza just laughed. Gloria Adler and Doctor Fowler showed no emotion.

"I am no fool, Fallon," Quinn said. "And had you made a play for that .38, I would have shot you dead."

Slowly, Fallon reached under his shirt with his left hand, while his right pulled the rawhide cord over his head. Using his fingers, Fallon pulled the double-action revolver from underneath his shirt, dragging the cord that was tied to the lanyard right out too. He held the gun toward Preacher Lang, who stood closest, but kept his eyes on Monk Quinn.

"I could use this on snakes down there," Fallon said.

Quinn shook his head. "I think you would be more inclined to use it on snakes up here." He laughed.

Preacher Lang snatched the pistol from Fallon's fingers, and shoved the Colt into his waistband.

Sighing, Fallon moved to the lariat, widened the loop and dropped it over his head, and then brought it up underneath his shoulders. He tightened the loop.

Maynard brought the end of the heavy rope away from the boulder, and pitched it into the hole in the earth. It landed with a faint noise and sent dust flying off the leather bags that it struck.

Preacher Lang laughed. "That sounded like that express man coughed."

"I don't hear any rattlers whirrin'," Morgan Maynard said, and backed away from the opening.

"Maybe they are restin', sleepin'," Preacher Lang said.

"You better hope so, Fallon," Yaqui Mendoza said.

"All right." Fallon grabbed a tight hold on the hemp rope in front of him. Captain Allan and Yaqui Mendoza took firm grips on the other end of the rope, and both men braced the rope against their backs and leaned away from the opening. Fallon dropped to his knees, nodded at the two men, and slid over the edge. Rocks and sand tumbled into the dark hole. Fallon grimaced as the rope tightened and cut into his shirt, his skin. He felt himself being lowered toward the bottom. He pushed the heavy rope away, but it kept coming back to slap his shoulders.

Above him came Preacher Lang's voice.

"What happens, Quinn, if Fallon gets kilt by a rattler?"

"You best hope that doesn't happen, Reverend," Monk Quinn said. "Because you go down to finish his job."

Fallon made himself look down. Fifteen feet was not that far of a drop, but Mendoza and Allan took their good, sweet time about lowering Fallon. And Fallon was in no hurry to reach bottom. He saw the bags, which pretty much formed a bit of a hill. He could see the body of Malcolm Conrad, and those dead yellow eyes that seemed to be staring at him, and his mouth, instead of locked in a scream, was laughing at him. He saw something else about the mummified corpse.

The hair seemed to be growing from the dead yellow skull, plowed in places by rats, likely to help with their nests.

As he inched his way deeper into the pit, he looked for snakes. Above him, Doc Fowler called out directions to the two killers lowering him. "About six more feet to go. Easy. Easy does it. Do you see any snakes, Fallon?"

The voice echoed in the pit.

Fallon shook his head. His throat felt as if it were covered with the grit and the dust and the sand that rose from the saddlebags below. He couldn't find enough moisture in his throat to spit. His boots touched the saddlebags, and he sank into them, feeling the hardness of the bullion in the pouches. When he thought he had firm-enough footing, he called out sharply, "All right. Stop. I'm at the bottom."

He sucked in a deep breath, slowly exhaled, and listened. Nothing near him rattled. He slipped the lariat's loop over his head, and knelt atop the bags. The rope began flying back to the opening, and he almost reached out over his head to try to grab it, but stopped, fearing that he might lose his balance and roll off the mountain of leather and into a family of rattlers.

He did call out, "Hey!"

"You don't need that rope, Fallon!" Captain Allan's voice called down into the hole. "You just need to do your job and get that heavy rope tied onto one of those bags."

"Check one first!" Monk Quinn's voice echoed in the tiny chamber of the chasm. "Make sure my gold's still there."

A few faces appeared at the opening fifteen feet above Fallon, who knelt atop the bags and found the buckled satchel. He touched it softly, listening, and fumbled with the buckle. At last, he slowly, carefully pulled the dusty brown leather covering up. Nothing rattled inside the pouch, and he moved both hands into it.

The gold felt hard, and cold, and he lifted the heavy bar out and held it up for the prying eyes to get a good look.

"Put it back in the bag," Allan yelled, "and tie the big rope around the center."

Fallon stared. "How do I know you pull me out of this once you've got all the bags up?"

"You don't," Monk Quinn's voice called out. "But here's something you do know. If you don't get to work, that wench is coming down with you. Only she won't get lowered down easy by a rope."

"Now you wait just a damned minute, Quinn!" That was Doc Fowler's voice, but the only answer was a violent blast that rang in Fallon's ears. He saw a shadow, then something falling into the pit. Fallon flinched, ducking from instinct and fear, and held his breath.

The body of Doctor Jerome Fowler crashed in the rocks and dirt and skins shed by snakes over countless years a few feet to Fallon's right.

Above him, Gloria Adler screamed in horror and cursed Monk Quinn furiously. Fallon saw Fowler, spread-eagled on the floor, eyes open, his head turned toward Fallon, a small hole in the center of his forehead. Just a little blood spilled out of the hole and dripped down across the bridge of his nose.

"You crazy fool!" Allan yelled. "You'll get those rattlesnakes down there all worked up. Then we'll never be able to get that gold out!"

Monk Quinn laughed. Fallon looked up, saw Gloria Adler's face, her arms reaching down toward Doc Fowler's dead body. Then rough hands clasped her shoulders and jerked her away from the opening.

"What about it, Fallon? You want the petticoat to join you and the good doc?"

Fallon could breathe again, and he heard only the echoes of Monk Quinn's threat. What he didn't hear . . . was the chilling rattles of any snakes. When the dust cleared from the impact of Fowler's body, Fallon saw something else . . . tucked under the ceiling of the den. It was another body, not quite as well mummified as the express agent. It sat against the wall, head tilted to one side, hands—or rather what was left of them—covering his nose and mouth. Fallon saw something glistening in the sunlight like diamonds. Broken bottles. Several of them. He turned his head to find other bottles on the rocks near the bags filled with gold, and he could make out the skull and crossbones on some of the shattered bottles.

That's when Fallon knew he did not have to worry about being bitten by rattlesnakes.

Getting out of this hole alive, though, remained a major concern.

CHAPTER FORTY-THREE

Breathing regularly again, Fallon slid the bullion back into the bag, which he did not bother to fasten. Next, he reached over and grabbed the big rope and brought it close to him. Working easily now, he slid the end of the rope underneath the center of the heavy leather that connected the two bags. He made the knot tight.

It felt cool in the hole, yet Fallon had to wipe sweat off his forehead with the back of his hand, and then he dried his hands on his trousers. He gripped the rope and tugged it hard.

"Ready!" he called out, and eased away from the first load of gold bullion.

"All right, Mendoza, Allan," Quinn ordered. "Let's get that gold out of there."

Above him came the grunts of the two men as they heaved on the rope. The bag inched upward and stopped. Yaqui Mendoza and Captain Allan were finding it a little harder to pull up two hundred pounds of dead weight fifteen feet than lowering a man the size of Harry Fallon the same distance.

The bags came up, and something long and slender

rolled down the saddlebags just below the one being pulled up. Fallon sucked in a deep breath as the rattlesnake toppled over toward him. It did not rattle. It did not strike. It rolled and stopped. Fallon looked up, but no one was looking down. He picked up the dead snake, also mummified, and tossed it toward the remains of the man who had poisoned it some time ago.

Just in time, too, because Preacher Lang's pale face peered over the edge. He grinned and turned toward the men doing the hard work. "It's comin', boys. Keep a-pullin'!"

Eventually, the saddlebags reached the top, and, hearing the commands from a straining Captain Allan—"Pull it up! Pull it up!"—Morgan Maynard and Preacher Lang knelt at the hole's edge to grab the leather. Fallon had to look away and keep his head down to prevent all that falling sand out of his eyes. He saw the revolver in the mummified corpse of the express agent. It was a Smith & Wesson. It didn't appear rusty. What were the chances that after six years, a Smith & Wesson would still fire?

The sand stopped spilling. Above, the outlaws hooted and hurrahed and hollered with joy.

"Quickly!" Monk Quinn's voice bellowed. "Quickly! Quickly! Quickly! The rope. We must get the rest out of the den."

The rope was untied from the first bags and sent down again.

He had the easiest job of the bunch. Allan and Mendoza had the hardest work, pulling up the saddlebags, one pair at a time. Eventually, they had to be spelled by Morgan Maynard and even Monk Quinn. Preacher Lang just helped bring the bags over the rim, although whoever helped the pale, weak murderer did most of that work.

While he waited for the bags to be hoisted to the top, the rope to be untied, and finally to drop back down, Fallon studied the hole he was in. It was, as far as he could tell, just a hole. No exit. No cave. Nothing that might be a way to get out of this. The only way out, Fallon finally convinced himself, was the way he had come down. Even the walls were too slick to climb fifteen feet. Fallon saw few, if any, places he could stick his hand or toes into for leverage. There was no other way out. If there had been, he had to figure, the corpse against the far wall would have found it. Maybe. He might not have had a chance.

He picked up one of the busted bottles, held the glass to his nose, and sniffed, and finally tossed it into the rubble of rocks, dirt, rattles from long-dead snakes, and skins of rattlesnakes from years past.

As the mountain of leather saddlebags filled with gold bullion was raised with each hoisting, Fallon saw the remains of dead rats and mice, some mummified, others down to skeletons. A few other bodies of dead snakes were tossed aside.

The rope tumbled down again, and Fallon busied himself tying the end to another pair of bags. He tugged on his end of the rope, and watched the bags slowly rise.

Clouds were passing overhead, dark clouds, and he wondered what time it was. How long had he been down here? He tried to count the bags, but they were jammed so tightly together, he knew that several of the eighteen remained.

Preacher Lang leaned over the edge. "Fallon!" he called out.

Fallon looked up.

The killer grinned. "You thirsty?"

Fallon shook his head, although he was quite thirsty. "I'm all right."

"Good!" Lang cackled. "On account you ain't gettin' none!"

The rope came down again. Fallon wiped his hands on the cotton pants he wore and went to work on another knot. He tugged. Preacher Lang laughed. The rope, and the leather bags, started upward, upward, and upward. The clouds stopped passing. No rain fell, yet the temperature felt cooler. Caves, he thought, usually kept a constant temperature, more or less, but this was no cave. Just a hole in the earth.

Much like a grave.

He found another dead snake. Fallon looked at the open mouth. One fang had broken off, the other curved out like a scimitar. He thought, *Can one fang of a rattlesnake that has been dead for years still hold enough venom to kill someone?*

Fallon laughed at the thought, and tossed the body away. His eyes fell on the Smith & Wesson on the dead man's body, and he wondered again if that pistol could still function. The weapon remained halfway out of the holster, as though inviting Fallon to roll the dice and give it a whirl. He looked at the glasses from broken bottles of poison. Maybe one bottle had not busted.

A heavy sigh escaped his lungs and mouth. That would be hoping for too much.

He looked at the opening above. The saddlebags were gone, and had been gone for a while. He could hear voices and movement above, but couldn't make out any words. Fallon tried to wet his cracked lips, but his tongue felt as dry as the mummy beside him. A shadow crossed his face, and he looked up to see the smaller lariat being lowered. This one held something, and that something, he soon realized, was a canteen.

Rising, Fallon reached up and let the canteen come into his hands. He untied the loose knot and began unscrewing the cap. Paranoia stopped him. He remembered the busted remnants of poison bottles all around him, and he looked up. Would Monk Quinn send poison down here? Fallon studied the rest of the saddlebags. That was a lot of money to leave behind.

Another shadow fell, and he saw Gloria Adler leaning over the edge.

"You got the canteen?" she called down, and smiled.

He held it up to her, but his throat felt too dry to actually verbalize a response.

She motioned behind her. "They're going down to bring up some of the mules and horses."

Fallon brought the canteen to his mouth. The water, tepid and with more than a taste of alkaline, felt wonderful. He gargled first, and spit it onto the floor. Then took a small sip, just enough to refresh and revive him. He drank again, more, but still not too much.

"Thanks," he called up to her, and sighed.

She was staring at the body of Doctor Jerome Fowler.

When her eyes returned to Fallon, he said, "It was quick. He didn't suffer."

"Too bad," she said. "He should have."

She looked behind her, and Fallon heard the voice of Preacher Lang. Gloria cursed him and turned back to Fallon, who had to guess that Lang had remained up to keep his eye on the woman, and to make sure she didn't try to get Fallon out of that hole or drop him a weapon. Again, he looked at the pistol in the holster on the mummy.

"Get that canteen out of that hole, missy!"

This time he heard Preacher Lang plain as day.

Gloria Adler turned back toward the cold-blooded killer. "Maybe you'd like to go down and take his place?"

"You can get pushed into that pit a lot easier than I can. Get the water out. He's had enough."

She looked back down at Fallon, her face apologetic. Fallon took another sip, then screwed the top back onto the canteen. His right hand reached out and grabbed the rope, and he managed to tie a loose knot on the canvas strap. As he did that, he studied the body of the dead Yuma doctor. A thought came to him, and he tugged on the rope and looked back up into Gloria Adler's eyes.

In a voice that never would have reached the young woman if he had not tasted the water, he asked, "Did Fowler carry a pistol?"

Her head shook.

Fallon swore.

She whispered into the pit, "I can try to get you one."

Instantly, he looked back up. "No," he said, louder than he had meant. He dropped his voice again into a whisper. "They'll kill you."

"What are y'all yakkin' about?" Preacher Lang demanded, and Gloria Adler brought the canteen above the rim. She disappeared, and he heard her tell the killer, "I'm just getting the canteen up. Or maybe you'd like to cross this desert without water."

"Shut up. And he don't get no more nothin'. Nothin' till we got the rest of that gold out of that hole."

More noises dribbled into the pit. Voices, too muffled to make out, and the clopping of hooves. Fallon wondered how many animals they had brought up. He had to guess all of them. They would start packing the animals now, so they could get out of this place as fast as possible. Fallon looked back at the saddlebags. He could count them now. There were that few, and they were spread out.

Six. They had hauled up twelve. Six more. He had just that long to figure out a way to survive.

The first pair of bags disappeared over the lip of the hole. Fallon moved over to the mummy and pulled the Smith & Wesson out of the holster. He tried to thumb back the hammer, but it would not move at all. Sand or dirt fouled the cylinder, and now he could see that the barrel was clogged. It wasn't rusted—well, not bad anyway—but he couldn't cock the weapon, and even had he been able to, most likely the weapon would have blown up in his face and hands.

He pitched it onto the ground near the remains of the dead express agent.

The rope fell back down, and Preacher Lang looked down into the hole.

"Hurry, buster. It's gettin' late in the afternoon." The fake preacher giggled. "I always love preachin' funerals in the late afternoon. Especially double funerals. And by that, buster, I don't mean you and the doc."

The man laughed as Fallon bent over and tied the rope around the leather. He tugged. The rope began pulling upward, taking another pair of bags to the surface.

Fallon found a rock. He laid it at his feet as the saddlebags rose above him. Another rock he pushed over with his boot, and he hefted it, shrugged, and set it beside the first one. So this is what it would come down to: he would be throwing stones at men with guns.

The saddlebags disappeared. The voices above him sang out with joy and almost immediately the rope fell back down.

Another bag. Finally, only one saddlebag remained to make the final six. By then, Fallon had gathered eight rocks that might be good enough to do the job. He could hide in the corner, with the other corpse, but they might let him live. Live for as long as one man can in a hole with no way out, and no water.

"Get that rope tied, buster!" Preacher Lang called out. "Last one, boys! Lord be praised, it's the last of the saddle-bags!"

Fallon hesitated. Lang found his derringer and aimed it. "One more load, buster. If you don't get it up here, since I don't think there are no snakes in that pit no more, I'll put a bullet in your belly and come down there to do that last one myself. Now." He swung the barrel away from the hole. "Or maybe I'll just put a bullet in Miss Jezebel's belly first. I got two shots."

CHAPTER FORTY-FOUR

Ignoring the rocks at his feet, Fallon moved to the last pair of leather saddlebags. He grabbed the rope, and secured the rope around the leather. He tugged, and looked at the slack. The boys up top were getting tired, or maybe just lazy. Lang climbed to his feet and grabbed the rope with his left hand.

"All right, Cap'n!" he yelled. "It's time to make our golden idols!"

Fallon jerked the rope. Preacher Lang screamed, and dropped into the pit. The killer landed on the mummified corpse, which disintegrated into a cloud of yellow and brown dust. Fallon leaped on the body, driving his knee between the preacher's legs, and bringing the palm of his right hand straight into the man's throat. He saw the horror in the killer's eyes, felt the larynx crush and heard the man try to suck in air that could not, would not, reach his lungs. The man gripped the Remington derringer, and Fallon pulled the two-shot .41 from Lang's fingers. By that time, Preacher Lang was already in hell.

Fallon rolled onto his back, bringing the popgun up, aiming at the sky.

No one appeared, and then Fallon heard the roar of chaos above him. Somehow, he thought he could make out Gloria Adler's screams. There was a gunshot. Another. But no bullets were coming down into the den. Fallon came up, keeping his eyes on the hole. Mules snorted. Some other noise came, like the roaring of a tornado, like the unleashing of total fury.

Fallon saw the rope, tight now, and he realized one end was wrapped around that boulder up top, and the other connected to two hundred pounds of gold bullion. He shoved the derringer into his waistband and lunged at the rope, which he gave a firm tug. Feeling minimal resistance, he reached up, gripped the hemp, and pulled himself up. One hand over the other, shimmying like when he had climbed trees as a kid. His eyes remained at the opening, and he wondered if he would be able to pull that Remington out of his waistband and kill anyone who dared look inside.

He reached up and pulled. Pulled. Pulled as hard, and as fast, as he could. Now he knew he heard gunshots.

A shadow appeared, and Fallon stopped climbing, just a foot or less from the surface of solid ground. Holding himself on the rope with his left hand, he shot his right to the derringer, and pulled it up, aimed, and saw Morgan Maynard pitch over the edge. Fallon ducked away as the body fell, barely missing his shoulder. The Remington slipped from his grasp, and he heard Maynard crash atop the body of Preacher Lang. Fallon looked down at the rising dust and the unmoving body of the gunfighter. He couldn't go back down to get the derringer. His right hand moved back, found the rope, and he pulled himself up. His head came up. He could smell the dung of horses, gunpowder, and what seemed to be rain. Mules ran all around him. He saw a saddled horse leap over a mound of rocks.

He dragged himself out of the hole. Yaqui Mendoza lay spread-eagled on the ground, sightless eyes staring at the clear sky, his chest riddled with bullet holes. Fallon looked for a weapon, but saw nothing near the dead bandit. He crawled over toward the saddlebags, and dived out of the path of a stampeding mule.

That's when he saw the machete Yaqui Mendoza had dropped. He rolled over. Grabbed it and came up as Monk Quinn leaped atop of a boulder, bringing his smoking six-shooter down at Fallon's stomach. Fallon let the machete fly. He saw Quinn's eyes widen, and saw the flame burst from the barrel of the killer's revolver.

But the revolver was turning away from Fallon because the top of Quinn's head was disappearing into a sea of blood, hair, and brains at the same time the machete was embedding itself deep into the outlaw's stomach. Almost at the same time, Monk Quinn was pitching forward, landing on Fallon's right, rolling over, and then sliding into the pit. Fallon heard the crash of the dead body below, and he came up.

Captain Allan was still out here. Somewhere. And so was . . .

Gloria Adler came around the rock. She was holding Allan's Winchester, which was smoking, and slowly, numbly, Harry Fallon realized that she had blown the top of Monk Quinn's head off. And if she held Captain Allan's Winchester, that meant . . . ?

"They're all dead," Gloria Adler said, and she lowered the Winchester and sank onto her knees.

They stood on the rim, looking at the last of the flood-waters pour out of the slot canyon.

"You see"—Fallon pointed at the dead farmer's fields—

"that's how they grew crops here. Soak the fields. Has to be a short growing season, just during the monsoons, but . . ." He sighed.

"When the water rushed out," Gloria said, "all hell broke loose. Captain Allan must have decided he could take the gold for himself. Or maybe it was Quinn. Hell, it was probably all of them. I don't even know who killed who first." Her brow knotted in confusion. "What happened to Lang?"

Fallon shrugged. "I brought him down to my level."

"Snakes?" she asked.

He shook his head. "There are no snakes. Not anymore." He gestured at the opening to the pit. "There's another body down there, and a bunch of broken poison bottles. My guess is that this prospector or bounty hunter or maybe a wolfer just happened along. Saw the saddlebags. Must have guessed that it was stolen loot. So he pitched bottles of poison into the pit. It caused a gas that killed the snakes. Only, he must have gotten too close to the edge and slipped in. He tried to get away but breathed in too much of the gas. He's down there too. With Conrad, the express agent, and . . ."

Gloria said, "They have plenty of company."

The mules and horses had calmed down, higher up the ridge. Fallon saw that most of the mules already had been saddled and loaded with the bags. Monk Quinn was wasting no time.

"So . . ." Gloria Adler asked. "What happens now?"

The bodies were up, wrapped in bedrolls, and loaded on the backs of mules or horses. As the water had receded or been soaked up by the roots of corn and cabbages, softening the desert ground, Fallon had buried the bodies of the dead farmer, his wife, the dog, and Doctor Jerome Fowler.

Burying the bodies, and getting the corpses, and the last saddlebag of gold bullion, had taken them into the night. Adler and Fallon had eaten raw corn, and the beans the farmer's wife had been cooking for their supper. They were not hungry, but knew they had to eat.

They slept fitfully, if they slept at all, and when dawn came, they stared at each other long and hard.

Fallon pointed to the horse Gloria had been riding, and the mule he had picketed beside it. The mule still held a packsaddle, and one of the saddlebags was on it, along with food, water, and Captain Allan's Winchester rifle.

She looked at the animals, and then back at Fallon.

"Who are you?"

He smiled. "Hank Fallon. Ex–deputy marshal. Paroled convict."

"I don't need that gold," she said.

"I'd give you more," he said, "but I knew you wouldn't want it."

"It's not yours to give."

"That's why I'm taking it back to Arizona." He drew in a deep breath. "It's a long story. But the mines and the law won't miss a few bars of bullion. And you'll need it to get to"—he shrugged—"wherever you're going."

"Vera Cruz," she said, "sounds nice."

"I've heard," he said, "the western coast is nicer. Not as many people. Or bounty hunters."

"Maybe," she said, "I'll go west."

"Be careful where you show off that bullion."

"I will."

He adjusted the gunbelt he wore and moved to the string

of mules. "Maybe," she said, as she walked to her horse, "one day you'll decide to see the western coast of Mexico yourself."

Fallon looked at her. "I have some personal business I have to take care of first. A few jobs I promised this fellow. But . . ." He turned away from her, tried to block her from his mind.

She rode south.

Hank Fallon rode toward Tucson.

He left the mules and the dead bodies in an *arroyo* just south of town, and rode to the little church. He found the confessional, and waited until he heard the wood slide open.

The voice was too young.

"No offense, *Padre*," Fallon said, "but I need to talk to the old priest."

The voice coughed. "Do you mean Padre Julio?"

"Let's try him."

A few minutes later, Harry Fallon smiled at the voice. "Did you say your fifty Hail Marys when you left the last time, Marshal Fallon? Have you tried to live better?"

Fallon laughed. "How did you know it was me, Father Julio?"

"I have heard no reports of the death of a man named Harry Fallon, but I have read a lot about a bloody escape out of Yuma."

Fallon lost the smile. "Well, bless me, Father, if you can bless a backsliding Methodist, for I have sinned."

"What do you wish to tell me, my son?" the priest asked.

* * *

When he had finished, he waited. The old man breathed heavily in the dark, and, at length, he said, "Would you like me to remember your late wife and child in the next Mass?"

"I'd appreciate it, Father."

"You're going back to Chicago?"

"I must."

"So this is good-bye."

"Who's to say?"

Another long silence, and then the old man on the other side of the confessional said, "Is there anything else I can do for you, Harry?"

Fallon let out a long breath. He said, "Actually, Father, there is. I was hoping you'd be able to send a telegraph as soon as I'm gone. I've written it out on a piece of paper."

"I suppose I can do this."

"Be careful that no one sees you."

"I am always careful. But as a priest, a poor man, I don't know if I have—"

"Don't worry, Father Julio. I can pay for the price of the telegraph. In fact, I've brought what we called a tithe back in my church." He cleared his throat. "Just be careful where you cash it in. I'd recommend this man I met down in Mexico, just below the border. I've written it on the note too. This place, it's not far. It's where I got my new duds. He takes a healthy cut, but . . . well . . . it's probably worth it."

Ten minutes later, Harry Fallon, dressed in black boots, black-striped britches, a yellow shirt, blue vest, blue ribbon tie, and black hat, entered a saloon. He made a beeline for the corner table in the back of the place, stood in front of Aaron Holderman, who was sipping a frothy beer, and waited for the detective to look up. When Holderman raised his head, his eyes widened in recognition.

"You . . ." he gasped.

"Get a horse," Fallon whispered. "And meet me at the south road in fifteen minutes. You've got some work to do, and a report to get to Mr. MacGregor."

The drunk blinked. "You mean . . . you found . . . you got . . . you done it?"

"Yeah," Fallon said. "I done it."

CHAPTER FORTY-FIVE

The little man sat in the green leather chair in an extremely large office in Chicago. He wore a brown suit with a tan vest and red tie, and he smoked a repulsive cigar. Sean MacGregor, president of the American Detective Agency, did not look happy.

Dan MacGregor opened the door, and let Aaron Holderman and Harry Fallon inside. The son of the detective agency's owner closed the door and leaned against the wall.

Holderman and Fallon walked to the desk the size of a battleship. Sean MacGregor laid the cigar in an ashtray.

"What the hell happened?" the Scot roared.

His anger took Holderman aback. The timid man wet his lips in confusion. "But . . . what . . . I mean . . . I wired you . . ."

"That you had the gold, all but a few bars! That Fallon brought it back, and the bodies of the dead men."

"That's right. Ain't that right, Hank?"

Fallon shrugged. "I gave you the gold, even the mules, and you gave me a receipt." Fallon patted the top pocket of his vest.

"Then . . ." MacGregor rose from his seat and slammed a newspaper, the *Chicago Appeal*, on the desk. "Explain this!"

Both men stared at the headlines in the lower right-hand corner.

PINKERTONS RETURN BULLION !

Detectives Discover Gold Stolen in Arizona Robbery Six Years Earlier.

RECOVERY OF TREASURE LONG THOUGHT MISSING BRINGS RELIEF TO MINES!

Amazing Story of Daring.

PRESIDENT PRAISES CHIEF.

Full Details of Exciting Story.

"It's gotta be a mistake, boss," Aaron Holderman stuttered.

"It's no mistake. Dan went to the depot himself. You want to show them what you found in the boxcar, Dan?"

MacGregor's son walked to the desk. He pulled a folded note from his inside coat pocket and gave it to Fallon, who glanced at it and handed it to the sweating, trembling Holderman.

> *Thanks,*
> *Allan*

"Allan." Holderman gasped. "The captain of the guards at the Yuma pen."

"No, idiot. It's the first name of Allan Pinkerton," the

elder MacGregor exploded. "That's all Dan found in the boxes. You fool. You loaded up the gold in Tucson and didn't bother assigning anyone to guard it—such as yourself? You just rode in the smoking car the whole trip. Did you even check on the gold once?"

"But those bars were in strongboxes, boss. Somebody must have tipped off the Pinkertons."

"Yes. Somebody." MacGregor stared at Fallon.

"I did my job," Fallon said. "I got the gold. And the dead bodies. I turned them all over to your man here. That's what you hired me to do. So don't blame me on anything that happened after that."

"But since the American Detective Agency can't claim any of that reward, you won't be paid a dime."

Fallon shrugged. "I'm alive. And if you're interested in what all I went through to get that gold to your boy here . . ."

"I'm not. Get out of here, Holderman. Wait. How much money did you collect from the Arizona authorities? For bringing in Quinn and those others."

The man shuffled his feet. "Well, I don't have most of it yet."

"What you get, you bring to Dan. That'll help with the loss of money your stupidity, your unprofessionalism, has cost this agency. Do you understand?"

The man answered with a timid nod, and left the room. Fallon started out the door, as well, but stopped when the old man called out his name.

When Fallon turned, Sean MacGregor said, "You owe me another job or two, Fallon."

Fallon laughed softly. "Do I?"

"That agreement you had me sign. I hear it went up in flames."

"Did it?"

MacGregor frowned.

"Is that what Holderman told you, MacGregor? The same man who couldn't keep almost two hundred thousand dollars in gold safe on a train from Tucson to Chicago?"

MacGregor found the cigar and sucked on it till he had it puffing again. He glanced at his son, then studied Harry Fallon.

"You want the man who framed you? You want the man who's responsible for the death of your family? You want that . . . you do another job for me."

"I think you owe me something for the job I just did for you."

"I'll pay you by not sending you back to the Illinois State Penitentiary."

Fallon shook his head.

"You'll get your salary. And time to clean up. And maybe I'll feed you a tidbit or two. But . . ." MacGregor opened a drawer and pulled out a file. "This might interest you. It's right up your line of work, Fallon. I've found your niche."

Fallon moved back to the large desk and the small man.

"And what," Fallon said, "is my niche?"

"Going to prison. And getting out."

Once he had settled into the chair, Fallon held out his hand and watched the small man push the folder across the massive desk.

Keep reading for a preview of the next
Hank Fallon western

NATIONAL BESTSELLING AUTHORS
William W. Johnstone
and **J. A. Johnstone**

BEHIND THE IRON
A HANK FALLON WESTERN

In this gripping thriller, America's greatest Western
storytellers take you inside the dangerous world of an
undercover agent—and the deadliest jail in America . . .

PRISON RIOT
Hank Fallon knows what it's like to rot behind bars.
To wallow in the filth of a rat-infested cell. To smell the
pent-up rage of cutthroat killers and thieves. Fallon
earned his freedom the hard way. He saved the lives of
four guards, got released early, and became a detective.
Then he went undercover, infiltrated a prison gang
plotting to bust out—and barely made it out alive.
Now they're sending him back. Behind the iron.
Straight to hell . . .

This time, it's the ninth circle, better known as the
Missouri State Penitentiary. His mission: get inside
the infirmary, look for a pregnant inmate named Jess
Harper, and find out where her bank-robbing boyfriend
hid the stolen cash. Problem is a rebellion is brewing
among the prisoners. Their rage is burning out of
control. An all-out savage riot is about to explode.
And Fallon's head is on the chopping block . . .

Look for BEHIND THE IRON—on sale now.

CHAPTER ONE

The little man in the extremely large—and very brown—office opened a drawer. He pulled out a file.

"This," the small man said, "might interest you."

What interested Harry Fallon right then was this thought about killing the man, and the little man's son, in the Chicago office, but Fallon didn't. Fallon would have to get past the other men outside the office doors, and out of Chicago. And then what? Besides, Harry Fallon still needed that pathetic, tiny man.

"It's right up your line of work, Fallon," the small man with the big head and big ideas said. "I've found your niche."

Fallon walked back to the large desk and the small man.

"And what," Fallon said, "is my niche?"

The small man grinned over his foul-smelling cigar. "Going to prison. And getting out."

Harry Fallon felt older than his thirty-three years.

With a heavy sigh, Fallon found the chair in front of the sprawling desk and sat. Grinning, the small man held the folder of papers in his little left hand.

The small man slid the folder across the massive desk.

Fallon opened the folder.

"Tired?" the small man asked.

Fallon felt no need to answer. Tired? Who wouldn't be exhausted? Just a short time ago, Harry Fallon had been at the Illinois State Penitentiary in Joliet, saving the lives of a few guards during a bloody riot, and that act of bravery, kindness, humanity—just a spur-of-the-moment decision, truthfully—had led to a parole for Harry Fallon, former deputy United States marshal for Judge Isaac Parker's court in Fort Smith, Arkansas. Fallon had been given a job at Werner's Wheelwright in Chicago and a place to live at Missus Ketchum's Boarding House near Lake Michigan. And then this small man had changed Fallon's life.

The small man was Sean MacGregor, president of this American Detective Agency, a man with dead, green eyes, and thinning orange hair streaked with silver. Sean MacGregor had a job he wanted Harry Fallon to handle, just a minor little bit of work. All Fallon had to do was break his parole—but MacGregor could make sure the authorities thought the ex-convict was living up to his agreement with the state of Illinois and the solicitor for the United States court. Go to Arizona Territory. Get arrested and sentenced to prison at Yuma Territorial Prison, also known as The Hellhole. Somehow make friends with Monk Quinn, a notorious felon and murderer who, six years earlier, had robbed a Southern Pacific train of some $200,000 in gold bullion. Escape from The Hellhole with Quinn. Cross the border into Mexico. And bring back Quinn, and any of his associates, dead or alive—preferably dead—

and return the gold. So that Sean MacGregor and his American Detective Agency could reap the glory and the rewards.

Somehow, Fallon had managed to do most of that, although the gold bullion wound up being recovered by MacGregor's rival, the Pinkerton National Detective Agency.

Somehow, Harry Fallon had managed to live through it all. When he had left Chicago for Arizona Territory he was an inch over six feet tall and weighed ten pounds shy of two hundred. Big man. Leathery. Rock hard. You had to be big and tough to get out of Joliet in one piece. After that short while in Arizona and Mexico, Fallon had returned with a few more scars, some premature gray hair in his brown hair, and about twenty pounds lighter. It had not been the easiest assignment in Fallon's life—and Harry Fallon had pulled some rough jobs riding for Judge Parker all those years ago. His eyes remained brown. His eyes rarely missed anything.

"Remember our little agreement, Fallon," Sean MacGregor said in his thick Scottish accent.

You didn't forget a little agreement like that.

The little man reminded Fallon, one more damned time. "You want the man who framed you? You want the man who's responsible for the death of your family? You want that . . . you do this job for me." He put the big cigar between his thin lips. "Savvy?"

The American Detective Agency's offices could be found on the top floor of the building in Chicago. Harry Fallon didn't know exactly what part of Chicago. He had scarcely had time to even see much of the city—just the depot and Lake Michigan (and the American Detective Agency's offices, of course) before he had been waylaid and brought to see the small little man in the massive but Spartan office of brown paneling, brown rugs, brown tables, and brown filing cabinets, with one window where the brown drapes were pulled tightly shut.

There was some color to MacGregor's office, of course. The lamp on his desk and the others on the walls had green domes. And the ashtray on MacGregor's desk was silver. The color of the folder was tan, which Fallon figured was as close to brown or green as MacGregor could find.

Fallon looked at the top sheet of paper. His stomach and intestines twisted into knots, but he showed no emotion. He merely wet his lips and turned to the next page. "You're sending me back," Fallon said dryly.

"Closer to home," MacGregor said. "Your old home. It's not like I'm returning you to Joliet to finish the rest of your sentence. Which I could do." He blew a thick cloud of smoke toward the ceiling, leaned back in his green leather chair, and chuckled. "I could even have you killed. I've had lots of people killed. And nobody would mourn the loss of a rogue deputy marshal, a paroled convict. Would they?"

No, Fallon thought sadly. The two people who would have mourned Harry Fallon were dead and buried. His wife and daughter. Murdered. While Harry Fallon was sweating and hardening behind the walls of Joliet.

"Dan," MacGregor called out to his larger, more handsome son. "Fetch Marshal Fallon a slice of cherry pie, would you?"

"Yes, sir," MacGregor's son said. Fallon kept looking at the pages. He heard the door open, saw some light filter into the dark brown room, before the door shut out the light and the fresh air. He went through the third sheet of paper and read the final page.

Carefully, he gathered the papers, tapped them on the big desk until they were even, and laid them back inside the folder, which he closed and left on the desk.

"Jefferson City," Fallon said.

"You've been there, I assume," MacGregor said.

"Just in passing."

"Well, you lived through Joliet and you survived Yuma. How hard could a little prison in a backwoods state like Missouri be compared to those two pens?"

Fallon stared. "The chances of someone recognizing me as a lawman or even a convict in Yuma were remote," he said. "But someone did recognize me in The Hellhole. Even though I'd never been in Arizona Territory till you sent me."

He tapped the folder. "I rode for Judge Parker's court in Arkansas and the Indian Nations. Missouri's just north of Arkansas. I arrested quite a few men who hailed from Missouri. I was born in Missouri. There's a pretty good chance that someone locked up there will know me."

"So what?" The small man dropped the cigar in the ashtray. "You're not the first badge-wearer to find himself behind bars. You can even use your own name this time. I don't think any warden or guard in Missouri will have enough brains or investigating skills to figure out that you're supposed to be on parole in the state of Illinois. And even if they do, they wouldn't be likely to give up a warm body and ship you back here to finish the completion of your original sentence. Be yourself, just another jailbird doing time."

The door opened. Light reappeared. The door shut. Darkness prevailed except for the lamps on the sprawling desk and the match that Sean MacGregor struck to light another one of his cheap, repugnant cigars.

Dan MacGregor slid a plate in front of Fallon.

"You like cherry pie?" Sean MacGregor said over his cigar.

"I prefer pecan," said Fallon, who hadn't tasted any dessert in years.

"Thaddeus Gripewater likes cherry pie," Dan MacGregor said. He spoke, unlike his father, without a trace of the Scottish Highlands. In the short time Fallon had met up with the MacGregors, he found few similarities between the two men.

Except this: A man would be wise not to trust either one of them. Fallon did not even think father and son trusted one another.

The younger man repeated the name: "Thaddeus Gripewater."

Fallon turned to look at the younger man. There had been no mention of any Thaddeus Gripewater in the four pages Fallon had just finished reading.

"Prison doctor at Jefferson City," Dan MacGregor explained casually but informatively. "You manage to get him a cherry pie, and he'll be putty in your hands, do anything for you, even get you to help him out in the prison."

He found the spoon and cut into the pie. He brought up some of the pie and smelled it.

"It's not poison, Fallon," Sean MacGregor said.

"There is some gin in it, though," Dan MacGregor said. "Thaddeus Gripewater likes gin, too. Probably better than cherry pie. You use gin to make your pie, and you'll rule the infirmary ward at Jefferson City."

After all those years in prison, Fallon found sweets unpalatable, and he didn't trust himself with alcohol, even if it had likely burned off while baking. He set the spoon on the side of the plate. "Thaddeus," he said. "Gripewater."

"It's his real name," Sean MacGregor said. "As far as we've been able to ascertain."

"His parents should be the ones in prison," Dan MacGregor said.

"So I'm supposed to get gin and cherries in prison and somehow bake the good doctor a pie, and get it from my cell—I assume I'll be a prisoner, again, right?"

"Well," Dan MacGregor said, "it never occurred to us to try to get you in as a guard." He smiled.

"They don't hire parole violators or disgraced federal lawmen," the elder MacGregor said. He did not smile.

Harry Fallon did not smile, either. He glanced at the plate and realized why Dan MacGregor had brought a spoon, and not a fork, with the dessert. A man who had spent ten years in Joliet could use a fork like an Indian could use a knife. Fallon envisioned the fork being pulled out of Sean MacGregor's neck, with blood spraying the dark room from the dying man's jugular vein, then slamming the fork between Dan MacGregor's ribs and into his heart.

"You still owe me something for the Yuma job," Fallon said.

"I told you already," Sean MacGregor said. "I didn't collect enough money, thanks to those damned Pinkertons. And whoever tipped them off that we had the gold bullion." He stared hard at Fallon, but Fallon gave nothing away. "Your payment is that I don't send you back to Joliet . . ."

Fallon finished the sentence. Hell, he had heard it enough: ". . . or another facility for completion of my original sentence."

The small man flicked ash from his cigar and smiled. "That's right."

"It's not enough," Fallon said.

"Dan will tell you something on your way to the train depot," Sean MacGregor said. "When you're finished with this assignment, we'll get you out of Jefferson City and get you across the border and back to your lovely boardinghouse near Lake Michigan. It's beautiful in the fall. Colder than a witch's teat, but beautiful. You should be back by October."

"I see."

"Cold will feel mighty good, Fallon," the small man said, "after spending a few months in hell."

"Yeah."

"Finish your pie."

"The cherries are too tart. I'll find a better recipe."

"You won't find it at Missus Ketchum's Boarding House," Sean MacGregor said. "Her meals are like sawdust."

"I wouldn't know," Fallon said. Which was true. He had yet to see the place where the warden at the Illinois State Penitentiary thought he was living. Likewise, he had yet to meet his alleged employer, Werner. Fallon didn't even know the wheelwright's first name.

"Dan will fill you in on the particulars," Sean MacGregor said as he set the foul cigar on the gaudy ashtray. "Do we have an agreement?"

"It depends on what Dan tells me," Fallon said.

"Fair enough. Aaron Holderman will be delighted to escort you to Joliet . . ."

Aaron Holderman worked for the American Detective Agency, but Fallon had known him in Arkansas and the Indian Nations, where he had run whiskey to the Indians, drunk what he couldn't sell, and used his fists on men, women, and children. He had spent time in Joliet, in Cañon City, Colorado; in Angola, Louisiana. He was exactly the kind of investigator a corrupt operation like the American Detective Agency needed.

"Yeah," Fallon said, "for violation of my parole, to finish the completion of my original sentence."

"No." MacGregor picked up his cigar. "You will face a new judge. The Almighty. Holderman will just be sending your dead body back to confirm that it is indeed Harry Fallon."

CHAPTER TWO

Out in the hallway, Dan MacGregor waited for a few other operatives of the American Detective Agency to head into other rooms. When the hallway was empty, he turned to Fallon and said, "The warden's name is Harold Underwood. He's the only one who should know you're working for us. You'll want to keep it that way. If an inmate finds out you're a detective, you're dead."

Fallon waited. "Is that it?"

The tall, handsome man glanced at Aaron Holderman before his eyes fell back onto Fallon. "No. There's another reason we picked you for this job."

Fallon let out a chuckle that held no humor. "I thought it was because I know how to rot behind bars."

"Mr. MacGregor's a man of his word," Aaron Holderman said. "He said he'd help you find out who killed your family, who framed you, and got you sent to Joliet. You listen to him. He'll help you out."

Now Fallon turned to the brute wearing the bowler.

The city hat was brown, as was the big man's ill-fitting suit. He probably wore brown to please the corrupt president of the American Detective Agency. The suit did not fit Holderman well, but even Chicago's best tailor would find it hard to outfit this mass of muscles.

Fallon studied Holderman, his mustache and beard, too brown it seemed to Fallon. The monster likely dyed his hair with shoe polish. The brass shield on his chest that identified him as a private detective was tarnished. The bulge underneath his left shoulder indicated a revolver. A Chicago billy club protruded from his brown boot. It would be hard for Holderman to run with a nightstick in his left boot. From the size of Holderman, though, it would be hard for him to run anyway.

Dan MacGregor, on the other hand, looked like he could run alongside a thoroughbred for six furlongs.

You're thinking of trying to escape, Fallon thought. *Stop it. You've a job to do. Just remember this is all for Renee. For Rachel. For justice.*

No, he was fooling himself. Ten years inside Joliet had changed him. He no longer wore a badge. Even the American Detective Agency had not pinned a shield on him. He was just being used. But Fallon kept figuring a way that he could use Sean MacGregor and his minions. But not for justice.

Revenge.

"What's the reason?" Fallon asked MacGregor.

"I'll tell you," the young detective said, "when I'm sure the walls aren't listening."

Holderman snorted.

Doors opened down the hallway, and voices became louder. Fallon could hear the footsteps behind him.

"All right," Fallon said.

MacGregor pointed. "Let's go."

They walked to the elevator. Aaron Holderman rang the button, and two awkwardly quiet minutes later the carriage arrived, the door opened, and the elderly black man said, "Headin' down, folks. Climb in."

Holderman moved in first, and Fallon started but felt something pull on the back of his vest.

"After you, Christina," Dan MacGregor said pleasantly, and gave a tall, attractive blonde woman his most handsome smile.

"Thank you, Dan," she said, and studied Fallon. "Who's your friend?"

"A lawman from way back," MacGregor said. "Working on a case with us."

She was already in the elevator. So were two other men. MacGregor let the last man, a thin man with huge spectacles, step inside, too, before he smiled at the black elevator man.

"You look crowded enough, Carlton," MacGregor told the black man. "And Holderman weighs more than three men and takes up the space of four. Run these good people down and come back up for us, will you?"

"Yes, suh."

"Aaron," MacGregor called out to the big detective. "Go on. Meet us at the depot. Make sure everything's ready."

"But . . ."

"Just do it," MacGregor said as the door closed.

He turned toward Fallon but said nothing until the creaking and clanging of the elevator revealed that it was at least two stories below them.

"There's one thing my father did not tell me to tell you, Hank," the handsome man said.

Hank, Fallon thought. *It's Hank now. Only my friends call me Hank.*

"Just one?" Fallon shot back.

MacGregor let out a genuine laugh. "One that I'm willing to share."

Fallon waited.

"Judge Parker sentenced you to fifteen years," MacGregor said.

Still, Fallon waited. He could hear the elevator begin its ascent to the top floor of the brownstone building.

"Parker was a federal judge." MacGregor's face showed no emotion. "So why were you sent to the Illinois State Penitentiary in Joliet and not the Detroit House of Corrections? Ever consider that?"

Fallon did not part his lips to respond.

"How many men did you send to Joliet? Other than Holderman, but if I remember right, you made that arrest in Illinois, after Holderman crossed the Mississippi around Cape Girardeau, and Illinois wanted him worse than Parker did."

That much was true. Fallon had arrested Holderman twice in the Indian Territory—another deputy had arrested him, too—but none of the charges ever stuck. So when Fallon had gone after Holderman all those years ago, across Arkansas, into Missouri, even into Kentucky briefly before back into Missouri, and finally into Illinois and made the arrest, he had found himself surrounded by some Illinois badge-wearers who wanted Holderman for stealing a horse, beating a blacksmith half to death, and robbing a

Mason of three double eagles he had been taking to an orphanage.

MacGregor went on. "You were arrested for robbery in the Creek Nation. They couldn't make the murder charge of that federal deputy against you, though the solicitor tried his hardest. That's a federal charge. Federal prisoners in that part of the country get shipped up to Detroit, Michigan. But you wound up in Joliet."

"So did Joey Kurth," Fallon said. Fallon had run into Kurth in Joliet.

"Yeah, but that was different," MacGregor said. "Kurth was arrested for running spirits and resisting arrest. But he was also wanted for a string of robberies in Beardstown, so Parker sent him to Illinois to be tried there, sentenced, and upon completion, returned to Fort Smith to get sentenced again. Just didn't happen."

Thanks to Kurth's untimely demise during the riots at Joliet.

"All right," Fallon said. "The way it was explained to me was that because I was a onetime lawman, with many, many men I had sent to prison serving their time—some of those sentences were for life—in Detroit, I was being sent to Joliet for my own safety." He shook his head, felt the gall rising again, and said again, his voice acid now: "Safety."

"Parker threw the book at you. You think he cared about your safety? He figured you betrayed him. From what I've read, Parker got you that job as a deputy marshal. He even talked you into reading for the bar. When you were accused of robbing that stagecoach, he felt like he'd been stabbed in the back."

The elevator arrived. The mechanical sounds echoed across the hallway.

"Did it matter where I wound up?" Fallon said.

"Detroit. Joliet. Neither one is quite the Drovers Cottage."

The doors began opening. "Chris Ehrlander was your lawyer, wasn't he?"

Fallon nodded.

The black man in the red jacket reappeared. "You ready, suh?" he asked MacGregor.

"Interesting," MacGregor said, keeping his eyes on Fallon, before he turned around. "Yes, Carlton. My friend here has a train to catch."

On the loud, grease-smelling elevator ride to the ground floor, visions of Judge Isaac Parker . . . of Renee DeSmet Fallon . . . of attorney Chris Ehrlander . . . of faces of men he had known as a lawman and as an inmate . . . all flashed through Fallon's mind.

MacGregor stared at the black elevator man in the red jacket. Fallon studied the back of Dan MacGregor's head. He remembered the man from some university in Illinois who had stopped in at the marshal's office in Fort Smith. The man talked to the marshal, the federal prosecutor, and the deputies who happened to be in town about how the shape of a man's skull could determine if that man were a criminal or a decent person. Fallon and everyone else in that room had figured the man was no better than the confidence men with their shell games, marked decks, and rigged faro layouts, but now as he stared at Dan MacGregor's head, he tried to re-member exactly what shapes the Illinois professor had said meant a man was a criminal.

The elevator came to an abrupt stop, and the jolt seemed to return Fallon's faculties.

He thanked the black man as he followed Dan MacGregor to the front door of the brownstone building. They stepped onto the sidewalk.

Chicago was crowded at this time of day. Fallon walked alongside Dan MacGregor. Neither man spoke, they simply bent into the wind and moved along with the herd of people.

This city wasn't for him. Too many people. No sense of order. No guard telling him where he needed to go or when he could hit the privy to relieve his bladder. No rolling hills and clear water of the Indian Nations. No wife. No daughter. And after spending what seemed like an eternity in that Hellhole called Yuma Territorial Penitentiary, after enduring the Snake Den, and some of the most ruthless cutthroats Fallon had ever seen—after escaping to Mexico and witnessing more carnage and destruction—Fallon just did not fit in with women in their bloomers and fine hats, men in their Prince Albert coats and shiny black leather shoes carrying grips and cases or umbrellas—even though the skies seemed clear.

"Here," MacGregor said, and he turned down another street, not as crowded, but far from deserted.

Why doesn't he hail a hack? Fallon thought. *It is a damned long walk from here to the depot.*

Another turn. Another. And then one more that led them down a narrow alley. A cat screamed, leaped out of a stinking can of trash, and bolted between Fallon and MacGregor.

MacGregor smiled, but the smile faded instantly.

The cat wasn't alone in the alley.

Four men came from behind a mountain of trash. Two carried baseball bats. Brass knuckles reflected off the tallest man. The fourth wielded a knife.

Fallon glanced behind him. Two other men, armed with revolvers, approached from the side street.